Keeping Up With the NEIGHBOURS

A Contemporary Christian Romance
Series 2

by

Tracy Krauss

Fictitious Ink Publishing
Tumbler Ridge, BC

COPYRIGHT

KEEPING UP WITH THE NEIGHBOURS
A Contemporary Christian Romance Series 2

Published by Fictitious Ink Publishing
Tumbler Ridge, BC, V0C 2W0

ISBN 978-1-988-447-308 (epub edition)
ISBN 978-1-988-447-292 (mobi edition)
ISBN 978-1-988-447-315 (paperback edition)

DISCLAIMER

DEDICATION & ACKNOWLEDGMENTS

This series is dedicated to all my wonderful friends from 'The Rock'. Newfoundland culture has a special place in my heart since so many people from there have a special place in my heart, too. You always make this 'come from away' feel welcome. This one's for you!

Thank you to a wonderful team of Beta Readers who gave me such valuable feedback during the writing of this sequel. Thanks to my sister Jane for letting me stay at her house (affectionately known as the 'Park Hotel') for much of the editing. Thanks to Priscilla Benterud for her ongoing editing of this series. Thanks to my writing colleagues and friends at 'Inscribe Christian Writers Fellowship'. You are a wonderful source of inspiration and encouragement. To all my family, especially my husband Gerald, I acknowledge your support and love. Finally, I thank Almighty God, who has given me stories to tell and the means with which to tell them.

Tracy Krauss

FOREWORD

Jed Malloy first came alive in **NEIGHBOURS Series 1** as a minor character who just wouldn't go away! Even though he had a small part to play in that first series, he made his mark with his quirky ways and 'down-home' manners. He soon became one of my favourites - and apparently yours, too, if reader feedback means anything! I knew I needed to continue the series and make Jed's large family the star. As I began to write, I discovered that every member of Jed's family was just as unforgettable as he was, each in his or her own way. It has been a fun ride getting to know these folks better. In the end, it was even more special for me to see some of them come to know Jesus as Saviour. Welcome to the neighbourhood!

NOTE TO READERS: This series is categorized as 'Christian fiction' because it has a strong redemptive message. However, there may be events that some Christians find troubling, such as the use of alcohol and references to sexual activity, although this always takes place 'off camera'.

The LORD doesn't see things the way you see them. People judge by outward appearance, but the LORD looks at the heart. (NLT)

1 Samuel 16: 7b

EPISODE 1

NEIGHBOURHOOD TANGLE

*J*ED

JED MALLOY SHUFFLED barefoot down the narrow hallway and let out an inadvertent groan. He was shirtless, bleary eyed, and his tongue was stuck to the roof of his mouth. The price of too much holiday cheer the night before.

He ran a hand through his thick brown hair, making it stand on end. He squinted when he reached the brightness of the main living space. Coffee. He needed coffee and lots of it.

A loud snore followed by a snort, a groan, and a sigh broke the morning stillness. The noises came from the living room couch. Jed grinned. He and his brother Zeb had bantered – okay, argued - far into the early hours. They'd consumed more alcohol than was good for them, trying to solve all the world's problems in one night. It was the way they operated. Always had. Good natured but competitive. As the closest brothers in age out of a family of nine, the battle had started early.

Bo and Reba, two of Jed's other siblings who were visiting for the Christmas holidays, had crashed earlier than he and Zeb. Bo was still sleeping on the floor in Jed's bedroom. Their sister Reba got the privilege of the spare bed. She'd passed out on the couch and Jed had moved her sometime after midnight.

Jed loved his family, but a week in their company was starting to take its toll. Too many late nights along with everything else it entailed and he was beginning to feel his age. Having to get up for work this morning was both a blessing and a curse. He felt like crap, but on the other hand it might bring some normalcy back into his life.

He made some extra noise as he prepared the coffee, banging a cupboard door here and a tin there, just for effect. If he had to get up for work, the rest of them might as well feel his pain. The growl from the couch brought another wide smile to Jed's face. When the coffee was ready, Jed filled an oversized mug and then clattered the coffee pot back onto the warmer. He took a tentative slurp, released a satisfied expletive, and shuffled from the confines of the galley kitchen to the living room only a few feet away.

Jed stood over his brother's sleeping form for a moment. Zeb was a giant. He was probably the only man who had ever beaten Jed in a fight. Not that Jed was small by any means. They were both above average height and broadly built, like Gramps on their Pop's side. But with a full red beard that contrasted with unkempt dirty-blonde hair, Zeb looked like a mountain man – or a grizzly.

At 32, Jed was the eldest boy in the family, but Zeb was right behind him at 30. They had one older sister who was 33, and then a string of siblings after. His parents were staunch Catholics who didn't believe in contraception – at least not in those days. Nine children in eleven years was the result.

Jed grabbed a stray cushion and thumped it across Zeb's head. "Wake up, ya lazy bugger. The days half over."

Zeb cracked open one eye and then shut it again. "Get lost."

"You're some crooked contrary this mornin'. I'm off to work. Don't sleep all day. And look after the kids. Don't let 'em wreck the joint."

"As if." Zeb's voice was muffled by the cushion.

"What's a matter? Can't handle yer liquor anymore, or what?" Jed's own head was pounding with the dullness of a hangover, but he would never admit it to Zeb.

Zeb told Jed exactly where to go and in no uncertain terms. Jed just smiled and downed the rest of his coffee. His brother was crass, but he'd missed him. He'd missed all of his family, but he was ready for a break. Even he had trouble handling more than one Malloy at a time.

JED SHUFFLED into the makeshift lunchroom and surveyed the inhabitants. He spotted his friend and co-worker, Lester Tibbett, sitting alone at a table made of plywood and sawhorses and headed his way.

It was the first day back to work after the Christmas break. Titan, the construction company that Jed and Lester worked for, was nearing completion of the downtown office tower. Despite some legal setbacks after an accident on site that had brought on an investigation, they were back on schedule.

Jed plunked down on an available folding chair, his lunch pail clattering on the wooden tabletop in front of him. "I miss takin' lunch in the open air, like we used to. I liked the whip o' the wind comin' at ya through the steel and cement." Jed took off his hardhat and set it off to one side and then proceeded to open his tin lunchbox and rummage around a bit.

"Those days are long gone since most everything's framed in." Lester was a clean-cut cowboy. A down to earth, no nonsense kind of fellow with high moral standards and a solid work ethic. His lean and sinewy frame was conditioned to hard labor and he was just a couple of years older than Jed. They'd become good friends since Lester and his sister had moved into Jed's apartment building last fall.

"That's your excuse, but we both know it's on account of the accident."

"The company has to think about their liability," Lester said. "Having a designated lunchroom is sensible."

"Course you'd think so, seein' it was you who almost bit the dust. But me? I don't like bein' boxed in." Jed exhaled - a prolonged sigh that came out more like a grunt.

Lester squinted over at his friend, his half eaten sandwich in mid-air. "Rough day?"

"My own fault. Stayed up too late, that's all."

"Ah, I see. You've been partying pretty hard since the family arrived." Lester's eyes held amusement with not a trace of sympathy.

Jed pulled out a sandwich and carefully unwrapped the cellophane. "Ya got that right, b'y. I 'ate to admit it but I'm feelin' it, too." He took a huge bite and then continued, the words garbled because of the food in his mouth. "I loves my family but I've 'ad just about enough." His distinctive Newfoundland brogue eliminated most 'h's' from the beginning of words.

"I've been wondering how you've been managing. Pretty crowded, eh?" Lester poured some coffee from his thermos into the lid that also served as a mug.

Jed nodded. His Adam's apple bobbed as he swallowed. "Sardines got more room."

"Now that Christmas is over, they'll be heading home soon, I imagine. You won't know what to do with yourself once they leave."

"Not till after New Year's." Jed mouth formed a lopsided bow. "Now that'll be some party."

"I'll just bet." Lester took a sip of his steaming coffee and surveyed his friend over the rim of the makeshift mug. He pointed at Jed's eye. "The shiner you were sporting on Christmas day is starting to fade."

"You should see the one Zeb's got now." Jed grinned. "That one'll be stickin' around for a day or two yet."

Lester shook his head and smiled. "I'm surprised Miss Peacock hasn't called the police on you. I heard her complaining the other day in the foyer when I was getting the mail."

"That nosy old bat can't keep her sniffer outta other people's business." Their neighbour, Millicent Peacock, had taken it upon herself to police the apartment building. Mostly she just banged on her ceiling with a broom handle, but she had threatened more than once to call the cops if the noise level didn't diminish to her liking.

"I don't imagine it's easy. Four Malloys under one roof…" Lester cocked an amused eyebrow.

"You got that right. I been tryin' but it ain't easy. Not Bo, so much. E's the quiet one of the bunch, if you can call any Malloy quiet. Now, Zeb…" Jed rolled his eyes heavenward. "We always did like to wrestle, me and Zeb, but I don't remember 'im bein' so strong last time we tried it. I could always whoop 'im but things is changin'."

"Too much beer and TV. You've let yourself get out of shape," Lester teased.

"Watch it or you'll be next."

Lester just smiled. He downed his coffee and started twisting the lid back in place on top of the thermos. "You'll miss it once Zeb goes back to Fort Mac."

Jed nodded. "You're right, I will. But…" He stretched his large frame. "My body won't. I feel like Hades warmed over." He rubbed a massive hand over his head, making the coarse dark hair stand out at odd angles. Then he looked straight at Lester. "What are you doing on New Year's Eve?"

"I'm not sure," Lester snapped his lunch kit shut. "You?"

"Probably goin' to the Urban Cowboy."

"Big deal. You go there all the time."

"True enough, but I'm told there's a live country band playin'. That oughta count for somethin'."

"I'll have to check with Sherri," Lester said.

"Oh right. You got the old ball and chain to consider now."

Lester smirked. "You're just jealous."

"Me?" Jed snorted in disgust. "No way, b'y. I loves my freedom too much to get tangled up with some woman."

"Sherri is more than just 'some woman'." Lester smiled congenially as he placed his hardhat on top of his closely cropped brown head. His sideburns peeked out by his ears. "When the right one comes along I'll be the first in line to watch you eat crow."

"Not likely, b'y." Jed waved his hand in dismissal. "I'm happy for ya, but ya won't catch me givin' up my freedom so easy."

"Famous last words." Lester stood to his feet and slapped Jed across the back. "I'll talk to Sherri about New Year's Eve."

"If she lets you off yer leash, you should come down to the Urban Cowboy tonight. You haven't been out in a while."

"Maybe." Lester turned to leave.

Jed sighed heavily as he watched his friend exit the lunchroom. He meant it when he said he loved his freedom, even if there was this hollow feeling in the middle of his gut.

JED ARRIVED at his apartment building after work, lunch pail in one hand and truck keys in the other. His usual MO was to stop and check his mailbox in the foyer before heading up to his suite. He was fumbling with the keys in an effort to find his mail key and only looked up when a sharp, "Ehem!" reached his consciousness.

Jed stopped in his tracks and let a sheepish grin spread from one corner of his lips to the other as his gaze made contact with the perpetrator of the sound. "Evenin', Miss Peacock." He nodded his head in the older woman's direction.

Miss Millicent Peacock was standing beside the long bank of mailboxes, her arms folded across her chest and her stare as impenetrable as the grey steel of her hair. "I'd like a word with you about the noise coming from your apartment at all hours of the day or night. There are laws about disturbing the peace in this city, Mr. Malloy."

Jed rattled the keys in his hand nervously. "Sorry 'bout that, Ma'am. My family are visitin' from Newfoundland. We 'aven't seen one another in quite some time, but they'll all be leavin' soon."

Miss Peacock tilted her head up and rose slightly on the balls of her feet. "It's only my generosity during this season of good cheer that has prevented me from calling the authorities."

"It'll only be a few more days. They're leavin' after the new year."

"That's not what your sister said." Miss Peacock arched one of her brows, daring him to explain.

Jed's own brows descended in a furrowed line. "You spoke to my sister?"

"Yes, at least I am assuming it was your sister. I went directly to your apartment this afternoon to ask whomever to turn their music down."

"Oh. I see." Jed rubbed the back of his neck and in the process dropped his keys. He stooped to pick them up and mumbled an apology.

"She was quite rude. 'Get used to it,' I believe she said."

"Get used to it?" Jed repeated.

"Yes. What does she mean, exactly? If you're planning on subletting, the housing authority will need to be notified."

"No, no. Nothin' like that." Jed straightened himself to his full height. "Reba just likes to get her back up. I'll talk to 'er. She'll be goin' back to Newfoundland soon enough, don't you worry. "

"My good will has almost come to its breaking point, Mr. Malloy. I won't stand for any more all night parties or loud music during the day. I hope I've made myself clear."

"Perfectly."

Jed watched Miss Peacock march away from the mailboxes, her heels clicking on the tiles underfoot until the sound was replaced by a dull thud once she hit the carpeted area near the elevators. He needed to have a talk with Reba. With all of them. They would have to tone it down for the next few days. The last thing he wanted was to get evicted.

JED UNLOCKED his apartment door and stepped inside. The canned laughter from a TV sitcom greeted his ears. He tossed his jacket in the general direction of the coat closet, kicked off his boots and threw his lunch kit on the counter with a clatter. "We need to talk about the noise. All of ya." The fact that he was practically yelling didn't register as ironic.

"Pipe down! We're watchin' a show." The voice coming from the living room was Zeb's.

Jed stalked into the living room and headed straight for the remote control sitting on the coffee table. With a decisive click the room reverberated with silence.

"What the - ! We were in the middle of a show!" Zeb sat forward from his reclining position on the couch, his reddish blonde hair half in his eyes; a beer in one hand. "Now who's bein' crooked contrary?"

Their younger brother Bo took up the only armchair, one foot resting on the other knee. "It's almost over." He spoke quietly, calmly, not out of fear, just practicality. He wasn't one to expend energy unnecessarily.

Bo was slightly shorter than Jed, but was a mixture of both older brothers. He had Zeb's blonde hair, only closely cropped, but Jed's square jaw, somewhat rounded nose, and the unmistakable Malloy mischief in the eyes. Folks back home always said you could tell a Malloy when you saw one.

With a grunt Jed relented and turned the TV back on. "As soon as it's over we need to talk." He flopped down on the couch beside Zeb, not even trying to figure out the silly situation on the tube. "Where's Reba?"

"Sh!" Zeb growled.

"In the bathroom," Bo supplied, ignoring Zeb's surly response.

Jed kept his mouth clamped shut for the next four minutes. He glanced over at Bo once or twice, glad for his younger sibling's calming presence. If it wasn't for Bo, he and Zeb might have killed one other by now, even if it was all in good-natured sport. Bo had been forthright with him right from the beginning. He was here to look for a job, but if nothing turned up within the next two weeks he was headed back home to Newfoundland.

When the television episode finished, Zeb lunged for the remote control but not before Jed could click off the TV. "I'm serious. My neighbour is gonna call the cops if we don't keep it down."

"Don't put it all on us." Zeb downed the contents of his can and then crushed it with one hand. He threw the mangled tin into the corner.

Jed frowned, but ignored the motion. "I'm not. I'm just sayin' is all. And apparently she came and talked to Reba. Either of you guys around for that?" He looked from brother to brother.

"I didn't pay any attention. Must a been in the can." Zeb settled into the cushions and closed his eyes.

"I know someone came to the door and Reba answered. Not sure what they said, though," Bo offered.

Reba appeared in the living room doorway. "What's all the fuss?"

Jed blinked. For a moment he didn't recognize the female standing there in his living room.

Jed's sister Reba was about five foot six in height, not tall by Malloy standards, but not short either. The sister he knew had thick red hair that normally fell in waves about her shoulders. This woman had jet-black hair. Her chocolate brown eyes stared at him from beneath a thick ring of black eyeliner. Her lips were also black.

"Reba Roxanne! What in blazes!"

Reba frowned and crossed her arms. "Don't call me that. Only Ma calls me by my full name."

"And what would Ma say if she saw ya?" Jed retorted. "What 'ave ya done?"

"What?" Reba spread her arms and looked down at her figure and then back up again.

"That." Jed made a corkscrew motion with his finger, gesturing up and down her body. "All that black makeup. And your hair! Ya gone and dyed it black!"

"So?"

"So?" Jed snorted. "God gave you a mane of red hair that any woman would kill for and you go and dye it black?" A suppressed chortle came from the couch. Jed turned an accusing glare upon Zeb and Bo, both smirking in their respective seats. "An' I suppose you two knew about this?"

"It's just some dye and a little makeup. Let the kid have some fun,"

Zeb said and then he chuckled. "Although I gotta say, Spitfire, it looks like 'ell."

"Thanks," Reba replied sarcastically. She shook her black mane. "Besides, I'm hardly a kid and it's not permanent. I'm not stupid. Angela says it'll wash out with just four to six washings."

"Angela?" Jed frowned.

"Yes, Angela." Reba sauntered into the room and grabbed up the remote. She flicked on the TV. Jed was too shocked to care. "You know. The hairdresser that lives in the building. The one who dates that cute French bartender. What's his name? Jacques?"

Jed grabbed the remote out of her hands and turned the TV down, but didn't shut it off altogether. "How do you know so much and when did you get this done?"

"I met them at the Urban Cowboy, remember?" Reba shook her head. "You're the one who introduced us. When I found out Angela did hair I thought it would be fun to try something different before I leave."

"Ma'll kill ya," Jed breathed.

"I remember 'er," Zeb said, nodding his head slowly. "Nice backside on that one." His teeth peeked out whitely from beneath the shagginess of his red beard.

"You're an animal," Jed shot in Zeb's direction.

Zeb just shrugged. "I likes a woman with a little meat on 'er. Seems to me you do, too, if I remember." He reached for the remote and Jed had to hold it at arm's length.

"Whatever." Jed threw the remote at Bo for safe-keeping. "Your mane is the least of my worries. My neighbour says you were rude to 'er today when she came to tell ya to turn down the music." Jed held Reba's gaze with his own.

Reba was not one to back down easily. Her chin tilted up. "Me rude? Ha! She was the one being rude. I just gave it right back to 'er."

"Except you forget that I have to see 'er after you goes home. Which reminds me. She says you said you might not be leavin'. Is that true?"

Reba rolled her eyes. "Of course not. I mean, I would if I found a job or something."

"And where would ya stay? Ya can't live with me permanent."

"What about Bo?" Reba chucked her head in his direction. "You said 'e could stay if 'e found a job."

"Exactly my point. We're packed in like sardines as it is."

Reba crossed her arms. "So Bo's welcome and I'm not?"

"I didn't say that!" Jed rubbed the back of his neck. "I'm just sayin' that this arrangement, as nice as it's been, isn't permanent. Lard tunderin' – ya don't think I'm daft enough to let all of yas stay with me forever, do ya? A course Bo's gonna get 'is own place, eventually – if 'e finds a job."

"And if I find a job?" Reba asked.

"We'll cross that bridge when we come to it, I guess."

Zeb chuckled. "I been scoutin' for a job around these parts, too. What if we all ended up livin' on Jed's couch?"

"Just remember I got first dibs," Bo said with a grin.

"All I gotta say is Lard 'ave mercy on us all!" Jed slapped his knees. "What say we go to the Urban Cowboy? I need a change of scenery before I go snakey. You bunch are drivin' me to drink."

They all laughed.

JED AND HIS siblings arrived at the Urban Cowboy just after eight. The interior gave a definite nod to the seventies with lots of neon, wood paneling, and several large framed posters of cowboys in designer jeans. Jed led the way through a maze of tables to the long bar that flanked one wall. The polished surface was almost as reflective as the mirror behind the counter.

Tad Roberts, a smooth headed black man of indeterminate age was behind the counter putting away some bottles. He and his son Cory owned the establishment, although Cory was nowhere in sight. Jacques Marcett, a resident of Jed's apartment building and also a very talented mixologist, was behind the counter as well, polishing glasses.

His dark blonde hair was pulled back into a ponytail and he sported a trimmed goatee and moustache. There was something about the Frenchman that reminded Jed of a fox, but he didn't say it to his face. Maybe the fact that Jacques had managed to land Angela Carravagio, the hairdresser Reba had been referring to earlier, made Jed feel somewhat cynical.

Jed shook his head. Scratch that. Angela Carravagio was a looker, at least in Jed's books, but she was welcome to Jacques if she preferred that scrawny frog to a real man. He wouldn't give Frenchie the satisfaction of knowing he'd been even remotely interested.

"I'll have what's on tap, " Jed hollered to Jacques as he leaned on the counter with his elbows. He turned to watch Zeb, Bo, and Reba sit down in a row on the counter's stools. "Don't get too comfortable. I plan on whoopin' someone's butt at a game of pool before the night is over."

"Hello, Jed. These must be the siblings you mentioned were coming for Christmas." Tad Roberts extended his hand in front of Zeb. "Tad Roberts. I believe we met already at the apartment social. I'm afraid I forgot your name, though."

"Zeb Malloy." Zeb's handshake was firm.

"An' that's my brother Bo and sister Reba all the way from Newfoundland." Jed gestured at the other two with his head.

"I call her Spitfire, but she'll answer to just about anything," Zeb teased. Reba punched him in the arm.

"Pleased to meet you as well." Tad nodded courteously. "Now what can we get for you folks tonight?"

The Malloys ordered their drinks – beer all around - and they settled in for a moment to quench their collective thirst.

"Surprised to see you here this fine evenin'," Jed directed at Tad.

"Somebody's got to work over the holidays." Tad smiled congenially at the group.

Jed nodded, remembering. "Your son Cory went to Vancouver for the holidays, didn't 'e?"

"That's right, although running this place isn't exactly my forte."

Tad glanced over at Jacques. "Good thing I have Jacques to keep things rolling. Otherwise I'd be hooped."

"He's a good boy, our Jacques." There was only the slightest sarcastic edge to Jed's tone.

"I'm trying to convince him to take my offer of promotion to manager, but he's still thinking about it."

"One can't be hasty." Jacques rolled a shoulder elegantly. "I'll let you know after New Year's."

"Well, I hope the answer is yes. Having to spend every evening here is cramping my style." Tad laughed. Jed knew Tad was talking about his new romance with Goldie Harper, a single mother who also lived in their building.

"If I become manager, what will you do? I'm the best bartender in the city," Jacques said, his French accent thick.

"I'll think of something," Tad said with a laugh. "But enough about that. I'm sure you didn't come here to talk shop with me."

"Came to blow off some steam. Thought Lester might show." Jed looked to the doors and then back again. "He hasn't been out in a while."

"What kind of experience does a fella need?" Bo kept his steady gaze on Tad as he took a swig from his stein.

Tad's attention swung from Jed over to Bo. He furrowed his brow. "Pardon me? Experience for what?"

"Bartending." Bo didn't blink. "I'm looking for a job."

Jed turned to Bo and punched him in the bicep. "What do you know about bartendin'?"

Bo maintained a calm face, although he leaned slightly away from Jed and clutched his arm. "I know a couple of things."

Zeb leaned further across the counter so that he could see Jed at the far end of the line-up. "Are ya stun, b'y? Bo took one of them fancy drink makin' courses. Last spring was it?"

"Mixology," Reba filled in. "Got the gift, so some people say."

Jacques had stopped polishing the glass he held and was surveying Bo closely. "How do you make a Boulevardier?"

Bo blinked and thought for a moment. "Bourbon, Campari, sweet vermouth and a twist of lemon." He hesitated before continuing. "Actually, make it an orange slice. More classic."

Jacques's head bobbed up and down. "Excellent."

"The Boulevardier is rather obscure, but it is making a comeback," Bo added.

"Now just a minute. How's bartending gonna pay the bills?" Jed asked. "If yer gonna stay and look fer a job, the oil patch is the place to be."

"That was rather arrogant." Jacques's nose tilted upward. "I pay my bills, and quite nicely I might add."

"You'd be surprised at how well people tip," Tad added.

Zeb guffawed. "Jed's such a cheap son of a - he don't know nothin' about tippin'."

"That ain't true and Jacques knows it." Jed pointed at Jacques with his half empty beer mug.

"When are you sissies gonna take me on in a game of pool? I'm tired of waiting." Reba downed the rest of her beer and clunked the mug down on the counter. "I'll have another, by the way."

"I'm with 'er," Zeb said. He shoved his empty mug in line with Reba's and then unfolded his considerable height from the barstool. "Let's go play some pool."

Tad stopped Bo by placing his hand on his sleeve. "Stop by with a resume. I mean it."

Bo nodded. "I will. First thing tomorrow."

Jed just shook his head. Silly fool kid. A big strong boy like Bo should be working a real man's job, not mixing sissy drinks next to the oh-so-smug Jacques. Not to mention, a permanent housing arrangement was probably in the cards, no matter what Bo said about finding his own place. Cheap rent was hard to come by in this city.

Not that Bo would be hard to live with, but Reba might start getting ideas next and who knew where it would go from there. Talk about cutting into one's private life! He might have to go back home to Newfoundland to find some peace!

THE POOL BALLS made a loud cracking noise as Zeb broke for the third game in a row. The siblings had teamed up – Zeb and Reba against Bo and Jed. So far, they'd each won a game so this one would be the tie-breaker. Zeb circled the table, sinking several balls easily before missing a shot. Bo was up.

Jed stood to one side leaning on his pool cue. Out of the corner of his eye he saw a familiar figure enter the establishment. He waved as Lester Tibbett and Sherri Chan headed his way. Lester was wearing a tan coloured cowboy hat that suited his physique and was holding possessively onto Sherri's hand. The top of Sherri's head was only up to Lester's shoulder, her sleek black hair framing her Asian features like that of a china doll. "Glad to see Lester could come out to play," Jed teased once the couple reached the pool table.

"Is that what he told you?" Sherri turned exotic eyes toward Lester and raised a brow.

"His words, not mine," Lester replied. "So who's winning?"

"Reba and I are about to kick some butt," Zeb answered just as Bo missed his next shot. "Looks like you're up, Spitfire."

Reba leaned across the table, one foot off the floor as she stretched to get just the right angle. A strong cut with the cue ball and one of her solids went into the side pocket. Two more shots and it was Jed's turn.

"Now I'll show youse how it's really done." Jed lined up to shoot. Out of the corner of his eye he noticed another figure moving just into his line of vision. Long, voluptuous chestnut curls, and a signature curve hugging dress accentuated her full figure in all the right ways.

Jed's cue wobbled and the white ball meandered toward its target, grazing the nearest striped ball before disappearing into the pocket. With a curse Jed straightened, thumping his cue on the floor for good measure.

Reba and Zeb let loose with simultaneous whoops and did a high five.

"Ya scratched!" Bo exclaimed. "I thought you said you had my back."

Jed growled a response and shrugged off his younger brother's hand. Then he made the mistake of glancing her way again and wished he hadn't. She was kissing that Frenchman, Jacques.

"Yeah, what's up with that?" Lester asked. "For a guy who likes to brag about how good he is at pool, that was amateur night for sure."

"Everybody misses once in a while," Jed mumbled. He kept his eyes focused on the pool table.

A grinning Zeb wasted no time in finishing the game.

IT WAS another short work week because of the upcoming New Year. The boss let them go early for which Jed was glad. This might be his last night with his siblings and he planned to bring the new year in with style. Zeb was scheduled to fly out to Fort McMurray the next day and Reba went back to Newfoundland the day after. Bo had only booked a one way flight, planning to stay for a longer time to look for work. If the job at the Urban Cowboy panned out, he would be staying for sure.

Jed had resigned himself to the fact - not that he really minded. Bo was quiet and clean. Not like Zeb. Or Reba. That girl set off a wildfire in her path. Makeup and curling irons or whatever the heck they were all over the bathroom. Not to mention clothing all over the spare bedroom floor. Jed was by no means a clean freak, but even he was beginning to feel uncomfortable with all the women's attire strewn about the house. Thankfully, all 'good' things had to come to an end.

As soon as Jed entered the apartment building he noticed Bo standing near the elevator talking to that Carravagio woman. A strangely familiar tightening of his gut occurred and Jed frowned. No woman had ever gotten to his insides the way that one did. It made him mad. He noted the way she placed a hand on Bo's arm and laughed up at him. She was dressed much more conventionally that day, not the usual revealing outfit. Still, women like that couldn't be trusted.

"I don't like that dye job you gave my sister," Jed called as he headed to the bank of mailboxes. He noticed a confused furrowing of her brow. Then the elevators opened and she disappeared inside. He ignored her as he got the mail. Bo was still standing there waiting for him when he was finished.

"That was kind of rude," Bo said as soon as Jed was by his side.

Jed grunted. "Just statin' a fact."

"It's not her fault Reba wanted to shock you."

Jed frowned and turned his gaze to Bo. "Shock me?"

"Of course." Bo laughed. "You don't think she actually likes the way she looks. She just does stuff like that to get a rise out of you. Or Ma. Or whoever she thinks is in charge at the moment."

"You watch yourself with that one. Women like her chew men up and spit them out again."

"Who are you talking about? Reba?"

"No, numskull. I mean that Carravagio girl. Don't think she wasn't trying to flirt. That kind always does. Nothing but trouble. Besides, Frenchie wouldn't like it."

"I wasn't flirting," Bo said, matter-of-fact. "Although she is kind of attractive, don't you think?" A mischievous smile was playing on Bo's lips.

Jed made a huffing sound deep in his throat. "Whatever. Just keep your nose clean. If you're gonna get a job working with Frenchie you can't be messin' with 'is girl."

"Jacques's got nothing to worry about. Least not from me."

Jed wouldn't count on it. That one was a looker and a flirt, and if he and Bo shared the same blood, he'd noticed it, too.

THE URBAN COWBOY was packed and it wasn't just with regulars. Jed's gaze flashed to some women perched provocatively on some stools just across from where he lounged at a small table with his siblings. He might have seen the girls before, but this time they weren't in the usual cowgirl costumes - the fake kind that real cowgirls wouldn't even dream of wearing. Instead, they were decked out in clingy, sparkly dresses with open backs. The kind that didn't allow for undergarments.

Not that he minded. Ringing in the New Year had its perks. He lofted his beer and smiled, only breaking eye contact when someone bumped him from behind.

"Which one do you want?" Zeb leaned over and flicked his head toward the ladies.

"Who says I wasn't planning on both?" Jed countered.

Zeb let out a raucous burst of laughter and slapped Jed across the back. "As if. You've turned into a monk as far as I can tell."

"That's cause I don't kiss and tell."

"I was hoping for a bit more than a kiss," Zeb said as he winked at the women.

"Go for it." Jed shrugged. "Just don't bring 'em back to my place. That would be awkward. Especially since you're sleepin' on the couch."

"You sure know how to kill the fun. Tonight's my last night in town. I deserve a good send off before I go back to Fort Mac."

"I'll just be glad to get your sorry arse off my couch."

It was good natured banter. The Malloy way. To an outsider it sounded like they were arguing, but it was their way of showing affection. When it came down to it, they fought tooth and nail, even as adults, but whoa to the person who dared cross a Malloy from outside the family. They'd have the whole clan down their throats.

Zeb stood up and downed the remainder of his beer. He thunked the stein onto the table. "Sure you're not coming? I don't mind sharin'." He grinned.

"Have at it." Jed took a swig of his own drink.

In truth, he really wasn't interested. There was a time that he would have gladly taken whatever he could get. But somehow the casual thing wasn't as fulfilling as it used to be. He wanted something more. A committed relationship like Lester and Sherri.

They were at a different New Year's gathering. When Jed had asked Lester about it, he just said they'd made other plans. Guess compromise was what it took when you had someone special in your life. Jed liked to tease his friend about the old ball and chain, but if the truth be told, he was jealous.

"Why so glum, chum?" Reba's voice cut into Jed's reverie. "You're gettin' behind!" She guzzled her own beer and then wiped her mouth with the back of her sleeve. Suddenly, a loud burp escaped and she laughed loudly.

"You better slow down. You'll be under the table before midnight," Jed said.

"I can handle my liquor," Reba said. She turned to Bo. "I think livin' out west so long made our big brother forget 'is roots." She flipped a long tendril of hair over her shoulder. The black was already beginning to fade.

"Not forgetting my roots. Just mindin' yours, seein' as you're livin' in my spare room."

"You're not my ma," Reba countered.

"Right you are. I'm yer worst nightmare."

"Come on, Bro," Bo cut in. "It's New Year's."

Before Jed could formulate a retort, Reba was waving frantically toward an approaching figure. "Come sit with us!"

Jed's eyes narrowed as he recognized Angela Carravagio heading their way, followed by a rough looking bald man who was wearing a leather jacket. He had a lot of tattoos and a long tapered goatee. Reba and Bo scooted their chairs to make room for the newcomers.

Angela's version of the 'shiny dress' was not as revealing as Jed would have expected. She usually liked to flaunt her assets, leaving little to the imagination. This dress shimmered in the dim light, the cowl neckline and flared skirt highlighting her curves but forcing onlookers to fill in the blanks. Jed found the more conservative style even more enticing than the usual show of skin. He frowned inwardly. She'd made it perfectly clear she wasn't interested in him, so why keep torturing himself? He was about to ask why she wasn't hanging out with her boyfriend when a voice interrupted his thoughts.

"Rocky Carravagio."

Jed blinked at the other man's extended hand. He stuck out his and they shook. "Jed Malloy. Nice to meet ya." He took in the other man's features after he released his grip. "Wait a minute. You're the brother. I remember seeing you at the Christmas party."

Rocky nodded vigorously. "That's right. I went with Angela. I don't recall if we actually met, but I do remember seeing you there."

"Me too. And this is my sister Reba and my brother Bo. Visiting from Newfoundland."

"Not visiting anymore," Bo interjected. "I'm startin' work next week as a bartender here."

"That's wonderful," Angela said. "It's nice that you don't have to leave us so soon."

"As long as Jed doesn't turn me out on the street, I should be good till I find my own place."

"Tough to get a place to rent these days," Rocky said.

"So, I've been told," Bo agreed with a nod.

"Oh well. It'll be nice to see you every once in a while, down by the mailboxes," Angela said with a smile.

Jed watched the conversation with disgust. Why in blazes was she so fired up happy about Bo sticking around? Didn't she already have a boyfriend? And Bo was lapping it up like a puppy dog starved for affection. Jed felt like slapping him upside the head!

When the conversation turned to hair colour and the fact that Reba needed her roots touched up, Jed had had enough. He pushed his chair back noisily.

"Where you goin'?" Bo asked.

"Getting another beer. They're so doggone busy the service is too slow." Jed turned on his heel to head to the bar where he usually liked to sit. Maybe there he could collect his thoughts - or get stinking drunk. One of the two.

He'd only taken one step when he froze in his boots. He blinked as his mouth dropped open. Perching on one of the high stools was a familiar curvaceous figure. She leaned over the counter a bit to receive a quick kiss on the mouth from Jacques the bartender. Then Jacques went back to spraying some soda from a nozzle into a tall glass.

Jed slowly turned to look back at his own table. Angela was deep in conversation with his sister. Or was it Angela? He pivoted again to gaze at the woman sitting up to the bar. She was wearing a strappy little black dress with a line of sequins around the plunging neckline. The skirt was riding dangerously high as she crossed one leg over the other; one spiked heel was caught in the rung of the stool while the other foot dangled. That was Angela Carravagio.

He glanced one more time at the look-a-like. So if the one at the bar was Angela, who was talking to his sister? They were obviously twins, but how had he not known? Was he the only fool who didn't? And if so, how could he admit his mistake?

For a split second, hope soared. If the other Angela really wasn't Angela, then he no longer had to worry about Frenchie. He thought of the few times he had seen her in the foyer and had assumed she was her sister. He should have seen the signs! Look-a-like Angela didn't wear too much make-up or clothes that were too tight. She seemed friendly and not as loud.

He took a step closer to the table. Then he noticed the way she smiled at Bo and the way he didn't seem to mind it. Had Bo known all along? The little rat! He was stealing her right out from under his nose.

Embarrassment washed over him. Of course that wasn't true. Hadn't he been the one to brag about being single? He'd set the example for all his siblings, except for the sisters back home. Fanny, Mary and Sissy all had families. But all five brothers - and Reba - were proud to still be single. No ball and chain for them. Ha. It was a lie and now he couldn't do anything about it because his own little brother was interested in his girl.

Jed turned away and headed for Zeb. If he was destined to be a bachelor his whole life he might as well make the most of it. His giant of a brother was sitting between the two girls they had seen earlier, one arm slung around each as they flirted and laughed.

"Hi ladies," Jed interrupted the threesome's conversation. "Did my brother tell ya he has a much better lookin' brother?" He slapped Zeb on the back.

The girls giggled.

"Eh, b'y!" Zeb's speech was only slightly slurred. "What you ladies say? Think we should let this big lummox join us?"

"Sure, he's cute," one of the girls said.

"And strong, too," the other added. "Are you really brothers?"

"Blood brothers through and through," Jed said with a grin. "Eh, barkeep!" he called a little more loudly. "How's about another round, eh? Let's bring this New Year in right!"

SLAP! The window blind whipped upward with a crash, flooding the bedroom with blazing white light. Jed shielded his eyes as some choice words erupted from his lips. He ducked under the blankets but gagged on the smell of his own putrid breath. As hangovers went, this had to be the worst.

"Can I borrow your truck?"

The voice was Bo's, barely registering beneath the dull buzz in Jed's ears. Jed told Bo to leave using a common metaphoric phrase ending with the word 'off'.

"Not till you answer me civil," Bo stated.

"What do you want?" Jed growled.

"To borrow your truck. Zeb's leaving and I thought I'd be nice and drive him to the airport instead of makin' him spend good money on a taxi," Bo explained. "And it doesn't look like you're gonna drive him."

Jed shook his head, immediately regretting the action. He took a steadying breath and opened one eye just a crack. "Zeb's leaving already?"

"It's already past noon." Bo chuckled. "And if it makes you feel any better, he's in about as much pain as you."

Jed grunted. He should get up and see his brother off. Who knew when they'd see one another next? With a groan Jed hoisted himself to a sitting position. After a moment's rest he swung his legs over the side of the bed. With effort he focused on Bo's sturdy figure, lounging in the doorway of the bedroom. The blow up mattress that Bo was using each night was already propped up against the wall and his sleeping bag was rolled neatly beside it. "Tell 'im I'll just be a minute and then I can take 'im."

"No need," Bo said. "I don't mind. Besides, you look like 'ell."

"Thanks." Jed still hadn't moved from the sitting position on the bed.

"And if you're worried about me getting lost, I'll use GPS. I think I can handle it."

The offer was appealing, there was no doubt about it. "Just let me get some coffee into my system and then I'll decide." Jed slowly stood up and managed to shuffle past Bo into the hallway and head to the bathroom.

A few minutes later, Jed emerged and maneuvered his body to the kitchen. Reba, Bo and Zeb were already sitting around the small formica table. The smell of coffee reached Jed's nostrils and he made his way toward the counter like a magnet to steel.

"You look about as good as I feel." Zeb's voice was gravelly.

"You both reek," Reba said, screwing up her nose.

Zeb narrowed his eyes. "I just took a shower."

"So? The alcohol is comin' outta your pores," Reba said.

Zeb laughed hoarsely. "No doubt." He rubbed his big hand through his thick beard. "We had some good time, eh, b'y?"

Jed joined his siblings and sat on the remaining kitchen chair. "Did we? I don't remember."

Zeb laughed, his eyes squinting with the pain of it. "Come to think of it, neither do I. I'm assuming we had a good time. Those were a couple of hot little chicks we landed."

Jed sipped his coffee. He didn't actually remember much about what happened beyond a certain point. He recalled sitting at the bar with the two women, and drinking some tequila shooters, which was always a mistake. After that there was some billiards, then the live music started and there was some dancing, some kissing after the count down to the new year… And then what? He looked sideways at Zeb. "Uh, how did we get home? Did we go somewhere else first?"

"If you're asking whether we got lucky, the answer is no," Zeb said with a sheepish grin. "Seems our lady friends don't do certain things on a first date."

Jed nodded. "So there are still a few moral people left in this world." Relief washed over him at the news, but he strained to maintain an 'I don't care either way' facade. He didn't like the idea of not remembering certain intimate details. Not to mention the fact that it felt like cheating, which was ridiculous since he wasn't even in a relationship with anyone.

"And as to how you got home, you took a cab, as planned," said Bo. "I made sure you got into the cab myself."

"Of course you did," Jed mumbled.

"Well, Andrea, Rocky, and Reba had to help." Bo laughed. "It's not easy getting two wasted Malloys to do anything once they've had too much to drink and think they own the world."

Jed frowned. "Andrea and Rocky? I don't know no Andrea and Rocky."

"Andrea and Rocky Carravagio," Reba explained as if to a child. "Of course you know them."

Andrea. So that was her name... Jed gulped down the remainder of his now cool coffee. He rose to get a refill, keeping his back to his siblings while he mulled this new information over.

He took another sip and then turned slowly, leaning against the counter with his backside. "So am I the only loser in this room that didn't know there were two of them?"

"I had no clue," Zeb said with a shrug. "In fact, I'm not sure what the 'ell you're talkin' about." He laughed.

"The Carravagio sisters," Reba said. "They're twins. Angela and Andrea."

"You mean the hottie that goes with that French bartender dude?" Zeb asked.

Reba nodded. "Exactly. That's Angela. The other sister's name is Andrea. They own a salon together. 'Gemini's'. Get it? Gemini's because they're twins."

"We get it," Bo said dryly.

"So you're telling me that you knew and you didn't say anything?

24

Just let me carry on like a fool?" Jed looked from Bo to Reba and back again.

"I knew," Reba said with a shrug. "I just assumed you morons did, too."

"I didn't," Bo admitted. "Although I wondered at times."

Zeb shrugged. "Whatever. I'm leaving in…" he consulted his cell phone sitting on the table in front of him. "Two and a half hours, so it really doesn't matter to me." He grinned. "It might make life interestin' around here for you fellas, though."

"What's that supposed to mean?" Jed asked.

Zeb shrugged. "Some healthy competition, that's all."

Bo put up his hands in surrender. "Count me out!"

"Don't you have an airplane to catch?" Jed asked sullenly.

"So I do. So which one of you lucky buggers is gonna take me to the airport?" He consulted his phone again. "With the stupid rules about getting there ahead of time, I'd say we better get going."

Jed downed the rest of his coffee, but Bo was already standing. "I'll do it," Bo offered. He looked directly at Jed. "You look like -"

"I know, I know! You already told me. So get going then and don't get lost or smash up my truck on the way. The drivers in this city are crazy."

Zeb's duffle bag was already sitting by the door so it was just a matter of saying one last good-bye accompanied by a bear hug and a few low intensity slaps on the back.

When Jed shut the door behind Bo and Zeb, the apartment felt suddenly quiet. Eerily so. He turned to say something to Reba but she had already disappeared from the kitchen.

With a sigh, Jed poured himself some more coffee. This first day of the new year was shaping up to be a long lonely one.

ANOTHER DAY PASSED and it was back to work for Jed. When he got home that evening, Bo was just leaving the apartment. "Where you goin'?" Jed asked.

"First night on the job," Bo said.

"Oh, right. You can take my truck if you like," Jed offered.

"No, I've got to figure out how to make my own way," Bo said. "Transit it is until I can buy myself a vehicle."

Jed nodded. He probably would have felt the same. "Looks like we'll be like two ships passin' in the night from now on. You workin' nights and me workin' days."

"G'wan," Bo said with a laugh. "You spend about as much time down at the Urban Cowboy as you do at home in the evenings, so I figure we'll see one another plenty."

Jed laughed. "True enough. Not tonight, though. I'm beat. Gonna eat some food and watch some TV and maybe even catch a few zees on the couch."

He waved good-bye and shut the door to the apartment. The holidays were starting to catch up with him and he was ready for a quiet evening at home.

Jed cleaned up from work and then went to the kitchen to rummage around in the refrigerator. Except for a turkey dinner on Christmas day, they'd been eating a lot of take out during the holidays. It was time to get back to some home cooking. "Reba, you here?" he called over his shoulder as he continued to peruse the contents of the fridge.

There was no answer. With a shrug, Jed found some farmer's sausage in the deep freeze compartment and threw it in the microwave to thaw. That and some frozen perogies with fried onions would make a tasty evening meal. He set to work, chopping, boiling and frying.

When the food was prepared, he left everything in the pots on the stove and grabbed a plate from the cupboard. Only slightly miffed that he didn't know where Reba was, but determined not to phone or text, he sat down in front of the TV with his plate and switched on a hockey game.

It wasn't until he was snoozing through the third period that he heard the latch on the apartment deadbolt click and he jerked to attention, his empty plate clattering to the floor. He let out a curse and scooped up the plate. Only a tiny dollop of sour cream had hit the carpet. He swiped at it with his finger, deciding that it blended in enough to leave for now.

"Do ya want some taken up? It's on the stove," he said as Reba hung her coat up in the closet near the door. One thing about family; you didn't have to translate when it came to Newfie expressions. He set his dishes in the sink and ran some water over them.

"No thanks. I already ate."

"You sure? There's lots." It was true. He'd cooked like he was making supper for the entire family, not just one person.

"I'm good."

"Well, that's debatable," Jed said with a grin. "I guess I'll be eatin' cold sausage and perogies for lunch tomorrow."

Reba leaned over his shoulder as he scooped some of the leftovers into a plastic container with a lid. "Why'd you make so much, anyway? Who'd ya think was coming for supper?"

"Nobody. I guess having youse around has made me feel like I was back in Newfoundland. I felt obligated to cook for the whole family and then some."

"I'll try one sausage, since they're already cooked." Reba reached into the frying pan with her fingers and grabbed a sausage. She bit into it without bothering with cutlery or a plate.

"Where you been?" Jed finished dividing up the food into containers - two days' worth of lunches.

"Just hanging out with the girls." Reba flipped her hair back off her shoulder.

Jed blinked. It was the first he'd noticed that Reba's hair was the right colour - a rich dark auburn. "You un-dyed your hair."

"No, I re-dyed it." She fluffed her hair with her free hand. "And don't say I told you so."

"Okay, I won't. But... I knew you'd see sense eventually." Jed grinned.

Reba rolled her eyes but smiled in spite of herself. "Angela did such a fantastic job of matching my real colour you can hardly tell, don't you think?"

Jed squinted and tipped his head to one side. Come to think of it, there wasn't the same variety in tone that Reba's natural hair had, but it was close. "She did a good job. So those are the girls you were hanging with?"

Reba nodded her head. "Good sausage." She nipped her fingers into the container before Jed could seal the lid and took another piece. Then she headed for the living room.

"You leave my 'ockey game alone," Jed called as he placed the food in the refrigerator. On cue the channel switched to the canned laughter of a popular sit-com. With a grunt he looked at the pots and pans, and decided against it. They could wait. He stalked into the living room. "I was watchin' that game."

Reba flipped back to hockey. "Okay, fine."

Jed settled himself in his chair and they watched for several minutes until there was a commercial break.

Reba cleared her throat. "So, what do you think about me staying on in Calgary?" She sat forward and added hastily. "I'm not asking your permission or anything. I just want to know what you think."

"Well, I guess when you put it that way, you can do whatever you please. As long as you have a job and a place to live." He stared at her pointedly.

"The first item seems to have fallen into place. Andrea and Angela offered me a job at Gemini's. Their business has really picked up and they need someone to work reception, do shampoos, things like that."

Jed nodded his head. "How much?" He didn't want to come off as negative, but that kind of a job probably didn't pay very well.

Reba tilted her head, her chin jutting out. Jed recognized the defensive move. "Just a bit over minimum wage to start. But I'll get part of the tips and if I do good, they said I can work into an apprenticeship."

Jed furrowed his brow. "You know anything about hairdressin'?"

Reba expelled a frustrated breath. "I took cosmetology in school so I know the basics. I even got a certificate." She shook her head. "You're so out of touch."

Jed shrugged. "Sorry for not knowing every single thing my

siblings been doing in the last few years. I didn't know Bo'd taken mixology so I figure you can cut me some slack if I didn't know you took cosmo-whatever you called it in school."

"Anyway, I've been thinking about doing it for a while now. It seems like now is my chance."

"Okay, but what about the living arrangements? You can't expect Bo to sleep on an air mattress for too long."

"I know," Reba said. "Who knows? Maybe me and 'im will get our own place and leave you to your bachelorhood forever."

"Suits me."

Reba hesitated. "So… you don't mind if I stick around then? For a while until I get my feet under me?"

"Course not. We're family." In Jed's mind that said it all. "I'm more concerned about what Ma's gonna say."

"She'll be fine. I'll get Sissy or Fanny to pack a few of my things and ship them out. The rest she can pack into the attic if she wants."

"I wasn't thinking so much about the stuff, as 'er losing 'er baby girl."

Reba rolled her eyes. "I'm hardly 'er baby. That's Pip's distinction."

Jed smiled at the memory of his youngest brother. Steve, or 'Pip' as he was called, was already 22 years old, a full ten years younger than Jed. That there were six other children between them wasn't the point. Pip represented Jed's own youth, which he sometimes felt was slipping away. Perhaps having Bo and Reba around would fill the void he felt inside at times.

"Well, just make sure ya let 'er down easy, my girl. Too many children leavin' the nest at one time might be more than she can take."

Reba straightened her stance and crossed her arms. "She's got five more at home not to mention the grandkids. She'll be fine." Her tone held more confidence than Jed suspected she felt.

He wrapped her in a bear hug.

"What's that for?" Reba's voice was muffled by Jed's shirt.

"Just cause I felt like it." He released her and smiled. She was frowning, but he could tell she was grateful for his support.

That was another thing about being a Malloy. Never admit to being scared.

~

ROCKY CARRAVAGIO HAD A SHAVED HEAD, a boat load of tattoos, and a scraggly goatee that ended in a point. He was sitting in one of the faux leather chairs at the front of Gemini's hair salon as Jed entered.

"Mind if I sit here?" Jed wasn't one to be easily intimidated, but he was glad they weren't meeting in a back alley somewhere.

"Course not," the other man said with a shrug. "I hear your sister is working for my sisters now. Small world." He smiled congenially, showing a gap where one tooth was missing. "You picking her up?"

Jed shook his head. "Gettin' a haircut. Thought I'd better give the place a try now my sis works here."

Reba rounded a corner and took up her spot behind the high reception counter. When she looked up her eyes widened in obvious surprise. "What are you doing here? I told you Angela offered me a ride after work."

Jed jumped to his feet and took the two steps to the counter. He rested his elbows on the shiny surface. "I know. I just thought that… uh… maybe you could squeeze me in for a haircut."

Reba narrowed her eyes suspiciously then perused the appointment book. "Angela could probably squeeze you in."

Jed peered over the edge at the appointment book. "What about Andrea? Is she free?"

Reba looked up, mischief in her eyes. "What's it worth to you?"

"How's about the fact that you're livin' in my apartment for nothin'."

"Only temporarily. Till I gets my feet under me."

"So you says."

Reba scanned the book with her pencil. "Come back in half an hour." She looked up. "And be prepared for some royal teasing once I tell Bo."

Jed frowned. "Keep yer mouth shut if you want to keep the spare room."

Reba shrugged. "Deal."

Jed waved to Rocky on his way out the door. He knew he wore a silly grin, but at that particular moment, he really didn't care.

JED ARRIVED BACK at the salon in exactly half an hour. Silly how nervous he felt. It was just a haircut. Reba seated him in one of those swivelling chairs that pumped up with hydraulics. She gave him a sly grin before walking away.

"Well, hello, there neighbour." Andrea's voice had a soft feminine quality.

Jed felt his insides tighten. "'Ello yourself."

"You're here for a cut?" Her fingertips touched his hair.

Jed squirmed in his seat. "Nothin' fancy. Just a trim."

"You've got nice thick hair." She continued to run her hands through his dark curls. It was torture. "Need a wash too, or just the cut?"

Jed cleared his throat. "Just the cut. I showered this mornin'." Letting her fingers massage his scalp for a prolonged period of time was out of the question. The cut was bad enough.

Andrea placed a plastic cape around Jed's shoulders and fastened it at the neck. Next she spritzed his hair down with a spray bottle and began combing it out. "So how long have you lived in Calgary, Jed?"

"Four years, give or take a few months."

"Do you miss Newfoundland?"

"Sometimes." He shrugged. "But it looks like Newfoundland is coming to me, now, what with Bo and Reba movin' to Calgary."

"Stay still," Andrea directed.

Jed glanced in the large mirror in front of him and wished he hadn't. Andrea looked as fresh and pretty as a flower in the soft pink smock she wore over her clothes. Not like her sister two chairs away who was wearing a V-neck that plunged way past decency. How did he ever get the two of them mixed up? Andrea was nothing like her sister Angela.

Andrea caught him staring at her in the mirror and smiled. His gaze immediately flew somewhere safe.

"We're very glad to have Reba working for us. She seems genuinely interested in the business and is a great worker. Very organized."

"That she is." Jed kept his eyes fixed on the counter top in front of him. Various blow dryers, curling irons and straighteners were plugged in and waiting in their dock. A tall clear vase-like contraption held combs and brushes in a turquoise blue liquid. There were a couple of magazines on the counter, too.

Andrea snipped away for a few minutes in silence. When she moved around to the front, she all but blocked his view. All he could see was her ample bosom staring him in the face. He shut his eyes.

"That about does it, I think. It wasn't very long to begin with, but you've got a nice crown. Your hair does exactly what it's told."

"The only part of me that does, I suspect." Jed grinned and risked looking in the mirror again.

Andrea smiled before swinging him around. She produced a hand held mirror so he could see the back of his head in the reflection.

"You can pay your sister at the front." She undid the smock and whipped it from his shoulders. Then she stepped on the hydraulic pump and the chair slowly descended.

"Thanks."

Angela walked by and waved. "Hi, neighbour. Fancy meeting you here."

"Hi, Angela," Jed mumbled. When she was safely past, he cleared his throat and spoke more quietly. "Say... You 'ungry? I'm just about gut founded. What say?"

Andrea blinked. "I beg your pardon?"

Reba appeared out of nowhere with a broom and began sweeping the dark fluff into a pile. "E's asking you out."

Jed felt the heat infiltrating his ears. "For a bite is all. If you're free, that is."

"Since you're my last client, I think I would like that very much."

"Good. That's just fine."

"I'd like to go home first, if that's alright." Andrea looked down at her serviceable smock.

"No problem. What time you be handy?"

"I should be home by five thirty. How about six?"

"Suits me. I'll meet you downstairs in the lobby then, at six o'clock."

"Looking forward to it." Andrea smiled.

"You g'wan." Reba made a shooing motion with her hand. "I'll finish the clean up and make sure this lummox pays 'is bill."

Andrea laughed. "Okay." She waved before turning and walked toward the back of the salon.

"Now if that weren't embarrassin'!" Jed let out with a puff of air.

Reba stood with her hand on her hip. "Which part? You askin' Andrea out on a date, facin' them both at once, or me overhearing everything?"

"All three."

Jed checked his watch one more time and then shoved his hands in his jeans pockets. Plaid shirts and blue jeans were about all he owned for clothing, but at least they were clean. The elevator doors swooshed open and he turned eagerly to greet Andrea. His smile faded when Bo stepped out.

"Off to work?" Jed asked. The answer was obvious of course, but he and Bo had barely seen one another yet that day so it seemed the polite thing to say.

"Yup. See you in the morning."

"Doubt that. You're still in bed when I wake up."

"Tomorrow is Sunday," Bo reminded.

Of course it was. Today was Saturday which is why he had time to drive all the way over to Gemini's for a haircut. "Right. I forgot. Maybe we should have Newfie breakfast tomorrow since all three of us will be home for a change."

"I hate bologna," Bo said.

Jed's eyes widened. "All these year's eating Ma's Newfie breakfast and you hates bologna? Well, I'll be giggered."

"Nobody gets away without eatin' everything on their plate," Bo reminded. "It was pure survival."

The elevator doors swished open once again and Andrea stepped out. "Hi, Bo!" she greeted warmly as she walked toward the men.

Jed frowned.

"Hi." Bo lifted a hand in greeting.

"Off to work?" Andrea asked.

Bo nodded. "You should stop by later. I'll mix you up something special. Virgin."

Jed's eyebrows shot up and his mouth dropped open. "Hey b'y! That was a mite inappropriate. What yer mouth."

Andrea just smiled. "He didn't mean it like that. Bo knows I don't drink alcohol, so he was just offering to make me something without," Andrea explained.

"Course, I knew dat." Jed clamped his mouth shut.

Bo gave his brother a quizzical look but continued talking. "Anyway, maybe see you both later."

Jed's gaze followed Bo out of the building.

"I, uh… I didn't know you didn't drink. Alcohol, I mean."

"Bo knows because he's mixed a few fancy drinks for me when I've gone with Angela." Andrea sighed. "She often needs a DD."

"I see."

They exited the building and walked toward the parking lot. Andrea pulled her coat more closely around her form. "That wind's nippy."

"It's still January," Jed replied.

"I don't want you to judge Angela," Andrea said as she slid into the open passenger door of Jed's pickup. "She's got some issues - don't we all - but she's just choosing to deal with hers in a different way right now. I'm sure she'll come around."

Jed was in the truck himself now. It was toasty warm since he had started it remotely while waiting in the lobby. He put it in gear and headed out of the parking lot.

"I'm the last person to judge somebody. Get the log outta your own eye before you go tryin' to get the speck outta someone else's."

"You know scripture!" Andrea fairly beamed at him.

Jed took a quick sidelong glance at the woman sitting next to him. "I went to Catholic school so I guess I'm not totally heathen."

"So you're Catholic?" she asked.

"Hm…" Jed rubbed his chin with his free hand. "I suppose I am for all intents and purposes. Been baptized and did my time as an altar boy if that's what you mean. Not sure I really believe in it much, though." He looked over at her again. "I take it you're religious?"

Andrea smiled and shook her head. "I hate that term 'religious'. I suppose to you I am, but I prefer 'in a relationship with Jesus'."

Jed tightened his jaw. Hoo-boy. One of those fanatics. Wasn't that just his luck. "So this not drinking thing… Is that part of your religion - I mean, your relationship?"

"It's just a personal choice, really. Drinking alcohol isn't necessarily bad; it's the overindulgence of alcohol that's the problem. I believe a person can have a glass of wine or a social drink on occasion as long as their conscience is clear and they don't get out of control by getting drunk. I just choose not to bother at all. I don't want to end up being a stumbling block to someone who is weaker than me and can't say no after they've had one."

"Hm. Never thought of it that way before." It was true, he hadn't. The consumption of alcohol had always been part of his life; part of his family. It was almost a cultural thing for him. He'd seen quite a few folks abuse it in his time, but most just saw it as a way to have some fun amidst the hardships of life.

"'Take heed lest this liberty of yours become a stumbling block to those that are weak.' At least I think that's how it goes."

"I sees you know your Bible well enough," Jed said.

"Probably not well enough, but… I try." She flashed him a smile.

They had arrived at their destination - a small Indian restaurant in a strip mall that was only a few blocks away. "I hope this is okay? I didn't think to ask if you cared for Indian food."

"Love it. Butter chicken is one of my weaknesses," Andrea said with a laugh.

Well, at least they had that in common.

JED AND ANDREA enjoyed a sumptuous Indian meal and were topping it off with cups of warm, authentic chai tea.

"I can tell your faith is important to you," Jed brought the subject up again. "Is that a family thing or something you decided after you left home?"

Andrea cocked her head to one side and leaned on her hand. "Hm… how can I put this? It was sort of a family thing, but we didn't grow up in a regular family. Our parents were killed in a car accident when we were young. Ang and I were nine and Rocky was already fourteen. Nobody wanted to adopt an entire family of kids, especially not at our age, so we went into foster care. We were never split up, but Rocky left as soon as he could at seventeen and joined the military. Ang and I were fortunate that our foster parents were nice people. Not the kind of horror stories that you hear all the time about abuse and what not. They were kind, caring people. Christian people. That's not to say we didn't have our share of troubles. We did." Andrea laughed and looked down at her mug. "Believe it or not, I was probably more rebellious than Angela when we were young. I didn't always like having to go to church and youth group and that, whereas Ang lapped that stuff up. Later, when I was about seventeen, I decided to give my life to Christ. Once we graduated from high school, Angela suddenly decided it was time for her rebellious phase. I'm still waiting for her to grow out of it."

"How many years has it been?" Jed asked.

Andrea flashed Jed an amused smile. "Is that your way of asking me how old I am?"

He chuckled. "Maybe."

"Twenty-five. As soon as we turned eighteen our foster parents had no choice but to let us go on our own. I think that's what turned Angela. In her mind - in mine, too, I guess - we were like their own kids. But suddenly after our eighteenth birthday, the government would no longer pay our foster parents for our care. We were expected to make a life for ourselves without their support."

"That seems cruel. No wonder she was pissed. I would be too."

"I understand why. They had other mouths to feed and if they let every foster kid just keep living with them indefinitely they wouldn't be able to afford it. They prayed with us before we left, but it still hurt. A lot." Andrea sighed and then straightened her shoulders. "But I've moved on. At least I had Jesus on my side. Unfortunately, it kind of turned Angela away from her faith."

"Then what happened?"

Andrea shrugged one shoulder. "We busted our butts. Got jobs and a tiny apartment. One of us went to school full time while the other worked full time and then we switched it up. It took us four years to do a two year program, but we did it. Certified in hair, aesthetics, and massage therapy."

"Good for you. And now you own your own salon. That's quite an accomplishment."

"We've worked hard for it." Andrea leaned forward. "Despite what you may think, Angela is very responsible when it comes to money. She's the brains behind our business. I'm the softy who takes stray clients in off the street and then only charges them half price."

Jed's eyebrows shot up. "You only charged me half price?"

Andrea nodded. "I figured with the minuscule amount of hair I took off the top, it would be highway robbery to do otherwise."

Jed ran a hand over his closely cropped head. "I guess I really didn't need a haircut yet..."

"I believe that she'll come around one day. Back to her faith, I mean. I've done a lot of praying. Even my brother has come to know Jesus. And that's saying something."

"Rocky?" Jed asked in surprise. "The tatts man?"

Andrea laughed. "A pussy-cat in tiger's clothing. Rocky was

dishonourably discharged for possession of marijuana - a big deal back when it happened. He maintains to this day that he was framed, and I believe him. The bitterness was eating him up until he came across an army chaplain he calls 'the padre'. Now he's living for Jesus. I don't know why I'm telling you all this." Andrea looked into Jed's eyes and smiled sheepishly. "I can tell you already think I'm a looney-tune or something."

"I don't think that. I think you're one brave gal, that's what I think."

There was a moment of silence as they held each other's gaze. Finally, Andrea shifted in her seat. "I like you, Jed. I really do. You seem like a nice, down to earth, honest man. But the Bible says that a believer shouldn't become unequally yoked, so until something changes, I'm afraid we can never be more than friends."

What the…? That came out of left field! "What are you sayin' exactly?" Jed asked, his voice hesitant.

"Just what I said. You're strong and attractive, too. And you're fun to be around."

"But…?"

Andrea sighed. "I know you coming to the salon today was not an accident. I'm flattered. On the other hand, I can't help wondering if it's really my sister you're attracted to, not me."

"Absolutely not! She may be a looker, but she's not my type."

"So you mean to tell me you never got us mixed up? Not even once?" Andrea looked pointedly right at him.

"No… well, yes. I didn't know there was two of you till New Year's," Jed admitted. He allowed a small half grin to lift the corner of his mouth. "Which explains why I wasn't always nice to you. I thought you were some kind of two-timing little… you know."

Andrea nodded. "I wondered. Sometimes it seemed like you liked me and then the next minute you were rude. I thought it was just the Newfoundland way."

"Never! We Newfies pride ourselves on bein' nice to everyone. Even come-from-aways."

"Come from aways?" Andrea repeated.

"Folks not from Newfoundland," Jed clarified.

"Ah. I see." Andrea lifted her chin. "In any case, none of that matters. As long as you're good with us just being friends. I wouldn't want you to have expectations beyond what I can give."

"Suits me fine," Jed lied. He hoped his smile was genuine.

"Good. I like you - and your family - a lot. I almost envy the bond that I see between all of you. Not that Rocky and Angela and I aren't close, but... it just seems less riddled with baggage, that's all."

"What you see is what you get," Jed agreed.

"Good. Now, how about if we go over to the Urban Cowboy and celebrate our new friendship? Bo promised me a drink and I expect him to deliver."

Bo. So that was her angle.

"Sure, I can hardly wait." Jed pasted on a smile and slipped from the upholstered booth.

Andrea chatted on the way to the Urban Cowboy but Jed paid little attention. All he could think about was how he had lost out again. Andrea made it sound like it was her religion that kept her from dating him, but in truth it was much closer to home than that. Andrea Carravagio preferred his younger brother Bo. And there was nothing he could do about it.

Except maybe drown his sorrows in a pint or two of beer. That was one relationship he could count on.

EPISODE 2

NEIGHBOURHOOD WATCH

o

IT WAS Saturday night and the Urban Cowboy was hopping. So was its newest bartender, Bo Malloy.

"Two more Mai Tais and three beer on tap," called a waitress as she leaned up against the long polished counter that ran all the way along one wall of the establishment.

"Soon as I'm finished this order." Bo simultaneously poured whiskey from two separate bottles into twin tumblers filled with ice. To the count of two he lofted the bottles high, letting the dual arcs of liquid gold splash against the rocks of ice below, before lowering them with a flourish.

"Wow. Gettin' fancy," Crystal, the waitress, commented. "You've been practicing." She set her tray on the countertop and leaned forward on her elbows.

"Busy is all." Bo flashed her a smile and then wished he hadn't.

It was obvious Crystal was flirting, the way she was sticking her behind out and swaying it in the aisle. She had a nice figure, no doubt about that, and her tight jeans - standard uniform for the place - hugged her rounded hips to perfection. But she was probably in her late thirties and her face was hardened by life. He didn't need that kind of complication.

"He is a show off," came another male voice with a distinct French flair.

Bo just laughed. Jacques Marcett, the manager of the Urban Cowboy, was pointing an accusing finger his way. Bo plunked two large steins of draft onto Crystal's tray, the frothy foam dripping down the sides. "Jacques's just jealous cause I know as much as he does. Maybe more." He grinned and glanced at Jacques, waiting for the inevitable tirade of cursing in French.

He wasn't disappointed. Jacques could let loose when he wanted to, which was more often than not. Good thing Bo's own French was almost non-existent, or he was sure his ears would be burning.

Bo finished Crystal's order and watched for a moment as she swung away from the counter, drink laden tray lofted high enough so as to maneuver past the crowd without getting bumped.

Country music blared in the background but was almost lost amid the cacophony of laughter and voices. The Urban Cowboy, a retro bar in downtown Calgary, was a hot location for wannabe cowboys as well as the real McCoy. Owned by a father and son team, it sported a country vibe complete with mechanical bull, lots of neon, wood plank panelling, and mirrors.

Bo jumped when Jacques slid up next to him. "Nice derriere on that one, no?"

Bo immediately straightened his shoulders. "No. I mean yes, but I'm not interested."

"No?" Jacques raised an aristocratic brow.

Bo turned back to the row of bottles behind the counter and stashed two empties underneath. "I like Crystal well enough, but not in that way."

Jacques shrugged elegantly and crossed his arms, leaning against the counter with his back to the crowd. "Perhaps you will change your mind. Crystal is not known for her... how do you say it? Choosing?"

"You mean she's not choosey?" Bo corrected.

Jacques nodded. "Yes. This is what I mean."

"Thanks," Bo retorted with a snort. "You make me sound like I've got the plague. For the record, she's not my type."

"Oh? And what is your type?"

"None of your business."

"Suit yourself. Just don't expect any advice - or sympathy - when the time comes." Jacques turned and walked further down the long counter, polishing as he went.

"Don't worry, I won't," Bo said under his breath. Not that he didn't like women, but he'd never made a connection with anyone that went any deeper than the physical. He preferred maintaining a certain amount of aloofness. It was less messy that way.

Bo had been working side by side with Jacques for a couple of weeks now. Jacques came off as snooty, but once you got to know him he was actually quite personable. His accent and the way he held his chin aloft, complete with pointed goatee, made him seem like he thought he was superior, but it really wasn't so. At least Bo didn't think so.

Bo enjoyed working at the bar. He had never been particularly ambitious, but the pay was actually pretty good, especially when tips were factored in. One of the best things about the job was watching the patrons come and go. Battles won, loves lost, schemes foiled. Flirting, wooing, maneuvering. It was all part of a grand game and Bo enjoyed the spectator aspect of the sport.

Just as he was about to get back to work Bo spotted his older brother Jed winding his way through the tables toward the bar. They made eye contact and Bo lifted his hand in a wave.

Jed was tall and broad with curly dark hair, a square face, and the distinct Malloy nose which was somewhat rounded - almost too cute for such an otherwise rugged face. People said Bo and Jed looked the most alike except for the hair colour, but then there was something about a Malloy that couldn't be mistaken. Perhaps it was the mischief in the eyes. Although Jed was slightly taller than Bo, they were similarly broad across the shoulders. Bo had never tested the theory, but he was sure he could take Jed in a fight if need be. Well, maybe. Jed did have experience on his side.

Jed plunked himself down on his customary stool at the bar.

"What'll it be, Bro?" Bo slung a towel over his shoulder.

"As if ya need ta ask," Jed said, his melodic Newfoundland accent coming across loud and clear despite the fact that he had moved away from the province years before any of the rest of the family.

With an amused grin, Bo filled an extra large stein with beer and slid it in front of his brother. "So? How was work today?" He mopped up the ring of liquid that was left behind from Jed's mug.

Jed guzzled a good quarter of the brew before answering. He set his stein down with a thump. "Fine. Be done that project right soon and then it'll be on to the next. Don't know what yet, but Titan always has lots of irons in the fire. I could probably get you on there if you wanted."

"So you said," Bo replied, a resigned smile playing at his lips. Jed didn't fully approve of Bo's current job. Not because Jed didn't drink - far from it. But to Jed, real men worked outdoors or did manual labor.

"I means it. Just say the word and I'll put in a good word for ya. Lard knows Titan could use a few more good men. Besides me and Lester, most of them lazy arses don't even know the meanin' of a day's work."

"Thanks, but no thanks," Bo responded.

"Why not? Regular hours, regular pay."

"We had this conversation already." Bo carefully pronounced the letter 'H' in 'had'. He'd been working on minimizing some of the more tell-tale aspects of his own Newfoundland accent. "I already have a job, I'm not interested in construction work, and I like what I do."

"Quit trying to steal my workers," Jacques interjected, coming up beside Bo and folding his arms, his stance wide. It was hard to tell if he was serious or not, but Bo suspected it was his version of friendly banter.

"That's a rotted thing to say about me own brother. You best not be testin' the Malloy loyalty."

"He wouldn't want to work for Titan anyway. He might fall down an elevator shaft," Jacques said.

"Now there's a low blow!" Jed blustered.

Titan, the construction company for which Jed worked, had suffered some nasty publicity before Christmas following an accident on site involving a worker who fell down an elevator shaft, but somehow managed to survive. Bo wasn't quite sure about all the details except for the fact that the man in question was Jed's friend, Lester Tibbett. The two hung around together quite a bit, often at the Urban Cowboy.

"I think that's enough, you two," Bo interrupted. He offered them both a placating smile. "People might think you're serious and that's not good for business."

"I'm just suggesting a real man's job," Jed said.

"I'm a real man," Jacques countered over his shoulder. He'd turned his back to Jed and was busy with some bottles, but he could still see Jed's reflection in the big mirror.

Jed snorted. "Says you."

Bo sighed. The exchange was beginning to grate on his nerves, good natured or otherwise. Why couldn't Jed just leave well enough alone? Why couldn't Jacques? It seemed they both wanted the last word, no matter how insignificant the topic.

"Just ask my girlfriend," Jacques continued. Bo saw Jed bristle slightly. He suspected Jed had at one time been interested in Jacques's girlfriend, Angela Carravagio, although Jed would never admit it outright.

"I might just do that," Jed countered.

"Go ahead." Jacques chucked his head in the direction of two approaching females, never actually looking in their direction, but using the mirror to his advantage.

Bo's gaze swung to the women in question. Angela and Andrea Carravagio were identical twin sisters who lived in the same building as all three men. They had long, luxurious brunette hair and curves that bordered on super-sized. The only real way to tell them apart was by the way they dressed. Angela loved to show off her assets by wearing revealing tops and tight fitting bottoms. Andrea chose a more conservative style, almost as if she were trying to hide her body, although it was a pretty hard thing to do. It was like trying to hide Mt. Everest behind a few trees. It just wasn't happening.

"What can I get for you, ladies?" Bo asked when they arrived, glancing at each woman.

Andrea sat down next to Jed while Angela leaned over the counter for a peck on the lips from Jacques. She and the Frenchman had been an item for at least a month and they certainly were not shy about public displays of affection.

"I'll take care of Angela," Jacques said with a wink.

"You always do," Angela responded and they kissed again.

"Get a room," Jed said under his breath.

Angela flipped her long hair off her shoulders and gave Jed a scathing look. Jacques couldn't hide the fox like grin beneath his goatee. He took Angela's elbow and they moved further down the counter out of earshot.

Bo let his shoulders relax and turned his attention back to Andrea. "What can I get for you?"

"I don't really care," Andrea said with a shrug. "Why not surprise me, but with no alcohol of course."

Bo nodded. "Of course. A virgin surprise, comin' right up."

Jed let out a snort, just barely audible. Bo glanced at his older brother, but let it go. Jed's posturing with Jacques had left him in fine form, which was a double shame since he'd been grouchy and non-communicative lately - a difficult feat for a Malloy since most of the family liked to talk one's ear off if given a chance.

Bo went to work on his version of a non-alcoholic sangria and in a few minutes placed the fancy pink drink in front of Andrea. As a final touch he dropped a little umbrella on top. "There you go. One virgin sangria."

Andrea took a sip. "Mm. Delicious." She smiled up at Bo and took another.

"You like it?"

"Very much. I hate to think about all the calories, though. I'll have to starve myself tomorrow."

"Don't be silly. You don't have to worry about that," Bo said.

"Are you kidding?" Andrea laughed out loud. "That's not a very nice thing to say to a fat person."

Bo blinked, not exactly sure how to respond.

"You're not fat." Jed was the one to utter the statement and his voice sounded gravelly. Angry almost.

Andrea made a little dismissive sound with her lips. "I'm hardly petite. I don't mind, really, but there's no use pretending."

Jed's scowl was even deeper than before. He cleared his throat and stood to his feet. "The pool table's callin'."

"What about your beer? Want a topper?" Bo asked.

Jed shook his head. "I'll get Crystal to fetch me another if I need it. She's always willing."

In more ways than one, Bo thought, but he kept the comment to himself as he watched his brother's hasty exit.

"He seems to be in a good mood," Andrea said, her tone sarcastic.

"Welcome to my world," Bo replied with a laugh. "Not sure what's gotten into him, but he's not the fun-loving older brother I remember. He's been a real bear lately, and I don't mean the cute and cuddly kind."

"I suppose we all have our issues," Andrea said.

"That we do," Bo agreed.

"Even you?" Andrea asked. "You always seem so even keeled."

Bo grinned and glanced to the pool tables where Jed was involved in a game. "In comparison, I suppose I am. Right now my biggest issue is finding my own place so I don't have to put up with Jed's sour moods."

A slight frown marred Andrea's features. "That could be tough right now. Places are hard to come by - especially decent places within a reasonable budget. Angela and I were so lucky to get our apartment when we did."

"I know, but things are pretty tight with the three of us," Bo said, "and I don't see Reba having the means to find her own place just yet, so…" He trailed off.

"Reba is a really good worker." Andrea and Angela had offered Bo's sister Reba a job at their hair salon and much to the family's chagrin, she'd taken it.

"It was good of you to take 'er on," Bo replied, "although our ma isn't so thrilled. She's some sore about it."

Andrea's mouth twitched.

Bo blinked. "What ya laughin' at?"

Andrea shook her head. "Nothing. You just sounded more like Jed than usual."

"Oh." Bo looked down and then up again and smiled crookedly. "It's hard to keep the Newfoundland outta the Newfoundlander."

"Don't apologize. Besides, I think it's kind of cute."

Bo blinked again, momentarily at a loss for words. Was Andrea flirting now, too? He cleared his throat, but before he could formulate an appropriate response, Andrea was speaking again.

"Anyway, you can tell your mother sorry about taking another one of her children so far from home, but her loss is our gain. We really needed another person at the salon, and Reba is learning fast."

"Ma's got lots more children and grandchildren to keep her occupied." Bo leaned on the counter. "But, since it's partly your fault that she stayed out here instead of going back home, maybe you can convince her to call a bit more often. I know Ma'd appreciate it."

"I'll see what I can do," Andrea said.

"I won't hold it against you if she don't listen," Bo said. "She's got the Malloy stubborn streak in spades."

"Is that what you call it? I'll keep that in mind." Andrea glanced toward the pool tables.

A flurry of activity brought their conversation to a halt. Two waitresses, one of them Crystal, swung up to the counter, forcing Andrea to lean to the side so as not to get bumped. Bo frowned but there was no use making a scene. Crystal rattled off an order and Bo started immediately mixing the drinks.

Andrea glanced to the side. "Well, I should probably see if Angela is ready to head home yet. Otherwise I'll be cabbing it alone. Thanks for the drink." She winked and lowered her voice. "Just put it on Angela's tab."

Bo grinned. "Gotcha." He glanced up to watch her retreating figure, while putting together the next order.

"Now wouldn't that just be quaint," Crystal said, her voice edged with sarcasm. "Both twins hooking up with bartenders."

Bo just shook his head. "We're just friends."

"You sure?"

"Definitely." He made the mistake of looking at Crystal.

She was smiling coyly and she raised one brow. "Good to know."

It was all Bo could do to keep the groan inside. So much for dodging that bullet.

Bo CLACKED the pen against his teeth as he stared absently at the light coming through the patio doors. There was a stark grid pattern on the carpet thanks to the sun shining through the railing on the outside deck. The actual view of the parking lot through the slats of the balcony railing was not especially inspiring. Still, he was determined to write a letter to his ma. It had been a month since he'd left the rocky shores of his home province behind and although he'd phoned her a couple of times, he knew she'd appreciate a letter in his own hand. She came across as hard-nosed, but she actually liked that kind of thing. She still carried the one letter she'd received from Jed four years ago in her purse and Bo was determined to do better than his older brother had.

He'd had plenty of time to think about what was eating at Jed, but he hadn't come to any conclusions. Jed was no longer the carefree hero of his youth. Or maybe he'd just never really known Jed that well. Jed was five years older than Bo, and naturally, Jed had been closer to Zeb, the next brother in line. Those two had carried on a constant battle, and not just of wits. Bo could distinctly remember them wrestling, and not always for fun. It was a wonder that one or the other hadn't gotten more injuries. Yet for some reason, the moment the blood was mopped up they seemed to be best friends again. The same bond he had with Will, who was one year younger than he was.

Sometimes Jed and Zeb had teamed up to torture the younger brothers, but Will usually got the worst of it. Pip was too small and Bo was too smart, but poor Will had taken a beating a few times. Mostly it was Will's own fault. He was a dare devil and Jed and Zeb could talk him into anything.

Bo shook his head. Nostalgia was a funny thing. He was actually remembering with fondness what amounted to unabashed bullying.

Bo looked down at the blank page in the coil bound notebook. One foot was resting on the other knee and the notebook was balanced on his leg. With a determined set to his jaw, he put the pen to paper. He'd avoid any negativity and stick to something positive.

Dear Ma,

Say hi to everyone back home, including Pop and all the rest. I am enjoying Calgary so far, although it is very different from home. It was good to see Zeb at Christmas time and Jed and Reba are fine, too. I told Reba to write you but she says she will just call instead. But I know how much you like a real letter, so here goes.

It's been three weeks now since I started at the Urban Cowboy. That's the name of the bar where I work in case you forgot. That mixology course I took has come in handy after all. (And you and Pop said it wouldn't.) Don't worry. Just because I'm mixing drinks for a living doesn't mean I'm indulging too much myself. In fact, it's probably a blessing in disguise because I am so busy working I don't have time to get into it.

I don't see much of Reba or Jed because they work during the day and I work nights. We are getting along fine and have settled into a routine. I do most of the cooking. Reba has the spare room and Jed and I share. I use a blow up mattress on the floor, but sometimes I switch to his bed once he leaves for work in the morning. (Don't tell!)

Reba is doing good at 'Gemini's' beauty salon. The owners (who are twins) say she is a very good worker and they seem to like her a lot. I hope you aren't too mad at her for staying. I think she just needed an adventure. Maybe you can come this way for a visit sometime and see for yourself.

The owner of the Urban Cowboy is very nice. Actually, it is owned by a father and son, Tad and Cory Roberts. I have never met the son since he moved to Vancouver, but the father is very nice. I get along with the manager most of the time, too. His name is Jacques Marcett and he is from Quebec. Sometimes he acts like he thinks he's better than anybody else, but I think it is just the way he is. He is actually a very good bartender and knows his stuff. I am learning lots from him. (But don't tell him that.)

Bo stopped writing and peered out the window. What else could he say? That he was lonely? That he wondered if he had made the right decision in moving west? Not that he needed a lot of people around all the time. He was a quiet person. Always had been. Of all his siblings he was possibly the quietest; some even said the most sensitive. That side of him was rising up these days now that he had so little contact with anyone outside of work.

He shook his head. He was being melodramatic. It was his choice to move away from home. Newfoundland held nothing for him anymore. He focused on the page again.

Do you know what's funny? My 'boss' Jacques is dating Reba's boss Angela. Isn't that a crazy coincidence? I've met some other nice people since moving here, too. A real cowboy lives in our apartment. His name is Lester and he used to ride broncs. He and Jed are good friends and he said he would teach me to ride the mechanical bull.

Bo stopped and looked at what he'd written. Better scratch that last part. Ma would worry if she thought he was doing something unsafe. He scribbled with the blue pen until the last part of the sentence was covered with ink and then continued.

The tips are really good. You wouldn't believe how much I make in one night. It's crazy. If things go well, I may rent my own apartment and let Jed have his own space back. Not that I'm complaining. You taught us to be grateful for a roof over our head. Well, I guess that's all for now. Take care.

Love Bo

Bo heard the key rattling in the lock. It was probably Reba home from work.

"Smells good in here," Reba called from the entrance. It was her standard line. Bo could hear her opening the doors of the small closet and stashing her coat before appearing in the hallway just off the living room.

"I had a craving for Ma's potato fish cakes. Not sure I succeeded but..."

"Smells good." Reba disappeared into the galley kitchen. "Ya make enough for Jed, too?"

"Depends on how many you plan on eating," Bo teased. Then he added, "Course. Don't I always? I'd never hear the end of it if I didn't." He heard the tell-tale clank of the frying pan lid as Reba put it back on the skillet. Then there was some rummaging in the refrigerator.

Bo had willingly taken on most of the cooking duties. It didn't make sense to cook for one person and they were family. Neither Jed nor Reba objected.

Reba joined Bo a few minutes later with a plate of fish cakes and some left over cold macaroni from the day before.

"Ya coulda nuked it." Bo made a face as he observed the large forkful of cold macaroni disappearing into his sister's mouth.

"Naw. Too much trouble and I'm starving. Besides, I like it cold."

"You just like food," Bo said with a grin. He cocked his head to one side as he watched his sister eat. She had a ginger complexion and fiery red hair with the temper to match. She could pack the food away, there was no doubt about it.

"What are you doing?" Reba asked, gesturing at the notebook still resting on Bo's knee.

"Writin' a letter to Ma. You should do the same."

"I told you, I'll just call 'er sometime." Reba took another bite of fish. "These are good, you know. You've got cooking skills as well as bartending skills."

Bo brought the conversation back around. "That's what you always say, but have you?"

"What?"

"Called Ma."

Reba furrowed her brow. "Um, yeah."

"When?"

"What are you, a cop?" Reba snapped. "I phoned 'er last week. Or maybe the week before…"

"After you left me the honours of breaking the news about you staying in Calgary."

Reba shrugged. "She and I have an understanding. No news is good news." She stood up and carried her empty plate to the kitchen, but continued in a louder voice. "I don't need you or Jed to play mother-hen with me. I'm a grown woman and perfectly capable of making my own decisions."

Bo doubted that. Reba was twenty-four, only three years younger than he was, but there seemed to be a world of difference in maturity level.

The Malloy siblings had all grown up to be tough. There was plenty of jockeying when it came to things like portion size at the dinner table, but they had always banded together against the rest of the world. They were a proud lot who didn't take things for granted, yet still enjoyed the simple pleasures in life. Rugged and independent, but the first in line to give the shirt off their back.

Except for the last two siblings. Maybe Ma and Pop were just tired by the time it got to number eight and nine, but Reba and Pip were spoiled brats in Bo's estimation. Reba was the princess; the youngest daughter who had been dressed up like a doll and lavished with every attention from the older girls until they left home and had children of their own. And Pip! As the true baby, Pip was never allowed to develop a sense of responsibility. The golden boy couldn't do any wrong.

Bo heard the lock rattling again. Jed was home. "Smells good in here," Jed echoed Reba's sentiments as he shed his work jacket.

Maybe Jed wasn't the only one slipping into a funk. With a sigh, Bo hoisted himself out of the chair and stretched. Just enough time to put the letter in an envelope and mail it on his way to work.

At least *he'd* done his duty as the good son.

Bo WAS busy attaching a new CO_2 canister underneath the counter. It was amazing how much soda they went through in one night. There was nothing worse than running out of CO_2 right in the middle of a rush.

He had his head bent under the counter, fiddling with the nozzle, when Jacques suddenly let loose with something in French. Bo smiled and finished the job before standing upright. He suspected it was best he didn't know what was said.

"What's up?" Bo asked.

"Nothing." Jacques swiped his phone with his index finger. "Just family." More cursing ensued.

Bo laughed. "Family? I know a thing or two about that. What's the problem?"

Jacques raised his arms dramatically. "My sister, she is coming for a visit."

Bo wiped his hands on a rag and then threw it in the sink. "I take it you two don't get along."

"No, that's not it."

"So what's the problem?"

"Viann, she is… how do you say?" Jacques furrowed his brow. "A spoiled brat?"

Bo laughed. "Younger sisters usually are. You've met my sister Reba."

"Viann is not just spoiled. She is difficult. Unreasonable at times."

"Sure it doesn't just run in the family?" Bo teased.

Jacques tilted his chin ever so slightly. "She is not my biological sister. She is the daughter of my father's second wife."

"Second wife?"

Jacques rolled his eyes. "He is currently on wife number four. Still, we were raised as siblings."

"I see." Bo leaned against the counter and crossed his arms. "Where is she living now?"

"Montreal." Jacques mumbled another curse under his breath. "I don't know why she's bothering to come. I'm not bailing her out this time."

"This is sounding more intriguing all the time," Bo said. "Dare I ask what you mean by 'bailing her out'?"

"No you may not. Now get back to work." Jacques turned his back on Bo, signifying an end to the conversation.

Bo's curiosity was piqued, but it was obvious Jacques wasn't about to share any more tonight.

Jed arrived a bit later along with his good buddy Lester Tibbett and Lester's girlfriend Sherri Chan. The lanky cowboy and the petite Asian woman made for quite a contrasting couple. The old saying that opposites attract must have been true in their case.

"Good to see you again, Bo," Lester greeted with a handshake.

"You, too. What can I get you?"

"The usual, I guess," Lester replied.

The threesome sat up to the bar and Bo busied himself getting their drinks.

"Did I mention that Patsi Mae is coming home this weekend for a visit?" Lester said to Jed.

"She's been workin' down at some ranch, right?" Jed commented.

"That's right. They winter horses," Lester said.

"And she likes it?" Jed asked.

"Of course. Patsi is a horse girl if ever there was one." Lester shook his head.

Bo slid their drinks in front of them - two beer on tap and a Tropical sunset cocktail with half the liquor - Sherri's orders. "And who is Patsi Mae?"

"Lester's little sister." Jed swivelled in his seat to look at Bo. "Maybe you and Patsi'll hit it off."

"Hey, now," Lester said. "I'm not sure I want my baby sister hooking up with a Malloy."

Lester's warning sounded amused, but Bo had to wonder how protective the older brother really was. "Never fear," he responded lightly. "I'm not in the market, so you can rest easy."

"I just wish she would have finished her first year of college, but…" Lester trailed off.

"I don't blame 'er. I'm not much of a college guy myself." Jed ducked his head at Sherri. "No offence."

"None taken," Sherri responded evenly. She was a college math professor. "Everyone has to make his or her own choices."

"It's the first time she's been home since she started." Lester took a sip of his beer.

Sherri placed a hand on Lester's forearm and leaned forward conspiratorially. "He misses her even if he won't admit it."

"Seems younger sisters are coming out of the woodwork. Isn't that right, Jacques?" Bo called to the other man who was several feet away scrutinizing something on his laptop.

Jacques just grunted.

Bo turned back to the group. "Jacques' sister is coming from Montreal and he doesn't seem very thrilled about it."

"You don't know Viann," Jacques said between tight lips. He rolled his eyes and mumbled something in French before clicking the lid down on the laptop and stalking off to the far end of the bar.

"I hears ya, b'ye." Jed shook his head. "Sisters are nothin' but trouble and I should know. I gots four of 'em!"

"They probably think the same thing about brothers," Sherri teased.

"Speaking of, here comes Reba." Bo gestured to the entrance where Reba and one of the Carravagio sisters were winding their way toward the bar. He assumed it was Angela, judging by her risqué outfit with its plunging neckline which left little to the imagination.

"We should grab a table so we can all sit together," Reba said as soon as she arrived. Bo had her beer waiting.

"Go ahead." Angela flipped her tresses back from her shoulder. "I'll wait here to see Jacques."

The rest of the group grabbed their drinks and moved to a round table nearby. Angela perched on one of the vacated stools. Jacques was busy counting inventory and Angela knew better than to disturb him. He'd given a quick wave, but went immediately back to jotting notes on a small pad of paper.

Crystal slid up to the bar and set her tray down on its surface. "Two whisky sour, a pitcher of draft and two vodka sodas - double."

"Comin' up." Bo went to work on the order. He glanced at Angela as he mixed the drinks. "Andrea didn't join you tonight?"

Angela shook her head in a somewhat disparaging way. "My sister prefers the company of books to real people."

"Makes sense when you don't drink," Bo defended with a smile.

"She's always been a party pooper," Angela said with a shrug.

"Don't you just hate it when people are such a buzz kill?" Crystal joined in the conversation, uninvited.

Bo plunked the drinks down on Crystal's waiting tray, avoiding eye contact. There was no point in encouraging her.

Once she'd taken her tray and left, Bo swung his gaze back to Angela. "So? Looking forward to meeting Jacques's sister?"

Angela's eyes widened. "His sister?"

"Yeah. She's coming for a visit." Bo hesitated. Maybe it was supposed to be a secret.

"I didn't know he had a sister." Angela's tone was clipped.

Bo blinked. "Oh. Technically, it's his step sister. The daughter of his father's second wife," he repeated Jacques' own words.

Angela's eyes narrowed to slits. "You don't say."

"Maybe he just forgot to tell you," Bo offered. Now what had he gotten himself into?

"Rather conveniently, I'd say. And what do you mean looking forward to meeting her? Is she moving here? Visiting? What?" Angela's tone was demanding; accusatory. As if Bo was embroiled in a conspiracy of sorts.

"I don't actually know much," Bo said. "I just assumed you knew. You'll have to talk to Jacques about it."

"I will." Angela stood up and marched to where Jacques was counting some bottles on an open shelf. "You never told me your 'sister' was coming." Her voice was laced with sarcasm and carried easily to where Bo was polishing glasses, trying not to eavesdrop.

Jacques swore in French. "Now I lost count."

"Too bad." Angela crossed her arms over her ample bosom. "You never even told me you had a sister."

Jacques sighed. "So? It never came up. Now you know." He continued counting.

"Oh wait. She's actually not really your sister at all. Is that right?"

Jacques finished counting under his breath, then jotted something down before answering. "Whatever is going through your head right now, isn't true. I've just been busy - as you can see."

"What else aren't you telling me?" Angela's voice rose.

"You're making something out of nothing," Jacques said.

"What if you're secretly in love with her?" Angela demanded.

"My sister?" Jacques' voice had lowered. "You're being ridiculous."

"Am I?" Angela hadn't lowered her voice. If anything it had risen.

Jacques sighed, swore in French under his breath, and then reached out to stroke Angela's arm. "Baby, listen. I just found out myself. And Viann and I... we don't always get along." Jacques pecked Angela's pouting lips with his own.

"You... you don't get along with her?" Angela asked.

"That's what I said." He kissed her again, lingering a little longer this time. "Now go sit down and let me finish my count."

The couple shared one more passionate kiss before Angela sauntered back to her stool and Jacques resumed his work.

Bo let a small smile crack his features. He had to hand it to Jacques. Despite the Frenchman's flaws, he knew how to handle women.

"He was telling the truth, you know," Bo offered. "I was here when he got the text and he wasn't too pleased about it."

"I hope what you say is true. I saw something exactly like that on a talk show, once. Step siblings that were having a secret affair because they knew their parents wouldn't approve."

"Maybe you're watching too much daytime TV," Bo said. "Besides,

Jacques's not like that."

"How would you know?" Angela gave Bo a sidelong glance.

"Well... I don't, I guess. But they say bartenders give good advice, so I'm advising you to let it go and not make a big deal out of it until you've at least met her."

"Hmph. Well, at least make me a drink. And this time make it a double."

Bo went to work mixing Angela's drink. He hoped Angela was taking his advice and at least thinking about giving the other woman a chance. He glanced up when he heard raucous laughter coming from Jed's table. Crystal had stopped beside Jed, either to chat or to take an order for another round. Just as Bo had looked up, both Jed and Crystal glanced his way. Although Bo couldn't hear the exchange, Crystal's laugh, a raspy smoker's sound, rang out loud and clear. Bo felt his own curiosity, laced with ire, rising. He wouldn't put it past Jed to have said something crude, and as for Crystal, he could only guess - and his thoughts were frightening.

This whole evening made him even more determined to avoid complicated relationships. He was very glad indeed that he didn't have to take responsibility for anyone but himself.

THE NEXT DAY, Bo met Patsi Mae Tibbett for himself in the foyer of the apartment. Lester entered the building carrying a duffel bag and was followed by a good-looking girl with blonde braids and typical cowgirl wear. Not the flashy pretend kind that girls liked to wear to the bar to show off, but the real thing. Plaid shirt, worn jeans, and cowboy boots. She was pretty and young looking, probably not more than twenty.

"Hi Bo! This here is my sister Patsi Mae," Lester greeted. He sounded proud, despite himself. He turned to his sister. "Bo is Jed's younger brother."

Patsi smiled warmly and extended a hand. "Well, if you're Jed's brother then I like you already. And the name is Pat, not what he said."

Lester shook his head. "I don't know why you insist on calling yourself Pat. You were christened Patsi Mae and I can't get used to calling you anything else."

Patsi sighed but she had a resigned smile on her face. "I see things haven't changed much since I've been gone. Good thing I'm only here for the weekend. Nice to meet you, Bo. And call me Pat, okay?"

Bo released her hand. "Deal. Pat it is."

"You heading to work now?" Lester asked.

Bo nodded in the affirmative just as the front doors swung open and Jed entered, stomping the snow off his boots on the large mat at the door.

"Well, if it isn't Miss Patsi Tibbett! Welcome back!" Jed dropped his lunch kit and backpack on the mat and took two giant steps forward, arms extended.

Patsi met him half way and allowed herself to get swallowed up in a bear-hug. "Good to see you, Jed."

"Ow ya gettin' on?" Jed held her at arm's length. "Look at ya! You're about disappeared, yer so rail skinny."

"Don't be silly. I'm just working hard," Patsi replied.

"Home for good, then?" Jed asked.

"Just visiting." Patsi glanced at her brother. "Now that I'm out from under Lester's thumb, I'm not going to get back under it quite so easy."

They all laughed, especially Jed.

"As if you ever listened anyway," Lester countered.

"True." Patsi took some keys out of her pocket and dangled them in front of her. "Hope you didn't change the locks or anything. I'm heading up now. Nice meeting you," she said to Bo and waved as she swung away from the men toward the elevators.

"I'm coming," Lester said. "Hold the elevator."

"You should both come down to the pub later, " Jed suggested to Lester's retreating figure. "It's Friday night."

"We'll see," Lester said over his shoulder before the elevator doors swished shut.

"So?" Jed elbowed Bo. "She's a pretty little thing, eh, b'y? Too young

60

for me but just right for you, I'd say."

Bo slipped back into his best 'Newfanese'. "Don't be a lummox. If Lester 'eard what ya just said, 'e'd string ya up."

Jed laughed heartily.

Bo shook his head, straining to keep the smile that wanted to creep across his face at bay. Trust his older brother to try and play matchmaker. Good thing he was just as stubborn as Jed or any of the Malloys. He wasn't about to bite, even if he wanted to.

LESTER, Patsi, Jed and Reba showed up at the Urban Cowboy about two hours into Bo's shift. He noticed that Reba and Patsi were already chatting and laughing like old friends as they approached the line of stools in front of Bo's section of the bar.

"We're gonna grab a table," Lester said to Bo. "Sherri and a few others are coming in a bit."

Bo nodded. "Sounds good. I'll send your drinks over with Crystal."

Lester, Patsi, and Reba headed toward the nearest table while Jed lingered behind. "I'm not waitin' on Crystal."

With a smile, Bo poured Jed's usual stein of draft from the tap and plunked the frothy mug down on the counter.

Jed saluted his brother with the mug before taking a swig. "Thanks, b'y. Join us when ya get a break."

Bo just shrugged. "We'll see."

A short time later, Lester's girlfriend Sherri Chan arrived with her brother Sherman and his fiancé Carmen Lamont. Bo had met them all in passing at least once. Jed had made sure of it, since Carmen's downtown coffee shop was one of his favourite daytime haunts.

From his station behind the bar, Bo couldn't hear their conversation, but the group seemed to be having a good time. He nodded and smiled once, keeping busy with a shaker full of crushed ice and vermouth, and tamped down the feelings of envy that were seeping in. Sure he'd met lots of people since moving to Calgary, but besides his own family, he didn't really have anyone he would call 'friend'."

Tad Roberts, owner of the establishment, was working this evening in place of Jacques. The older, black man approached just as Bo poured the martini into the wide mouthed glass. "Must be just about time for your break," Tad said.

Bo blinked and let his gaze meet Tad's. "Not yet, I don't think."

"I'm your boss and I say it is," Tad said. He smiled congenially and chucked his smooth head toward the table where Jed and the others sat. "Why don't you go join them for a bit?"

"Oh... that's not necessary. You might get busy and -"

"No arguing," Tad interrupted. "You look like a lost puppy."

"Not sure that's a compliment, but, if you say so..." Bo tossed the towel from his shoulder onto the back counter and rounded the bar. When he reached the large, oval table, he pulled an extra chair from nearby and swung it around, ready to straddle. "Mind if I join you? Boss says it's time for my break."

"Please!" It was Carmen Lamont who spoke up. She had a ready smile and her teeth stood out whitely against the darkness of her skin. Large colourful earrings danced at her lobes. "Your brother was just telling us about your family and I think we need some clarification."

"Shoot." Bo crossed his arms along the back of the chair.

"Jed said your mother had nine children in eleven years." Carmen looked at Bo expectantly, waiting for him to deny it.

Bo nodded. "That's right."

"Told ya!" Jed bellowed. "And youse thought I was lyin'."

"Is it only eleven?" Reba said, her brows furrowed. "I thought it was thirteen."

"Reba's never been good with math," Bo said.

"Watch it!" Reba punched Bo's bicep with her fist.

"Ow!"

"Start at the top," Carmen directed.

Bo took a deep breath and began. "Fanny is the oldest. She's married to Joe and they got three kids."

"Then there's me," Jed interrupted. "I came along one year later and I'm the best looking outta the lot."

"Still living in a fantasy," Reba chirped.

Everyone laughed.

Bo picked up the narrative. "Next is Zeb. He's two years younger than Jed. Then one year later came Mary. She's got two kids and -"

"She's married to a chucklehead," Jed put in.

"Jed doesn't get along with Mary's husband Trent," Reba said in a staged whisper.

"He's a son-of-a-you-know-what. Thinks 'e's better 'an everyone else just cause he's a fancy come-from-away doctor," Jed said loudly.

Bo ignored Jed's outburst and continued. "Sissy Suzanne came exactly one year later and she is married to Hank..." Bo grinned before continuing, "whom Jed greatly approves of because he is a fisherman. They have four kids."

"I loves my b'y Hank, I do," Jed interjected.

Bo took up the genealogy again. "Then right after Sissy is me and then Will. That's seven kids in eight years."

Carmen rolled her eyes. "I'm exhausted just thinking about it! How did your mother do it?"

"My mother's a saint!" Jed made the sign of the cross over his chest.

"That she is, to have put up with you," Bo put in.

Everyone laughed again.

"But you stopped at seven in eight years," Sherri reminded. "Who's next?"

"Will is just a year younger than me," Bo said. "Then our parents got smart and left a couple years between the last two. Reba is the second youngest and then Pip."

"Pip?" Patsi repeated with a raised brow.

"Short for Pipsqueak." Jed grinned. "Real name is Steve. Zeb labeled 'im Pipsqueak as soon as Ma brought 'im home and it stuck."

"And there you have it," Bo finished. "Fanny is thirty-three and Pip is twenty-two, so that's nine kids in eleven years."

"Little Pip." Jed shook his head. "Seems like 'e should still be in grade school."

"Time flies, Bro," Bo said. "He's not a baby anymore, that's for sure, even if he acts like it. Anyway, I should be getting back to work, now."

He stood but before he could swing his chair back to its rightful table, he spotted Jacques entering with a slender woman on his arm. She had bleached blonde hair, perfect makeup, and a designer cream coloured wool overcoat belted at the waist. A coordinating scarf and fashionable boots that were quite impractical for the winter conditions completed the outfit.

"Angela's not going to like this," Reba said under her breath.

"It's his sister," Bo explained. "He went to pick her up from the airport, but I'm surprised he brought her here straight off. I thought she'd want to rest up after her long flight from Montreal."

"She looks like that after traveling all day?" Patsi asked and opened her eyes wide. "She looks as fresh as a daisy."

Reba laughed. "I hate her already." The two younger women shared a giggle.

"I better get going," Bo said again.

He scurried to make it back to his station behind the bar and arrived at the same time as Jacques and his sister. "I wasn't expecting you back tonight," Bo said.

"Evidently," was Jacques' sardonic reply.

"I told him to take a break," Tad defended, coming alongside Bo. "He looked like a lost puppy."

Jacques frowned. "A lost puppy?" Jacques' French accent made it sound like 'poopy' instead of 'puppy'.

Bo laughed outright. "A lost 'poopy', eh?"

Jacques just shook his head, although a smile tried to peek out from under his moustache. He gestured to the woman standing patiently beside him. "This is my, uh… sister. Viann-Patrice."

An imperceptible nod was all Viann mustered and she certainly didn't smile.

"I'm Tad. Nice to meet you." Tad stuck his hand out. Viann stared at it a moment and then just nodded again, the faintest bit of disdainful superiority marring her lips. Tad dropped his hand.

Jacques said something in French under his breath and Viann straightened her spine. "You are the owner?" she asked in a low but melodic voice laced with a strong French accent.

Tad nodded. "So it says on the lease. Your brother keeps things running, though. He's the real brains behind the business." He smiled congenially, never one to take offence.

"And this is Bo," Jacques went on, nodding in his direction.

Bo opted for a nod instead of a handshake. "Pleased to meet you."

A muscle moved in her jaw and she acknowledged him with another nod before allowing her gaze to sweep the room.

"She wanted to see where I worked instead of going to my apartment," Jacques explained hurriedly. "So, this is it." He made a sweeping gesture with one arm. "And now that you're here, I'll get you a drink?"

Viann nodded her assent and perched on the edge of one of the stools.

Tad stopped Jacques from coming behind the bar with a hand to his chest. "Let Bo handle it. You're supposed to have the night off, remember?"

With a shrug Jacques complied. "I am not used to this side of the counter." He said something to Viann in French and gestured to a nearby table but she shook her head, so he sat next to her on a stool.

Bo smiled over at Viann. "What can I get for you?"

She spoke to Jacques and he interpreted. "She'll have a Cosmo."

"Comin' right up," Bo said.

"She's kind of particular about her Cosmos," Jacques said.

Bo gave Jacques a withering look and went to work on the girly drink.

"Patrice. That's a nice last name," Bo said conversationally. "French I take it?"

Viann blinked and then looked directly at Bo for the first time. "My last name is Marcett. Viann-Patrice Marcett." Her accent was even thicker than Jacques's.

"My, uh... father adopted Viann legally," Jacques explained.

"Of course," Bo responded, ducking his head as he finished the drink. He set the ruby filled glass in front of her.

Viann grasped it with delicate fingers and took a sip, her gaze averted.

Bo looked up when Reba and Patsi approached.

"Hey, Jacques," Reba said loudly. "We hear your sister is here visiting." She immediately turned to Viann. "I'm Reba and this is my friend, Pat. You could say we're part of the establishment around here."

"More like our brothers are part of the furniture," Patsi said and then giggled.

Viann blinked and then let her gaze rest first on Reba and then Patsi.

Jacques cleared his throat. "This is my sister, Viann-Patrice Marcett. Reba and Patsi both live in my building," he informed Viann. She didn't respond other than to give a slight nod.

"Not me," Patsi corrected. "I'm just visiting. And it's Pat."

"This is real ironic if you ask me," Reba continued. "All these siblings in one place. Me, Bo and Jed; Pat and Lester; Sherri and Sherman; and now you and your sister." She stopped, her eyes losing focus for a moment before she blurted, "We can have, like, a sisterhood!" She raised a fisted hand and giggled.

"I've never had a sister," Patsi said.

Reba leaned in, a little too closely. "I've got three and believe me when I say you aren't missing much."

"I'm telling Fanny you said so," Bo said from behind the counter.

"Oh, you know what I mean," Reba said with a dismissive wave. "I love my sisters, but they were always so girlie. I got on better with the boys."

"Me too!" Patsi said. "I was definitely a tomboy growing up."

Viann finally spoke, but it was in quiet French.

"What was that?" Reba asked.

"Her English isn't that good," Jacques explained. "She said nice to meet you. We're probably heading home now."

Bo had his doubts about whether that was what she'd really said, but he kept a noncommittal smile pasted on his face.

"Oh. Okay. Well, nice meeting you, too." Reba waved.

Viann stood elegantly, leaving much of the dark pink liquid still in the glass.

"I will see you tomorrow," Jacques directed at Bo.

They watched the pair wind their way toward the exit and disappear into the night.

Bo went to pick up the half empty drink that Viann had left behind and Reba stopped him. "Hey! Don't waste it. Give it to me."

"Absolutely not," Bo said sternly, and whisked the glass out of her reach.

Reba shrugged, too much alcohol making it impossible for her to argue further. She turned to Patsi. "That's not what she said, you know." She blinked, trying to focus on her friend's face.

"Who? Viann?" Patsi asked.

Reba nodded. "She didn't say 'nice to meet us'. She said we were a couple of bit-"

"Since when do you speak French?" Bo interrupted.

"Since I took it in high school," Reba said, refocusing on Bo with effort. "Not everyone in the family dropped it at the first chance."

Bo considered this. "It might come in handy if she's going to be around for a while."

Reba frowned. "Why should you care?'

Bo shrugged. "I don't. Just sayin' is all."

Reba had lost interest in the topic already. "Looks like the rest of them are getting ready to leave, too. Well, except for Jed." She blinked at Patsi. "You wanna stay for a while longer with me? We can share a cab later. Or…" she looked to Bo, "catch a ride with Bo when he's done."

"I'd say you've already had enough fun for one evening," Bo said. "I'm going to have to cut you off."

"Phooey on that!" Reba scoffed. "We can't go home yet. Pat's only here for the weekend."

"I don't think I better on my first night home," Patsi said. "Lester wouldn't like it."

Reba sighed heavily. "What's with everybody and their rules?"

What indeed. It seemed everyone had a different set of expectations and navigating through them was a lot like walking a high wire.

∾

Bo busied himself in the kitchen, rustling up some French toast for himself and his two siblings. It was Saturday - a rare opportunity for the three of them to spend some time together before he had to go to work in the evening. It seemed like they didn't spend much time together except at the Urban Cowboy and then that couldn't really be considered quality time since Bo was working and Reba and Jed usually ended up drunk.

Make that Jed. Reba had overindulged the night before, but she normally knew her own limits, especially on weeknights. Jed on the other hand didn't seem to have any boundaries. Bo wondered how his older brother managed to get up every morning and go to work. In fact, he was beginning to get worried. If Jed wasn't already an alcoholic, he was on a fast track to making himself one.

It was already past eleven in the morning, not an unusual time for Bo to be getting up since he always worked late, but Reba and Jed still hadn't shown their faces.

"Breakfast!" Bo called, slipping the last pieces of golden brown French toast onto a platter and then placing it in the oven to keep warm.

Reba appeared a few minutes later, hugging her pajamaed body and shuffling her bare feet. She inhaled deeply as she came to stand beside Bo who was washing the prep dishes in the sink. "Smells good. Even if I am a bit hung over."

"Get some food in your stomach first thing," Bo said. "And a glass of orange juice. Some people don't eat cause they don't feel good, but eating takes the edge off. Gives your body something else to do besides try to absorb the alcohol."

Reba went to the refrigerator and took out a jug of orange juice. "Okay, if you say so." She found a tumbler in the cupboard and poured herself a glass of the bright orange liquid. By the time she'd downed the entire thing Bo had two pieces of French toast on each plate.

"We're not waiting for Jed, are we?" Reba asked. "He could be in bed for hours."

"True. He can microwave his if he ever wakes up." Bo set Jed's plate on the counter and proceeded to doctor his own plate with butter and syrup.

They dug into their food for a few minutes until Bo spoke again. "So… do you think Jed is drinking a bit too much these days?"

Reba cocked her head to one side and held her fork aloft. "Compared to what? I mean, we haven't seen much of 'im these past few years so it's tough to tell if it's over the top or just normal for 'im."

"I'd say it's over the top." Bo pointed his fork at Reba. "I see a lot of drinkers. Some come every day but only have one or two. Some come once a week and get hammered but don't drink for the rest of the week. Practically since Christmas time, Jed's been drunk every day. The body can only take so much of that before it becomes dependent."

Reba shrugged. "Jed's a big boy. I'm certainly not going to be the one to warn 'im." She finished her breakfast and took her plate to the sink, dumping it into the water that remained from the previous clean up.

"Not sure if I want to be the one either," Bo said wryly. He started running some more warm water into the sink. "Do you want to wash or dry?"

Reba frowned. "Oh. I might not have time. Pat and I are going to the mall."

"Suck it up, Princess." He tossed her a towel before starting to wash.

Reba caught it and sighed. "Okay, okay. Too bad Pat has to leave so soon."

"You two really seemed to click." Bo placed a plate in the rack.

"Working on a ranch sounds like fun. Some people have all the luck."

Bo laughed. "You've never ridden a horse in your life."

Reba tilted her chin. "So? I could learn. Besides, I said it sounded like fun, not that I was going to quit my job and do it."

"True enough."

"I wonder what it would be like, though." Reba leaned on the counter, the plate and towel still in her hands. "Working on a ranch. I wonder if there would be any good looking cowboys there."

"Ah, now I get your sudden interest." Bo shook his head with a grin. "Haven't you seen enough cowboys down at the Urban Cowboy?"

"Those aren't real cowboys, just wannabees. Well, except for Lester and 'e's, well, too old and already taken."

"Watch it, Sis. I hope that isn't the reason you moved to Calgary. To hook up with a cowboy."

"And what if it is? I needed a change of scenery. I'm tired of the local boys." Reba cocked her head to one side. "Speaking of which, what made you want to move so suddenly? It's almost like you're running away, but I know you didn't have a girlfriend so…"

"Change of scenery, like you said." Bo abruptly took his hands from the soapy water and dried them on her towel before taking it and the plate out of Reba's hands. "I'll do the rest since it was my idea to make breakfast. You go get ready or whatever."

Reba scrutinized him for a moment under narrowed lids. "Hm. I think there's more to this mystery than you're letting on."

"My offer ends in ten seconds," Bo said.

Reba laughed. "Okay, I'm not gonna argue." She gave Bo a peck on the cheek. "But I'd say my oh-so-casual-and noncommittal-brother might be hiding something."

"Out." Bo snapped the towel, just grazing her bottom.

"Ow!" Reba squealed and jumped away. "You know you can't keep stuff from me," she shot over her shoulder as she left the small kitchen for the bathroom.

That part about being casual and noncommittal stuck in his craw because he knew it was true. He'd had the interest of plenty of girls over the years, but no one had ever stood out. It hadn't really bothered him much before, but now he wondered if the whole Malloy clan had commitment issues.

Mostly he'd left for the change of scenery, like he'd said, but now he wondered if it had to do with needing some distance from the constant stigma of being one of the Malloys. Well, that particular trait had followed him west. The expectation that he would get into trouble, breaking a few hearts along the way, had never really suited his personality. As much as he'd never felt heartbroken by any of the girls he'd dated, he doubted that any of them had given him a second thought either. And that stung. Was that his lot? To be relegated to a life of mediocrity?

Thousands of miles and things really hadn't changed that much. He was still labeled as one of 'the Malloys', and so far, as nice as the girls were that he'd met, no one stood out beyond friendship.

With a sigh he went back to the dishes and finished up. Once done he sauntered to the living room and flopped down on the couch, simultaneously flicking on the TV with the remote.

Jed appeared a few minutes later, bleary eyed and unshaven. His dark hair was sticking out in all directions.

"Morning." Bo smiled. "Although it's past noon already. I made some French toast. You'll probably want to nuke it."

Jed grunted and shuffled to the small galley kitchen. A few minutes later he appeared with a full glass of orange juice and a plate of breakfast. Bo smiled again. It was Jed who had advised him on the necessity of eating a good breakfast and drinking orange juice to curb the effects of a hangover. Obviously, Jed was taking his own advice.

Jed set his glass on a small end table and then slowly lowered himself into his armchair. He balanced the plate on one knee and ate in silence. Bo knew better than to disturb him too much until he had his sustenance. They both focused on the handy-man renovating a turn of the century house on TV.

Jed grunted again and set his empty plate on the floor. "Makes it look so easy. Probably has a whole crew doing the real work when the camera's not there."

Bo nodded in agreement. "Probably." They watched for a few more minutes. "I've been looking at a used car. Nothing fancy. Just a tin box for getting around."

"You got enough money?" Jed asked.

"I didn't move here completely broke," Bo said.

Jed let out a grunt. "Should let me take a look. You don't want to buy a piece of crap."

"Too late. I got the plates yesterday. All I need to do is pick it up."

"What make?"

"An older Volkswagen Golf. Should be good on gas and the price was right."

"Like I said, probably a piece of crap."

Bo smiled. "Thanks. Since I'm a better mechanic than you, I'm not worried."

"Doubt that." Jed let out a huge yawn. "I can take you later if you want."

"That'd be great." Bo cleared his throat. "I was surprised to see you in bed this morning when I woke up. When I got home last night you weren't here."

"What are ya? A cop?" Jed growled under his breath.

"No, just wondering. You left the bar just before I did, so I assumed you took a cab with Reba."

"Caught a ride with someone else," Jed said.

"Oh." Bo thought for a minute and then raised his brows. "Oh…" he said in understanding. "You mean Crystal." Bo had seen the waitress flirting openly with Jed during the course of the night. Guess his big brother could only hold out so long.

"Got a problem with that?" Jed said with a scowl.

"No." Bo focused on the TV again. "She has a kid, you know."

Jed rubbed his head, leaving a rooster's comb in his hand's wake. "I know." He sighed heavily. "But she's nice enough and well, she was willing so… a man's gotta get his needs met somehow."

"Wow. If that isn't the most eloquent thing I've ever heard."

"Not trying to be eloquent, just stating a fact. Besides, I'd had a few drinks."

"Speaking of…" Bo hesitated. "You ever think you might drink a bit too much?"

Jed pinned Bo with daggers for eyes. "Don't forget you're sleeping under my roof." He hauled himself up onto his feet. "And get your own ride. I'm busy."

Bo listened to Jed's shuffling retreat all the way down the hall. With a sigh he got up and retrieved the plate from its resting place on the floor. So much for some quality time with his siblings.

Bo took a cab to the address of his car purchase. He'd seen it in an online ad, talked to the owner a few days ago, and met to exchange the cash and other particulars yesterday while the insurance office was open. All that was left now was to bring the plates and pick it up. He was looking forward to the independence, no matter what Jed said.

After running a few errands, Bo arrived back at the apartment block in the late afternoon. He pulled into visitor parking, and cut the engine. Not the best option but it would have to do for now. He doubted that the housing authority would notice on the weekend, but he was going to have to pay for an extra parking spot or try to find parking on the street each day since each suite only had one allotted parking spot.

Bo stomped his boots off in the foyer as he entered the building, not bothering to look up until someone spoke.

"Nice haircut."

He jerked his head up to see Andrea and Angela Carravagio standing near the mailboxes.

"Oh. Thanks." He wasn't sure which one had made the comment.

"I didn't see him at the salon, today," Andrea said to her sister. "Did I miss something?"

"Not that I know of," Angela responded.

"Oh, uh…" He rubbed the nape of his neck, which suddenly felt itchy with microscopic hairs. "I was in a hurry so I just went somewhere close by. Sorry."

Andrea laughed. "Forget it. We were just teasing."

"Oh." He nodded and smiled. "Haha."

"I'm not," Angela said. "Reminds me of someone else who shall remain nameless."

At Bo's confused expression, Andrea filled in the blanks. "We invited Jacques' sister Viann down to the salon, but she refused. Politely, of course, but…"

"Pedicure, manicure, massage, hair extensions… anything she wanted," Angela said, her tone miffed.

"Maybe she's just tired," Bo said. "Or she didn't need any of those things. She did just get here."

"Oh, I could tell exactly what she was thinking." Angela flipped her long hair from her shoulder. "I guess we're not good enough for her. She's such a snob."

"Well, maybe she's just shy," Bo tried. He wasn't sure why he was bothering to defend Viann, since her attitude last night did seem a bit snobbish, but he felt obligated none the less.

Angela rolled her eyes. "And it was so awkward having her there last night when Jacques and I were… well, you know." She looked pointedly at her sister. "If somebody would let up on her 'no sex' rule in our own apartment, it would make things a lot better for the duration."

Bo raised his brows but kept his mouth shut. He glanced at Andrea, whose lips were pursed into a tight line.

"That has always been my deal, so if you want to keep rooming with me you'll have to get used to it."

Angela just rolled her eyes. "Whatever. We need to get moving if we're gonna have things ready by six." She started for the elevator and then stopped and turned back to look at her sister. "You coming?"

"In a minute." Andrea cast her gaze down toward her feet. With a shrug, Angela marched the rest of the way and hit the button.

"What's happening at six?" Bo asked when the elevators had swished Angela away.

"My brother Rocky is coming over for dinner tonight." Andrea gestured lamely toward the elevator. "Sorry about that. She can be so embarrassing at times."

Bo chuckled. "Not to worry. I'm Jed's brother, remember? I'm used to embarrassing."

"Right…" Andrea's eyes focused downward again. "There was actually something I wanted to talk to you about…"

"Sure. Go ahead."

The front door of the building opened and Jed walked in, looking first at Andrea and then Bo.

"Any mail?" Jed said with a grunt.

"Just a few flyers. It's Saturday," Bo replied.

"That your crap box out there in the visitor parking?" Jed directed at Bo.

"If you mean the spanking new-to-me Golf, then yes."

"You bought yourself a car?" Andrea asked, smiling.

Bo nodded.

"You'll have to be careful," Andrea said. "Apparently we're in for a record snowfall tonight."

"Not worried. I've seen some doozies back home," Bo said. "At least here it's not so cold as it is back in Newfoundland. That wind can bite when it comes off the North Atlantic."

Jed huffed. "Mary, Martha, and Joseph! As if she cares a wit about the weather back home! Mighty pathetic if all ya gots to talk about is the weather."

"Right." Andrea blinked rapidly. "I'm probably keeping you both from something and I do need to get upstairs and help Angela prep the food. It's Rocky's six-month anniversary, so we're celebrating. Been sober for half a year."

"If I would have known I could have picked you up a nice non-alcoholic wine to go with your dinner," Bo said.

"That would have been nice. Next time I'll remember to ask your advice."

"Non-alcoholic wine?" Jed snorted. "Doesn't sound like much of a celebration to me."

Andrea levelled her gaze at Jed. "It is when you're an alcoholic."

Bo coughed and shifted his feet at the awkward silence that followed.

Andrea straightened her back and took a deep breath. "Well, I better not keep you two any longer."

"Um, you said you wanted to ask me something," Bo reminded.

"Oh, it was just about the wine," Andrea responded, overly bright. "I was wondering if you knew of any good non-alcoholic kinds but I don't think we'll bother. Thanks." She turned abruptly and walked the short distance to the elevator and pressed the button. The door opened almost immediately. "Shall I hold it for you?" she asked.

"You go ahead," Jed said gruffly, simultaneously blocking Bo from moving forward.

Andrea disappeared into the elevator and the doors swished shut.

Bo crossed his arms. "What if I was ready to go up?"

"Were you?" Jed snorted as if he couldn't care less.

"Did you want to talk to me about something?" Bo asked.

"Not particularly," Jed said with a shrug. "Just didn't want to be trapped in an elevator with 'er."

Bo frowned. "What's gotten into you? Andrea's a nice person."

"So you keep telling me."

"If I didn't know better, I'd say you were jealous, which is ridiculous, since you went and hooked up with Crystal last night."

Jed rubbed the back of his neck, but before he could formulate an answer, the second elevator opened and Viann Marcett stepped out. She was wearing the same cream coloured designer jacket and boots with heels - not very practical for the mounds of snow that had been piled up around the parking lot by the snow plough.

"Evening Miss Marcett," Bo greeted congenially.

"Oh. Hi." It was like she hadn't even registered the fact that the two men were standing right in front of her until Bo spoke.

"Going somewhere?" Bo asked.

Viann sighed. "Jacques asked me to drive his vehicle to the Urban Cowboy," she replied in her thick accent. "He and his boss went there earlier and his girlfriend is busy, apparently."

"Is that a problem?" Bo asked.

Viann shrugged her delicate shoulders, the fur collar of her coat lifting a few strands of her perfectly waved blonde tresses. "I am not sure I even know how to get there. And with this snow…" She gestured eloquently with her hands.

"I can drive it for you," Bo offered.

Relief visibly relaxed Viann's tense shoulders. "It is not too much trouble for you?"

"I was just on my way," Bo said.

"Oh you were, were you?" Jed muttered under his breath.

"Yes, as a matter of fact. I don't need anything from upstairs, so we can get going."

"Bo to the rescue again," Jed said as he slouched toward the elevator.

Bo ignored the jibe. It was his opportunity to find out what made the elusive Viann-Patrice Marcett tick. And for some odd reason, he was looking forward to it.

THE STREETS WERE deep with the grimy tan of snow mixed with sand and salt, an oatmeal like substance that left vehicles a fuzzy brown all the way from the running boards to the windows.

Bo concentrated on maneuvering his way through the ruts. It was a good thing they'd left earlier than he normally would have. They'd need the extra time under these conditions.

"Thank you for offering to drive. I do not think I would have managed so well," Viann said.

Bo glanced at her profile for a second. She was definitely attractive, but it was hard to tell if it was the facade of makeup and grooming or the real person. She had a narrow, aquiline nose and smooth neck. The fur collar piled near her chin made her look like a movie star from a by-gone era. "No problem. I'm glad to help. Did Jacques say why he and Tad had to go early today?"

Viann shook her head. "No. We don't... how do you say? Communicate much."

Which begged the question, why was she here? Bo wanted to ask it, but wasn't sure it was appropriate. Instead he asked the next best thing. "How long are you staying?"

Again that delicate shrug of shoulders. Apparently she had trouble communicating in general.

Bo concentrated on the road ahead of him. "Must be nice not to have any timeline." He hesitated before diving in. "You don't have a job to get back to? A boyfriend?"

"No - to both."

"Independently wealthy?" Bo asked and flashed her a grin.

"I, well… I have my allowance. But then that is none of your business." She turned her face to look out the window at her side.

"Your allowance?" Bo couldn't help the twinge of sarcasm.

"Don't judge." Her tone was angry, upset. "We can't help it if we come from a wealthy family."

"We? You mean you and Jacques?" Bo glanced her way again. Sparks flashed in her blue eyes.

"Don't play dumb. I know what you are trying to do, but it won't work."

"Hold on, now. I don't even know what I'm trying to do! And as for judging, I'd say you pretty much have that department sewed up."

Viann inhaled sharply, then tilted her head upward with practiced distain. "I don't understand. My English isn't good."

Bo shook his head and laughed. "That excuse has worn itself out. There's nothing wrong with your English. And as for you and Jacques coming from a wealthy family, I had no idea."

After a short silence she spoke. "I apologize for seeming… how you say? Snobbish? I just don't like being around strangers."

"You're shy," Bo supplied, albeit somewhat sardonically.

She nodded. "Yes."

"Fair enough. But shy doesn't mean you have to turn your nose up."

She frowned. "Turn my nose…?"

"The snobbish part. Not talking to people when they talk to you, for example."

"If you don't know what to say, it is best not to say anything. That is what *mon pere*, er… my step-father taught me."

"Jacques's dad?" Bo asked.

She nodded. "Yes."

"I see. So tell me more about the rich part. If your family is so rich why is Jacques working in Calgary as a bartender?"

"This is his… how you say?" She furrowed her brow. "His amour. His love."

"His passion," Bo supplied.

"Yes!"

"I get that," Bo said with a nod.

"But this was not good enough for mon pere. Jacques has made his own way without the help of his father's money. I thought you knew this."

Bo shook his head. "Not a clue. Mind you, I only met the guy recently myself. Probably not the kind of thing he would want to go around sharing, anyway. 'Hey, did you know I am actually from a wealthy family from back east but I chose to throw it all away and become a bartender instead?' Definitely not something you wanna share around."

"You may laugh, but it has been hard on Jacques. It is not an easy family to belong to."

"I don't know. Hand me downs times nine, plus wolfing down your portion of food so you could be the one to get seconds seems like my definition of hard times."

"You are making fun of me." Viann's expression closed.

"No, not making fun of you," Bo responded. "Just trying to understand, is all. So, let me get this straight. You're here on your step-father's dime for an undetermined amount of time because…?" He looked over at her as if to gain the answer to his question.

"I think I am finished speaking with you now," was all she said. She settled back into her seat and stared straight ahead.

So much for getting inside the head of a wealthy debutant. Viann was a paradox of insecurity and downright snobbery. Reconciling the two was going to take some work.

Without warning, a car came hurtling forward from a side street and rammed directly into the rear passenger side of Jacques's vehicle. It slid to the side, skidded sideways, and landed with a soft thud in a snow bank.

Thankfully, the impact was soft enough that the airbags did not inflate. Bo felt a nasty pain in his left knee where it had hit the dash and a slight jar to his neck. His seat belt had tightened into a death grip on his chest and he quickly undid it to gain some breathing room. He looked to Viann. "Are you alright?" he asked, leaning toward her.

She nodded her head, her eyes squeezed shut. "Yes, I think so."

Bo tried opening his own door, but it was wedged against the bank of piled snow left by the plough. "Take off your belt," he said to Viann, "and we'll see if your door opens. I need to get out to assess the damage."

Viann's door did not open on the first try.

"Let me help," Bo said. He leaned across her body while she strained back against the seat to give him more room. "You hold the handle and I'll push. Ready?" After two good pushes the door popped open with a horrible groaning of metal on metal. It sounded as if the hinges had been rusted for a thousand years.

A young man in a plaid scarf was on the other side of the open door, peering into the car. "I'm so sorry! I didn't see you, honestly. I thought the way was clear, but the banks are so high…"

"Just help her out of the car and then we'll talk," Bo said somewhat gruffly.

The stranger grabbed one of Viann's arms and helped her hoist herself from the vehicle. Bo scrambled over the centre console and emerged from the passenger side. A quick assessment of the damage showed that the impact had landed on the rear passenger side. Any sooner and Viann's door would have been crumpled and she might have been badly injured. He quickly glanced her way again. "You sure you're okay?" he repeated.

She nodded mutely. He noticed she seemed unsteady on her feet but it could be due to the ridiculous heels on her boots. They were poking down into the snow, keeping her off balance.

"Good thing you weren't going any faster. " Bo gestured at the damaged car. "What were you thinking?"

"I came to a complete stop," the man defended himself. "I tried to see if the way was clear but honestly I didn't see any lights so I assumed it was clear." He reached into his pocket and pulled out a business card. "Here's my information. My insurance will cover it."

"It won't be mine," Bo mumbled. He already had his cell phone to his ear. The police had to be notified immediately and neither party could leave the scene until the authorities had taken a look.

Once the police were called, Bo dialed Jacques. He noticed Viann was starting to shake, either from the cold or from shock. He wrapped an arm around her shoulder and waited for Jacques to pick up. When the other man did, Bo took a deep breath and then explained what had happened. As expected, Bo had to hold the phone away from his ear to accommodate Jacques's tirade on the other end. The conversation ended with Jacques asking to speak to Viann.

Bo removed his arm from around her shoulders and held the phone out to her. "He wants to talk to you."

Viann took the phone in trembling hands and put it to her ear. Her voice, husky with emotion, sounded even more exotic in her native tongue. Bo waited until they were finished and then put the phone back in his pocket.

"He said not to come in to work tonight," Viann relayed.

"Yes, he told me," Bo responded.

"And that you should take me to a hospital to get checked over just in case."

"He told me that, too."

Suddenly Viann burst into tears. With wide eyes, Bo enfolded her in his arms. He stroked her hair. "It's okay. You're just in shock."

The fur of her jacket tickled his nose, so he tilted his head up, looking at the sky. A few stray snowflakes fell into his eyes and he blinked. After a moment when her tears had subsided, he held her away from him. "You gonna be okay? I have one more call I should make."

She nodded and sniffed.

He found his cell phone once again and punched in Jed's number. "Hi, Bro. Yeah, we had a little accident on the way." Bo glanced at the perpetrator who was standing apart from them, making his own calls. "Some dummy rammed right into the side of us. I had the right of way, but the snow banks are so high he apparently couldn't see so he thought he'd just go ahead anyway. Dumb. We're okay, but Jacques wants me to take Viann to the hospital just in case. We might need a ride."

"Stay where you're to till I comes where you're at," Jed bellered in typical Newfie fashion.

"Cops aren't here yet, so that won't be a problem. I imagine they've got a few such accidents to deal with tonight." Just as he said it Bo spotted the tell-tale red and blue flashing lights in the distance. "Scratch that. They're on their way."

"So am I, so stay put!" Jed barked before hanging up.

VIANN STOOD QUIETLY SHIVERING as Bo finished up with the authorities. Gone was any air of superiority. If anything, she looked like a little lost girl on the verge of tears. There wasn't much he could do about it at the moment, but he was thankful for Jed's speedy arrival. His older brother was seeing to the tow truck and they could soon be on their way to the hospital.

As the tow truck pulled away, Jacques' sleek vehicle behind, Bo was finally able to focus some attention on Viann. "You cold?"

She shook her head. Tears were pooling in her eyes and she made no attempt to brush them away.

"It's gonna be okay," Bo repeated himself. He brushed a tear away with the pad of his thumb, letting it linger longer than necessary on her smooth cheek. Their eyes locked for a second and then she glanced away.

"Get in, kids," Jed bellowed from the driver's side of his truck. "This taxi service is leavin'."

Bo let his arm drop to his side and then moved to yank the passenger door open. He held onto Viann's elbow as she hoisted herself up into the passenger side and slid across the bench seat. Bo got in next, ignoring the stiffness in his own neck and shoulders, and closed the heavy door with a clunk.

The drive to the hospital wasn't silent. Jed made sure of that. But other than answering Jed's direct questions, Bo really didn't feel much like small talk. He silently slipped one gloved hand overtop of Viann's, between them on the seat. She didn't acknowledge the touch but she didn't move away either. It wasn't much comfort, but it was the least he could do.

She seemed genuinely undone by the ordeal. After checking in at the desk, they took off their coats in the emergency waiting room and sat down to wait.

"Well if this ain't some way to spend a Saturday evening," Jed said as he plunked down across from where Bo and Viann sat side by side on a vinyl sofa.

"Thanks for the rescue," Bo said. "We can take a cab if you want to get going."

"Don't be daft."

Bo acknowledged the sentiment with a slight grin. Nodding was out of the question. He felt like a wooden soldier, his back rigid in protective mode. Without looking down, he let his hand find Viann's again on the seat between them, this time unencumbered by leather and wool. Her hand was narrow and fragile like a bird's. But it was warm and soft and fit perfectly under his own.

He risked glancing her way, moving his neck as little as possible, and their eyes met. The corners of her mouth turned up ever so slightly before her lashes fluttered downward. The movement of those exotic wings was enough to make his own stomach flop like a duck.

After waiting for half an hour, doctors confirmed that both Bo and Viann suffered from a slight case of whiplash. Pain killers and rest were all that was prescribed. On the way home, Viann kept her own hands safely locked in her lap. The spell had been broken.

Jed and Bo accompanied her to Jacques's apartment. "Thank you for everything," Viann said as she fumbled with the keys. She squinted as she attempted to put the key in the lock and they fell to the carpet.

"Let me," Bo offered. He bent at the knees to retrieve the keys but before he could stand up, Jed was reaching for them himself.

"Give me them keys," Jed exclaimed as he wrenched them out of

Bo's hand. He unlocked the door with swift efficiency, swung it open, and then handed the keys back to Viann.

"Merci." She turned her entire torso to look at first Bo and then Jed.

"Hold it right there!"

Bo turned his body in the direction of the voices that had just emerged from the elevator. Angela, Andrea and Rocky Carravagio were walking at a brisk pace toward them.

"Jacques called and told us what happened," Angela exclaimed.

"You poor dear! Are you hurt badly?" Andrea asked.

"We both suffered a bit of whiplash," Bo informed.

"Jacques insisted we make sure Viann was looked after once she made it home," Angela continued. "Why are we standing around in the hall? Get inside." She ushered Viann through the doorway. Andrea and Rocky followed.

Jed peeked around the door jamb into the apartment. "Nice digs."

"Andrea and I are both trained in massage therapy," Angela said from inside the door. "You both need a good neck massage."

"I think I'll just head downstairs," Bo said. "I'm beat."

"Andrea, go with them and look after Bo," Angela ordered. "I'll stay here and look after Viann."

Bo lifted his hands in front of his chest in a stop signal. "No no! I'm fine. The Doc prescribed some pain killers. I'll just go with that for now."

They said their good-byes and then Jed and Bo headed down one flight to their own apartment.

Bo poured a glass of water and downed two of the pills the doctor had prescribed. Then he made his way to the living room and lowered himself gingerly onto the couch beside Jed. Once settled he let out a little self-depreciating laugh.

"What's funny?" Jed asked.

"Nothing, really."

"Sure as heck can't be the mess you made of Frenchie's car. He won't be a happy camper and I wouldn't be smilin' about it if I was you."

"Jacques'll come around when he talks to the insurance agent."

"Let's hope so."

"I was just thinking how you think you know a person and then you find out you were wrong," Bo said.

"Who we talkin' about?" Jed asked.

"Nobody."

"Lard tunderin'! Ya can't give a teaser like that and then not tell!"

"I don't want to gossip."

"I was about to offer you my bed tonight, but I'm thinkin' better of it."

Bo turned his whole body to the right so he could have a better look at Jed. "Did you know that Jacques actually comes from a wealthy family back in Montreal? Viann said he and his father disagreed on Jacques's choice of vocation."

"That's a nice way of putting it. Sounds like Frenchie's father has some sense."

"Not if it tears the family apart."

"That's a good one!" Jed's laugh held little humour. "Just cause you got a sore neck, don't mean you're gettin' away with things."

"I beg your pardon?" Bo asked. "Because I have an opinion about people being able to choose their own occupation?"

"Not that! I don't like the way you been conducting yourself, lately."

Bo knit his brows. "Now I'm confused. Just what are we talking about?"

"You and your flirting. I seen the way you were cozyin' up to Viann, and I don't think it's fair to Andrea. She's a good woman and deserves better."

Bo blinked, his neck remaining still. "Now I'm even more confused. Me, flirting? You're barking up the wrong tree, Bro."

"You can't tell me you aren't interested in Andrea Carravagio. I seen the way you two get along."

"Because we're friends," Bo said. "Nothing more."

Jed frowned. "That's what you say, but I don't trust you."

Bo frowned. He wasn't in the mood for this. "And why should you care? You're dating Crystal now." He looked sideways at his brother without moving his neck.

"That was just a thing -"

Bo cut him off. "Seems to me you're the one who should be ashamed. You obviously like Andrea, but not enough to stop you from sleeping with another woman."

"You're cock-eyed crazy," Jed said with a snort.

"Am I? I'm worried about you, Jed. You're on a fast track to I don't know where, and it's got me worried."

"Typical. We was talkin' about you and you go and turn the tables around to point the finger at me."

Bo sighed. "Nobody's pointing fingers. Deny it, then. You don't actually like Andrea Carravagio."

Jed hesitated but then answered. "Nope." He crossed his arms over his chest.

"You're lying through your teeth and you know it."

Jed shrugged. "Maybe, but we both know there's no use pursuin' a girl like that one. Her religion is important to her, for one thing, and she said she'd never hook up with a guy like me."

"She said that?" Bo felt himself softening toward his older brother.

"Yup. Said we could never be more' than friends." Jed said. "It would take a miracle. Something that never happens to black sheep like us."

"Speak for yourself."

"So you do like her?" Jed asked.

Bo threw his arms in the air and then winced with the pain of it. "No! I don't like her as anything more than a friend. I already told you that. I don't like anyone as more than a friend."

"Even Frenchie's sister? She's pretty, that's for darn tootin'."

"My brother the match maker." Bo hoisted himself from the couch with a grunt. "Enough for one night. I'm off to get some shut-eye."

"Mind if I watch some TV?" Jed asked.

"Course not." Bo stopped on his way toward the hall leading to the bedroom. "You're not going out? It's still pretty early. At least for you."

"Nah. Think I'll stay home for a change."

"Maybe miracles do happen."

"The only reason I'm lettin' ya get away with that is cause you're injured. Otherwise, look out."

Bo made his way toward Jed's bedroom. The pain killers were starting to make him drowsy and he could hardly wait to lie down. Even more, he was afraid of what he might say if they also loosened his tongue.

Viann wasn't just pretty. She was beautiful and he couldn't quite fathom the way his insides were scooting around in his chest at the mere thought of her. Either these were some strong drugs, or he had just been hit by cupid's arrow for the first time in his life.

POTS AND PANS clattered in his dream, rousing Bo from the deepness of sleep. He opened his eyes, realizing the clanging was probably Jed in the kitchen. He'd forgotten all about the events of the night before - until he tried to move and a sharp knife of pain sliced through his neck and lower cranium.

He took a deep breath and rolled to his side where he was able to push himself up using one arm, all the while keeping his head and neck perfectly still. That collar the doctor had given him last night was going to come in handy, he could tell.

After using the washroom, he maneuvered like a robot toward the sounds coming from the kitchen.

"Morning, Bo," Jed greeted. "Newfie breakfast comin' up."

"Not sure I'm hungry," Bo said.

"Too bad. You'll eat it anyway," Jed said. Using a fork, he flipped some bologna that was frying in the skillet.

A knock sounded on the door. Bo walked to the entrance and bent his knees so that his eye was level with the security hole. Jacques. Bo slowly stood and then unlatched the deadbolt and swung the door open for his boss.

"Good morning," Bo said. "Come on in."

Jacques stepped tentatively inside the door.

"Mornin', Jacques," Jed greeted. "Just in time for breakfast. My specialty."

"I already ate, thank you," Jacques said. "I just wanted to thank you for looking after Viann yesterday. And…" Jacques looked to his feet for a moment before continuing. "I wanted to apologize for yelling at you over the phone. It wasn't your fault. The insurance company verified that this morning."

"Thanks," Bo said.

"Pull up a chair! Can I at least get you a coffee?" Jed asked.

"Sure. Coffee would be fine." Jacques sat down at one of the kitchen chairs while Jed busied himself pouring the coffee. He plunked two mugs onto the table.

Bo lowered himself into one of the other chairs and picked up the fresh cup of coffee. "How is Viann feeling this morning?"

Jacques shrugged. "Sore, as I suspect you are as well. Angela is giving her another massage later today so that will help." He looked at Bo. "You should get a massage as well."

"I'll keep it in mind, but frankly, I don't like the idea of someone touching my neck. It gives me the heeby-jeebies."

"Suit yourself."

Two plates with toast, bacon, fried bologna, hash-browns, and eggs appeared in front of both men at the table.

"As I said, I already ate." Jacques pointed at the plate.

"Just try it," Jed said. "There's plenty."

Jacques popped a piece of bologna in his mouth and chewed. "Surprisingly good," he said with a nod.

Jed joined them at the table and all three ate for a few minutes in silence.

Jed pointed his fork at Jacques. "Well, b'y, you sure had me fooled."

"How so?" Jacques took another bite.

"Working as a bartender when you come from a rich family."

Bo frowned. "Jed!"

Jacques blinked but quickly tempered his surprise. "Oh that. It's no secret."

"So you don't deny it?" Jed asked.

"Why should I?" Jacques shrugged elegantly. "I never asked for handouts, if that's your question. But that is all in the past."

"Sorry about that," Bo offered on Jed's behalf. "It's really none of our business."

"Maybe not, but I'm not one for beating around the bush," Jed said. "If she's not even your real sister, and she's got access to money, why is she here? She's not too friendly."

"Jed!" Bo turned his frame to face Jacques again. "Just ignore him -"

Jacques held up his hand to silence them both. "Viann is…" He took his time with another sip of coffee. "Viann is… how do you say it? She has low self-esteem."

"How can that be? She's beautiful!" Bo said before he could stop himself.

Jacques' eyes swung to meet Bo's and the latter lowered his gaze. "Outward looks do not always filter into the soul. Viann suffers from deep insecurity. She was abandoned by her biological father only to be re-abandoned when her mother and my father got divorced."

Jed nodded in understanding. "Now I get it. Daddy issues."

Bo just closed his eyes and sighed.

"She has made herself unreachable to protect herself. She is attracted to men similar to my father. Powerful men. Men hungry for success. In their eyes she is a nice trophy, yes? She looks good on the arm of such a man, but soon he abandons her for another more beautiful or of more benefit."

"So she's running away from a relationship gone bad?" Bo asked.

"It is a cycle." Jacques sighed. "And because she is not my biological sister, I tell myself I should not care. But I do. She is the only real family I have." Jacques straightened in his seat. "I am the only man that has not let Viann down. Even if I complain about her, I will not turn her away. She can stay here as long as she wishes." Jacques put his hands on the table and stood abruptly. "And now I have work to attend to. Tad's son Cory is coming back to Calgary and we have a few … issues to work out. Thank you for the breakfast. It, how you say, hit the spot."

Jed saw Jacques to the door. Bo sat twirling his fork between his fingertips until he could formulate the words that were on his mind. When Jed got back to the table Bo spoke up. "How could you ask such personal questions like that? It's embarrassing."

"So what? I always say what's on my mind." Jed took another bite of his mostly cold breakfast.

"Besides the fact that it's none of your business, I asked you not to."

Reba entered the kitchen. "What's not Jed's business?"

"Nothing. It's not your business either," Bo said.

Reba just shrugged. "Somebodies not in a good mood today." She sniffed. "Smells good in here. Any left?"

"A bit. Jacques ate most of yours," Jed said.

"I thought you said there was plenty," Bo pointed out.

"Ma always taught us to feed company first," Jed reminded. "I couldn't let 'im go 'ungry."

"No biggy. I'm in a rush anyway," Reba said, taking a piece of bologna from the pan and popping it into her mouth.

"Where ya headed?" Bo asked.

"Pat's."

Jed checked his watch. "It's Sunday and she probably went to church with Lester."

Reba furrowed her brow. "Oh right. She said her brother would probably make her go. Not sure what people see in it, but..."

"Ma wouldn't like to hear you talk that way," Jed said.

"You're one to talk," Bo observed.

"That's different," Jed defended himself.

"How?" Bo asked.

"Well, it just is. If I walked into a church, lightning might strike. It's too late for a son-of-a-gun like me, but you, young lady, should be thinkin' about your spiritual side."

"What a hypocrite! Besides, Ma knows I quit going to church." There was a defensive edge to Reba's voice.

"Your boss goes to church," Bo stated.

"Who?" Reba furrowed her brow again.

"Andrea."

Reba nodded. "That explains a few things."

"Leave her outta it. She's a fine Christian woman and you could take some lessons," Jed said.

Reba just rolled her eyes and swung her gaze to Bo. "And just how do you know so much?"

"I'm the bartender. People tell me things." He grinned.

Just like Jacques had told him what he wanted to know about Viann - despite the fact that he'd protested. Now all he had to do was put the information to good use.

Bo stood outside Jacques' apartment door, shifting from one foot to another. He rapped again. He was sure he'd heard movement inside but no one was coming to the door.

He was just about to abandon his post when he heard the chain rattle and the door swung open. His practiced greeting got stuck somewhere between his tongue and his lips when he saw what was on the other side.

Viann stood, wrapped in a large towel, one hand grasping the fluffy terry material near her chest while the other held the door ajar.

"Hi." It was all that managed to come out of his mouth.

"Hi."

"I didn't mean to interrupt."

"Angela just gave me a massage. I was about to take a shower."

"I can come back later."

"No, no. Come in." She grasped the towel more firmly and gestured with her free hand.

"You're sure?"

"Yes. Angela and Jacques just left, so…"

"I just wanted to see how you were feeling."

"Much better. The massage helps."

"So I'm told." Bo gestured to the padded collar at his neck. "I opted for the extra designer look."

Viann smiled. "I took mine off to shower. Excuse me while I change? I will be right back."

Bo lowered himself onto the couch. The apartment was a mirror image of Jed's yet looked completely different because of the elegant furnishings and strategically placed art on the walls. A few minutes later, Viann emerged from a bedroom wearing an identical collar to his and a silky bathrobe that clung to her slim form. The towel probably offered more coverage.

Bo averted his gaze and spoke to the floor. "Doc said not to get dependant on the collar. I figure I'll see how it feels tomorrow and probably get rid of it before work."

She lowered herself into a chair opposite. "You will go to work tomorrow?" She sounded genuinely surprised.

"If I feel up to it. There's no workman's comp at the bar. If you don't work you don't get paid."

"I will speak to Jacques."

"I'd prefer you didn't," Bo said quickly.

"You are proud. Like Jacques." She smiled.

The gentleness of the look she offered melted the last vestiges of insecurity away. Bo smiled back. "Part of the Malloy genes, I guess."

"I've been thinking about what you said yesterday," Viann started. "In the car. About 'turning my nose up'?"

"Oh that!" Bo made a dismissive gesture with his hand. "I had no business being so rude. I shoulda kept my big mouth shut."

"No, you are right. I was behaving as a snob and I apologize. One cannot make review of the book by the cover."

Bo laughed. "Don't judge a book by its cover. I think I misjudged you, too, and I'm sorry."

"Good. We will start over, then. As friends." She stood up and offered her hand.

Bo stood also and grasped her hand, savouring the feelings of warmth that travelled along his body at such a simple touch. "Friends."

"And now I would like to shower, if you don't mind."

Bo let go of her hand. "Of course." He turned to make his way to the exit and then stopped, turning slowly so as not to upset his own equilibrium. "Maybe we could seal the deal sometime over dinner."

"That would be very nice."

Bo knew he was grinning all the way back to his own apartment. The hope in his heart had quite successfully blocked the pain in his neck.

~

Bo stepped out of the elevator and into the foyer. It had been three days since he'd seen Viann last. His neck was feeling better and his heart had never been more alive.

He smiled when he recognized Viann on the other side of the glass outer doors. Just the person he was hoping to run into. It was time he made his offer official and ask her out to dinner.

He stopped in his tracks ten steps from the doors. Viann was not alone. She was holding onto a man with an expensive trench coat. He had slick dark hair and hipster glasses. Bo squinted, recognizing the face, if not the man himself.

Then it dawned on him. It was the doctor who had treated them the night of the accident. Viann went up on tiptoe so as not to bend her neck too much and kissed the man right on the mouth. Then she smiled, waved, and let herself into the building.

"Hello, Bo," she greeted with a sing song lilt to her voice. "On your way to work?"

"Um, yes," Bo said. "Say, was that the doctor who treated us after the accident?"

"Yes. I went for a follow up appointment and he was so kind. He asked me out for dinner and well…" Viann giggled. "His name is Martin. Dr. Martin Lawler."

"Oh."

"Well, see you. Have a nice time at work."

Bo watched her retreat into the confines of the elevator, a coy smile still playing about her lips.

His heart thudded into the pit of his stomach. With a sigh he slung his scarf over his shoulder and pushed through the glass doors. Maybe he was just destined to be alone.

EPISODE 3

NEIGHBOURHOOD REBEL

EBA

"I'M SO excited I'm gonna burst!" Reba swept a pile of dark curls into a dustpan and dumped it in the trash. Gemini's, the salon where she worked for the Carravagio twins, was closing for the day and the three women were doing their final clean up.

"Why's that?" Andrea Carravagio asked.

"My brothers Will and Pip are arriving tonight from Newfoundland. We'll be gettin' on the beer soon as they land, it's like."

Andrea blinked once as she tried to mentally interpret what was just said. "Goodness! There sure are a lot of you!"

It was true. Reba was the second youngest in a family of nine children - not such a novelty in her home province of Newfoundland as it might be elsewhere. She had moved west to Calgary, Alberta just a couple of months ago with her brother Bo. They'd joined their eldest brother Jed and currently still lived with him. It was tight, but soon enough she and Bo planned on getting their own apartment if they could find one that was reasonable in price.

"Are they anything like the rest of you?" Angela, the other owner, asked.

Reba furrowed her brow and thought about it for a few seconds. "Depends. I mean, look at you two. You're exactly alike and yet you couldn't be more different." It was true. The Carravagio sisters were identical twins and as far as the physical went, they were equally big boned and curvaceous. But Andrea was as soft spoken as the pastel colours she favoured, while Angela was brash and bold like the revealing clothes she preferred.

"Are they more like Jed or Bo?" Andrea asked.

"Neither. Will is the least Malloy like as far as looks, although he has Jed's dark colouring. And Pip's just a scrawny version of Zeb."

"The brother from Fort Mac," Angela said with a nod. "I remember him."

"He's coming down for a visit, too," Reba explained, not able to contain the excitement in her voice. "It's been awhile since we were all together. The only ones missing will be my three sisters, but they have kids. And my parents, of course, but they don't count."

"How fun for you!" Andrea exclaimed.

"I know, eh?"

"Well, ladies? We ready to lock up?" Angela looked around the room for any last tasks. Since they all lived in the same apartment complex, Reba had been fortunate to get a ride to and from work each day with the sisters since starting work at Gemini's.

When they arrived at the apartment building, Reba jumped from Angela's small vehicle and jogged to the building, not bothering to wait for the other women. It was March, and although spring was around the corner, snow was piled along the perimeter of the parking lot.

She skidded to a stop inside the building when her brother Bo met her in the foyer. "Are they here yet?" she asked, breathless.

"No. Jed went to the airport to pick them up." Bo was big and broad, like most of the Malloy men, with a ginger complexion and sandy blonde hair.

"What? I thought they'd be here hours ago!" Reba scowled.

"I think Pip got the times mixed up when he tried to convert Newfoundland time to Alberta time. He forgot about the extra half hour. Anyway, I'm off to work and Jed is going to bring them straight down to the Urban Cowboy from the airport. I told him they'd be too bagged after such a long flight, but you know Jed."

"What about Zeb? What time does he get in?" Reba asked.

"Driving down. I imagine he'll hook up with us there as well."

"It's gonna be some crowded tonight!" Reba said with a grin.

Bo grimaced. "Tell me about it. Jed was a bear when he left. Said maybe he'd have to find his own place if the rest of the family keep coming."

Reba just laughed. "Listen, if you have a minute, I'll just run up to the apartment and then we can go together. There's no point in me staying behind."

Bo glanced at his watch. "Hurry. I gotta be at work."

"I'll be two minutes." Reba fled to the elevator and pushed the button then jumped inside when the doors swished open. This was going to be the best night ever!

THE URBAN COWBOY was ramping up for a typical Friday night. It was decorated in a retro ranch style and sported lots of neon, a large area for pool and even a mechanical bull. A long black counter flanked one side of the establishment with a mirrored wall behind that made the place look bigger than it was. Bo had taken his place behind the counter, and next to him was the manager, Jacques Marcett, who also happened to be Angela Carravagio's boyfriend. Reba fidgeted on her stool, watching the entrance in the mirror.

Country music blared on the sound system but was almost drowned out by the laughter and cheering around the pool table that was typical of the bar scene. When the front door opened, an even louder cheer went up as a string of Malloys entered.

"Whoo hoo!" Reba jumped off her stool and ran full tilt right into

Zeb's arms. He was a giant of a man with shaggy hair and a ginger beard.

"Hey, Spitfire!" Zeb swung her around and then set her down in front of Will who did the same.

Will Malloy had a trim athletic build, not as square as the other Malloy men, but every bit as powerful. His dark good looks were more refined that the others, too. Pip, on the other hand, had the typical Malloy rounded features, but was much slimmer than his elders Jed and Zeb.

After a sufficient ruckus, they moved en masse to the bar to do it again with Bo. Hands pumped and backs slapped amid many loud expletives.

Bo finally pulled himself from Will's bear-hug and turned to Jacques. "These are the rest of me brothers. This is Will and this is Pip. And you probably remember Zeb."

"I remember." Jacques shook each hand in turn, never wincing despite the extra pressure applied by Zeb.

Reba just stood and watched, not even attempting to wipe the foolish grin from her face. These were her men. And she was proud to say it.

"First drink is on me," Bo said.

"First drink is on the house," Jacques corrected, his French accent coming through.

Bo and Jacques lined up the drinks - beer all around except for Pip who ordered a vodka and water.

"Who drinks that?" Jed asked.

"Millions of Russians can't be wrong," Pip replied. He lofted his glass with a mischievous grin and took a drink.

Jed shook his head. "Who ever heard of a Russian Newfie?"

"Don't knock it. Closest thing to screech you can order legally," Pip said.

They all laughed.

"Who's for a game of pool?" Zeb suggested.

The group moved to a large round table near the pool tables and the banter continued. It was hard to keep track since so many conversations were going on at once. News from home, Pop's health, the sisters, nieces and nephews… it seemed like more than just two months since Reba had left Newfoundland. She missed it. Missed the folks. But it was time to make her own way, too.

One of the waitresses, Crystal, hovered nearby. "Aren't you going to introduce me?"

Reba narrowed her eyes. Crystal and Jed had a relationship of sorts. Sex was more like it. Reba didn't really like the other woman. Not that she was a person to be judgemental, but Crystal seemed desperate. Willing to use her body for a little companionship.

Jed shifted in his seat and made the introductions. Crystal rested her free hand on his shoulder while he did so.

"Well, nice to meet you." When Crystal moved away, Zeb and Pip both made a suggestive noise, almost in unison, then laughed.

"So the waitress serves up more 'an just drinks?" Zeb asked.

Jed shrugged. "We're just friends."

"Not the story I heard," Reba said.

"Shut up yer prate," Jed said with a scowl.

"Who's for pool?" Zeb asked again. "Last time me and Spitfire beat the crap outta Jed and Bo."

"I'll let you kids have at 'er," Jed said.

"Okay. Me and Pip against Will and Reba."

It was fun having the brothers all together, Reba decided. And tomorrow her friend Pat Tibbett was also coming for a visit. Life didn't get much better than this.

THE DOORBELL SOUNDED and Reba jumped up from her half sleeping position in the recliner. She'd been expecting the interruption. Her friend Pat Tibbett had arrived the night before and was coming over bright and early. Bright and early was a stretch considering Reba and her brothers had stayed until closing at the Urban Cowboy, but Reba and Pat didn't get to see one another that often, so she was willing to make the sacrifice.

Reba stepped over Pip's prone body where he lay sprawled out on the living room floor. As soon as she opened the door, Pat threw her arms around her neck.

They hadn't really known each other long, and had only spent a limited time together, but the two girls had hit it off like best friends. Pat's brother Lester Tibbett lived downstairs and was one of Jed's good friends. It was how they had met.

"I'd invite you in, but as you can see, floor space is at a premium." Reba gestured to the living room. Pip was on the floor in a sleeping bag, Will was on the couch. Bo normally slept in Jed's room on a blow up mattress, but he had pulled it into Reba's room for the night so that Zeb and Jed could share Jed's room.

Pat glanced around the room. "You want to go out for coffee?"

"Sure." Reba looked over her shoulder at Pip's sprawled form. "I'll take Jed's truck. He won't be up for a while anyway."

"Want to go to the Brew?" Pat said. "I know it's all the way downtown, but I haven't been there in ages."

"Sounds good."

The drive to the coffee shop was filled with chatter as each girl filled the other in about recent life events. "I might actually move back at the end of the month," Patsi said.

"Really? That's great!"

"Most of the horses go out to pasture by springtime, and the work will slow right down. I was thinking of asking Carmen and Tamara if I could get my old job back."

"So that's why you wanted to go to the Brew."

"Not the only reason, but partly. Also, I have to come back to the city at the end of March anyway for my friend's wedding."

"Cool. That should be fun."

Pat looked down at her hands. "I suppose. Actually, it'll be super awkward. I used to date her brother."

"That is awkward."

"It's one of the reasons I left when I did."

"It's too bad when that kind of thing comes between friends."

"I know. Anyway, Megan - that's my friend - had a really hard time of it. Her family all but disowned her for dating an immigrant. His name is Emmanuel and they really love each other."

"How romantic."

"At first they said they wouldn't have anything to do with her if she kept on going with Emmanuel, but apparently they came around when they found out she's pregnant."

"A grandchild? That'll do it."

"They aren't having a big wedding. Just something at the court-house, which is ironic considering her parents are lawyers. She wants me to stand up with her. I was the only one who was still nice to her. I couldn't say no."

"Really? You stuck by 'er?" Reba glanced across at her friend. "That's good of you considering you and 'er brother broke up."

"Of course." Patsi looked sideways at Reba. "That's what friends do."

"Of course."

They'd reached the Brew and Reba parked out front.

As soon as the little bell rang over the door, Carmen Lamont came running and squeezed Pat around the middle. "We missed you! How have you been?" Her dark chocolate face was split by a wide, red lipped smile.

"Fine. This is my friend Reba."

"I think we've met. You're Jed Malloy's sister?"

"That's right."

"How are the renovations coming?" Patsi asked.

Reba looked around the coffee shop. It had a nice vibe - relaxed and intimate, with warm colours that made one want to have a cuppa.

"Excellent. We hope to have our grand opening in April." Carmen gestured to a wall that was obviously temporary. By the look of it they were expanding into the space next door. "The last thing to come down will be that wall. It'll be so nice to have more space."

Patsi and Reba ordered coffee and a muffin and went to a high table.

"So tell me more about this old flame," Reba said once they were settled.

Patsi sighed. "Brett was… preoccupied with himself and his friends. I didn't realize it at first, but he's a player and was only interested in one thing."

"Most guys are," Reba agreed.

"He was ashamed of me when we were around his rich friends. And his mother hated me. Probably still does." Patsi looked down at her lap. "Anyway, it was best that I dumped him when I did."

"So you dumped him?"

Patsi nodded. "Although I'm sure he has a different story. It's kind of convoluted. Brett was the brother of my best friend, but then he also used to DJ with this guy named Cory Roberts, who owns the Urban Cowboy."

Reba scrunched her brows. "I thought an older guy named Tad owned the bar."

"He does. Cory is his son. They're partners, I guess. Anyway, it made it awkward cause Lester and Jed liked to go there and then when Lester hooked up with Sherri, her brother Sherman is like best friends with Cory and then Carmen started dating Sherman and the other owner of the Brew, Tamara, started dating their other friend Steve… It was like, everywhere I turned, I was running into someone I knew that knew Brett or that had a connection to him somehow. I just had to get away."

"Sounds complicated. It's why it's best not to mix friendship with romance."

"It is complicated." Patsi straightened. "But now that I've had some time and distance, I'm fine. I'm totally over him and other than having to see him at the wedding, I'll probably never run into him again." She leaned forward. "You know what was really awesome, though?"

"What?"

"Brett's snotty parents got caught in some kind of embezzling scam. The case is still in the courts but it's put their own practice in the tank."

"And that makes you happy?" Reba asked.

Patsi shrugged. "Not really. But like Miss Peacock would say, they got what they deserved."

"Miss Peacock?" Reba asked.

"OMG!" Patsi slapped the table. "Don't tell me you haven't run into Miss Peacock? That nosy old lady who lives in our building?"

"Oh, that lady!" Reba made a dismissive gesture. "I told 'er off the first day I moved in."

They both laughed.

"I'm sure glad to have a friend in this city," Patsi said.

"What about what's 'er name? The one getting married?"

"Megan? Yeah, she and I are friends, too, but not like we used to be. It's -"

"Complicated," Reba finished and they both laughed again.

"So enough about me. How are you going to stand being so crowded now that your whole family is here?"

"It's not the whole family," Reba said. "And it's only temporary." She stopped and smiled. "Besides the fact that my head feels right loggy, it was sure good to spend time with them last night."

"Tell me more. What are they like?"

"Why? You looking for a boyfriend to take to the wedding?" Reba grinned.

"No, although that might be fun. Just for spite."

Reba's smile faded. "You should steer clear of my brothers. Especially Pip."

"I was only kidding. Sheesh."

"I knew that."

"So? Your brothers?" Patsi prompted.

Reba straightened and forced a bright smile. "Well, Jed's the talker of the family - as you know already - and kind of like the second father next to Pops."

"The bossy older brother. I know all about it," Patsi said.

"Zeb's been dubbed the 'animal', for obvious reasons. Bo is the quiet, sensible one. Will is the daredevil. And Pip is, well, Pip's the baby. He's the spoiled one."

"You sure? I heard Bo say the same about you last time I was here," Patsi teased.

"Typical middle-child syndrome. Bo has a chip on his shoulder."

"And what about you? What do they call you?"

Reba smiled widely. "Zeb calls me Spitfire. He has nicknames for everyone. He's the one who gave Pip 'is name. It's short for 'Pip-squeak'. His real name is Steve."

"Nice. I'm glad I only have to put up with one brother. I can't imagine five of them telling me what to do."

"I can hold my own."

"And how's your job working out?"

"Job's good. Angela and Andrea are good bosses, and I suppose we're friends, too, although being friends with your bosses can be awkward at times. They're not much older than me but they seem older. Not sure why."

"People are just different."

"You got that right. They're like Jekyll and 'yde, and I don't just mean one is one and one is the other. Angela's a piece of work some-times. She's so bossy and loud - something I'm used to coming from a family like mine, but then sometimes I see a different side to 'er. Like she's just putting on a front cause she's hurt. And then Andrea acts like a little church mouse most of the time, timid as all get out. But once in a while she gets stubborn and then watch out!"

"Jed still have a thing for her?"

"You saw that?" Reba surveyed her friend curiously.

Patsi shrugged. "Lester may have mentioned it."

Reba shook her head. "Talk about stubborn. Jed's got that award sewed up. I think they like each other but there are 'issues', apparently. Anyway, he keeps hooking up with Crystal, so I'd say 'is chances with Andrea are over."

"The waitress?"

"You got it."

"And what about your love life? Any prospects?" Patsi raised her brows and smiled.

"Not sure anyone can keep up with me." Reba threw her napkin on the table. "So, are we going shopping or what?"

∼

By THE TIME Reba and Patsi got back to the apartment, the Malloy men-folk were up and about. Reba ushered her friend into the small living space where five brawny males sat on every available seat.

"Well, 'ello, Patsi," Jed said as soon as he saw her hovering in the small entrance between the galley kitchen and the living room. "Visiting again so soon? Miss me or what?"

Patsi smiled back. "I had a few things to look after this weekend and then I'll be back again in a few weeks for my friend's wedding."

"Anybody I know?" Jed asked.

"Maybe." Patsi looked down at her toes. "My friend Megan McMillan is getting married."

Jed's brows descended into a straight line. "The same McMillans that got caught on that Nudara Oil case?"

"Yes. One and the same."

"If I recall, you also used to date the brother. What was 'is name?" Jed asked.

"Brett," Patsi supplied.

"Good grief, that's enough questioning," Reba exclaimed. "For those that don't know, this is my friend Pat Tibbett. Her brother lives downstairs and is a friend of Jed's, which is why 'e thinks 'e can be so nosy."

"We met last time you were here," Bo said.

"And I remember you from my Christmas visit," Zeb put in. He winked. "I never forget a pretty face."

Reba rolled her eyes and then gestured to Will and Pip. "So these are my other brothers, Will and Pip."

Pip jumped off the couch and approached Patsi with an outstretched hand. "Pleased to meet you. Is it Pat or Patsi?"

"Pat will do." She took his hand and shook it, then looked at her feet as she withdrew a step. "Well, I suppose I should get going. I've got a few other errands. Nice meeting everyone."

"I imagine we'll be seeing you again tonight at the bar," Jed said.

"Probably." Patsi waved and took her leave.

"Seems nice enough," Will said. "What did you say she does again?"

"I didn't say." Reba glared in his direction then turned to Pip. "And what was that all about, playin' the gentleman knight? 'Pleased to meet you.'" She mimicked. "I only seen you act that way when you got ulterior motives. Or a bet to settle."

"You wound me!" Pip put a hand to his chest. "Can't a fella be sociable without ulterior motives?"

"You gotta admit, she's a looker," Zeb put in.

"How would you know?" Reba shot back. "You got eyes like a caplin goin' offshore. Not sure how you can even see outta dem."

Pip slapped his knee at Reba's insult, a reference to Zeb's blood-shot eyes from a hangover.

"That's enough. Reba's got sense for once," Jed said. "Lester'd string the first one of ya up to make a move on 'is sister. And I'd be next in line when 'e finished with ya."

Bo leaned forward in his chair. "To answer your question. She works at a ranch down south that boards horses for the winter."

"A real live cow-girl." Pip grubbed his hands together. "Even better."

"Now what'd I just say?" Jed said sternly. "Lard tunderin'! You got cauliflowers for ears?"

"Who? Me?" Pip gestured at himself, still grinning.

"You may look like an innocent young pup but I know the truth." Jed shook his head.

Reba pointed a finger as close to Pip's face as she could without touching it. "Don't even think about it." She straightened and looked around the room at the rest of her brothers. "That goes for each an every one of ya. Last thing I need is you wreckin' the only friend I got in this town."

As she marched down the hall, Reba heard Zeb say, "What bee got into 'er bonnet?"

"YOUR BROTHER NOT COMING THIS EVENIN'?" Jed asked Patsi when she joined the Malloy table later on that evening at the Urban Cowboy.

"No. He and Sherri had other plans. He said to say hi, though, so 'Hi'." She gave a mini-wave to the group in general.

"I'd say things are gettin' serious between them two," Jed said.

"Maybe."

"Who's for pool?" Zeb asked.

"You're up for more? After me and Reba beat the arses off you last night?" Will said with a laugh.

"Only cause buddy was reelin' pickled afore we even started," Pip replied.

"A rematch it is, then," Will said and stood up.

"No way. I wants a new partner," Zeb said. "Not some nish who cries for his momma every time he misses."

"Fine. I'll take Pat and you can have pretty boy." Pip gestured at Will.

"Yer on!" Zeb stood as well.

"You don't mind?" Patsi sought Reba's eyes with her own.

"Course not. I can only take so much of these lummoxes. Go show em how it's done."

Reba watched as the foursome maneuvered their way to the pool tables. Zeb and Will were jostling each other in typical Malloy fashion, but Pip was hovering close to Patsi, whispering something in her ear that made her smile, guiding her through the crowd with the palm of his hand on the small of her back. It wasn't until Jed spoke that Reba realized she'd been frowning.

"I wouldn't put too much stock in it. Patsi's not a fool."

"But Pip is," Reba retorted.

Jed frowned. "Lard knows if I can figure what came between you two. Ya used to be so close."

"It's nothing. And you're probably right. Pat's leaving tomorrow anyway and Pip'll be gone before she moves back."

"What say we sit up to the bar for a bit? I think I just seen an old friend talkin' to Bo. I'll introduce ya."

Reba glanced in the direction of the bar. Indeed, Bo was in conversation with two black men, one whom she recognized as Tad Roberts, the owner, and the other a younger and much handsomer man with a head full of dreadlocks tied into a huge mass that stuck out like a giant bun. She shrugged nonchalantly. "Sure. Let's go."

As soon as they reached the counter, Jed stuck out his hand and pumped the younger man's for a good ten seconds. "If it isn't Cory Roberts, back from the bright lights of Vancouver. I thought you'd abandoned us for good."

"Couldn't stay away," the other man said. Up close he was even more attractive than Reba had first assessed. Athletic looking, with well-developed biceps bulging beneath the tightly woven material of his long sleeved T-shirt, white against the dark chocolate of his skin.

"Meet my little sister, Reba," Jed was saying. Reba blinked back to reality, focusing her gaze on the man's smiling face instead of daydreaming about being swept off by an African prince in some remote jungle.

"Cory Roberts."

They shook hands, Reba on auto-pilot as she tried to make sense of her own sudden incapacitation. The man was a god, plain and simple. "Nice to finally meet you. Tad talks about you all the time," she mumbled.

Cory flashed his gaze to where his father stood. "Hopefully all good."

"You know it," Tad responded with a laugh.

"I'll tell you what he really says behind your back," Jacques put in, his goatee twitching with repressed laughter.

It was like they were a long lost family and the prodigal had just come home.

"So, are you just visiting?" Jed asked. He was sitting up to the bar now, Bo having provided him with a beer.

Reba looked down and saw that there was one in front of her as well. She took a sip and then wiped the froth off her upper lip with the back of her sleeve.

"I've moved back," Cory said.

"And what about that pretty gal you was seein'?" Jed asked. "She back, too?"

"Um…it didn't work out," Cory said.

"Oh. Sorry to hear it."

"Anyway, I'm back now, so dear old dad can get back to his own retirement plans, which I hear are going very smoothly with a certain lady named Goldie." Cory smiled over at his father.

Jed, Bo and Jacques laughed at the joke. Reba knew Tad had a girl-friend named Goldie that lived in their building, but she'd never really had any dealings with her - or Tad, other than to see him occasionally at the bar.

"I told him that time mends all wounds, but it'll be tough for a while," Tad continued on his previous vein.

"Dad..."

"Her career was more important to her in the end. I warned him about dating an actress, but..."

"Dad, I seriously think that's enough. Nobody wants to hear all the sorry details."

"I don't mind," Jed said.

"Jed!" It was Bo who scolded this time.

"Listen. Things just didn't work out, okay? End of story," Cory said, his tone definitely indicating that the line of questioning had come to an end. "What I'd like to know is, what the heck am I going to do now that Dad went and gave my job to Jacques? And to top it off, he went ahead and hired even more help. I think I'm out of a job." He was smiling but there was definitely a sudden edge of tension in the air.

After a moment of awkward silence, Jacques spoke up. "Of course, you are still the boss..."

"And as part owner, you can take back the run of the place," Tad picked up where Jacques left off. "I was only here to help you..."

Cory burst out laughing, doubling over for several seconds. "Gotcha! I was only kidding. I am so glad to have good employees to come back to." He turned to Bo. "And Jacques says you're a good bartender. As good as he is."

"Not my exact words..." Jacques said.

Bo grinned. "Thanks. That's high praise coming from him."

Cory sighed and looked around. "I missed this place. It's good to be back."

"Glad to hear it," Tad said. "I plan to make myself scarce. Once Goldie and I get married the last thing I want is to be hanging around down here every night. No offence."

"What? You and Goldie are getting married?" Cory asked. "I was only kidding about -"

Tad put up a hand to stop him. "I haven't asked her yet, so don't go spreading rumours. But soon, I hope."

"What's this?" Patsi sat down on the stool next to Reba.

"Nothing, nothing!" Tad said.

"Hey, Pat! Great to see you again." Cory leaned over the counter and he and Patsi shared a cheek to cheek hug. "How you keeping?"

Reba let out an inaudible sigh.

"Good. I moved out after Christmas, or maybe you knew that already," Patsi replied. "Been working on a ranch down south, wintering horses."

"Right up your alley."

"Still into the music business?" she asked.

"Hoping to do more of it now that I'm back in Calgary. It was pretty competitive in Vancouver. Hard to get any gigs. At least here we're more established so I should be able to pick up where I left off. At least that's what I'm hoping." Cory's attention was suddenly taken by another patron wanting to shake his hand. "Hey! Good to see you, too!" He directed a quick wink at Patsi and Reba before moving further down the counter to talk to the new person.

"He's yummy," Reba said under her breath. "Why didn't you tell me you were friends with such a 'unk?"

Patsi frowned. "A yunk? Oh, you mean hunk!"

"That's what I said."

"I did. Yesterday," Patsi said. "Remember? He and my ex play music together? DJing?"

"Oh. Right." Reba waved a dismissive hand. "You get tired of pool? Or was it the company?"

"The company's fine," Patsi replied. "But I'm not the best player so

I thought I better take pity on poor Pip and let someone else step in." She turned to Jed. "They're waiting for you. You're my replacement."

"On it!" Jed downed the rest of his draft. "Now you ladies stay outta trouble," he said before making his exit.

"I also wanted to make sure I spent some time with you before I leave again," Patsi said once Jed was out of earshot. "Your brothers are nice but…"

"Pip was coming on to you, wasn't he? That little weasel!"

"It's fine! I'm just not really in the market right now, if you know what I mean."

Relief flooded through Reba's body. "Good. I'll tell him to keep his distance."

Patsi placed her hand on Reba's forearm. "Don't do that. I don't want to embarrass anyone. Besides, I'm leaving tomorrow right after church. No harm done."

Reba nodded. "Okay." She really shouldn't have been worried. Pat wasn't like her other friends. She swallowed the last of her beer and smiled.

Score: Reba one. Pip zero.

REBA LOOKED up from her phone as Jed entered the living room. He stood for a moment, gazing around the body strewn floor. "Jumpin' Jehoshaphat! This is about to drive me snakey!" He ran a hand through his dark crop of hair, making it stand up at odd angles.

"You need a haircut," Reba said. She turned her attention back to the tiny screen. She was curled into the only available chair.

Jed stepped over a sleeping bag cocoon which presumably held Pip's body. "No time. I'll do it myself."

"Looks like you did that already - and it's terrible, by the way. I'll book you an appointment."

"Nope. Not goin' back there." Jed shoved Will's feet to the side and sat down on the end of the couch. Will made a grunting noise and curled into himself a bit, allowing Jed more room.

"Why not? Andrea and Angela are good hairdressers. You liked the cut that Andrea gave you that one time."

"What I want to know is, when am I ever gonna get my apartment back?"

"Soon, I hope." Bo was standing in the hall entrance. "I was thinking about apartment hunting this afternoon."

"What about me?" Reba asked. "I thought we were going together."

Bo lifted a shoulder. "I figured you'd want to spend today with your friend. Wanna come?"

"Yes, I want to come," Reba exclaimed. "Pat had to go to church with her brother, and then 'e's taking her right to the bus depot."

"Right. I forgot they went to church regular. Seems like it's a popular activity. Maybe I'll have to try it sometime," Bo said.

Jed made a snorting sound, but didn't say anything.

"How soon do you want to go?" Reba asked.

"As soon as you're ready. I already made a few calls and have some showings lined up. We can grab a coffee to go."

"Mind you're back before suppertime," Jed said. "Zeb's takin' us all out for supper tonight and you wouldn't want to miss out on a free meal. Especially not when Zeb's payin'."

A thought that had lodged in Reba's mind found its way out on their way to the first appointment. "What'd you mean back there when you said you might try going to church? Seems to me it's not something you just try on, like a pair of shoes. Either you go or you don't."

"I don't know. Just something I've been thinking about lately." Bo glanced over at his sister. "Lots of people we know believe in God."

"I believe in God."

"Okay, fine. But I mean really believe, like they mean it. Lester and Sherri, Tad and Goldie. Even your friend Pat must believe if she goes to church."

"It makes 'er brother happy."

"Not the best reason, but I suppose it's valid since she doesn't get to see him much."

Reba furrowed her brow. "I know Andrea and her brother Rocky are both religious like that. We've talked about it a few times, but I never really paid it much attention. They have their beliefs and I have mine."

"I've talked to Tad about it a lot," Bo said and then chuckled. "Kind of a funny conversation to have while serving up alcohol in a bar, but Tad is a really good man. He explained things in a way that made sense to me. Different from what I've heard before. He's very open about his beliefs but he doesn't come across as judgemental. It makes me curious, is all. He seems genuinely content with life."

"Don't go getting all religious on me, now," Reba said.

"Or what?" Bo asked and grinned. "You won't be my roommate?"

"You know what I mean. Don't go changing. You're the only really stable one of the lot."

"Thanks, I think."

"Um... do you think Tad's son Cory is that way too? Religious, I mean?"

"I couldn't say, exactly. I only just met him, same as you." Bo glanced her way. "Why do you ask?"

"No reason." Reba focused her gaze out the window.

"You like him, don't you?"

"Maybe. That a crime?"

Bo laughed. "No. Just seems a bit premature. By the sounds of things he's just getting over a relationship. You don't want to be his rebound."

Reba lifted a shoulder nonchalantly. "A rebound might be fun."

Bo shook his head. "I'm the stable one - your words. Take it from me. I don't want to see you get hurt."

"Says the guy with no experience at relationships. Maybe you should try getting hurt. It might do you some good."

"Maybe I have and didn't like it."

Reba considered this for a moment. She glanced over at Bo's profile. He was good looking in his own way. Not handsome like Will, and not quite brawny enough to attract attention like Zeb. Even Jed could get women just by sheer force of character, and Pip - well, Pip's confidence seemed to work in his favour, not that she liked it. But Bo was just kind of… ordinary. Ordinary, stable Bo. She'd never really considered before that he could be lonely. She thought he just chose to live that way.

"You want to talk about it?" she asked.

"Absolutely not." He grinned.

"Fine. I won't ask again."

"Good. Don't."

She sat for a few seconds then burst out. "Anyone I know?"

"Thought you said you wouldn't ask again."

"Quit bein' a scut and tell me. Do I know 'er or not?"

"Maybe."

"You can't expect to be my roommate and keep those kind of secrets from me," Reba said reasonably.

"If we become roommates, and if the opportunity presents itself, and if I feel like it, you'll be the first to know."

"Fine." She sat back in her seat and went through the possibilities one by one - and came up blank. This little mystery was going to take some serious espionage.

TRUE TO HIS WORD, Zeb took the entire clan out for a meal that evening. The Fortune Cookie Family Restaurant was old school, decorated in gold and red with pastoral Chinese paintings on the walls.

"Just like old times." Zeb shook his head as he looked around the table at his siblings. "Now all we need are Ma, Pops and the other three sisters."

"You make it sound like the last supper," Bo said.

"It is! For me, anyway. I'm the one who's gotta head back to Fort Mac first thing in the morning."

"Good thing. My place is startin' to feel like a sardine can," Jed said.

Their waitress came and distributed plastic covered menus. "How are you this evening? My name is Lily and I'll be your waitress." She was tall and slender with long raven hair pulled back into a swinging ponytail.

Zeb smiled broadly. "What's good? I'm buying."

"Well… that depends on what you feel like eating. Were you planning to order several options and share, or did each of you want to order individually?"

"Let's get lots of different dishes and share," Reba suggested. "That way we get to try more things." The others agreed.

"I'll just give you a few minutes to read the menu and then I'll be back."

Pip watched the waitress retreat to a counter where an older Chinese man was sitting reading a paper.

"What are you starin' at," Will asked, giving Pip a shove in the shoulder.

"Nothing," Pip said.

"You're a pig," Reba said, never taking her eyes off her menu.

"None a that, now," Jed said. "You don't want your lack of manners gettin' back to Lester."

"What he said," Zeb agreed with a grin. "Besides, this is my last night."

"As if a Malloy had any manners to begin with," Will chimed in.

"Speak for yourself," Pip objected.

"Wait! What?" Reba interrupted the brotherly banter. "Why would your friend Lester have anything to do with - anything?"

"Didn't you know? This here restaurant belongs to 'is girlfriend's family. In fact, I expect he'll be showing up later on before we even get outta here. Sunday night family dinner. Or so I'm told."

Lily arrived back at their table. "Are you ready to order?"

"These lummoxes haven't decided what they want yet," Zeb said. "How about you just surprise us?"

"Well…" Lily leaned across Zeb's shoulder and pointed at the menu. "Why don't you try the dinner for six? It comes with a nice variety."

"Sure. Only make it for eight."

"Are you sure? That seems like an awful lot of food," Lily said.

"You seen the size of these brutes?" Reba asked.

Lily laughed. "Okay. Um, so, you're friends with Lester Tibbett?"

"How'd you know?" Jed asked.

"I didn't mean to eavesdrop, but I heard your conversation a couple of minutes ago."

"And how do you know Lester?" Jed asked.

"Sherri and I are cousins. All in the family, and all that." Lily smiled. "Well, I better get this order to the kitchen." She bowed before leaving.

"I like that. Respect. And her English is so perfect!" Zeb exclaimed.

Reba rolled her eyes. "Course 'er English is perfect, you dummy. She's Canadian. It's better 'an yours!"

"I won't deny that," Zeb said with a laugh. "You're some testy these days, Spitfire. What's eatin' ya."

"And please don't say 'woman' stuff," Pip said. "If that isn't an excuse!"

"How would you know since you've never been a woman?" Will asked.

"I'm not testy," Reba said, her voice sounding only slightly miffed. "I just meant you shouldn't judge 'er cause she's Asian."

"That's not what he was talking about and you know it," Pip said.

"Nobody asked you."

The verbal volley continued for a moment until Jed interrupted. "Whoa now! Quit actin' like juveniles."

"I'm not the one acting juvenile," Reba said.

Bo interjected before Pip could form a comeback. "Can't we have a decent meal without all the drama?"

"What drama?" Pip directed a glare at Bo instead of Reba.

"This." Bo made a circle in the air with his forefinger. "I'm not sure what's going on but I think it has something to do with Pip taking an interest in your friend Pat. Am I right?"

"What?" Pip screwed up his face. "I never -"

Reba jumped in before he could finish. "Never what? Take advantage of every friend I introduce you to, and then drop 'em like a hot potato once you get what you want?"

"Hold on now. That's not fair. I never took advantage of no one."

"No? Then why'd Brianna come crying to me after you broke up with her? And Erin? Neither one of 'em will talk to me now, thanks to you."

"You and Brianna?" Will interrupted. "Brianna Johnston? You mean you two…?"

"He didn't tell you?" Reba asked. "See, even he's ashamed that he ruined the best friendship I ever had."

"Can I help it if the ladies find me irresistible?" Pip asked.

Zeb laughed outright.

"It's not funny. I think he purposely tries to make it with every one of my friends so that he can laugh later on when they won't speak to me."

"Seems to me true friends wouldn't hold it against you," Bo said reasonably. "Even if your brother looks like Pip."

The brothers all laughed.

Reba's mouth twitched but she kept it as straight as possible.

"Come on, Spitfire." Zeb put one of his massive arms around her shoulders and squeezed. "Pip can't help being who 'e is any more an you or I."

"Meaning?" Bo asked. "Impulsive? Hot headed? What?"

"Meaning, passionate," Zeb said and looked square at Bo.

Jed and Will whooped. "If that don't beat all," Jed said between sputters of laughter.

"He may have something there," Bo said. "It's the red hair coming out."

"Exactly!" Zeb nodded with satisfaction.

"I think you should cut Pip a bit of slack," Bo continued. "He's only here for a little while, and Patsi seems like a level headed person, so I don't think you really need to worry."

"Not to mention Lester'd skin ya alive if you messed with his sister," Jed put in for good measure.

"I think you're just worried because of Pip's track record," Bo said. "That was in the past and you two need to move forward. Let bygones be by-gones."

117

"Who made you the psychiatrist?" Will asked.

"Didn't you know? Bartending is the next thing to psychiatry. Told you I was good at more than just mixing drinks."

"Bo's one to give advice," Reba said. "Pining away for some mystery woman."

The moment she said it she wished she hadn't. The hurt look in Bo's eyes said he wouldn't soon forget the betrayal.

"What's this, now?" Will asked. "You been holdin' out on us?'

Bo shook his head. "Reba doesn't know what she's talkin' about. Besides, here comes our food."

"You won't get outta it that easy,' b'y," Will said and slapped Bo across the back. "For now I'll let it pass cause I'm some gut-founded."

Lily and another young man brought two large trays laden with steaming dishes. As the food was passed and the banter continued, Reba stole a glance first at Bo and then around the table at the rest of the brood of burly men. She'd hurt the only one who took things to heart. As for the rest of them, they could hold their own and would eventually surface, still breathing.

REBA CRANED her neck to get a better view of her reflection from the backside. She nodded with satisfaction. The new jeans were a splurge on her tight income, but the way her butt looked right now was worth it. Andrea Carravagio approached and Reba swung around to meet her face to face.

"Looking good. Going somewhere special?" Andrea asked.

Reba smiled and took another peek at herself in the full-length mirror. Gemini's salon had several mirrors - a luxury that was sorely lacking back at Jed's. "Just the Urban Cowboy."

"Oh?" Andrea raised a brow.

"Haven't you heard?" Angela said in passing. "Cory Roberts is back in town."

Reba frowned. "That's not why -"

"Really? Not what Jacques said."

Reba flipped her dark red curls behind her shoulders and turned away from her reflection. "So?"

Angela raised her hands in mock surrender. "I'm not judging. Just stating a fact."

"Sometimes men don't like a woman to come on too strong. It makes you look desperate," Andrea advised.

"A strategy that seems to be working quite well for you," her sister Angela threw over her shoulder.

Reba winced. Angela's words were hurtful and catty. Andrea was a truly nice person and it was hard to see the two sisters at odds, even though Reba herself was used to sibling rivalry.

Andrea seemed unfazed by the remark and tucked the last of the clean towels onto a shelf. "I'm just waiting for the right guy."

"Does such a man exist?" Reba asked.

"I want the man God has in store for me. I'm not saying it isn't hard sometimes, but it's teaching me patience."

"She's waiting to get struck by lightning," Angela said with a smirk.

"You probably deserve the perfect guy," Reba said, ignoring Angela's jibe, "but I definitely don't have the patience to wait around for 'im to appear outta thin air."

"So you are planning to attract Cory Roberts' attention." Angela folded her arms across her chest and leaned on the doorframe.

"Maybe…I don't know! I just thought maybe it was time I did something for myself for a change. Lord knows I've been catering to my family for too long, already."

"Tell me about it!" Angela exclaimed. "Jacques's life is hardly his own any more since the precious Viann arrived." She crewed up her face in disgust.

"She's still here?" Reba asked.

"Is she ever," Angela said. "At least she doesn't bother us as much now that she's dating that doctor."

Reba shrugged. She hadn't really noticed whether the other girl was around or not, but then why would she? They had nothing in common and as far as Reba could tell, Viann Marcett was a snob.

"She's not that bad," Andrea defended. "I think she's just had some hard times. Most people act a certain way because of something from their past."

Reba agreed wholeheartedly, which is exactly why she needed to move out of the shadow of her own past. It was time to leave Pip, Bo, Will, Jed, and even Zeb behind and do as she pleased. With or without their consent.

~

"HI, CORY," Reba said as she sat up to the bar. "Have you seen my brother around?"

Cory looked over at Reba and smiled. "Hi, yourself. Which one?" He'd been talking to a young man sitting on the stool right next to her.

"Bo." She smiled back.

Cory leaned over the counter a bit. "It's his evening off."

"Oh, right." Of course, she'd known that already. Bo had taken Will and Pip on a little day trip somewhere, so they wouldn't be around to spoil her plans. Jed, on the other hand, could show up at any time, but she would just have to deal with him if he did anything embarrassing.

"What can I get for you?" Cory asked.

Reba swung her free leg a bit. What would a girl on the prowl choose? Something girlie, no doubt, which didn't sound that appealing next to her usual beer. "Um, you can surprise me," Reba said.

"You two know each other?" the man next to her asked. He was good looking, probably in his early to mid-twenties with styled blonde hair and dark brown eyes shaded by sinfully long lashes.

"This is Reba Malloy. Correct?" Cory asked. She nodded. "Her brother is the new bartender."

"Pleased to meet you Reba. I'm Brett McMillan."

"Hi."

"Brett and I do some DJing together."

"That sounds like fun. Where do you play? Weddings? Graduations?"

"Not that kind of DJing," Brett said with a slight laugh. "What we do is more like composing. We remix a song with a new beat, maybe add a bass line, or speed it up. You know, make it more danceable."

"Oh, I see." She wasn't really a big fan of electronic music, but she didn't say so.

"Cory, here, is the master," Brett continued, gesturing at his friend behind the bar. "I'm just the apprentice."

"Don't sell yourself short," Cory said. "Your mashups are fresh." He set a pink, frothy drink in front of Reba.

She took a tentative sip and tried not to wince at the sweetness. "I'd love to hear you play. Either of you."

"Maybe we can arrange it sometime." Brett winked and lofted his own glass in a salute.

Reba smiled. She'd come to the Urban Cowboy with her sights set on Cory Roberts. Now she had choices - a dilemma she was willing to embrace.

"WHAT IN BLAZES WERE YOU DOIN' last night?"

The toast halted midway to Reba's mouth as she looked up at Jed, standing over her with hands on hips.

"Do you mind? I'm tryin' to get some breakfast in my gut before I have to go to work."

"Flirtin' all over them boys like a two dollar hussy."

Reba rolled her eyes. "Stop being so paternal. Besides, your morals ain't so high and mighty. Look at you and Crystal."

"That's different."

"Why? Cause you're a man? Get with the times, Bro. Women have needs too."

Jed slammed his palm down on the table.

"Sh," Reba warned. "You'll wake Bo and the others."

"If I thought you actually knew who it was you were flirting with last night I'd skin ya alive."

Reba screwed up her forehead. "What do you mean?"

"Brett McMillan."

"Yeah? So?"

"Blazes, woman! He's the scoundrel that broke your friend Patsi's heart."

Reba blinked. "Seriously?"

"Seriously."

This was news. She thought the name had sounded familiar. In fact, come to think of it, Pat had shared something about her ex playing music with Tad's son Cory. But she just hadn't put two and two together.

Reba took a bite of toast, determined not to show weakness in front of one of her brothers. "No need to get your snot in a knot. I was just having a bit of fun. No harm in that," she said while chewing.

"There is if you're too tipsy to know what you're doing."

"Says the resident alcoholic," Reba scoffed.

Jed ran a hand over the dark bristles on his head where his hair used to be - recently shaven so he didn't have to visit a hairdresser. "Remember whose roof you're under."

"How could I forget? You won't let me."

Bo shuffled into the kitchen, still wearing his pyjama trousers but no shirt.

"You're up early," Jed said to Bo.

"Can't sleep with all the ruckus."

"Jed's stickin' 'is nose in where 'e shouldn't - again," Reba said with a huff.

"Cause she was throwin' herself after the menfolk last night at the bar."

"And I missed it?" Bo asked with a grin.

"I wasn't throwing myself at anyone. We just had a few drinks is all. Maybe a little dancing..."

"To top it off, it was with Patsi Tibbett's ex-boyfriend," Jed continued.

"What about Patsi Tibbett's boyfriend?" Pip was standing in the doorway, looking sleepy-eyed.

"None of your business," Reba snapped.

"Oh, I get it. Now that the shoe is on the other foot, you're not so eager to talk," Pip said.

Reba let out a disgusted sigh as she pushed away from the table. "I'll be some glad when you go back to Newfoundland."

"About that…" Pip rubbed the back of his neck. "I been thinkin' about stayin' on for a bit longer after Will leaves. I'm outta work anyway, so I might see if there's any prospects around here."

Jed turned squarely to look at Pip, his hands on his hips. "And when were you gonna let me in on this?"

"Soon. Bo says I can stay with 'im once he gets 'is own place, so it won't be no imposition."

Reba swung to glare at Bo. "I thought you and I were moving in together?"

Bo just shrugged. "I figure it's the least I can do. Jed's been good about having all of us, so I'm just trying to pass it on."

"If you're mad about what I said the other night at the restaurant - about you likin' a mystery woman, I was just fooling," Reba said.

"I'm not mad," Bo said quietly. Reba had her doubts.

"I've been meaning to ask you about that." Will had now joined them.

Reba threw up her hands. "Can't a person have any peace around here?"

"My feelings exactly," Jed said.

"This is crazy. I need to get to work," Reba said and pushed past Will and Pip who were effectively blocking the small entrance into the hall. She stopped and turned. "And don't be surprised if my stuff is gone when you get home tonight."

"Where you going?" Jed asked.

"Not sure. Away from this craziness, that's all." She slammed into the bathroom and leaned against the door for a moment to cool down.

She'd left Newfoundland to get away from her parents and three controlling older sisters. Now her brothers had taken over, and she'd had enough.

~

"YOU SEEMED quiet on the way to work this morning," Andrea observed as she mixed up some hair colour. She and Reba were in the back room of Gemini's salon, a space which wasn't much bigger than a closet.

"Had a bit of a fight before work is all," Reba answered. She was making an inventory of the colours that they needed to order.

Andrea whisked the creamy concoction in a wide mouthed bowl using a paddle shaped brush. "With Jed?"

Reba let out a small snort. "With all of them. It's definitely getting too crowded for my liking."

"But the others will be going home soon, right? Plus, you said Bo made a down payment on an apartment, so... Things should settle down soon."

"Except, now Pip wants to stick around and Bo said he could stay with him. Not sure I can handle it."

"You were so excited he was coming for a visit."

"I forgot what an arse he can be sometimes," Reba said.

"Sometimes it's the people we're closest to that irritate us the most." Andrea laughed. "I should know. Angela drives me crazy, and I certainly don't approve of the things she does most of the time, but I can't imagine my life without her."

"I guess." Reba hesitated and then just blurted out the request that had been on her mind all morning. "I don't suppose you'd have an extra couch I could use for a night or two?"

"That bad?" Andrea's brows had risen. "I don't mind, but I'd have to run it by Angela."

"Run what by Angela?" Angela was standing in the doorway.

"I'll let you tell her about it," Andrea said. "I need to get this hair colour on Mrs. Dupre."

Angela stood to one side as Andrea squeezed past. Then she turned to Reba expectantly.

"I asked if your couch was free," Reba said in a rush. "Been havin' some fights with the brothers. Of course, if you say no, I'll just suck it up. But I could use a breather, that's for sure."

Angela shrugged. "I don't mind. I'd offer you my bed, except I don't spend as many nights at Jacques's anymore." There was a definite twinge of irritation in her tone.

"Viann," Reba stated.

"I should be jealous, but…"

By the sounds of it, Angela was jealous, but Reba chose not to point that out. "Say… What do you know about Cory Roberts?"

Angela surveyed Reba out of the corner of her eye. "Other than the fact that he's back and apparently single? Not much. He and Jacques get along, but I haven't had much to do with him outside the bar."

"Maybe he's still in love with that other girl."

"Renee? Who knows? Sounds like you're interested."

"Maybe." Reba shrugged. "What was she like, anyway?"

Angela shrugged. "I didn't really know her that well. She's related to Carmen, who dates Cory's best friend, Sherman Chan."

"What I meant was, is she pretty?" Reba asked.

"I guess so. She's an actress so she'd have to be."

"Hmph." Reba frowned.

"But you're here and she's not, so that's a point in your favour. If you like him why not give it a shot?"

Reba sighed. "I need to do something before I go bonkers. Might as well go back home if I don't."

"I heard him tell Jacques about a show this weekend that he and his friend are playing."

"Brett McMillan."

"You know him?" Angela looked genuinely surprised.

Reba nodded. She wasn't sure she wanted to meet up with Brett again. Despite her denial, she had been coming on to him the other night - maybe more than she'd intended. But alcohol would do that to a person.

"It's settled, then," Angela said. "You'll come with me to the show, since you're my new roommate, at least for a while."

"Are you sure?" Reba asked.

"Of course. It'll be fun. Besides, I need something to make Jacques jealous and this'll be the perfect excuse."

"Jacques's not coming?"

Angela waved her hand dismissively. "He's working. It'll be perfect."

Reba frowned. The last thing she wanted was to be used as a pawn between Angela and her boyfriend, but the prospect of meeting Cory Roberts outside of his normal work environment was more enticing.

REBA ARRIVED with Angela at the private club where Brett and Cory were DJing. The atmosphere was casual chic with low couches and groupings of chairs instead of the bar room style that Reba was used to at the Urban Cowboy. General lighting was almost non-existent and Reba was glad for the shimmering fabric of Angela's top which enabled her to see where she was going as she followed the other girl into the depths of the club.

"We'll get as close as possible to the stage," Angela yelled back at Reba. "Our ears might get blown off, but we're here to be seen!"

Reba just nodded and followed as closely as possible through the crowd. She didn't really understand the music. Scratching and dub-step weren't really her forte. She was more of a country music girl at heart.

Angela waved at Cory when she got close enough for him to notice her. He smiled and nodded but was obviously otherwise occupied. Both he and Brett wore large padded headphones and were grooving to the beat. Reba wished she had a set of those headphones. It was just so loud!

Several songs later, the music stopped and Cory told the crowd they were taking a short break. Reba was secretly relieved. The canned dance music was a pleasant reprieve.

Cory leaned in close to Brett, saying something into his ear. Brett had a large pair of earphones on his head, one padded cylinder propped up so that he could hear what Cory was saying. They both looked her way, and then Cory slapped Brett on the back and jumped down from the platform and headed their way.

"Hey, thanks for coming. Brett'll be glad to see you." Cory smiled at Reba.

It wasn't Brett who she wanted to please, but she smiled and nodded. Before she could think of something witty to say, Cory was excusing himself to go talk to someone else.

Who was she kidding? A man like Cory Roberts could have his pick of women. He was definitely out of her league.

Angela elbowed Reba in the side. Her gaze followed Angela's to several meters away where a familiar figure stood talking to Cory. Viann.

Viann was dressed to the nines in a chic short dress and high boots, her golden hair bouncing around her shoulders and back. She was hanging on the arm of a sophisticated man in his mid to late thirties. He had a polished look about him with well coiffed hair and glasses that gave him a distinguished air. Despite the fact that she was obviously with another man, the fact that she knew Cory brought on a sudden twinge of jealousy deep inside Reba's gut.

"It figures she'd be here to spoil the evening," Angela said.

Reba rubbed her temple. She felt a headache coming on. "I'm not sure how much more I can take. I'm getting a headache."

"Absolutely not!" Angela exclaimed. "You haven't even made your move on Cory and I didn't help you get all dolled up to leave before you see some action!"

Reba looked down at her outfit, a typical 'clubbing' ensemble that was low in the front and much too short. "Maybe I just have to face facts. He's not into me."

"Nonsense. You need more alcohol to help you get loosened up."

"I doubt that," Reba mumbled but before she could protest further, Angela was already gone.

"Thanks for coming." Great. It was Brett looking all handsome and expectant.

"Taking a break?" Reba asked. Of course he was, but it was the only small talk she could think of.

"Wanna get some fresh air?"

Reba tossed the wisdom of such a suggestion around for a moment and then nodded. Her headache won out.

They walked to the exit and stepped outside into the parking lot. It was chilly and Reba had left her coat inside.

"Here, you must be freezing." Brett removed his jacket and placed it around Reba's shoulders.

She snuggled into the warmth from his body heat, all the while feeling miserable.

"So?" Brett asked. He smiled crookedly, his handsome face coming a bit closer as he peered into her eyes. "What do you think?"

"Um… you're nice and all -"

Brett laughed. "I meant the music."

"Oh." She returned his amused smile. "The truth?"

"Please. Although I get the feeling I'm not necessarily going to like it."

"I'm sure you're good at what you do, but I don't think I'm really into the electronic thing. I'm more of a country music fan."

"Fair enough."

Reba cleared her throat. "And while we're being honest I think there's something else you need to know."

Brett shoved his hands into his pockets. "Okay…"

"I like you. I really do."

"But?"

"I know about your past relationship with Pat Tibbett, and, well, she and I have become good friends. I won't jeopardize that."

He nodded slowly. "Good to know." He took a deep breath and looked up at the nearest street light. "How is she?"

Reba blinked. The tone of his voice was definitely one of regret; that of a man who wasn't near being over the relationship.

"Okay, I think. I guess you'll get to see for yourself soon enough at your sister's wedding."

Brett let out a little chuckle. "I was hoping to ask you as my date. I thought it would make her suitably jealous." His eyes, which surveyed

Reba, were crinkled in amusement. "Guess that's out of the question now."

"I'd say so." Reba slung the jacket off her shoulders and handed it back to Brett. "We better get back inside."

As if on cue, Cory swung through the exit, scanning the outdoors until his gaze lit on the two of them standing on the sidewalk. "Let's go, man. Save the intimacy for later. Next set starts now."

Reba frowned, protest on the tip of her tongue, when a shuffling sound met their ears. A well-dressed man came into view, half dragging a woman whose high heels were making it difficult for her to keep up.

"But why are we leaving now?" The French accent was unmistakable.

The man stopped in front of an expensive car and released Viann's arm with an extra shove that sent her stumbling into the side of the car. "I wanted you to meet my friends, not argue with them."

"You just want a show piece." Viann stuck out her chin.

"Don't be ridiculous. I just didn't expect you to share your opinions so... forcefully. It was totally embarrassing and uncalled for."

"Abortion is murder."

He pointed his finger in her face. "My colleagues are well respected physicians."

"It makes no difference to me. It is still murder." She swung her hair back and stood a little straighter. "I am Catholic."

The man raised his hand as if to strike, but then lowered it slowly. "Come on, Princess. Can't you just be beautiful? That's all I ask."

"A puppet. That's what you want."

His eyes narrowed. "You should be so lucky. There are plenty of women in this city willing to dance to my tune."

Viann hung her head. "I am sorry. Can we go back inside, now? I won't talk to anyone else. I promise."

The man took her quivering chin in his hands and kissed her lightly on the mouth. "Okay. Don't let it happen again." He put his hand on her elbow and they turned to walk back the way they came. Cory stepped forward and blocked their path.

"I don't have any money," the man said.

Cory laughed humourlessly. "Just because I'm black doesn't mean I'm going to rob you."

"Cory!" Viann let out in a squeak.

The man squinted at Cory in the dark. "Oh. It's you."

"You deserve better than this creep, Viann," Cory said.

"It's nothing. Just leave us alone," Viann said, her voice near a sob.

Reba ignored the other girl's plea. "Everyone has the right to their opinions, Viann. Even you."

"Jacques isn't going to like it when I tell him about this," Cory said.

The doctor threw up his hands. "I've had enough. I hope you enjoy finding your own way home." He stalked off, leaving Viann to cry in earnest.

"Good riddance," Reba called after him.

"Now look what you've done!" Viann cried.

"You don't need that creep," Cory said.

"Thanks to you I am alone again! Always alone!" Viann shook Cory's hand off her arm and stalked a few feet away.

"Viann -"

She held up a hand. "Stay away from me. You just ruined my life!" She punched some numbers into her cell phone.

"Do you need a ride?" Reba asked, approaching slowly.

"I need nothing from you."

Viann the snob was back. Reba shrugged and turned away.

"You go and start the next set," Cory said to Brett. "I'll be in as soon as I know she's safely on her way back to Jacques's."

"I can wait with her," Reba said. "I'm going home myself anyway. We can share the cab."

Viann glared in Reba's direction but didn't deny her the ride.

"You're sure?" Cory asked.

Reba nodded.

Cory embraced Viann's ramrod straight body and gave her a squeeze. "You deserve better. It's gonna be alright." He was obviously more than a little concerned over Viann's welfare.

Reba watched Cory and Brett go back inside the club, a wave of music reaching out to her when the door opened, but just as quickly thudding into silence when the door closed behind them. Kind of like her own prospects.

So much for making an impression. The one she had made was all wrong and now all she had to show for it was the pleasure of a forty-minute cab ride with a disdainful rival.

The story of her life.

EPISODE 4

NEIGHBOURHOOD UPSTART

IP

SPRINGTIME IN CALGARY. The chinook winds had blown in and taken with them the last vestiges of winter. Pip Malloy stood gazing out at the Rocky Mountains in the distance - a craggy strip of purple and white that separated the sky from the flat lands. From this vantage point on the viewing deck of the Calgary Tower, he could see for miles. Literally. It was beautiful - different from the crash of waves against rocks of his native Newfoundland, but the expanse of sky and sheer distance between himself and the mountains, standing like sentinels to some forbidden kingdom, filled him with a sense of awe.

He and his closest brother, Will, had come west for a visit just two weeks ago. They had four siblings who lived in Alberta. Jed, the eldest male, had been here the longest and worked in construction. Next was Zeb, who lived a seven hour drive north in the city of Fort McMurray where he worked in the oil patch. The most recent to relocate were his brother Bo and sister Reba. Bo worked at a downtown bar and seemed to genuinely enjoy the science behind bartending. Reba was apprenticing at a beauty salon.

That left three sisters back in Newfoundland. It was doubtful that any of them would be moving since they all had families. But him? That was another matter...

He had announced the other night that he was planning to stick around for a bit longer and look for work. He was currently unemployed, so it seemed like an ideal time to check out the prospects. Of course, there were some members of the family who weren't so keen on him staying. Jed, for one, had cautioned him that their Ma would not stand for any more of her children moving so far away - especially her baby.

Pip remembered her words before he'd even left home: "Don't go gettin' any ideas, b'y! Enough of me offspring 'ave flown the coop." Of course, he had assured her that it was only a visit. Oops.

And then there was Reba. For some reason she seemed miffed with him. It was nothing new. They had always fought. She still harboured resentment toward him for dating a couple of her friends. It's not like he'd forced them or anything. He just liked to have fun and each one of them had approached him first. But Reba didn't see it that way. In her mind it was some kind of weird competition - as if being her friend meant she had exclusive rights to a person.

Pip pushed off the railing and walked back along the circular indoor deck in search of his brothers, Bo and Will. The viewing deck gave a three hundred and sixty-five degree view of the city and surrounding area. Part of the platform spun at a very slow speed, so theoretically, you could stand in one spot and see everything there was to see.

"So? What do you think?" Bo asked.

"Nice view of the mountains," Will said.

"I can't believe you've never been here before," Pip directed at Bo.

"Jed's not much for sightseeing," Bo said. "I guess I was waiting for someone to go with me."

"I wonder if there's any work at Banff or one of the other parks around here?" Will shoved his hands into his jeans pockets and gazed out over the scene before them.

"Ma'd kill you," Pip said.

"Says the pot to the kettle," Will retorted. "Doesn't seem like you're too worried."

"I thought you said they were hiring you back on at the camp grounds back home," Bo said, always the practical one. "You might lose it if you apply for something else."

Will shrugged. "I was just kidding anyway."

"Well, we should get going. By the time we get back to Jed's he should be home and ready to take you to the airport." Bo nodded at Will. "Sorry I couldn't do it, but I have to get to work."

"No problem." Will gave Pip a sidelong glance. "You sure you're not gonna jump on the plane with me tonight? There's still time to change your mind."

"Nope. I feel adventure calling my name," Pip said. They stepped into the elevator along with several other people and the doors swished shut.

Will grinned. "Oh, really? And what does it call you? Steven or Pip-squeak?"

Pip punched Will in the arm, not with much force since the confines of the elevator prevented any momentum. "It calls me Master, cause I'm takin' charge."

Will shook his head with a snort. "As if. You can't even take charge of your own laundry."

"Ma still doin' your laundry?" Bo asked as the doors opened again and the folks in front of them filed out.

"I don't ask 'er to, she just does it," Pip said with a shrug. "You know how Ma is about a couple of socks lyin' on the floor."

"If you move in with me, I won't be doin' your laundry," Bo said.

"I wouldn't expect you to," Pip replied.

"If 'e moves in with you, that'll be the least of your worries," Will said to Bo.

"Meaning what, exactly?" Pip asked.

Will shook his head. "Babies…"

Bo grinned and finished the sentence in unison with Will. "They always want their way."

~

"WELL, THAT'S THAT," Jed said. "It was good to see Will again. I just hope Ma ain't too upset when only one son gets off the plane." He and Pip had just dropped Will off at the airport and were on their way home.

Pip glanced across the interior of the truck to look at his older brother's profile. Jed held the steering wheel loosely in his left hand as he used his right to switch on the radio. They were about ten years apart in age and in many ways, Pip viewed Jed as a second father. He respected Jed's opinions, but at the same time he knew he had to do things his own way. He wasn't the baby everyone treated him as. "She'll be fine."

"I reckon we'll find out one way or t'other. Not sure she'll take it as easy as you seem to think."

Pip crossed his arms and looked out his own window. "It's not fair that you can leave home, but I can't. It's not my fault I'm the youngest."

"Course it's not your fault, but it's the facts." Jed looked over at Pip and grinned. "Just like bein' the oldest means everyone expects you'll bail 'em out when the time comes."

"I don't need bailing out."

"Not now, maybe, but the time'll come."

"I'll be outta your way soon enough once Bo moves into 'is new place."

"About that…" Jed cleared his throat. "Now that Reba's got 'er nose outta joint and is stayin' with them Gemini ladies, you could sleep in the spare room if you want. Bo won't have a bed for you to sleep on, or even a couch for that matter, till 'e gets settled."

"I'll think about it. If I find a job, I'll move, though," Pip said. "I can find a second hand bed."

"You seem awfully sure you're gonna get work. Things are slowin' down a bit these days. What kind of experience you got?"

Pip shrugged. "Construction. General labourer." He grinned. "Tim Horton's."

"Well, I guess there's always that." Jed was silent for a moment and then spoke up again. He kept his eyes fixed on the road ahead. "You know, I shouldn't even be tellin' you this, seeing as Ma is gonna be some upset and all."

"But...?" Pip prompted.

"An opening just came up at Titan, where I work." Jed glanced at Pip. "General labourer."

Pip raised his brows. "What's the pay like?"

Jed blew out a snort. "As if that should be your first question! It's a job, numbskull! A few dollars more than minimum wage. Plus, you could catch a ride with me if you don't move in with Bo. Although, I'm not sure I should even be tellin' you about it."

"Where do I apply?" Pip asked.

"I wrote it all down before I left work. I can take your application in tomorrow and you can call in the morning. Although, I'm not sure why I should be encouragin' you," he repeated.

Pip smiled inwardly. It was just like Jed to pretend not to want him to stay, even if he did. "Wanna go to the Urban Cowboy to celebrate?"

"You haven't got the job yet," Jed warned with a scowl.

"I'm not worried. Once they meet me in person, my charm will win 'em over."

"You are some full of yourself, you know that?"

"I learned from the best." Pip grinned. "You."

THE ATMOSPHERE at the Urban Cowboy was electric. Glowing neon, wood paneling, and a shiny granite bar along one wall with a counter-to-ceiling mirror behind it was the backdrop for the mingled cacophony of canned country music and live laughter, punctuated occasionally by the crack of pool balls. Pip could see why the place was so popular. It was country comfort straight out of a movie.

Bo waved in their direction as Pip and Jed wound their way through the tables to the bar. "Will get off okay?" Bo asked when they arrived.

Jed plunked himself onto a stool. "Yup. I don't envy 'im. That's a long flight with a couple of stop overs. Add the time change and 'e won't get home 'til noon tomorrow."

Bo filled two steins with draft and set the frothy golden liquid in front of his siblings. "Anyone contact Ma to let her know Pip's not coming?"

"Not my job." Jed took a slurp of his beer.

"It's three and a half hours later back home. Ma'll be in bed already," Pip said as he took a drink of his own beer.

"If that ain't an excuse." Jed shook his head. "Ya coulda called earlier, or even a couple days ago, for that matter."

Pip shrugged. "Like you said, not your problem."

Cory Roberts, owner of the establishment, slid behind the bar with a large poster in hand. He nodded at Jed and Pip, his dreadlocks bouncing. "Good to see you. How's it going?" He didn't wait for an answer but turned to Bo. "When you get a minute do you think you could find a spot for this behind the bar?" He held up the poster.

"Sure. What is it?" Bo asked.

"Another bull riding competition. The last one went over so well, I wanted to try it again."

"Lester'll have to defend his title," Jed said.

"That's the idea," Cory replied.

"If his girlfriend doesn't put a stop to it first." Jed grinned.

"Your friend Lester?" Pip asked. "Pat's brother?"

"One and the same. He's the real deal when it comes to cowboys."

Pip took another swig of his beer. "What kind of prize money we talkin' about? Maybe I'll enter."

Jed blew out a snort. "Lard tunderin'! If that don't sound like the cocky bugger you are!"

"Why? It can't be that hard. All you gotta do is hang on for dear life, by the look of it."

"I'll leave that up to you to figure out." Cory smiled, his teeth white against his dark skin. "Just make sure you sign the waiver beforehand for insurance purposes." He turned and walked further down the length of the bar to talk to the manager, Jacques.

"Will will be disappointed he missed it," Bo said. "That sort of thing is right up his alley."

"Unless he decides to move west, too," Pip said.

"Sh!" Jed put a finger to his lips. "Don't tempt the fates. Ma'll be in 'er grave next if youse don't stop."

"Here comes Reba." Bo nodded toward the entrance. "Either of you talk to her since she stormed out the other day?"

"For a couple minutes." Jed shook his head. "She came for some of 'er stuff, but wasn't too talkative."

"I'm surprised at how angry she seems - with all of us," Bo said.

"With you, you mean," Pip said. "She's always been angry with me. Even as kids."

Jed finished off his beer. "She'll come around. She's a lot of pride, that one."

They watched as their sister approached and purposely walked right past them on her way to see Cory Roberts. Reba was an attractive woman, but tonight she must have decided to display her assets a little more forwardly than was usual, in skin tight black leggings and a low cut top. She made eye contact once on her way by, but then swept her gaze away with a flip of her red mane.

Pip watched for a few seconds as his sister flirted with Cory and Jacques - a risky business since her boss at the salon was currently dating the French bartender. He looked away when Jed swore under his breath. "Wanna play some pool?"

"That sounds like a mighty good idea," Jed said with a nod. "Can't stand to watch 'er throwing 'erself at every breathing male like that. But she's not gonna listen to me."

Pip agreed but didn't say anything. The hypocrisy of his sister's actions wasn't lost on him, but he was no judge and jury. If everyone would just keep their noses out of each other's business, things would be just fine.

~

"How's the first day so far?" Lester Tibbett smiled and took a bite of his sandwich. It was Pip's first day on the job at Titan Construction and they had gathered in the lunch room for their break. So far, he hadn't really done much.

Pip shrugged. "Can't complain. I've been the gopher mostly, so it's hard to say."

Jed laughed. "Usually the newbies get the rotten jobs. Just wait. Your time's comin'."

The construction company was still working on a new high-rise building in downtown Calgary. The structure itself was complete, but there was still a lot of finishing and interior work to be done.

"Patsi is arriving today on the bus," Lester said. "I couldn't take the time off, but Sherri is picking her up and dropping her off at the apartment."

"For good this time?" Jed asked.

Lester nodded. "So she says. Carmen and Tamara promised her a job at The Brew so... We'll see how it goes."

"I guess she just needed a break," Jed said. "From you as much as anything." He laughed at his own joke.

"I don't deny it. It's hard being the older brother. It's my job to protect her, but I've come to see that it's not always possible."

"Maybe you should let 'er alone to make 'er own mistakes," Pip said. "We don't always need protection."

Jed scowled in Pip's direction. "No one's talkin' about you."

Pip just shrugged.

Jed turned his attention back to Lester. "When you gonna put a ring on that gal's finger?"

Lester blinked and focused on Jed. "Come again?"

"Sherri, dumbnut!" Jed said with a laugh. "When you gonna make an honest woman of 'er?"

"None of your business. Besides, we've been dating less than six months."

"That all?" Jed shook his head. "Seems like an eternity."

"That coming from the sworn bachelor," Lester said with a grin.

"My brother can be quite the hypocrite," Pip offered.

"Runs in the family," Jed quipped back.

Lester lightened the mood with a chuckle. "Play nice, kids."

PIP AND JED arrived home after work just moments behind Lester. The cowboy was locked in a full embrace with his sister, Pat - or Patsi, as Lester and Jed called her.

"I'm next," Jed said, spreading his arms wide for a hug.

Patsi giggled and complied. "It hasn't been that long, but it seems like ages. Once I decided to move back, it seemed like the time went so slow!"

Jed released her and there was an awkward moment when she stepped back and surveyed Pip, standing there waiting. She cleared her throat. "Nice to see you again, Pip. I thought you'd have headed home by now."

Pip shrugged. "I got a job at Titan, so I thought I'd stick around for a while till I get sick of it."

Jed rolled his eyes. "That's arse forward if I ever seen it. Talkin' of quitting after the first day."

"I never said anything about quitting. Just don't want to get tied down. Gotta keep my options open."

"Anyway, nice to see you. I want to get upstairs and change," Patsi said. "I'm meeting Reba later at the Urban Cowboy. Maybe we'll see you there."

Lester and Patsi disappeared into the elevator while Jed went to check the mailboxes. Pat was nice looking and she seemed fun, but Pip wasn't sure she was worth the flack he'd get from Jed, nor the risk of trouble with the protective older brother. On the other hand, dating Pat might be just the ticket to set Reba in her place.

He was tired of his sister's immature attitude when it came to his love life.

~

PIP SCANNED the Urban Cowboy for any sign of Pat and Reba and zeroed in on them at a table not too far from the bar. He waved at Bo on his way by and headed straight for the two women.

"Hi, Pip," Patsi greeted with a ready smile. "Join us."

Pip sent Reba a triumphant signal with his eyes and pulled out a vacant chair.

"Really? I see enough of this joker." Reba let out a small laugh which didn't match her sour expression.

"Oh?" Pip opened his eyes wide in innocence. "You've hardly spoken to me all week."

Patsi glanced furtively from one to the other. "Am I missing something?"

"Don't ask," Reba said.

Pip angled his body away from Reba and focused his attention on Patsi. "So, how was your long bus trip?"

Patsi opened her mouth to answer but then suddenly ducked her head. "It's Brett."

Pip turned around to get a look at the object of Patsi's sudden discomfort. If he wasn't mistaken, it was Brett McMillan, Patsi's former boyfriend and the cause of much of the tension between Reba and the rest of the family of late. He was leaning on the bar with one elbow, talking to Cory Roberts.

"I should have known!" Patsi let out a frustrated sigh. "He and Cory used to play gigs together all the time. He was bound to come here and hang out now that Cory is back." She cast apologetic eyes at Pip. "Brett and I were a thing once, and I just didn't want to have to run into him on my first day back, even though I'll have to meet him at his sister's wedding, soon."

"We can pretend to be a couple if you want," Pip offered. "I don't mind."

"I'll just bet you don't," Reba said under her breath.

"Really? You wouldn't mind?" Patsi looked hopeful.

Pip reached across the table and took Patsi's hand in his. "Anything for a friend." He didn't miss Reba's rolled eyes at the gesture. He also noticed that she was squirming in her seat.

By this time Brett had reached their table. "Hello Pat, Reba. I see you two know one another." He took in Pip and Patsi's clasped hands. "And I see you have another friend here as well."

"My brother, Pip," Reba said. "I think you met already."

"Oh, right." Brett's smile didn't reach his eyes.

Patsi seemed to have missed the tension that Pip's possessiveness was causing. Instead, she turned her gaze to Reba. "You and Brett know each other?"

"Um, ya," Reba said brightly. "Met here a couple of times. Bound to happen, seeing as it's Jed's favourite hangout and Bo works here…"

Brett's eyes narrowed ever so slightly and he placed a hand on Reba's shoulder. "You make us sound buddy-buddy, Reba. I'd say we're past that stage, wouldn't you?"

Patsi's eyes widened, betrayal evident in their depths. "Is that so?" She blinked rapidly and tugged her hand out from under Pip's grip. "Of course, that's totally fine with me." She stood abruptly. "Um, excuse me for a minute. I need to go to the washroom." She practically sprinted toward the ladies' room sign.

Reba stood also and directed her index finger toward Pip. "This is your fault. Again. Don't expect me to ever talk to you from now on."

Both Pip and Brett followed Reba's retreating figure with their eyes as she traced Patsi's trail.

Brett slowly turned around and fixed an icy stare on Pip. "If you hurt her, I'll kill you."

Pip blinked, but then sat up straighter. "Same goes if you hurt my sister."

"I'm not interested in your sister. I intend to get Pat back, so be ready." Brett laughed, not a speck of humour in the sound. "But if your sister comes in handy while doing it, I can't guarantee the outcome." He pushed away from the table and strode away.

This was going way beyond teaching Reba a lesson. Pip didn't want to see either of them hurt, but more than that he needed to preserve his own skin.

~

"HOLD THE ELEVATOR!"

Pip put a hand on the doors until Patsi scooted inside.

"Um, sorry about ditching you last night like that." She kept her gaze focused on the floor of the small space.

"It's alright. You were upset," Pip offered. "It's not easy running into an old flame."

Patsi glanced sideways at him. "Speaking from experience?"

Pip just shrugged. "I guess."

"I wouldn't know. I've only had one serious relationship." She stared straight ahead.

"And in fairness to Reba, she didn't know you and Brett were a thing when she… well, when they… well, anyway. You get the picture." He looked up at the ceiling with a sigh. "Although, I don't know why I'm defending her."

"Cause she's your sister. I get it," Patsi said. The doors swished open on Patsi's floor. She hesitated, not leaving the elevator. "Um, is there somewhere we could talk some more? I feel as if there are a few things I need to explain."

"Sure. Jed and Bo took a load to Bo's new apartment." They were silent as the doors swished shut again.

"Bo's moving?" Patsi spoke up.

Pip nodded. "I was going to move in with 'im but then it made more sense to stay with Jed since we work at the same place now." He sighed. "Another reason for Reba to be mad at me."

Patsi frowned. "What do you mean?"

They'd reached Jed's floor and stepped out of the elevator. "Reba has a lot of resentment toward me for some reason. Probably cause I was a cuter baby." He grinned. "She'd planned to move in with Bo but then got rotted when she thought I was taking 'er place. It was only supposed to be temporary and now she's free to do it if she wants, but she's mad at Bo, now, too, and stubborn as all get out." He shrugged as he unlocked the apartment door. "She's got issues."

Patsi followed Pip inside. "I probably overreacted last night. Like you said, how was she to know who Brett was? And besides, he and I haven't been together for months, so technically there's no reason for her not to see him."

Pip led Patsi into the living room and flopped onto the couch. "Excuse the mess." He gestured to some clothing strewn about the floor. "I'm supposed to be moving my stuff into the spare room while they get Bo set up. Not that I have much. I just came with one suitcase."

"So, do you think she'll accept my apology?" Patsi asked. She propped her feet up on the coffee table.

"Maybe. Reba's got a stubborn streak so it depends on 'er mood."

"What happened to make her so angry with you?"

"I started dating one of her best friends back in Newfoundland." Pip stopped and smiled. "Brianna. Well, actually, I dated two of her friends - Brianna and Erin." He cleared his head with a shake. "Anyway, when Brianna and I broke it off, she wouldn't talk to Reba anymore. I told her a real friend wouldn't do that, but she wouldn't listen. She blames me for losing 'er friend."

"I know the feeling. I met Brett through his sister Megan. She was my only friend in Calgary. It would have been easier to never see Megan again, but that's not what real friends do."

"Exactly what I said to Reba."

Patsi sighed. "And now I have to go to Megan's wedding next weekend and see Brett all over again. At least I got the first meeting over with. It'll be easier next time, right?" She looked hopefully at Pip.

"I suppose it depends on how deep the cut is." He surveyed her delicate features. She looked innocent and naive, despite her past with Brett McMillan.

She looked ceiling-ward. "Deep, although I know I have to just get over it." She looked directly at Pip. "He was ashamed of me. Of who I am. In the end, he caved in to what his parents wanted. They were going to cut him off financially."

"That's terrible." Pip sat up a little straighter.

Patsi shrugged. "Megan says he's made some changes for the better. He's not letting his parents push him around as much and he went back to college this semester. He plans to go into law like his parents." She gave a slight smile. "Let's hope he doesn't follow in their footsteps too closely."

"Meaning?" Pip asked.

"They're involved in that Nudara Oil scandal. You didn't hear about it?" When Pip shook his head she continued. "Some kind of cover up with a politician or something. I don't really understand it all, but they're up on some kind of charges. Not that I wish bad luck on anyone, but it serves them right for being such hypocrites."

"Some people's kids," Pip said.

"I know it's a lot to ask, but I was wondering how serious you were last night when you said you'd help me out?" She surveyed him expectantly.

He blinked, taken aback by the turn in the conversation. "Um, I meant it. What do you need?"

"I would really appreciate your support at the wedding. Since Brett thinks we're dating anyway, it wouldn't be too big a stretch for me to bring you along."

She turned soulful eyes on him and that was the end of it. "Of course. I'd be honoured." In typical Newfie fashion he pronounced the silent 'h' in honoured.

Now what was he getting himself into? He tossed around the idea of telling her what Brett had said to him last night, but decided to keep that information for another day. He might need it.

"PATSI TELLS me you're going to her friend Megan's wedding with her this weekend." Lester Tibbett's words were casual, but there was a definite edge of warning in his cadence.

They were working side by side on the job site, installing the trim around some windows in one of the offices.

"That's right." Pip kept his gaze away from Lester's penetrating stare.

"Should I be worried?"

"I doubt it. Jed been spreadin' rumours about me?" Pip tried for a chuckle.

"No. I'm just over protective, as Patsi would say. But I'm all she's got, so if you want to date her, you'll have to put up with it."

Pip took a deep breath. He couldn't tell Lester that the arrangement wasn't exactly 'dating'. "Not to worry. I won't lead 'er astray if that's what's worryin' you."

"That's exactly what's worrying me. She's just come around in her faith and I don't need a hot blooded young man like you messing her up."

Pip forgot his determination not to make eye contact and faced the other man with a frown. "What does that mean, 'Come around in her faith'?"

"My sister is a Christian. Didn't she tell you?" When Pip didn't answer, Lester continued. "So am I, so watch your step."

Pip was still frowning. "But… you hang out with Jed. You go to the bar…"

Lester stopped what he was doing and turned to Pip. "Be careful not to judge people. Only the Lord knows what's inside here." He pointed to his chest. "Have you ever seen me drunk?"

Pip shrugged. "No. But then I haven't known you that long."

"Point taken. I've been feeling some conviction about that, but that's not my point. The point is, Patsi's faith is weak right now, and she's been hurt - bad. I don't want it happening again."

"Okay. I'll keep that in mind."

Lester smiled. "And just because I'm a believer doesn't mean I won't enjoy whipping you good if you don't take my advice."

~

FOR A 'SMALL' wedding, it was fancy enough as far as Pip could tell. The hotel conference room was decked out in lace and other typical wedding finery; mini-lights glowed around the perimeter and the soothing strains of a three piece string ensemble did not inhibit conversation. Not like any wedding he'd been to before. Back home raucous laughter and uninhibited dancing were encouraged by Celtic fiddle music - that and the free flow of alcohol. Lots of it.

Pip took a sip from the long necked bottle of fancy craft beer that he'd opted for and tried not to make a face. He wasn't much for fancy cocktails and since the only other alternative was wine or craft beer, he'd stuck with the latter. The positive side of it was he probably wouldn't end up with a hangover.

His gaze rested on the bride and groom. She was pretty and petite with an unmistakable baby bump that no amount of lace could hide. He was olive skinned and of Latino descent, judging from the accent. Her parents were nearby, coiffed and pressed into plastic perfection. Then there was Brett McMillan, whom Pip had so far managed to avoid, and next to him was Malibu Barbie personified. Nobody had a tan like that at this time of year unless it was sprayed on, not to mention the bleached blonde hair. Not that he minded the view…

"Thanks for coming. I know it's kind of boring when you don't know anybody…"

Pip blinked and turned his attention back to Patsi, sitting next to him at the round table. "No problem. It's interesting to see how the other half lives."

"Now that people think we're dating, maybe you'd like to come to The Brew's grand opening, too." Patsi smiled and then looked down at her hands. "I mean, if you want to. No pressure."

Pip swallowed. "Um, yeah. What do you mean grand opening? They're already open."

"They've been doing a major renovation," Patsi explained. "Tamara and Carmen - my bosses - bought the space next door so they could expand. It's going to be really cool, with an art gallery, a small place for musicians to play and have book readings." Patsi laughed. "Not that I'm into that stuff much, but it looks really nice. Carmen's boyfriend Sherman Chan drew up the plans."

"The same Sherman Chan who's the architect of the building Titan is working on?"

"Yes!" Patsi brightened. "And not only that, but he's Sherri's brother. You know Sherri? My brother Lester's girlfriend?"

"All in the family, it seems. And people call us hicks." Pip took another swig of his beer. He was getting to the bottom of the bottle and this time he couldn't help the sour face.

"You're funny." She perked up and waved at someone behind him. "I think Megan wants me for something. Probably more pictures. I'll be right back."

Pip felt for Patsi. She didn't fit in with this crowd either, but as Megan's one and only bridesmaid, she had duties to perform and was standing up to the scrutiny like a trooper.

He picked up the bottle and swirled the last bit of foam around in the bottom. Another beer didn't appeal to him at the moment. Maybe a glass of water would go down better.

"I'm surprised you came. I thought we had an understanding."

Pip glanced up at Brett standing next to his table. "Only thing I understand is that Pat's not into you anymore. So go blow off steam somewhere else."

"This is my sister's wedding. You have no right to be here."

"I do if I got invited." Pip gestured to a chair. "If you got something to say to me, sit down. If not, take a hike."

Brett hesitated before sitting down. He clasped his hands on the table in front of him. "Look. I want to be honest with you, okay?"

"Okay..." Pip picked up the empty bottle and then set it down again. He was wishing for that next beer after all.

"I get the feeling you're not really that serious about her."

"What makes you say that?"

"I asked around."

Pip frowned. "Who'd you ask? I'm new around here."

"You forget that Cory Roberts and I are pretty tight. Plus, I do know your sister, Reba."

"Ah…" Pip nodded. Of course Reba would stick her nose into things.

"I won't stand by and watch Pat become just another notch in your belt." Brett's jaw had a determined set to it.

"It's not like that -"

"I mean it." Brett looked him in the eye.

Pip purposely relaxed his shoulders and lounged against the back of the chair. "You're one to talk. She told me about you. How you broke her heart."

"It wasn't exactly that way. She broke my heart, if you must know the truth. I love her."

"She said you wouldn't stand up to your parents. Were ashamed of 'er. That don't sound like love to me."

"It was complicated and I was… dumb. I never should have let her go."

"Seems to me she did what she wanted to do," Pip said.

"With you?" Brett asked.

Pip shrugged, trying hard to remain nonchalant under Brett's scrutiny. "Sure. Why not?"

"Because you'll never love her the way I do," Brett said.

"That's something you need to take up with 'er, isn't it?'

"I intend to." Brett stood up. "And by the way, I've noticed the way you can't take your eyes off my cousin Ophelia. For the record, she'd never go out with a scumbag like you."

PIP WAITED in line at the bar. He could use another drink after that little meeting with Brett. There was only one bartender and no waitress, so folks had to wait in line to get their drinks. This time he was up for something a little stronger than beer.

He wasn't quite sure what to make of Patsi Tibbett. She'd hinted at wanting to date him for real, with her suggestion that he come to the grand opening of the coffee shop where she worked. He liked her well enough and usually wasn't one to pass up on such an offer. Then again, things could get way more complicated with Patsi than he was ready for. She had baggage, there was no doubt, not to mention Lester's warning. He also suspected that she wasn't over Brett by a long shot, and according to him, he still loved her. So why all the melodrama? Why not just say it like it is? Something he was beginning to appreciate more and more about back home.

He stepped up to place his order - a double shot of vodka with a little water. He noticed another fancy concoction languishing on the counter beside the bartender. "Thought you weren't allowed to drink on the job." He nodded to the untouched drink. "My brother's a barkeep. That's how I know."

"It's not mine," the bartender said. "I'm keeping it safe for someone while she uses the ladies' room." He gave a small laugh of disgust. "Apparently she doesn't even trust people at a family wedding. But here she comes." He set the drink up within reach beside Pip's vodka.

Pip glanced at the woman in question, approaching from the corridor that led to the washrooms. "That's cousin Ophelia for you. These California types," he added in a staged whisper. "I was going over to talk to her anyway. I'll take it with me." He scooped both drinks before the bartender could protest and headed off to intercept the lovely Ophelia.

"Here you go, m'lady." He grinned disarmingly. "Barkeep kept it safe and sound." He lofted the frothy pink drink but didn't hand it over just yet.

Ophelia blinked, her long false lashes sweeping her cheeks like butterfly wings. "I beg your pardon?"

"Bartender saw you coming and asked me to deliver your drink. Where you sitting?"

Her gaze flickered instinctively to a nearby table, although she kept her mouth shut.

Pip headed straight for the table without waiting for confirmation and set both drinks down. "Ophelia, right? Brett and Megan's cousin?"

"Um, yes. That's correct. And you are?"

"Name's Steve Malloy, but my friend's call me Pip." He extended a hand.

Ophelia ignored the proffered hand. "Right. You came with Megan's friend." Her tone held a touch of superiority.

"That's right. So?" He gestured for her to sit down.

"I never said you could join me," Ophelia pointed out. "Your girl-friend might get jealous."

"Don't worry about that. We're just friends. I'm here for moral support." Pip winked. "But don't tell your cousin. I think she's tryin' to make him jealous."

Ophelia stood for a moment longer and then finally lowered herself into her seat.

Pip immediately sat down, too. "So how are you related to the McMillan's?"

"My mother and Aunt Elaine are sisters."

"Aunt Elaine...?"

"Brett and Megan's mother."

"Of course! I knew that!"

"Are you sure?" Ophelia narrowed her eyes. "You're not one of those wedding crashers, are you?"

"Course not."

Ophelia tilted her head to one side and scrutinized Pip with her lusciously fringed eyes. "You're not from around here, are you?"

"Why's that?"

"Your accent. It's different than the rest."

"I could say the same about you." Pip grinned. "I'm from Newfoundland. And you?"

"California." She flipped her hair off her shoulder.

Pip slapped his knee and laughed out loud. "I knew it!"

"Knew what?"

"I said to the bartender that you were from California and I was right."

Ophelia sat up primly, her mouth narrowing into a line. "How could you tell?"

"Nobody has a tan like that this time of year unless they come from somewhere like California. I just had a feelin' is all. Are you staying long?"

Ophelia shrugged one delicate shoulder. "A couple of weeks. I don't visit very often. But Megan is my only female cousin, so I felt obligated." She shivered slightly. "It's so cold here! I don't know how you stand it."

"This is nothing. You should see the weather we get down in Newfoundland. If I 'ad a jacket, I'd offer it to you, but I left it on the back of my other chair."

"Very gentlemanly. I'll keep that in mind. Here comes your non-girlfriend." Ophelia cast her glance at Patsi's approaching figure.

"You've met Megan's cousin Ophelia, I see," Patsi said, not sitting down.

"Yes, your 'boyfriend' and I were just chatting about the weather." Ophelia emphasized the word 'boyfriend' and raised a brow before sipping from her straw.

"True story. I wouldn't mind lounging on a beach in California about now," Pip said.

"Um, right…" Patsi focused her eyes downward.

Ophelia sat up straighter. "Do sit down. I'd like to hear all about how you and your boyfriend met."

"We don't want to bore you," Patsi said.

Pip noted the stressed look on Patsi's face and a rush of compassion overcame him, no matter how much he wanted to stay and talk to Ophelia some more. He stood to his feet. "Nice meeting you. Maybe we'll see you around before you go back to the States." This time when he offered Ophelia his hand, she took it and a warm sensation filled his body.

He let go of Ophelia's hand abruptly and grabbed Patsi by the elbow, propelling her toward their original table.

"What's your rush all of a sudden?" Patsi asked.

"No rush. I just didn't want to make you uncomfortable. You know, trying to explain the whole dating thing when it's really not happening."

"How kind." Her tone didn't exactly support the statement. "She seems fixated on the fact that you're my 'boyfriend'. Do you think Brett's said something to her?"

"I wouldn't worry about it."

"If we were actually dating, I might be jealous."

"Posh!" Pip blew some air out his lips. "She's way out of my league and knows it."

"I didn't think you cared about that kind of thing."

Pip shrugged. "I don't. But in her case, I couldn't be bothered. I'd say her personality goes about as deep as her tan."

Patsi laughed. "I couldn't agree more. She seems like such a snob. The whole time I was helping Megan get ready, she kept talking about the latest wedding trends in L.A. As if Megan needed someone trying to spoil her big day by finding fault with everything."

"Some people's kids." Pip shook his head.

"You said it."

Pip glanced Ophelia's way. For a snob, she sure was a looker.

PIP AND JED stood beside the elevator in their apartment building, waiting for it to come back down to the foyer. Lester had probably beat them home from work and now they had to wait.

It had been an interesting day, if interesting meant that Lester had grilled him about his activities on the weekend. He thought about setting the cowboy straight about a few things, first and foremost the fact that he and Patsi really weren't dating. But to explain to her overprotective brother that she was using him to make Brett jealous, just didn't seem like such a good idea. Lester might not take it too well.

The front doors opened and in walked Reba with the Carravagio sisters, Angela and Andrea.

"Hi, Jed. Pip," Andrea Carravagio said as she took her place beside the men.

Jed stiffened and offered an almost undetectable nod. Andrea's eyelashes fluttered and she focused on the closed metal doors of the elevator.

"Nice to see you ladies," Pip filled in the awkwardness. "You managing with Reba under foot? Must be a lot to put up with at work and at home, too."

"Shut your mouth," Reba quipped.

Andrea laughed softly. "She's no trouble at all. I hardly even see her after hours."

"Cause she's always down at the Urban Cowboy," Jed said under his breath.

"So? You are too," Reba said.

The elevator doors finally swished open. Jacques Marcett, manager of the Urban Cowboy, stepped out, followed by an attractive woman Pip hadn't seen before. Jacques's eyes widened when he saw his girlfriend, Angela, standing on the other side of the doors waiting for the elevator.

"It's rather early for your shift." Angela's tone sounded slightly miffed, as if she was accusing him of something.

Jacques shrugged. "I promised Viann I would help her with some errands before work." He planted a quick kiss on Angela's lips. "I'll see you later?"

"Of course," Angela said. Her lips formed a pout as soon as they piled into the elevator and the doors had shut behind them.

"How you enjoying your new job so far?" Andrea asked Pip conversationally.

"Good. Just fine," Pip said.

"The nerve of that Viann," Angela said to no one in particular. "Jacques and I hardly ever get any alone time since she arrived. You'd think she'd want to go back to Montreal since things didn't work out with that doctor."

"I second the motion." Reba crossed her arms and leaned on the far wall of the small space.

"Who is she again?" Pip asked.

"Jacques's sister," Andrea said.

"Step-sister," Angela clarified. "Sometimes I think she's trying to break Jacques and I up."

"Not if Cory has his way," Reba added. "You'd think he was the brother the way 'e fusses over 'er."

"Only he's not her brother, is he?" Angela said. "Neither one of them are. If there's one thing I can't stand it's a woman like her pretending to be helpless."

"Exactly. Makes me sick," Reba agreed.

Pip looked from Reba to Angela and smiled. "Ladies! Do I detect a hint of jealousy?"

Angela and Reba responded in unison, Angela's unequivocal, "Absolutely," countered by Reba's resounding, "No!"

Jed made a snorting sound. "Lard tunderin'! The whole place has become a soap opera, and no mistake."

Pip just laughed. "What you need is someone to distract this Viann person while you get your own affairs in order."

Reba gave Pip a withering look. "And I suppose that someone would be you?"

"Sure. Anything for the cause." He grinned.

"Casanova strikes again!" Jed rolled his eyes.

"I think you should just let things work out the way they're supposed to," Andrea offered.

"I think you've got a pretty lofty opinion of yourself if you think you can make an impression on Viann," Reba said.

Pip went up on the balls of his feet and puffed out his chest a bit. "What can I say?"

"Well, this is one time when you have my blessing," Reba said. "Not that I think you can pull it off."

The elevator stopped and the doors opened. Pip and Jed stepped out. Pip saluted the three women before the doors shut again.

"What in blazes you doin' now?" Jed asked Pip as they walked down the corridor toward their apartment.

"Mending fences between Reba and me," Pip said.

"What in tarnation?" They stopped in front of Jed's apartment and he dug in his pockets for the key.

"Reba's sights are set on Cory Roberts. If I can keep Viann away from Cory, Reba might just get over this bout of ornery she's carryin' toward me."

Jed clucked his tongue as he let them in. "And what about young Patsi Mae? Lester won't be happy if you just drop 'er like a hot potato."

Pip shook his head. "There's nothing between Pat and me. She asked me to pretend to be dating to make 'er old boyfriend jealous."

"Mary, Martha, and Joseph! Lester'll hit the roof if 'e finds out."

"Then don't tell," Pip said simply.

"Like I said. It's a soap opera."

Pip had to agree, except the prospects of himself as the lead male had definite advantages over the supporting role he'd been playing so far. Lights, camera, action!

"You coming or not?" Jed stood in the living room entrance, arms crossed.

Pip pointed the remote at the TV and flipped to a different channel. "Not right now. Gonna stay home and relax a bit, I think. I might come by later if I feel like it, but don't worry about me. I'll take a cab."

"Why do I get the feeling you're up to something?" Jed shook his head.

"Cause I don't want to spend every night at the Urban Cowboy like you? Maybe you should think about getting a life."

Jed grunted and headed toward the exit.

Pip waited for five minutes to be sure Jed was out of the building, and then left the apartment as well. He'd already called Angela Carravagio and set up a meeting, so now all that was necessary was to figure out a plan.

He took the elevator down to the lobby and sat down on the cushioned bench near the mailboxes. He checked his phone twice and waited. About ten minutes later, Angela Carravagio emerged from the elevator. "You don't waste any time, do you?" she said.

"That's me, a man of action," Pip said with a grin.

Angela sat down beside Pip. "I honestly don't know if this is such a good idea. If Jacques finds out, he'll be more than just upset."

"I just need a way to meet Viann again. Leave the rest to me."

"Cocky, aren't you?" Angela observed with a raised brow.

"Confident. There's a difference."

"What's in it for you?" Angela asked.

"Besides the fact that Jacques's sister is a looker?" Pip responded. "It's a way to try and make peace with Reba. She and 'er friend Pat had a falling out and she blames me."

"Patsi Tibbett? Lester's sister?" Angela shook her head. "You do get around."

Pip just smiled. "If Viann is out of the picture long enough for Reba to make a move on Cory, I figure she'll forgive me and all will be right with the world."

"She has been a bit testy, lately. Even I've noticed." Angela sat up straighter. "So... I was thinking we could go up to Jacques's together. Pretend that I thought it was his night off or something. Somehow we need to convince her to come out with us somewhere. A walk, drinks, coffee, anything... Then when I get a call from Andrea I would have to leave and you two could be alone."

"Andrea will play along?" Pip asked in surprise.

"Of course not. I'll pretend it's a call from Andrea."

"And what if Viann won't budge from the apartment?"

"That's where your charm comes in," Angela said. "What's the matter? Not feeling so sure of yourself anymore?"

"I got this." His bravado suddenly didn't match what was on the inside. He stood up and stretched. "Okay. Ready when you are."

They took the elevator up to the fourth floor where Jacques lived and knocked on the apartment door. "Hey, it's Angela," Angela called softly near the doorjamb. After a few more minutes the rattling of the safety chain preceded the door opening.

"Jacques is not at home," Viann said.

Angela furrowed her brow. "But... I thought it was his night off?"

Pip had to hand it to the woman. She was a good actress.

"He has already left for work."

"Oh. Well, can we come in for a minute, at least?" Angela asked. She added in a stage whisper. "I was looking at this cute little side table for Jacques, but I want to make sure it'll fit. He really liked it the other day when we were out shopping and I thought it would be a fun surprise if one day it just showed up."

"Um… of course." Viann's gaze flickered to Pip but she didn't say anything else.

Angela strode into the room as if she owned the place. "By the way, this is my friend Pip. He's new here."

"Nice to meet you." Pip extended his hand. "And you are…?"

"Oh, I'm sorry. I just assumed you knew," Angela said. "This is Jacques' sister, Viann."

"Viann. That's a nice name. Not sure I've ever met anyone with that name before."

Viann nodded, avoiding his hand. "As I have never met anyone named 'Pip'."

Pip laughed. "My real name is Steve, but nobody calls me that - except my Ma when she's angry and wants to make a point."

"He's one of the Malloys," Angela said. "They just seem to keep coming out of the woodwork. I promised I'd show him around a bit. Introduce him to some new people."

"I know who he is," Viann said.

"Hope what you heard wasn't all bad," Pip said with a grin.

The apartment was a mirror image of Jed's, just with nicer furniture. Angela sauntered around the space, tilting her head to one side as if considering the placement of the imaginary side table. "I don't know. Maybe it's too big…"

"Jacques's taste is very select," Viann said. "Quality always comes first. It's the way we were raised."

Angela inhaled sharply but didn't respond to the bait. "I noticed. He prefers picking out his own gifts, so maybe it wasn't the best idea."

"Since that's settled, what say we go out for a drink or something?" Pip suggested.

"I avoid the Urban Cowboy unless absolutely necessary," Viann said.

"We could try somewhere different for a change." Pip looked at Angela. "Any ideas?"

"There's a nice Italian restaurant right around the corner with a lounge. Why don't we go there?" Angela suggested.

"I was planning to stay in tonight," Viann said.

"You stay in every night," Angela countered. "It'll do you good to get out."

"Since when do you care about my welfare?" Viann folded her arms across her chest.

Angela let out a sigh. "I know I haven't been the nicest to you so far, but I can see how close you and Jacques are, and I decided it was time to apologize. I'm trying to reach out. Be nice."

"I can't believe you'd rather spend time with me than go see Jacques," Viann said. "There's more."

"If you wanna know the truth, I wanted to meet you after seeing you in the elevator today," Pip cut in.

Viann raised one elegant brow. "And that is supposed to make me say yes?"

Pip shrugged. "It's the truth. Come on. Let your hair down a little and come out for a drink with us. Just one. Then you can come back and watch TV or whatever it is you were gonna do."

"Why should I?" Viann asked.

"Cause I said please and cause you secretly think I'm kinda cute?" Pip said.

Viann's mouth turned up ever so slightly at the corners. "Just one hour."

PIP SAT down at the bar beside Jed and signalled for Bo to bring him a draft. Then he turned to his older brother and grinned.

"Well, don't you just look like the cat that ate the canary?" Jed surveyed Pip up and down.

"I've got the gift and I don't mind sayin' it."

"Just what might you be referring to?" Jed asked.

"Just came from havin' coffee with Viann Marcett and she's agreed to go out with me again tomorrow night."

"So you were serious? About goin' after 'er?" Jed shook his head.

"Course I was serious. It's a win-win for everybody involved. She's lonely, I'm available, and it gets 'er outta Reba's way."

"A lot of good that's doing." Jed chucked his head toward their sister. She was sitting up to the bar a few feet down from them talking to Jacques. Cory was nowhere in sight.

"Well, it might gain a few points with Angela and Jacques," Pip offered.

"You sure about that? Seems to me Jacques is awfully protective."

"You're sure some ornery. Points with Angela, then."

"And what about Patsi? Lester won't be pleased if he finds out you're two timing 'is little sister."

"There's nothing between Pat and me. If anything she's been using me to make Brett jealous."

Bo finally set Pip's stein of beer in front of him. "Wasn't purposely ignoring you. Just busy is all. So what's this about Pat?"

Jed cleared his throat. "Nothing. Just Pip being Pip. So? Busy for a weeknight, eh?"

Pip ignored Jed's attempt at changing the subject. "I was just telling Jed how I charmed Jacques's sister Viann into going out with me tomorrow evening."

"And I said he better watch it or he'll have Lester Tibbett to contend with," Jed said.

"To which I said mind your own damn business cause me and Pat are just friends," Pip countered.

Bo blinked. "What do you mean 'charmed' 'er?" For some reason he'd forgotten to enunciate his 'h's' the way he'd been practicing.

"You know, convinced 'er to go on a date. What are ya? Daft as well as slow?" Pip shook his head. "People think she's a snob, but I think she's actually just shy or something. Nothing that the old Malloy charm can't fix, though." He winked.

Bo's gaze went from Pip to Jed and then back again.

"I told 'im it was a bad idea," Jed said. "Ya can't go about toyin' with people's feelings for your own gain."

"You make it sound devious or something. Besides the fact that it's a win-win for everyone, I'd be lyin' if I said I didn't find 'er attractive. I might even get lucky."

A muscle ticked in Bo's jaw. A split second later he reached over the counter and grabbed Pip by the collar, lifting him a few centimetres off the stool. "If you so much as lay a hand on Viann, you'll answer to me." He released Pip and let him slide back onto his seat.

Pip smoothed the front of his shirt. "Jumpin' Jehoshaphat! What's got into you?"

Jacques approached and stood beside Bo. "Whatever it is, it's not happening here." He directed a stern gaze at first Pip and then Bo.

"It's nothin'," Jed said. "Just some sibling love is all."

"You Malloys may like to wrestle amongst yourselves, but not here. Not if you still want your job." The last part was directed straight at Bo. Jacques waited for a moment to make sure his message had gotten across before turning his back on them.

Bo's features had transformed into an immobile mask. "This isn't a game, little brother. I mean it." He strode several feet away and turned his back on them, busying himself by polishing some glasses with extra vigour.

Reba approached, concern written on her face as she sat down next to Jed. "What was that all about?"

"Seems the sane one of the bunch has some red blood in 'is veins after all," Jed said.

"What happened?" Reba asked.

"All I said was I was going on a date with Viann." Pip blew out a disgusted puff of air.

"Seriously?" Reba let out a scoffing snort. "I never thought she'd fall for the likes of you."

"She hasn't fallen yet," Jed pointed out. "And by the looks of Bo, you'd better make sure she doesn't."

"You're no fun," Pip said. "Besides, Bo's got no claim to Viann that I can see."

Reba glanced at Bo's broad back and nodded. "So that's how it rolls... I wondered who'd gotten under Bo's skin. When I asked 'im about it he wouldn't say."

Pip furrowed his brow. "If Bo likes Viann Marcett, why's 'e playin' it so close to the chest?"

"Who knows. You're all like a bunch of women," Reba said. "At least when I want something I go out and get it."

"Like you're going out and getting Cory Roberts?" Pip asked. "And how is that going for you seeing as 'e isn't anywhere to be found?"

"None of your business." Reba tilted her head upward.

"At least when I set my mind to getting a girl, I actually score," Pip said.

He just wondered if the cost was going to be worth it.

"That'll be fifteen fifty." The cabby craned his neck to look at Pip and Viann in the back seat of the taxi.

Pip dug in his pocket and came up with a debit card. "You sure you want to go to the Urban Cowboy? We could try somewhere different," he said to Viann as he entered his pin number. They had just enjoyed a nice dinner together and he'd been surprised by her request to end the evening by going to the Urban Cowboy.

"Are you ashamed to be seen with me?" Viann asked. She batted her eyelashes and he knew she was teasing.

He laughed. "Of course not. I just thought it might be awkward with your brother and all." He thought it might be awkward for him with his brother, but he didn't say it.

She allowed a prim smile to cross her lips. "Exactly."

Pip shrugged. "Okay. You're the boss." Something told him she was playing her own kind of game - at his expense. He didn't mind, really. Viann was a beautiful, sexy woman and he was ready for whatever she had in mind. In fact, he was hoping for it.

Viann slid her arm through his as they entered the Urban Cowboy and he responded with a smile. Yep. She definitely had more in mind than friendship. He caught a glimpse of Jacques, Cory and Bo having a conference behind the counter and suddenly realized that any one of those men could have reason to thwart this evening's final outcome.

"We should find a more private table," Pip suggested, veering her away from the bar.

It was too late. Jacques had already seen them. Viann waved and smiled and two more pair of eyes followed Jacques's nod. Cory's eyebrows rose in surprise while Bo looked like a thunder cloud about to burst. Ooo boy...

They sat down and Crystal took their order. Jed was up at the bar in his usual position. Pip was pretty sure he saw Jed shake his head once, but he was one to talk. Apparently he and Crystal had a relationship of convenience going on. Talk about a hypocrite.

Pip reverted his attention back to Viann. "So? This place as riveting as you remember?"

Viann just shrugged.

Pip let out a nervous laugh. "I get the feeling you're on a mission and it doesn't really include me."

Viann blinked and focused on Pip's face. "A mission?"

"A plan. An ulterior motive for coming here tonight."

"And you don't have a plan of your own?" Viann asked.

Pip swallowed. Just what had she overheard?

Viann shrugged and smiled. "I think you're letting your... how do you say it? Imagination run a race for you."

"Letting my imagination run away with me, you mean."

Viann nodded. "That's what I meant."

"Well, hello. I wasn't expecting to see you here." Cory Roberts set their drinks down in front of them. He kept his eyes focused on Viann, as if Pip were invisible. "It's such a nice surprise, I thought I'd bring your drinks myself. How are you?"

"I am fine. And you?" Viann responded.

"Busy, as you can see." Cory finally made eye contact with Pip. "I didn't know you two knew each other."

"We just had dinner," Pip said. He allowed a triumphant smirk to toy with the corners of his mouth.

"Angela introduced us." Viann placed a hand on Cory's forearm. "She was worried that I was lonely and convinced Steve - I mean Pip - to cheer me up. She couldn't join us, unfortunately."

"I wouldn't mind cheering you up. You know that." Cory smiled.

Pip frowned. He was about to say something nasty when another person suddenly joined them.

"Hi guys. Enjoy your date?" Reba stood next to Cory, touching his shoulder with her hand. Viann dropped hers from Cory's forearm.

"A date was it?" Cory asked, looking from one to the other.

Viann preceded her words with a tinkling laugh. "You almost sound jealous." Her gaze flashed momentarily to Reba, triumph in their depths.

Reba's eyes narrowed but she didn't say anything.

"I better get back to the grind," Cory said. "Maybe I'll see you later?"

"That would be nice." Viann smiled and they all watched Cory retreat back to the bar.

Reba turned her flashing gaze toward Pip. "You and I need to talk later, too." She turned on her heel and headed back to the bar to sit with Jed.

"What's got into her?" Viann asked and took a sip of her cocktail.

"The question is, what's got into you?" Pip asked.

"I don't know what you mean."

"I think you do. It's obvious you're using me to make Cory jealous."

"You know nothing."

"No? Seems pretty obvious to me. I'd play along except I don't want to alienate my sister any more than I have to."

Viann made a small snorting sound. "Your sister means nothing to me."

His hopes for some extra-curricular activity with Viann later on crashed along with his interest in her. "In that case, I think I'll go join my brother and sister up at the bar. You 'ave a nice rest of the evening. Alone."

Before he could stand up, another person was standing at their table. Pat.

"Um… Pip. I… Nice to see you." Patsi's gaze swung to Viann. "Viann. It's been awhile. Not sure if you remember me."

"Of course." Viann's recognition lasted only a second and she veered her interest elsewhere.

"You two know each other." Patsi twisted her hands in front of her.

Pip sighed. "Appears so."

"And you're here... together."

Viann swung her gaze back toward Patsi. "We just went out for a magnificent dinner. Didn't we, Pip?" The way she said his name sounded like a caress and she placed her hand on his arm.

Patsi blinked. "Oh. Well, I guess I should go. See you around."

"Pat, wait!" Pip's words fell on deaf ears. Her crestfallen features were in such stark contrast to Viann's cat like smile that it sent a sudden shiver down his spine. Who was this Viann Marcett and what had he gotten himself into? He pushed his chair back. "Well, that's enough fun for me for one evening. Not sure what your game is Miss Marcett, but I'm throwing in my cards."

"My game? That is rich."

"Meaning?"

"Don't play stupid. I know what you're doing."

Pip's brows rose. "Do you, now? Maybe you'd like to let me in on it."

"That... that... woman my brother is so infatuated with paid you to get me out of the way."

Pip blinked. "Is that what you think this is?" She wasn't too far off. Except for the money part, it was true.

Viann shrugged elegantly. "She hates me and wants me out of Jacques's life."

"And how do you figure I fit in?"

"You are to distract me. She knows if Cory and I... well, I won't want to leave and go back to Montreal. Your sister is in on it, too, no doubt."

Pip let out a chuckle. "Not sure if I should be offended or not. Wouldn't you want to stay if you and I hooked up?"

Viann surveyed Pip under hooded lids. "You're not the committed kind. You will break my heart and I will rush back to Montreal."

"Pretty elaborate plan if I do say so," Pip said.

"But you don't deny it."

"If you think it's all a game, why not play along? It might be fun for both of us."

"So it is a game? And Angela is behind it?"

Pip hesitated for a moment before replying. "Well, I wouldn't put it that way exactly…"

Viann's eyes narrowed. "She will be sorry when I tell Jacques what she has done. She doesn't realize who she is dealing with."

He wouldn't disagree.

Viann rose from her seat.

Pip stood also. "Now where are you going? You're not gonna make a scene, are you?"

Viann laughed. "I don't make scenes. A few words are all I need."

Pip lowered himself back into his chair with a sigh and watched Viann's hips swing elegantly as she marched toward the counter where her brother worked. A few moments after, she was heading for the exit. He supposed he should have made sure she got home safely, but the fun had been sucked out of the entire evening and he didn't have the energy to care. As he watched her leave, another pair entered the establishment. Brett and his cousin Ophelia. It didn't rain but it poured.

He put up his hand to signal for a waitress and Crystal came to take his order. "Make it a vodka and water this time. Double."

"Trouble in paradise?" Crystal asked.

"You could say that."

"I wouldn't be too upset. I like Jacques well enough but people say his sister is a real snob."

When Pip saw Bo approaching with his vodka and water on a tray, he almost bolted for the door. Instead, he strove for as casual a posture as he could muster and waited for the boom.

Bo set the drink down in front of him. "I thought I told you to leave Viann alone."

"You're not my boss."

"No, but I could get you thrown out on your ear quick enough."

"Threats. They don't suit you, brother." Pip added a splash of water to his drink and took a sip.

"I don't know what she said to Jacques, but whatever it is she sounded upset and now Jacques is upset."

Pip shrugged and took another sip. "This isn't the only watering hole in town."

"You're missing my point." Bo sat down on the edge of the chair opposite. "Stay away from Viann. You're not serious about 'er and you know it. She's had some bad times and she'll only get hurt with the likes of you."

"You seem to know an awful lot. Not sure the precious Viann is as vulnerable as you make it sound, though."

"I'm warning you."

"Warning me of what? You have no claim to Viann. Not that I can see. If you're that fired up about 'er you shoulda gone after 'er when you 'ad the chance."

A muscle ticked in Bo's jaw and he stood up abruptly. "Thank goodness I didn't let you move in with me. I'd be throwin' you out on your ear."

"The Lard answers in mysterious ways," Pip said and lofted his glass. "So Ma says."

Bo swung around and stalked back to his post. Pip smiled to himself. He should have ordered another drink before he let him go.

"Looks like you're feeling pretty satisfied with yourself. Reba was right to steer me clear of you."

Pip glanced up. "Pat! I think we need to talk. Why don't you sit down?" He gestured to a chair.

"I don't think there's much to say. It's pretty clear you're a playboy, like your sister said."

He closed his eyes for a milli-second, took a deep breath, and then reopened them. "Sit down, okay?"

She hesitated for a moment but then sat down.

He leaned forward in his chair. "First of all, it's not like Viann and I were on a real date. It was more of a favour - for a friend."

"Like you and me," Patsi stated.

"Exactly! It's not like we're actually dating, either. So there's no reason for you to be all snarky about it."

"I'm not being snarky."

"You said yourself it was just to make Brett jealous," Pip continued. "So if anyone should be feeling used, it's me."

"I know, but…" Patsi sighed.

Pip reached for her hands across the table. "What?"

"Brett's no good for me. And Lester will kill me if he thinks I'm still interested. I thought that maybe you and I…" She trailed off.

Pip had a sinking feeling in his chest. "You thought what?"

Tears had begun to form in the corners of Patsi's eyes. "Oh! This is just so embarrassing."

"It's alright. I won't laugh." He squeezed her hands encouragingly.

"I thought… I thought… I thought that maybe we could start dating. Like, for real." She sought his eyes with her own.

"Pat, I like you - a lot. But…"

"Just not in that way," she finished for him.

"I'm sorry."

She pulled away from him abruptly and bolted for the washrooms. Pip sighed. This night was turning out to be one for the record books. He'd successfully ticked off multiple people without even trying.

"I'm surprised to see you smiling after that."

Pip glanced up. It was Reba again. "Why not? I've done nothing wrong."

Reba made a sound of disgust. "No? Not by the look on Pat's face."

"That's none of your business."

"Maybe not, since you've already ruined our friendship. But what about your little escapades with Viann earlier? What have you got to say about that?"

"You didn't seem to mind the idea the other night when we talked about it," he countered.

"Except you let her flirt with Cory right in front of me. Not exactly the master of love you make yourself out to be."

"Can I help it if he's not interested in you?" Pip asked.

Reba let out a frustrated breath. "This isn't how it's supposed to go."

"You're telling me!"

Someone cleared his throat nearby and they both swung around.

"Jacques!" Pip and Reba said in unison.

"So it is true what Viann said. That you have planned some terrible trick to get rid of her."

"I don't know what you're talking about," Reba denied.

"No?" Jacques didn't look convinced. He turned a haughty gaze toward Pip. "Then what are your intentions with my sister?"

"We went on a date. That's it. Got a problem with that?" Pip added for good measure.

"Oui. I have a problem. A big one. Your own brother says you are two timing and this is all some kind of game. A bet."

Pip rolled his eyes. "I should have known Bo would stick his finger in where it's not wanted."

"I will not have my sister's emotions toyed with in such a way. She is fragile."

"What about my emotions?" Pip asked.

"You will finish your drink and then you will leave," Jacques said. "Both of you."

"You can't do that -"

Jacques cut off both of their protests. "I can and I will."

"But our own brother works here," Pip said.

"And Jed - what about 'im?" Reba added.

"I doubt Jed is in on this, but keep your mouths shut, or I will ban him also."

"You can't do that," Reba protested. "I know my rights."

Jacques scathing stare pierced through Reba. "You know nothing. If I find that either of you have contact with Viann again, I will find a way to terminate your brother's employment. Have I made myself clear?"

"Perfectly." Pip put a steadying hand on Reba's arm to keep her mouth shut. They waited while Jacques stormed away.

"Now look what you've done!" Reba hissed.

"Me? You're not exactly Miss Innocent."

"That French snob forgets who he's messin' with. Nobody threatens a Malloy and gets away with it." Reba rolled up her sleeves as if getting ready for a fight.

"Don't you dare do anything stupid. You heard what he said. Bo and I might not be on best terms right now either, but you won't spoil his job."

"You're a terrible person. I wish you'd go back to Newfoundland." Reba stalked away, brushing past Jed on her way to the exit.

"You here to lecture me as well?" Pip asked as soon as Jed sat down.

"Seems to me there's a boat load of drama tonight where you're concerned."

"Not my fault. Can I help it if the whole city's gone mad?"

"I want a word with you. Alone."

Pip glanced up, drink in mid-air. It was Brett McMillan. Of course it was. "Take a number," Pip said and downed the rest of his vodka.

"Whatever you got to say, you can say in front of me," Jed said.

"Not sure that's a good idea," Pip said, "but the way this night is going… why not? Things couldn't get much worse." He sat up straighter and pasted a blasé smile onto his face.

"I thought I told you to stay away from Pat," Brett said as he lowered himself into a chair.

"First of all, I don't take orders from you. Second, I came with someone else, so shut your trap."

"How could you? When you knew Pat might come here?" Brett asked.

Pip shrugged. "You should be happy."

"I told 'im it was a bad idea," Jed put in.

"You're not helping!" Pip said.

"Listen to your brother." Brett said. "She's so upset she won't talk to me either."

"Which is a darn good thing," Jed said. "Lester would clean your clock - both of yas - if he knew youse were fightin' over Patsi."

"Jed! Keep outta it!" Pip thumped the table in exasperation. "Me and her are just friends and as for the likes of you," he pointed at Brett, "you're the one what broke 'er heart, so don't be blaming me for her tears."

"Just stay away from Pat. Do you understand?" Brett stood abruptly and stormed away.

There were a couple of minutes of awkward silence after Brett left them alone.

"This table's a regular revolving door," Pip said with a laugh.

"Lester thinks you and Patsi are dating. He's gonna be upset when 'e finds out the truth. And as far as that fella goes," Jed chucked his head behind him, "He'll hit the roof if he finds out that scoundrel is after her again."

"Not my problem," Pip said.

"I think it is. The moment you pretended to be dating 'er, it became your problem."

"You know what? I'm sick and tired of everyone's advice tonight, okay?" Pip pushed his chair back and stood up. "See you tomorrow. Maybe."

Pip grabbed his coat off the back of his chair and slung it over his shoulder as he made his way to the exit. This had to be the worst night of his life.

As soon as he stepped out into the fresh, night air, he shivered and shoved his arms into the sleeves of his jacket. It was spring, but that didn't mean the wind couldn't bring a chill.

"You look like you're ready to run for it."

Pip twirled around and saw a woman standing under the protection of an awning, just out of the street light's glare. She was puffing on a cigarette and after one last drag, threw in onto the sidewalk.

"Ophelia. I didn't know you smoked." He wasn't sure why that was the first thing out of his mouth and he felt suddenly awkward.

"There's a lot you don't know about me." She stepped out of the shadows.

"True, I guess. I saw you and Brett arrive earlier."

"And I saw the people lining up to give you a piece of their minds."

Pip let out a derogatory huff. "You saw that, eh? Not sure what all the fuss is about."

"I thought you said the little country girl wasn't really your girl-friend," Ophelia said.

"She's not."

"My cousin seems awfully upset."

"Not sure why. Besides, he has no right."

"And what was with the bartender? And your brothers and sister?"

"Who told you they were my brothers and sister?" Pip asked.

"Brett, of course." She smiled.

"For the record, there is nothing between me and Viann, either."

"Viann?"

"Jacques's sister."

"Ah…" Ophelia nodded knowingly.

Pip put his hands in his pockets. "It's not like it seems. I'm not really that kind of guy."

"What kind of guy?"

"You know. Two-timing. A player."

"That's too bad."

Pip blinked. "Beg your pardon?"

"I said, too bad. I was hoping to find some action around here, but maybe I'll have to go somewhere else."

A slow grin spread across Pip's face. "What'd you have in mind?"

"Not sure." Ophelia raised a brow invitingly. "Why don't you surprise me."

"Serious? With you?"

"Sure. This cowtown has me bored stiff."

"I'm not from this cowtown, remember?"

"Exactly." She smiled coyly. "Plus, I'm feeling a tad naughty tonight, if you get my drift."

Pip took a step closer and reached for Ophelia's shoulders. He let his gaze linger a moment on her eyes, smouldering with promise between the long, false lashes, and then he focused on her luscious mouth until he had covered it with his own. She tasted of nicotine, but he didn't mind. His blood was already boiling and he knew this was the best way to wipe away any thoughts of the disastrous evening he'd just endured.

He stopped kissing her and stepped back, not letting go of her shoulders. "I don't imagine Jed'll be home for a while yet. Wanna come to my place for a drink?"

"Perfect."

They kissed again, more quickly this time, and then he raised his arm for the taxi that was just pulling up in front. Ophelia slipped her arm through his and they jogged to the waiting cab.

"Am I gonna get in trouble with your cousin over this?" Pip asked as he held the back door open for her.

"Do you care?" she asked.

"Not particularly."

EPISODE 5

NEIGHBOURHOOD FREEDOM

*W*ILL

WILL Malloy inhaled deeply and let the musky scent of moss mingle with the salt sea air that wafted up from the coastline below. From this vantage point atop a cliff on the western edge of the island, he could see for miles. The roughhewn landscape stretched out before him, one of the most beautiful, if not rugged, sights he'd ever laid eyes on. Undulating greenery was shocked by jagged rocks that jutted out like spikes on the back of a dinosaur, stopping abruptly at the sea where the water clawed at the shore. It was primitive, unrefined, and utterly breathtaking.

He'd worked at the regional park for the past four seasons in a row. It was the kind of work he loved - physical, outdoors, and always changing. He liked working with his hands. The sense of honest accomplishment he got from maintaining the trails, cutting firewood, or providing security from wildlife when necessary, more than made up for the relatively low wages and the seasonal nature of the job.

Heck, he'd even had to do latrine duty. The job required a varied skill set and he was ready, willing, and able.

He was lucky to get pogey in the winters, or employment insurance as it was properly called, and he also managed to score the occasional job creating cross country ski trails and such. It left him plenty of time to pursue his own passion for snowboarding in the winter; less for BMX biking in the summer.

It was a good life. Not too much stress and few responsibilities. Yet... Something stirred within him. A memory of the majestic Rockies whose grandeur could not be paralleled, even by the vista before him, nagged at the back of his mind. If he could get work near Banff or Jasper, he would take it in a heartbeat. The snowboarding would be unprecedented, not to mention the biking. Despite the fact that he loved this place, he was ready for an adventure and the restlessness that had first surfaced on his recent trip to visit family in Alberta had not abated.

He knew what his mother would say. She was already reeling from the fact that five of her nine children now lived in the western province - had flown the rocky shores of their beloved Newfoundland and would not get home very often to visit. Was he willing to become the sixth?

He'd made some inquiries when he'd been in Calgary - unknown to family on either side of the continent - and had found an ad for a general labourer at a private campground just outside the National Park limits. After some doubling back he'd sent in an application and his resume. He was determined not to get his hopes up, but with his experience and willingness to do just about anything, he just might have a shot.

Will loved the outdoors, whether it be the ragged beauty of Newfoundland's coast or the way the rolling prairie met the wall of mountains back in Calgary. He just wanted to get out there and experience it. All of it.

The distinct scent of moose filled his nostrils and he snapped himself out of his reverie. Coming across a full-grown moose was no joke, even in the spring when they were less aggressive than during the fall rut. The large mammals were plentiful in Newfoundland, a hazard to vehicles and a nuisance for outdoorsmen despite the fact that they provided meat for most tables. Fortunately, a keen sense of smell probably alerted the beast to his presence far before his own olfactory sense had kicked in. Moose were naturally shy, so it was probably well on its way by now and he wouldn't have to use his flare gun to scare it away.

Will lumbered down the slope, sliding on some gravel along the way, to his waiting work truck - a white pick-up with the campground logo splashed across the side. He tucked the flare gun into its holster behind the seat and then swung himself into the driver's side. He glanced down at the cell phone sitting on the serviceable upholstery beside him. There was no cell service this far out, so he'd left it where it was. Sometimes he wished for a life totally off the grid with no cell phones and no worries. Now that would be heaven.

As expected, his phone started beeping about ten minutes down the road. He would have to stop at the camp office first before heading home for the long weekend off, and he could check it then. Not that he was expecting a call from anyone other than his ma. To entertain the notion that it could be the campground in Alberta calling was just setting himself up for disappointment. No, it was likely just Ma. She was right anxious that he come home for Easter this year and he was glad he'd managed to wrangle it, especially if it kept her happy for another couple of months. If he was going to lower the boom and follow the rest of his siblings out west, he needed to score a few points first.

"WHAT'S THAT?" Will covered one ear with his hand as he pressed his cellphone up against the other. "The kids are makin' such a ruckus I can't hear ya." He walked down the narrow hallway in his parent's two-story home and took the stairs two at a time. Once upstairs, he had to maneuver sideways to avoid two of his young nephews as they scooted past.

Inside one of the bedrooms, he shut the door. He and his brother Bo, closest in age and in most every other way, had shared the room as teens, and evidence of their interests still hung on the walls. A Montreal Canadiens pennant, BMX biking posters, and a shelf full of Will's various sports trophies next to Bo's collection of mysteries and westerns kept the room frozen in time.

"That's better." Will lowered himself onto one of the twin beds, its springs creaking in protest. "Everyone's here for supper and it's a zoo. Now, repeat that last part."

Bo was on the other end. "I don't know what to tell you. You've got to follow your own dream, not let your life be dictated by others."

Follow his dream? It might be a lot easier said than done. "I've got a telephone interview on Monday. They called me on the way from camp last night. By the sounds of it, they want me, and the interview is just a formality."

"So what's the problem?" Bo asked.

"Pays about the same, but I'd lose my seniority for next year if I change my mind and don't like it."

"But?" Bo prompted.

"But there's something about it. Not that I don't love it here - I do. I don't know how to explain it, exactly. I just feel in my gut like it's something I should do."

"Then do it," Bo advised. "You're only young once. Don't let Ma or anyone else talk you out of it."

Will rubbed the back of his neck. "That's just it. Ma doesn't know yet."

"When you planning on telling 'er?" Bo asked.

"Soon." Will let out a guffaw. "I hate to bring it up on Easter weekend."

"You can't put it off."

"I know."

He did know. The longer he avoided talking to his mother the angrier she would be. He was better off just biting the bullet and getting it over with as soon as possible.

"Say 'ello to everyone," Bo said. "Tell 'em I love 'em."

"Even Trent?" Will asked, his mouth a rueful grin.

"You know I don't mind Trent," Bo replied, referring to their sister Mary's husband. "It's Jed that doesn't get along with 'im."

"I'll be sure to pass it along - although Ma might not want to hear it. She feels betrayed as it is."

They said their final goodbyes just as Will's mother was hollering up the stairs for everyone to come to the table. With a sigh he pocketed the cellphone and headed down. Time to meet the firing squad head on.

The dining room, although fairly large in size, was crammed to overflowing with a long table surrounded by chairs, stools and even a couple of crates in order to make sure everyone had a seat. The Malloy family was staunchly Catholic and had the large family to prove it. Will's father, or 'Pops' as they called him, was seated at the head of the table, a steaming platter of turkey in front of him, already carved and waiting to be passed. He was large and squarely built like most of his sons, with a mop of salt and pepper hair that testified to a perpetual need for a haircut.

Ma hovered near his right elbow, not willing to sit until everyone else was securely in their places. "Sit your behinds down before everything is cold." She was only five foot two, her once auburn hair now a shade of faded peach, and she'd grown thick around the middle as the years went by. But she ruled the family with a sharp eye and a ready tongue. It was a brave soul who crossed her intentionally without good reason.

The rest of the family scurried to find their seats. Will's eldest sister Fanny and her husband Joe lived nearby with their three children. Mary, her two children, and her physician husband Trent had come all the way from St. John's for the occasion. His sister Sissy and her fisherman husband Hank were also present and beat the rest when it came to offspring at four. With the addition of Will, there were eighteen at the table - a small number compared to some years when the younger children had to eat separately at a card table in the living room.

Once everyone was settled, amid much shuffling and scraping of chairs, Ma held her hands out and a sudden silence descended on the family. Dutifully they grasped one another's hands, encircling the table. "Go ahead and say grace," Ma instructed her husband.

Pops mumbled a practiced prayer of thanks for family and food followed by a chorus of 'Amens'.

"There now." Ma beamed. "Start passin' the grub before it gets cold."

If there was one thing Newfoundlanders did well, it was feed people. Bowls mounded with vegetables, and platters of turkey and ham, made their way around the outer ring. A heaping bowl of bright purple mash, a family favourite at this time of year, consisted of potatoes mashed together with pickled beets and mayonnaise.

Will was glad for the cacophony of chatter. He was trying to summon up the courage to let the family in on his plans.

"Is the park ready for tourist season?" Joe asked Will from across the table.

"Getting there. You know how it is. Cleaning up after the winter months is a lot of work, but it'll be ship shape by the long weekend in May."

"That long?" Mary asked. "It seems they could get things ready a bit sooner than that."

"Nobody is stopping tourists from coming any sooner. But the weather can still turn nasty. Especially in the high places. You know that." Will smiled over at his sister. She had his same dark colouring, as did Jed and Fanny, but Mary usually wore a sour look on her face. Money obviously didn't buy happiness.

"It sure seems strange without Bo and Reba and Pip here," Sissy said. She had a ruddier complexion, partly from the outdoor air and partly because of her strawberry blonde hair.

"I miss Uncle Pip," her youngest, John, said, his freckled face sporting a frown. "And Uncle Bo."

"Not Aunty Reba?" Fanny asked the youngster. As the eldest child, she felt it her right as well as her duty to help parent all her siblings' offspring.

"Leave 'im alone," Ma interjected. "He's only four, 'e is."

"Never too young to learn manners," Fanny quipped and tilted her head up. "Speaking of Bo, was that 'im on the phone earlier?"

"Um, yes. He said to wish everyone a happy Easter and that 'e loves you all and misses you."

"If 'e misses us so much why'd 'e move so far away?" Ma asked with a sniff.

Will braced himself. Here it comes.

"I don't know," Pops said. "I guess young people 'ave to figure things out for themselves."

"He coulda talked to me in person instead of passin' along a message," Ma continued. "At least Reba and Jed did that much. And Zeb, all the way from Fort McMurray."

"You make it sound as if it's more difficult to telephone from Fort McMurray than Calgary," Mary noted with a shake of her head.

"Pip didn't call?" Fanny asked with a raised eyebrow.

"Probably 'ad to work today," Ma said with a shrug.

"Of course he did," Mary put in sourly. "The golden one always gets a pass." She made a point to carefully pronounce her 'h's.

"Why would 'e work when Jed didn't?" Fanny put in. "I thought they worked at the same place."

"They do," Will said. "And as for Bo, 'e actually did have to work today, so that's why 'e didn't have time to talk to everyone."

"Trent had to book time off from the clinic so we could drive all this way, but I don't see anyone making a fuss over that." Mary sniffed.

Trent turned purposefully toward Will. "I didn't hear much about your trip out west," he said, changing the subject.

"Lard of a duck! I don't wants to hear any more about that godforsaken part of the country," Ma declared. "Gone and stole all me bairns!"

"Thanks a lot, Ma," Sissy said with a laugh. "Hank and I aren't goin' anywhere." She glanced around the table. "And I think it's safe to say the same for the rest of us."

"I should 'ope so," Ma said.

"What do you say, Will?" Hank said with a smile. "The western bug didn't get you when you was there?"

Of course, Will knew Hank was only joking. Of all his brothers-in-law, Hank was the most congenial and would never think of saying anything if he thought it would cause trouble. But he had, and now it was time to set the record straight.

Will cleared his throat and the room went suddenly quiet. Even the children seemed to sense that something important was coming next.

"As a matter of fact, I've tossed the idea around, so to speak."

The silence stretched, taut and awkward until Ma broke it with a cry. "How could ya? After everything?" She pushed back from the table and fled from the room with a sob, not waiting to hear the rest.

Will blinked, stunned by his mother's outburst. In all his years he'd seen her rant, threaten, and even curse... but burst into tears? Never. He pushed himself back from the table as well, rising slowly to follow her.

"Sit down," Pops ordered, his tone gruffer than usual. "She just needs a minute to pull 'erself together is all. Fanny? Sissy? Why don't you bring on the dessert? I know your ma made a cupboard full of pies that she wouldn't want goin' to waste."

The two women got up and did as they were bid, exiting to the kitchen off the dining room. Gradually, quiet conversation resumed as Joe and Hank discussed Hank's new fishing boat, Mary fussed over one of her sons, and Trent tended to the other. The rest of the children engaged in hushed giggles and a game of poking one other. That left Pops and Will.

Pops leaned on the table with his elbows. "Can't say I'm surprised."

Will's brows rose. "Really? What makes you say that?"

"Just a feelin'. In my gut."

Will nodded but was silent.

Pops surveyed him out of the corner of his eye. "Must be quite the draw for you to leave the park behind."

"Nothing's official yet," Will said.

"Still... Seems to me I need to visit this place for myself, seein' as all my children are want to pull up stakes and move there."

"You should. You and Ma both. Maybe a trip this summer if you can swing it."

Pops shook his massive head. "Not sure your Ma'll want to, least not right away. She's madder than a wet hen and stubborn besides. She won't agree to visit just outta spite."

"I feel awfully bad about it, but…"

"You're young and want to experience the world while you can. I understand." Pops winked. "Not that I want to see you go, but don't worry too much. She'll get over it."

Fanny and Sissy entered, laden with two pies each.

Will hoped Pops was right and that she'd get over it sooner rather than later. There was nothing worse than angry good-byes.

WILL SHUFFLED BEHIND BO, stopping as he unlocked his apartment door and swung it open. The interior of Bo's Calgary apartment was shrouded in darkness. It was past one a.m. mountain time and they had just come from the airport. Will was beginning to feel the jump back in time creeping up on him. He yawned widely. "'Scuse me."

"You'll be tired after your flight and it's way past your bedtime according to Newfoundland time. I won't keep you up." Bo switched on the kitchen light and Will had to scrunch his eyes.

"I might need a minute or two to unwind," Will said and found his way to Bo's couch. He sank down into its depths. There wasn't much other furniture to speak of in the room save a couple of crates that had become a makeshift bookshelf.

Bo sat down on the couch beside Will. "It took me a 'ole week to adjust when I first got here." Bo had been practicing pronouncing his 'h's, but at this hour - and in Will's company - he let himself slip back into pure, unadulterated, Newfoundlander.

"Don't have a week," Will replied. "One day and then it's off to orientation and then work for real." He smiled broadly. "Who woulda thought?"

"Who indeed? Certainly not Ma." Bo smiled and gave Will a playful elbow in the ribs. "I can't believe you actually did it. Not sure I coulda stood to see Ma cry."

"Pops took my side, so it made things a bit easier," Will said. This time he tried to stifle the yawn. "Thanks for letting me stay, by the way."

"What'd ya expect?" Bo countered.

Will shrugged. "I coulda bedded down at Jed's I suppose, but I woulda had to wake 'im."

"I just got off work, so I was up anyway," Bo said.

"This seems more natural." Will surveyed the spartan living room. It meant sleeping on the couch at either place, but he was more used to sharing with Bo than with Jed. They'd always been close.

"I definitely think it's for the best." Bo's tone was somewhat cryptic.

Will knew that there had been some infighting among the clan since his last visit, but he wasn't sure how bad it really was. "So, I filled you in on the rest of the family on the way from the airport. Now it's your turn. How are things?" he asked.

"Zeb never calls. Reba still has 'er nose outta joint. Jed drinks too much for 'is own good. And Pip..." Bo let out a derogatory snort. "Pip may have crossed one too many lines, even for my liking."

"What kind of lines?"

"Not sure it's my place to say," Bo hedged. "Let's just say 'e's up to no good and doesn't seem to care a wit who 'e steps on in the process."

Will chuckled. "Ma won't be pleased, but she'll blame it on the water or something."

"You're not going to tell 'er?" Bo pinned Will with a stony stare.

"Course not," Will said and smiled to ease the tension. Whatever was going on had Bo strung up tight. "I'm no spy. Just concerned if the family is splitting apart at the seams."

"Not splitting apart, really. Just suffering from spring fever."

"Spring fever?" Will shook his head. "Now you're talking in riddles. What does that mean, exactly?"

Bo tilted his head in thought for a moment. "The twitter-pated kind."

"Huh?"

"Don't you remember that old cartoon?" Bo waved a hand dismissively. "Never mind. Love sick."

"You don't say. I hope it's not catching!"

"Reba's chasing 'er tail around Cory Roberts, the owner of the club where I work and 'e doesn't even seem to notice. Pip's gotten 'imself in deep with more than one girl and now 'e's got their brothers mad at 'im, too. And I'm almost certain Jed has a crush on a woman in our building - Andrea Carravagio, one of the twins who owns the salon where Reba works. But 'e's too stupid to make a move, so instead he's sleepin' around with one of the waitresses. It's a twisted mess."

"Sounds like a reality TV show."

"Exactly." Bo shook his head.

"And what about you? You didn't mention yourself. Is that part of the equation, too?"

"No. Nothing like that for me," Bo answered quickly - perhaps too quickly, if Will read things right.

Will slapped his knee. "I know you too well, b'y! This is me you're talkin' too, remember? You caught the bug the same as the rest! I haven't forgot that conversation back at the restaurant."

"Well..."

"You was never very good at keepin' secrets. Not from me. So who's your poison?"

Bo's eyes narrowed, ever so slightly. "Not poison."

Will shrugged. "Okay. What's 'er name, then?"

Bo hesitated and then sighed, a deep exhalation that came right from his core. "Never mind. She doesn't even know I exist."

"That's not what I asked."

"If I tell you, you have to promise not to use it against me."

"Would I do that to you?" Will asked. "I'm the one who always has your back."

"True." Bo sighed again and glanced up at Will. "You'll think I'm crazy."

"Try me." Will sat back and folded his arms across his broad chest.

Bo opened his mouth and then shut it again and shook his head. "Forget it. I'm over it and there's no use even talking about it."

"For the love of Mary, Joseph and -"

"Okay, okay!" Bo interrupted. "Her name is Viann. Jacques's sister. Jacques the bartender?"

Will nodded. "I remember Jacques. So what's the issue? Does she know how you feel?"

Bo shook his head. "I doubt it. Well, maybe…" He sighed. "We were getting along good enough but then she took up with this doctor. Then when he broke 'er heart she went into hibernation. Or so I thought. Then I find out Cory Roberts - my boss - might be after 'er."

"The plot thickens."

"You could say that."

"That can't be good. Is the feeling mutual? Between 'er and 'im, I mean?" Will asked.

"Not sure. That's where it gets complicated. Now Pip's gone and stuck 'is nose in."

"Pip?" Will frowned. "Is your girl one of the girls you mentioned 'e was after?"

"She's not 'my girl', and yes. Pip says it wasn't anything, but who can ever tell with 'im? I hate to say it about my own brother, but 'e's a slimy little beggar, that one."

"Now you're sounding like Jed," Will said with a smirk. "Speaking of, what's Jed got to say about all of this?"

"Not taking sides, at least not that I can see," Bo said. "But it's made things awkward. I'm just glad I moved into my own place before it all hit the fan."

"And Reba?"

"She's mad at Pip for any number of reasons, not the least of which, she's taken offence on behalf of 'er friend, Patsi Tibbett."

Will nodded. "I remember 'er, too, I think."

"Which makes it doubly awkward cause Jed's good friends with Patsi's brother Lester and now that they all work together - Jed, Lester and Pip - Jed's walkin' a tightrope."

Will rubbed his dark head. "Wait a sec. I think you lost me somewhere."

"Patsi is another of Pip's conquests. Patsi, Viann, and now some new girl called Ophelia - all at the same time." Bo let out a disgusted snort. "He says 'e was just doing a favour for someone, but the story is so convoluted I can't imagine anyone believes it."

Will whistled softly. "Pip does know how to make a ruckus, doesn't he, our little brother?"

"A ruckus you call it? I can think of a few other choice words."

Will felt the yawn coming on long before it hit and this one he couldn't hide. "Phew. Sorry about that. As for your predicament, I don't know what to say."

"My predicament?" Bo asked.

"Your love sickness."

"We were talking about Pip, not me."

"Either way, I'm the last man to give advice when it comes to romance. I just head for the hills and let it pass."

"Your time will come," Bo said. "When the right one comes along."

"If I end up looking as pathetic as you, no thanks." Will grinned and then gave Bo a good punch in the arm. "Take it on the chin, b'y. You'll get over it."

"Maybe," Bo mumbled. "But you said yourself you're not the best one to give advice."

"So I did." Will yawned again, loudly.

Bo hauled himself up off the couch. "Sorry. I'm keepin' you up too late as it is. You'll want to get some shut eye and I'm on your bed."

"I don't mind. Once I'm outta town you won't be seeing that much of me."

"You're welcome to stay whenever you're in the city," Bo said. " I kinda miss your company."

"Sounds like a good deal to me," Will said. "I'll need a headquarters, so to speak."

"It's settled, then. You can stay with me. You're the only one who listens. The rest just like to hear themselves talk."

"If that isn't truth, I don't know what is."

~

WILL GLANCED to the left and then to the right, trying to decide if he really wanted to be at the Urban Cowboy on his last night in Calgary. Jed had been talking non-stop since they arrived and somewhere in the discourse he had tuned out.

Bo was behind the counter, mixing drinks and serving customers, looking efficient and cool despite the revelations of the night before. Further down the line was Jacques, brother to Bo's love interest, looking like a sly fox talking to Cory Roberts, the smooth talking owner with a head full of dreadlocks. Will didn't recognize anyone else, which was just as well. He didn't plan on getting too comfortable in the developing family soap opera. When he told Bo he'd rather head for the hills, he'd meant it. Fresh air, exercise, and a dose of adrenaline now and again had managed to keep him on the level when it came to women. He intended to keep it that way.

Surprisingly, neither Pip nor Reba had joined them. Reba had made an excuse about meeting some other friends, and apparently Pip was sick. Will had just shrugged it off, determined not to be offended, but it did seem out of character - for both of them. Reba loved nothing better than to be included with the 'men' when it came to a party, and Pip was never sick. Maybe he was laying low for safety's sake. Will grinned at the thought.

"I don't see as it's funny," Jed said, pointing a finger in Will's direction.

Will blinked, trying to reorient himself to the conversation. "What's that?"

"Although I suppose a fella like you thinks bull riding is a cake walk, seeing as you have no fear in ya."

"Bull riding?"

"The mechanical bull riding competition I was tellin' you about," Jed said. "Lard tunderin'! Yer ears full a wax or what?"

"Oh… the bull riding competition. When is it again?" Will's interest was slightly piqued, although he doubted he would be in town for the event.

"Right there on the poster." Jed pointed to a large poster taped to the mirror behind the counter. "I figured the daredevil in you would be rarin' to enter."

"Not sure about that, but it might be fun to try it once," Will said with a shrug. "Where is it?"

"Just around the corner. Course, if my friend Lester were here 'e could give you the proper advice. Lester's the real deal when it comes to rodeo ridin'. Probably wouldn't mind, even if he is still mad at Pip."

"I'm not Pip." Will shrugged. "But it can't be that hard."

"Eh, Cory!" Jed hollered toward the other man. "My brother wants to give that bull a whirl."

BULL RIDING HAD BEEN A MISTAKE. It definitely wasn't as easy as it looked and Will had the sore muscles to prove it. He did some arm circles, trying to work the kink out of his left shoulder where he'd fallen hard the night before. But his interest had been piqued. He was never one to run away from a challenge. Perhaps some lessons from Jed's friend Lester were in order after all.

"Got a bum arm?"

Will's attention shifted back to his new boss, Jeremiah Reynolds, a man with grizzled facial hair and a long ponytail hidden under a ball cap with the campground logo stamped across it. "No, no. Nothing like that. Just a kink. I'll be good as new tomorrow."

"Hope so. Your application looked good, but I don't want to find out you're a dud." The words were gruff but Will detected a twinkle in the grey eyes peeking out from under the brim of the hat.

Will laughed. "I promise you. I'm no dud."

Jeremiah stretched and then pointed to the A-frame log house to his left. "That about does it for now. Maizy'll be expecting us for lunch. After, I'll take you on a tour of the perimeter and then you can come back and fill up the firewood bins. Can't let you slack off too much on your first day."

"That's why I'm here," Will said.

Jeremiah stopped in his tracks and stared at Will. "To slack off?"

Will blinked. "No, to work."

The older man smiled. "Good. Come on, then, before she sends the posse out after us."

Will followed behind Jeremiah's quick but stilted gait toward the house.

His new boss had picked him up bright and early at a large shopping mall on the south end of Calgary and they'd headed the forty-five minutes to Jeremiah's family owned property. The foothills rolled and dipped as they wound their way off the main thoroughfare that led to Banff National Park. The roller coaster hills reminded him somewhat of the rugged landscape around Grosemore in Newfoundland - minus the sea, of course - a place near his home that was dear to his own heart.

When they arrived at the campground, it wasn't quite what he was expecting. Somehow he thought it would be different than the campgrounds back home; grander. It seemed pretty rustic. Ramshackle, even, but one place was pretty much like the other, he supposed. A large log building near the gated entrance served as the office, shower house, laundry facilities, and a small store that stocked the basic essentials - things like matches and insect repellent that tourists might have forgotten to pack. There was no getting past it to the neatly ordered camp sites carved out among the trees. You stopped at the office or you didn't get in. It was as simple as that.

Once past the main building, the grand tour continued. Jeremiah and his wife, Maizy, lived in a log home just steps from the office, while a row of bunkhouses for the hired help - three buildings in all - were tucked farther away from the general public. These were next to the machine shed and other maintenance buildings. There he'd gotten the low down on all the equipment that he could and could not use, plus a list - more or less - of tasks that he could expect to perform. It seemed a little less organized than what he was used to at the regional park back home, but it was a private business, after all, so Mr. Reynolds was free to run it however he saw fit.

Will ducked his head as he entered the cabin. Not that it was small, but the A-frame construction meant that head room was at a premium on the outer edges of the building. He followed Jeremiah's example by washing his hands at a sink in the porch area and then stepped further into the house - an open concept kitchen, dining, living room with a loft above.

"Come sit." Maizy Reynolds gestured to the long plank table fitted with bench seats on either side that dominated the space. She was younger than Will would have expected, judging by the age of her husband. "You must be the young man from Newfoundland Jeremiah was so fired up about. I'm Maizy."

"She's the real boss around here," Jeremiah said with a grin.

"He was so impressed by your application, he said, 'Maizy, we have to get that young man here before he changes his mind.'"

"She's exaggerating again," Jeremiah said gruffly. "General labourers are a dime a dozen."

A First Nations' man of indeterminate age was already standing beside the bench, waiting for the rest to sit down. "That's not what you told me," he said.

"This here is Buck Stone," Jeremiah introduced. "He does some guiding and such when the need arises. Otherwise, you two will be working together a lot of the time." Jeremiah wagged a finger. "And don't believe a word he tells you."

"Pleased to meet you." Will shook Buck's hand.

During the course of lunch, he learned that the campground had been in operation since the 1950s, started by Jeremiah's grandfather when he saw an opportunity to entice tourists with an alternate site so near the park. A cooperative arrangement had been reached that was still upheld - unprecedented in today's management of lands adjacent to national parks. There was a strict code of ethics to be maintained, however, in terms of ecosystem integrity. No new development was allowed, which probably explained the rustic appearance of the buildings.

After lunch, Jeremiah took him on a tour of the perimeter, as promised. It was someone's job to make sure no one snuck into the camp through the stretches of wilderness that surrounded the establishment. Worse yet, if someone started a campfire without permission, it could result in a wild fire that could devastate the area.

Later that evening, Will finally had time to unpack the few belongings he'd brought with him. He'd travelled light, figuring he could buy whatever he needed in the city on his next visit. It was only a forty-five minute drive to the outskirts, so he might even head to town on occasion for an evening out. Especially if it meant practicing on that bull. Somehow the thought of mastering the beast had gotten stuck in his craw and he was hard pressed to let it go.

The bunkhouses were miniatures of the main house - three tiny A-frames in a row that left even less head room than the original, except when standing dead centre. Not that it mattered much since there were two bunk beds on either side, so you couldn't walk near the outer edges anyway. That meant that the bunkhouses could sleep twelve if need be. As it was, there was only himself and Buck that he knew of. Apparently, they would hire a couple of summer students once the busy season hit, but Buck said not to worry about losing his privacy. The students would have to share, not them.

He'd had to laugh at that. "I'm used to being crammed in like sardines." It was true.

As he put away the last of his belongings, he couldn't help thinking about his siblings and their troubles. If anyone was able to talk sense and make peace, it was Bo. Yet, apparently he was just as messed up as the rest of them. It got Will to worrying. What if he was next?

WILL HOPPED on one of the quads and headed out to do his rounds. It was common practice to scout the outer perimeter of the campgrounds before the evening set in. There was nothing of consequence and he was about to turn back when he noted something out of place in the distance. He pulled out the miniature binoculars that were part of his issue and adjusted the lenses until he focused on the object in question. His eyebrows rose in surprise when he registered what it was.

A person was standing on the precipice of a hill, a steep valley stretching out before him or her with a magnificent close up of the Rockies in front. It looked like the person was painting a picture.

Will revved the engine and maneuvered the all-terrain vehicle through a break in the fencing. He followed the rugged footpath through the brush and trees, dipping and swerving through ruts and sharp turns until he came out on the other side at a clearing. The woman - he could see she was a female now - was about twenty yards away. She was standing beside a portable easel, paint palette in one hand and brush in the other.

She turned when the noise of the quad got closer and although he couldn't see her eyes beneath the large plastic framed sunglasses that covered half her face, he could imagine she was glaring at him all the same. Her mouth was drawn into a petite line.

He pulled up as close as he dared and cut the engine. The tinkle of tiny bells attached to the easel faded on the breeze. "This is kind of an out of the way spot," he said.

"Exactly the point."

"That's a very pretty picture you're painting."

"That's a very noisy machine you're driving," she retorted.

"Just doing my job, Miss. No harm done."

"Except for the wildlife that you just scared half out of their wits, not to mention the greenhouse gasses that monstrosity has just belched into the atmosphere. This is supposed to be a pristine environment."

"Like I said, just doin' my job. The boss asked me to check the perimeter, so I was checking the perimeter."

"As you can see, I'm outside the property line," she said. "So you can be on your way." She turned back to the painting.

Will let it go and got off the machine. He approached the easel to get a closer look. "Very nice."

"It's just a sketch for a bigger piece."

"So you're a real artist?" Will asked.

Her mouth twitched. "Don't I look like a real artist to you?"

"Not sure. My Nan used to dabble, but other than that I have nothing to go by." He grinned. "And you definitely don't look like my Nan."

Actually she did in a way, if one took her strange clothing into account. It reminded him of something a hippy would wear. She wore a long, patterned skirt, an oversized sweater, and high topped hiking boots. Her long brown hair fluttered in the breeze, mindless of the bandana that was supposed to be holding it off her face. She looked like a flower child straight out of the sixties, despite the fact that she was probably only in her mid-twenties.

He watched her dabble for a while, fascinated by the way she was able to make slashes and blotches look like something real. Suddenly she turned, brush in mid-air. "Are you going to stand there all day? I thought you had work to do."

"Um, right." Will straightened up. "Since I'm here, mind me asking how you got all the way out here?"

"I walked, of course."

"Oh." He nodded, taking the information in. "Are you staying at the campground?"

"I suppose you could say that."

"I could give you a lift back. I know you don't like the noise and fumes and all, but it gets dusky pretty quick in the shadow of the mountain."

"I'll be fine, thanks. I want to catch the last rays of sunlight before the sun sets."

"Can't you just take a picture or something? We're in grizzly country, you know. It could be dangerous out here all alone."

If he could see behind those ridiculous glasses he figured she was probably giving him her best glare. "I'll be fine. This isn't my first time." She jingled the bells on the easel to make her point.

He didn't feel good about it, but short of hauling her off cave man style, there didn't seem to be much he could do about it. "Suit yourself." He sauntered back to the machine, and then turned before mounting. "Mind if I ask your name at least? In case the boss asks?"

"Marigold. He'll know."

Will nodded. "Okay. I'm Will, by the way."

"I know."

Will's eyebrows rose. "Is that so?"

"It is. Now get going before you spoil my painting all together. The light is perfect now and I don't have a moment to waste."

"I could wait…"

"Go!" The directive held enough force that Will didn't hesitate. He hopped on the quad, revved the engine, and high tailed it back the way he'd come. Marigold may be foolish, but she was also feisty and he wasn't about to stick around for a second command.

"NICE OF THE boss to let you have an evening off," Jed said. "So's you're liking it, I take it?"

Will nodded. They were sitting together at the Urban Cowboy, up at the bar where Jed usually perched. "As long as I'm back in the morning, I can come to town any night of the week once the work's done. Not that I think it's a good idea," Will added. "But since you figured Lester would be willing to give me some pointers tonight, I made sure of it."

"And your friend - what's 'is name? Buck? He gave you a ride. How come he didn't stay for a lager. I'd like to meet 'im."

"Me, too." Reba was sitting on Will's other side. She was in one of her moods again, which seemed to be more frequent according to Bo, but at least she'd agreed to join them.

"Stop acting desperate," Will said to her, "He's way too old for you, and he doesn't drink anymore, so he says. But he has a daughter in town that he comes to visit once a week, so he didn't mind." Will tapped his naked wrist where a watch should be. "As long as I'm ready by eleven, just like Cinderella."

"That's midnight, and you're no Cinderella," Reba quipped.

Jed checked his own wrist where an actual watch resided. "Wonder what's taking Lester?"

"His girlfriend probably won't let 'im outta the house." Reba made a sour face and took a swig of her beer.

"You always this pleasant or is it for my benefit?" Will asked.

"It's her new persona," Bo said, joining them on the other side of the counter.

Reba stuck out her tongue, grabbed her drink, and marched away toward the pool tables, presumably to watch some burly cowboys involved in a game.

Will scrunched his brows. "What's got into her?"

"Nothing she didn't bring on 'erself," Jed said.

"Apparently she and Angela Carravagio had a falling out." Bo chucked his head toward Jacques Marcett, the bartender and manager who was working down the line. "They broke up and Angela blames Reba. It's Angela's sister Andrea that's keeping the peace. Seeing as they work and live together, though, it's not good news. I almost feel sorry for her."

Will surveyed Bo through narrowed lids. "I think you enjoy the gossip. Working here has changed you."

Bo just shrugged.

"Like I said, nothing she didn't bring on 'erself," Jed said. "If she'd quit being so all fire stubborn, she could move back in with Pip and me."

Bo pointed toward the entrance. "Here comes Lester and Sherri. Be prepared for some aches and pains."

"Who made you the expert?" Will asked with a grin. "When was the last time you rode a bull?"

"Once was enough. I don't want to break my neck," Bo said.

Lester Tibbett and Sherri Chan joined them. Sherri sat in Reba's vacant seat while Lester stood behind her. "So I hear you want to learn to ride the mechanical bull?" he directed at Will.

Will nodded. "I tried it once and it wasn't as easy as I thought. Maybe you can give me some pointers."

"Why?" Lester asked. "What's your motivation?"

Will thought about it for a moment. "The challenge, I guess. What made you want to be a rodeo cowboy?"

"Stupidity," Sherri supplied and they all laughed.

"Will's a man's man," Jed answered for him. "Loves sports - any kinda sports. Baseball, 'ockey, dirt bikes, camping -"

"Since when is camping a sport?" Bo threw in.

"Never mind 'im," Jed continued with a wave of his hand. "He loves the outdoors, Will does. Hunting, camping. You name it."

"Sounds like Will's your favourite," Lester said with a grin.

"More like his guinea pig," Bo said. "Too stupid to say no whenever Jed and Zeb came up with some hare-brained scheme. It's amazing he's alive."

"Will's a dare devil, I'll give you that, but we never forced 'im to do nothin'. Always went willingly." Jed smiled broadly. "Willing Will. That's 'im!" He turned to Bo. "Remember that time we tied 'im onto 'is bike and sent 'im down McGregor's hill?'

"Don't pin that on me." Bo held up his hands. "It was all you and Zeb."

"The poor little bugger was reciting the rosary all the way down at the top of his lungs!" Jed slapped his knee. "I handy bout died!"

"They thought it was funny," Will interpreted at the confused expressions coming from Lester and Sherri. "Meanwhile, I almost did die."

"Goodness!" Sherri shook her head. "It's a wonder any of you survived."

"Well? You ready for that lesson or not?" Lester asked.

"Ready as I'll ever be," Will replied.

Jed signalled for Cory to come join them so that he could run the machine.

"It's all in the hips, actually," Lester said as they made their way around the corner to the area where the bull lived.

Will nodded. This time he was ready.

"Once I got some pointers from Lester, it went a lot smoother." Will chucked a few pieces of firewood on the stack he and Buck were making in one of the bins at the campground.

Buck straightened the wood into a neat row. "You'll fit more in if you do it right. Makes for less work in the long run."

"Oh right." Will slowed his movements to match Buck's more methodical ones. "He said it's all in the hips, and he was right."

"Until you fall and break a hip and then it's quits," Buck said.

Will looked over at the older man in surprise. "Are you talking from experience?"

Buck nodded, his dark hair falling into his eyes as he bent to fetch the next bundle of logs. He wore it slicked back in front, almost like a throwback to the greaser era, and when he worked, it tended to get in the way. "Rode bareback. Was pretty good at it, too, till I got injured."

"You should come with me to the Urban Cowboy next time and watch. You might have some good pointers. I'm thinking about entering the contest, although I know it's a long shot. It'd be fun."

Buck shook his head. "No thanks."

"Why not? I know you don't drink, but you could have pop."

"I'm diabetic."

"Well, water then. Or coffee."

Buck stopped what he was doing and straightened his back, pinning Will with the directness of his stare. "I'm a recovering alcoholic. You don't tempt an alcoholic by asking him to a bar."

"Oh." Will blinked and looked down at his toes. "Sorry. I didn't think."

"When I said I like to go to town and visit my daughter, I wasn't lying. But I also go to my AA meeting, first."

They continued working for a few more minutes in silence. Then Will spoke up. "This AA meeting. Can anybody go?"

Buck glanced over at Will. "Of course. You want to come?"

Will shook his head. "Not me, but I know someone who might... benefit."

"You can't force someone else to stop drinking," Buck said. "They have to want to do it. Then it's up to them - with the help of their higher power, of course."

"Higher power? What in blazes is that supposed to mean? Like native stuff?" Will stopped abruptly and blinked before continuing. "I mean, sorry about that, b'y. I didn't mean it to be disrespectful."

Buck chuckled. "It's okay. For some, yes, they do rely on those kind of spiritual beliefs. Others focus on an object - any object. For me, it's Creator God, the same one who came in the flesh as a man called Jesus. That is my higher power."

"Hm." Will nodded. He hadn't supposed Buck to be a religious sort, but then lots of things were taking him by surprise these days.

WILL BUMPED ALONG THE TRAIL, letting his body sway with each tilt and jolt of the quad, relaxing his muscles to meld with the flow instead of trying to absorb the shock. Fluidity; becoming one with the animal - or in this case the machine - instead of working against it, was the key to staying on for the full eight seconds. At least according to Lester Tibbett. A quad was no substitute for the mechanical bull, but there were some parallels, and Will had come to value these evenings when he could take the machine out and test his mettle, full tilt - out of earshot of the boss, of course.

It was something to look forward to at the end of each day - a little adrenaline rush... Not to mention that meeting Marigold on the bluff just outside the perimeter had also become something he looked forward to.

Most days she was there, in the same spot. The days she wasn't he felt a strange sense of disappointment, although they didn't talk much. Mostly he commented on her painting, which was amazing in his eyes, and she mentioned the fact that he was contributing to the depletion of the ozone layer. It was a comfortable repartee which he'd come to enjoy over the past two weeks.

She was a bit of an enigma, Marigold. Like her name she was a flower that adorned the grassy slopes but didn't seem to exist anywhere else. He'd never come across her in the campground proper, and when he'd asked Buck about it once, the other man had given him an amused stare and shook his head. "That's for her to tell you. If she wants to, that is."

As expected, Marigold was outside the fence in an area a little farther down the sloping hill than was her usual spot. Her hair was fluttering about in the wind, never seeming to get tangled despite the tendrils that constantly floated about her face like a mermaid's in seawater. His heart picked up its pace just a bit and he attributed it to the extra hike down the slope in order to get to her.

Slightly out of breath, he offered his usual opening line as he slid into position beside her. "Nice painting."

"Thanks." She wiped her hands on the thighs of her jeans, already spotted with colourful testaments to the day's work.

"You're a little off the beaten path today," he observed. "Trying to hide from me?"

"You certainly couldn't hide from anybody on that noisy thing." She smiled over at him, whisking a strand of hair off her cheek as it whipped about her face.

His breath caught in his throat. For a millisecond he had the strongest urge to bend down and kiss her right there on the spot. Before he could act on it, a grunt registered in his ears and the hair on the back of his neck bristled. It was an unmistakable pig-like snort... only it wasn't a pig.

"Sh!" Will put a finger to his lips as he barely made the sound. "Don't move."

Ten yards away a black bear rose up on its hind legs and sniffed.

Marigold reached out to grab hold of Will's forearm and they stood like statues for several eternal seconds. Then the bear thumped down on its front feet and lumbered away.

"I told you it was dangerous out here alone," Will said, still using a hushed voice. "What if it woulda been a grizzly?"

"I have a flare." She laughed nervously. "But I've never had to use it. I might forget how."

"And I don't even have that," Will said with a shake of his head. "Left it on the quad. Pretty careless of me."

"I'll say. My father won't be happy to hear his favourite employee almost got himself eaten by a bear. What would you have done if it hadn't just taken off?"

"Put my arms out and made myself bigger like this so he thinks I'm bigger than he is." Will demonstrated by raising his arms in a hulking fashion. Then he dropped them and turned toward Marigold, his brow in a furrowed line. "What did you just say? About your father, I mean?"

"That he likes you. A lot. Never heard him sing the praises of someone like he does about you."

"Hm." Will looked out at the lengthening shadows creeping over the mountain in front of them. "That's what I thought you said. So you're the boss's daughter…"

"You didn't know?" She looked genuinely surprised. "I thought he'd sent you out on purpose to keep an eye on me."

Will shook his head. "No clue."

"And if you had known, would you have tried to kiss me earlier?" She smiled coyly up at him and he grinned in response.

"No clue about that one either, although I may have thought better of it. I don't want to get fired."

"Then let's pretend you didn't know." She tilted her chin up, challenging him to kiss her now, if he dared.

He didn't need to be asked twice. Their lips came together with the smoothness of vanilla pudding; a swirling of toffee and honey and all things sweet.

She pulled away suddenly, taking a step back as he released his hold of her arms. Her chest rose in little huffs and she licked her lips - those tantalizing lips - and habitually whisked a strand of hair from her cheek. "I think I'll take that ride back to camp tonight. I'm not sure my legs will carry me after that bear scare."

"The bear scare is it?" He smiled and lifted a brow.

"Yes, the bear scare. You don't think one little kiss from a lumberjack like you would make me unable to walk straight."

"A lumberjack! While I'll be stun! Been called a lot of things but never that." They were back to fencing with words, which was probably for the best. At least for now.

Marigold was already busy packing up her painting gear. "Don't tell me. I'm sure my ears would burst." She bent over, her jeans tightening around her hips.

Will shook his head to clear his thoughts from running rampant. "Need a hand?"

"I'm fine." She folded the telescoping legs of her easel into themselves. "I have a system and you'd just get in the way."

"We lumberjacks do that."

"Precisely." She stood erect, all her gear either inside or attached to one compact backpack. "Ready."

He offered her his hand and they climbed the hill together, steadying one another in their ascent. He was loath to let go but it seemed awkward to hang on once they'd reached the quad. "Your chariot, m'lady."

She surveyed the rugged machine with dubious eyes. "I suppose I'm not really contributing to global warming since you were going to have to ride it back anyway…"

"Get on or I'll leave your arse to the bears." Will was already on the quad, revving it to life.

She did as she was told, grasping him firmly around the middle with both arms.

"Hang on!" With a jump forward, Will let it rip. There was nothing like speed - and a pretty woman hanging on for dear life - to boost a man's self-esteem.

"So this is where you hide when you're not painting on the hill." Will stood with hands on hips outside what he mistook for a garden shed behind the main house.

Marigold was outside, a pitcher of water with paint brushes in it in her hands. "It's my summer studio. There's no water and no heat, so I only use it in the summer."

"What do you do the rest of the year?"

"I'm part of an artists' co-op in the city. We share the studio space and I have an apartment there, too. But I find it's so much more inspiring here. Plus I can help my parents out if they need me. Give Mom a break running the office so she can make meals for guys like you." She smiled.

"Much appreciated. Your ma's a good cook."

She nodded. "Well, maybe I'll see you later when you do your rounds."

Will frowned. "You're going back there? Even after yesterday?"

She tucked a strand of hair behind her ear. "Of course. I've been going there for years. I'm not stopping now."

"But -"

"No buts about it. It's time we humans learned to coexist with our fellow creatures. That bear has more right to that hill than I do."

"You should take a gun," Will said.

"I have my bells, remember? And my flare." She smiled. "I got Buck to show me how it works again, just in case. I'll be fine." She turned to enter the small shed.

"Wait! Can I see what you're working on?" Will asked.

"Absolutely not!"

He blinked, surprised at the force in her voice.

Her countenance softened. "It's just this thing I do. Not let anyone see a painting before it's finished."

"I saw your paintings on the hill. All of 'em."

"Those aren't finished paintings," she explained, as if to a child. "Those are sketches for paintings."

"Oh." He looked down at his work boots.

"If you want to see my finished paintings you'll have to come to my next show."

"When is that?"

"It'll be up for a month at this nice little coffee shop downtown called The Brew. The owners are very good about letting local artists show their work. This Saturday is the grand opening of their newly renovated space and they've asked me to be part of it."

"This Saturday, eh?" Will rubbed his chin.

"Of course, I wouldn't expect you to be there for the opening since you have to work. My own folks aren't going until the following week. But you can go some other time. It'll be there for a whole month."

"You're probably right. Well, I better get back to work. Those weeds aren't gonna whack themselves. Good luck this Saturday." Will waved and headed back toward the machine shed.

His mind was anywhere but on the grass and weeds that needed to be trimmed around the buildings. It involved thinking of a way to get Saturday off so he could surprise Marigold. He hoped his status as the boss's favourite worker was strong enough to pull it off.

"This is the first time you've taken me up on staying over since you started work," Bo said to Will. "What's the occasion?" He slung a white towel over his shoulder and leaned on the counter.

Will picked at the label on his bottle of beer. "I've got a little… thing I want to attend tomorrow."

"A thing," Bo repeated, his tone laced with sarcasm.

Will sat up straighter. "Ya, a thing. None of your business is more like it."

Bo shrugged. "Just as well. I have a 'thing' I'm going to tomorrow, too."

Will nodded. "Good. Then it's settled."

"Why so mysterious?" Bo asked.

"Not being mysterious," Will hedged. "Say… you ever heard of a place downtown called The Brew?"

Bo's eyebrows rose a notch. "Sure. That's where I'm going tomorrow, with Jed. It's the grand opening of their newly renovated place. Lots of people we know will be there."

Will frowned. "You don't say."

"Don't tell me that's the 'thing' you were talking about?"

Will nodded. "It so happens I know the artist whose work is going to be shown there."

"You don't say," Bo repeated Will's words. "This artist wouldn't happen to be a female, would she?"

"Maybe." Will grinned in spite of himself. "Make sure not to invite Pip." He was kidding of course, but it did irk that he wasn't going to be able to surprise Marigold without the whole family witnessing it.

"I doubt he'll be there. He's laying low these days, especially around certain people. Patsi Tibbett works there, and Lester's girlfriend's brother, Sherman Chan, drew up the reno plans, so they'll probably all be there, too."

"Poor kid. I should stop in and see 'im before I head back to camp tomorrow evening."

"Pip's a big boy," Bo said. He apparently wasn't too sympathetic toward his younger brother's self-inflicted seclusion.

Will surveyed Bo out of the corner of his eye. "Don't you think it's time you buried the hatchet? Brothers shouldn't stay mad at one another so long. It's not natural."

Bo just shrugged. "I'm done being the mediator in this family. It's more trouble than it's worth since no one listens anyway. The job's open if you want it."

"I can't believe the steadiest one of the bunch has become such a cynic," Will said. "Moving out west hasn't done you no favours."

"Maybe not, but I'm not moving back either. Just looking out for myself these days, that's all."

Will shook his head and finished his beer. He was no mediator, like Bo, but one of these days he was going to have a heart to heart with each and every one of his siblings. He normally just ignored the drama and went fishing instead, but this was getting out of hand. Right after the art show, the next time he got time off, he was going to figure out what to do about it.

THE BREW, a trendy coffee shop in downtown Calgary, was nestled under the shadow of the surrounding high-rises, and apparently had all kinds of connections to Jed and his group of friends - or so Jed tried to explain on the way over. "The place is owned by a real pair of lookers. Course, don't tell 'em I said so," Jed said. "Carmen goes with Sherman Chan, Lester's girlfriend Sherri's brother. He's also the architect who designed the building we've been workin' on. Then there's Tamara. She lives in my building. And of course, Lester's sister Patsi works there, too."

Will nodded. "Bo told me."

"Did 'e tell you they make the best pastrami sandwiches in the city?" Jed asked, craning his neck around to look at Will in the back seat.

Bo chuckled, making eye contact with Will in the rearview mirror as he drove. "I think I missed that detail." They were driving together to the grand opening since the parking downtown was sure to be a nightmare.

"I'm still surprised that Reba didn't come. Pip I can understand, but I thought Reba and Patsi were good friends." Jed shook his head.

"Maybe she still finds it awkward," Bo said.

"Dare I ask?" Will leaned a forearm on the headrest in front of him.

"Long version or short?" Bo asked.

"Short," Will said.

"Reba was caught coming on to Pat's ex and Pat still has feelings for him. Then Pat wanted to date Pip, which he obliged, which made Reba mad cause of all the baggage with Brianna -"

Will interrupted with a smile. "Ah... Brianna."

Bo grinned. "Yes, Brianna."

"Who's Brianna?" Jed asked.

"Just a girl from back home," Will supplied. "After you'd already left." He turned back to Bo. "So, go on."

"Anyway, Reba thought it was that whole scene over again," Bo continued, "which isn't far off because now she and Pat had a falling out when Pip ditched Pat for Viann. Oh, and then ditched Viann for Ophelia. I think that pretty much sums it up."

"You're bein' a bit hard on the b'y," Jed said. "I think 'e feels right bad about the mix-up, and according to 'im, it was Patsi's idea to pretend to date in order to make the other fella jealous."

"I can't believe you're sticking up for him," Bo said. "Although I suppose you get to hear his sob stories often enough, it's bound to affect your grasp on reality." His speech started to thicken, as it often did when he got upset.

"He's hurting but good over that last one, too, b'y! If truth be told, he's a sorry mess after she up and went back to California without so much as a good-bye."

"One night with Pip made 'er come to 'er senses," Bo said.

Jed shook his head. "I'm not sayin' he's without fault, but I think it's time we let 'im be. Reba's made 'er own bed, too, as far as I can tell." Jed gave Bo's profile a sober once over. "As did you, I reckon. Can't blame nobody but yourself if things didn't turn out the way you wanted with Jacques's sister."

"Says the sage who can't make up 'is own mind about what 'e wants in a woman," Bo said under his breath.

"Okay, that's enough friendly chit-chat for one day," Will interjected. "Once we get there I want you two to behave. Got it?"

The atmosphere in the vehicle remained strained for another few minutes until they arrived at their destination. Bo parked half a block up from the entrance and the fresh air did them all good as they walked toward the sandwich board on the sidewalk that announced the grand opening.

The interior was warm and intimate despite the ample seating and high ceilings. Most of the tables were occupied, the hum of conversation blending with a backdrop of soft jazz created a cocoon of sound that enveloped the soul. Other people milled around the outer perimeter, coffee mugs in hand, as they perused the art that was hanging on the walls. Based on Jed's description, Tamara Spence was working behind the counter, her long dark hair and exotic First Nations' features making her a striking woman by anyone's standards. Patsi Tibbett was beside her and greeted them with a friendly wave when they walked through the doors.

He'd never been to the coffee shop before so had nothing to compare it to, but he supposed the newly renovated section was off to the left, where a small step up led through wide open French doors into another part of the establishment. Jed had already made his way to where Lester and Sherri stood. Another man of Chinese descent was also standing with them along with a lovely woman with dark skin and dancing earrings. He supposed that must be Sherman and Carmen, whom Jed had spoken of in the car on the way over.

Besides them he didn't recognize anyone else. The person he really wanted to see wasn't in sight. Maybe she was on the other side of the French doors.

He started in that direction but got waylaid by a hand on the arm. "Free coffee today." It was Patsi Tibbett. "Lattes, house blend, whatever you want. Can I get you something?"

"Um... just a bottle of water, I guess. I don't drink coffee as a rule."

"We don't do bottled water here. The plastic bottles are so bad for the environment. But we do use a reverse osmosis filtration system, so I can get you one of those."

"That's okay. I just came to look at the art."

"Then go right ahead." She gestured to the walls. "There's some really nice work as far as I can tell."

Will glanced around the room. As far as he could tell they didn't look anything like Marigold's work. He cleared his throat. "Can you tell me if you have any paintings by Marigold Reynolds?"

"I know there's more in the new part. Why not take a look?" She smiled again and then turned to greet another customer who had just come in.

Will stepped into the newer section and surveyed the room. It was just as packed but still no Marigold in sight. Then he glanced to the walls and his heart took a leap. He recognized that scenery, although there was something different about it, too.

He strode to the nearest painting and then blinked as the subject came into focus. In the foreground was a bright meadow sprinkled with colourful flowers and lush grass. A woman dressed in a peasant style dress was picking some of the flowers, a pleasant smile on her face. In the background was the rugged mountain scenery he had seen Marigold painting so often. But as his eye was drawn deeper into the image, he noticed that some of the flowers were dark and

lifeless, taking on a grotesqueness of shape that made him feel
unsettled. Along the horizon the mountain morphed in places to
become the silhouette of a factory with smoke billowing out of its
stacks.

He was so absorbed in the imagery that he jumped when someone
touched his arm.

"What are you doing here?" Marigold's tone, although hushed,
seemed pleased.

He smiled. "Surprise! I wanted to come and see for myself, so I got
the day off." He drank in the sight of her, dressed as she was in a
bohemian print dress with a large orange flower in her hair.

"I can't believe you managed it on a Saturday. What did you do?"

"I have my ways." If the truth be told, he'd promised Buck he'd
clean the septic tank alone next time if Buck would vouch for him and
say he had business in the city that couldn't wait. It was true, in a way.
This was important business, at least in Will's mind.

Marigold's gaze went to the painting. "So? What do you think?"

"It's... very intriguing," he said, not quite sure how else to describe
it. "What are you trying to say exactly?" he ventured.

She blinked and then gave him an unbelieving look. "That pollu-
tion is poisoning our planet."

"Oh. Of course. That's what I thought."

"Do you like it?"

He nodded. "Sure. It's just... different than I thought it'd be. Not
as... pretty."

"Art doesn't have to be pretty. It's about the message. Come on. I'll
show you."

They spent the next half hour looking at the pieces that Marigold
had brought with her - five in all. Each one had a social or political
message hidden within the landscape. He never knew art could be so
deep - or so exhausting to look at. He was just happy to bask in her
company, never mind hear about the paintings, as skillfully rendered
as each one was.

"So this is where you got to." It was Jed, coming up behind them,
and as usual, speaking a decibel louder than convention dictated.

"What I don't get is how you can paint a perfectly nice piece of God's green earth and then spoil it with all that nastiness."

Will saw Marigold's back stiffen and he quickly intervened. "Jed, this is the artist, Marigold Reynolds. And this is my brother Jed." He added in a staged whisper, " Don't mind 'im. He's known for speaking before 'e thinks."

"Nice to meet you," Jed said, not embarrassed one whit by what he had said earlier. "You're a pretty thing for 'aving such a dark outlook on life. Are you depressed?"

"The world can be a dark place," she responded, her chin tilted in defiance. "Life isn't a bed of roses."

"Now if that ain't the truth and I knows it. But it's enough I gotta live it without lookin' at it in pictures, too."

"Somebody has to speak out. Industry is ruining our planet and I won't wait on the sidelines while it happens."

"Industry is what heats your 'house and provides electricity. Lard tunderin'! All these Greenpeacers 'aven't a clue when it comes to -"

"That's enough," Will interrupted. "I didn't come here to listen to you get ornery or to talk disrespect."

"Am I missing out on the fun?" Bo had just joined them as well.

"I was just sayin' -" Jed started.

"He was just sayin' he was about to go somewheres else," Will said.

Bo raised a brow and looked at Jed.

Jed just shrugged. "Nice meetin' ya, anyway." They watched him walk away back through the French doors.

Once he was gone, Bo stuck out his hand. "I'm Bo, the nicer brother."

Marigold looked quickly at Will and then back at Bo. "You brought the whole family?"

Will rubbed the back of his neck. "Not exactly. There's six more of us, but these are the only two that tagged along."

"I didn't tag along," Bo said. "If I recall, I told you I was coming here long before you even knew the place existed." He turned to Marigold and smiled. "I didn't get your name. Probably because my dumb brother didn't introduce us properly."

A smile tugged at the corners of her mouth. "Marigold. Marigold Reynolds."

"Pleased to meet you Marigold Reynolds. And for the record, I think your paintings have a much needed social conscience. They're very direct and express the times we live in to a 'T'."

"Why thank you." Marigold smiled up at Bo.

For a moment Will felt a bolt of jealousy, but then when Bo flashed him a smile, he relaxed. "When in tarnation did you become an art critic?"

"It's because I read," Bo said. "You should try it sometime."

WILL GOT a ride back to the campground later that afternoon with Bo, but he didn't see Marigold for another three days. Apparently she had some work to do in the city and stayed at her apartment. When he did finally see her again, it was outside her studio shed. It was late evening and she had just shut the door behind her, while he was heading to his bunkhouse. It was a warm night - the warmest he'd experienced since moving west, and a few threads of lightning flashed across the sky, illuminating the tree tops.

"Back to work already?" he asked. "I thought you'd take a day or two off."

She shrugged. "I just had something in my head that I had to get on canvas. But it's getting too dark now. The shadows aren't good, so it'll have to wait until tomorrow."

Will inhaled deeply. "Feels like a storm is brewing."

"I love storms. Especially in summer. They're so full of raw energy. It makes me want to stay out in it and paint."

"You should see the doozies we get back home in Newfoundland." He whistled under his breath. "Now there's a sight!"

"I've often wanted to visit Newfoundland. I hear it's very beautiful."

"Wild and rugged." He grinned. "Like some of the folks. Sorry about my brother, Jed. He actually has a good heart. He just says what's on 'is mind is all."

"I've had worse criticism," Marigold said and waved a hand dismissively. "I liked your brother, Bo, though."

"Who knew he could be such a charmer?" Will said and laughed.

The lighting flashed again and this time thunder followed close behind.

"We best be getting inside," Will said.

"No, let's stay out and experience it!" Marigold opened her arms wide and turned her face to the sky in readiness for the rain that had just started to sputter down.

"You're a crazy woman, you know that?"

"So I've been told." She grinned up at him.

"Come on!" He grabbed her by the hand and pulled her toward her studio. Before she could protest he'd shoved the door in on itself and pulled her inside out of the rain, which had started in earnest now.

"No. I don't want you to -"

"I already saw your paintings in town, remember?" He smiled at her silliness and turned to have a look around the room. He could just make out the shadows of some shelves and an easel with a large painting propped on it. It was too dark to see what was painted on its surface, however.

"No, I think we should go," she said, her voice a little more urgent now. She grabbed his hand and pulled him toward the door.

"It's raining cats and dogs out there. Besides, it's pitch dark and I can't see a blasted thing anyway."

A clap of thunder accompanied by instantaneous lighting illuminated the small space. In those few seconds he saw what was on the canvas.

"It's... um. Is that me?" He hadn't really needed to ask. His own likeness, slouched against the quad with arms crossed, had stared back at him.

"It's not finished," she said, breathless.

"But, it is me, right?"

He saw her head bob in the dark.

"Is that what you couldn't get out of your head?"

She nodded again.

He took a step closer, the air suddenly crackling with more than just charged electrons from the storm. The urge to kiss her was strong - stronger than any common sense he may or may not have possessed. "May I?" he asked, his voice a hoarse whisper.

When she nodded a third time he took her mouth with all the force he'd been holding at bay for all these weeks and she met him with just as much urgency.

The pulse pounding in his ears drowned out the rain pelting the roof. They crashed in time against the door frame with the next roar of thunder and then slid to the rough wooden floor.

Outside, the storm raged, the perfect metaphor for what was happening in the tiny shed.

EPISODE 6

NEIGHBOURHOOD CUPID

*EB*

ZEB LOOKED out the window of the turbo prop airplane as it circled
the sprawling city of Calgary, Alberta. He worked a 'fourteen and
seven' schedule in the oil sands in the northern city of Fort McMurray
and sometimes he just needed to get away on his days off. It would
have been cheaper for him to drive to Calgary, but it took at least
eight hours on a good day and he didn't want to waste any time on his
week off from work.

Most of the time he stayed put, often fishing or hunting in the
warmer weather and snowmobiling in the cold months. There was
usually a fair bit of partying, too. But sometimes he just needed to get
away for a while and Calgary was his usual choice since his eldest
brother Jed lived in that city. Actually, several of his siblings lived
there now, having recently moved from their home province of
Newfoundland. He knew his parents - especially his mother - weren't
too happy about it, but kids grew up and had to live their own lives.

One of these days he would take a flight back home to the east coast, but not this time.

His younger brother Will was entered in a bull riding competition on the weekend at a local watering hole and Zeb didn't want to miss it. Will had been dubbed the daredevil of the clan, although Zeb recalled from their childhood that most of Will's adventures had been inflicted by either himself or Jed. Poor young bugger.

Zeb stroked his shaggy red beard and smiled. He was looking forward to the visit. He hadn't seen the gang in a couple of months and it was high time the Malloy clan got together again. It was sure to be a rocking good time.

The light aircraft sped toward the ground and hit the tarmac with a bump followed by a whoosh as it slowed to a stop. He fished for his cell phone in his jacket pocket and disabled 'flight mode' so he could call a cab. Normally he'd call Jed for a ride, but his arrival was a surprise and he wanted to keep it that way. He could hardly wait to see the look on Jed's face.

"LARD TUNDERIN'!" Jed stood wide mouthed at the door to his apartment. "What the…? Why didn't you call for a ride?"

"You gonna let me in or what?" Zeb asked, a grin splitting his beard.

"Ya big lummox!" Jed swallowed Zeb in a bear-hug followed by several slaps on the back - their usual greeting.

Once out of Jed's grip, Zeb pushed past his brother and then dumped his duffle bag unceremoniously in the hallway leading off the living room. He peered around the room, noting a few dirty dishes and beer cans on the floor near Jed's favourite chair. "Do I get the spare bed this time or is it the couch? I can never keep track of the strays you keep."

"The place has been a regular flop house, that's for sure," Jed said. "But it's just me and Pip now, so I guess you can take the couch."

"I'm surprised you're here and not down at the Urban Cowboy,"

Zeb said. He took his cell phone out of his back pocket and consulted the time. "It's only nine o'clock. Right early for a lush like you."

"Tryin' to slow down," Jed said. "Sides, it's a work night."

"As I recall that never stopped you before."

"Tryin' to be a better influence on the young 'uns."

"Ha! That'll be the day."

"Can't fault a man for tryin'." Jed grinned. "But now that you're here, how's about a beer?"

"I thought you'd never ask."

Zeb settled himself on the couch while Jed went to the kitchen and cracked open two beer. He returned and handed one of the cans to Zeb, and then sat down across from him in his easy chair.

"Where's Pip at?" Zeb asked before taking a long swig. It went down smooth as silk and he smacked his lips.

"Not sure. He's in a bad way these days," Jed said.

Zeb frowned. "Bad way how?"

Jed shrugged. "Female troubles, mostly."

"Got bit by the love bug, or what?"

"Maybe. He's been right rotted the last little while, not to mention he's in Lester's bad books as well as Jacques's."

"What he do?" Zeb asked.

"Two timing with both their sisters."

"Patsi Mae?" Zeb asked. He remembered Jed's cowboy friend Lester and his little sister Patsi, and the fact that she had just moved home.

Jed nodded. "I told 'im he was nut jiggered to mess with 'er in the first place, but Pip doesn't listen too well."

Zeb grinned. "That's our Pip. And who's the other one?"

"Jacques, the bartender from the Urban Cowboy?"

"Right, right."

"His sister Viann is visiting from Montreal. Then there was some other girl who I never met who has connections with those McMillans from that Nudara Oil scandal. Pip hasn't been the same since she took off back to California. But then again, not sure what he was thinkin', tryin' to keep 'em all on a tether at one time."

"Just sowin' his wild oats, I guess. You and I done the same once upon a time." Zeb guzzled from his can of beer.

"I never had three at once!" Jed declared.

Zeb's smile was smug. "No? Your loss." He burst into full on laughter a few seconds later at the look of outrage on Jed's face.

"Jumpin' Jehoshaphat! The last thing I need is you comin' around puttin' notions in the boy's head!"

"Seems to me he already gots the notion," Zeb said with a raised brow.

Jed was about to bluster again but let out a deep sigh instead. "I expect you're right. I just hate it when the family is turned topsy-turvey."

Zeb shook his head. "My, but that sounds old! Next you'll be checkin' into the old folks' home!"

"Can I help it since everyone of 'em has landed on my doorstep? It's a worry and no mistake." Jed looked over at Zeb. "And you're not far behind, neither."

"Me? What ya talkin'?" Zeb waved a dismissive hand.

"You're nearly as old as me."

"So?" Zeb crushed his beer can and threw it near Jed's head. Jed ducked and it landed on the floor with the others. "Sounds like you're forgettin' what it is to be young and free. Let 'em be."

Jed emptied his own can of beer and set it beside his chair. "I swear the girls are gettin' younger every day."

"Sounds good to me." Zeb stretched out his legs and put his hands behind his head.

Jed frowned. "Soon there won't be any good ones left and the young ones won't be interested in old beggars like us."

"Is that what we're talkin' about, now? Your sorry arse love life takin' a nose dive?"

Jed shrugged. "I don't know. Maybe. Sometimes I feel as old as Methuselah."

"You need a change of scenery, b'y. You're right depressing." Zeb surveyed his brother beneath narrowed lids. "You and Crystal still an item?"

"Nah. Broke it off." Jed sighed. "She was gettin' too demandin'. Wanted more than I was willing to give."

"See? You're still yourself after all."

"Not completely happy about it, though."

"Why?"

Jed rubbed the top of his head so that his hair stood on end. "Not sure. Maybe I'm lonely. Sometimes I see my life stretching out before me and it all looks the same." Jed looked to Zeb with a pointed stare. "And don't you go blabbin', neither. I've only admitted it to you and not a soul other."

"So you think you might be ready to settle down, then?" Zeb asked.

"If the right girl comes along, maybe."

"Got anyone in mind?"

"That's as far as I go, b'y. You won't get another word outta me." Jed slapped his knees and then stood up.

"Hm. Well, this bachelor ain't never gonna change. You can count on that."

Jed shook his head as if he weren't convinced. "Whatever. I'm about to hit the hay, anyway. Nice chatting. Make yourself homely. There's more beer in the fridge."

"Okay. What time do you expect Pip?"

"Lard only knows," Jed replied. "Say, you wanna meet for lunch tomorrow? Tomorrow's Friday and sometimes me and some of the others go to this little coffee shop for lunch. I'm payin'."

"Then for sure it's a go," Zeb said.

Jed excused himself and Zeb swung his legs up on the couch to get more comfortable. He flipped on the TV and scanned through the channels for something interesting enough to keep him awake until Pip got home. The sports broadcast flitted from highlight reel to highlight reel and Zeb felt his eyes drooping as he stroked his beard.

Perhaps his older brother really was reaching an age when he longed to settle down. Or maybe it was just the beer talking. He'd noticed Jed had already had a few when he arrived. Drinking alone wasn't a good sign.

As for himself, he was staying free and single for the long haul. There was no question about it.

~

ZEB STEPPED across the threshold and immediately inhaled the deepest breath he could muster. The Brew, the downtown coffee shop where he was meeting Jed and Pip for lunch, smelled like heaven - a mixture of rich coffee and fresh baking that hit him in the nose and reminded him that he hadn't eaten anything yet that day.

When he opened his eyes, he saw that there was a mixture of high tables, comfy chairs with coffee tables, and some regular kind, but most of the latter were already occupied. A slight frown marred his features. He didn't really like those fancy low ones - or the high ones either. He liked sitting up to a regular table to eat.

"Can I help you?"

Zeb looked up and instantly recognized the blonde haired girl behind the counter. He smiled broadly and strode her way. "Patsi Tibbett, right?"

"Yes! You remembered. You're Jed's brother. I recognized you the minute you walked in."

"Nice place." Zeb glanced around. He noticed a pair of other women working as well - one with dark skin and the other First Nations, but both very attractive. The owners, if he remembered correctly. "Jed talks about it a lot. Hope he knows what he's talkin' about."

"I guess you'll find out. So… What can I get for you? When you came in you looked kind of lost."

"I'm meeting Jed and Pip for lunch. Got any regular seats?"

"Oh." Her tone didn't quite match the bright smile on her face. "Why don't you try the new part. I'll tell them where you are when they get here."

She gestured to some French doors and he nodded his thanks before heading that way.

"Can I bring you a coffee while you wait?" Patsi called after him.

He gave her the thumbs up before stepping into the newly renovated part of the establishment. He found a seat and Patsi brought him a steaming mug of coffee and a laminated menu. It was only a few minutes later that Jed joined him.

"Where's Pip?" Zeb asked as Jed got himself situated.

"Doesn't like showing 'is face here," Jed said. "Remember? I told you about it last night."

Zeb's bushy brows descended over his eyes. "I don't recall."

"Pip and Patsi? One of his conquests?"

"Oh! That!" Zeb nodded. "Now I remember. How's that been for youse at work? Lester and you and Pip all working for the same outfit?"

"It's been a strain all around, I won't lie," Jed replied. "But Lester's a good sort. He don't hold nothin' against me. It's his sister he's most worried about." Jed looked around the table as if he'd just noticed something was missing. "And why isn't Bo here? I thought you was going to ask 'im to join us?"

"I did. The first thing outta his mouth was, 'Is Pip coming?' I told him, 'Yes,' since I thought he was, and low and behold if he didn't say he was busy and couldn't come." Zeb shook his head. "I'm beginning to see what you meant about topsy-turvy. I had no idea things were actually this bad between them."

"Oh, it's bad, alright. Reba's nose is outta joint, too. Mad at both of 'em, but especially Pip, and even our Will's gone and got himself tangled up with some strange artist type."

Zeb's eyes widened. "Will, you say? G'wan!"

"Yes, b'y!" Jed gestured to some of the art hanging on the walls of the cafe. "See dat? Will's artsy-fartsy girl painted the disturbing ones."

Zeb squinted at the nearest painting. "Looks alright to me."

"Not that one, ya stun! Look behind ya!"

Zeb swung around in his seat and perused the painting for a few minutes. "Looks like mountains."

"Look closer."

Zeb squinted again and then opened his eyes wide. "Oh! Is that a skull hidden in the smoke? Cool!"

Jed shook his head and let out a disgusted sigh. "Never mind. She's a gatch, that one. Thinks she's all that, and then some."

"I guess as long as Will likes 'er," Zeb offered.

"He's close lipped, our Will. Been to town to practice on the bull but there's nary a word about the girl. Marigold's 'er name, if I recall."

"He coming into town tonight or tomorrow?" Zeb asked.

"Tomorrow in time for the contest. Had to wrangle a few things to get the time off, being as tourist season's about to begin in earnest."

"I see." Zeb nodded. He did see. His whole family was in need of a psychiatrist as far as he could tell.

"Now, how about we order some pastrami sandwiches? They make the best there is."

"Go for it - since you're payin'."

They both laughed.

ZEB WAITED outside Bo's apartment complex for Bo to buzz the entrance and let him in. If Bo wasn't going to come and see him, then he was going to see Bo - and maybe get to the bottom of all the family drama that was causing so much commotion.

Once inside, he took the elevator to the correct floor and then knocked soundly on Bo's apartment door. Bo was right there to open it after only one rap.

They did the usual hug and slap routine, and then Bo ushered Zeb into the living room. It was sparse to say the least, with only one couch, a few shelves made of crates, and no TV in sight. "Livin' the life of a monk, I see?" Zeb said, looking around.

"It'll come. I'm not into a lot of stuff."

"Got any beer?" Zeb asked.

"Not at the moment. I see enough alcohol at work."

"Hmph." Zeb grunted and sat down on the couch. Bo lowered himself beside him.

There was a moment of awkward silence before Bo spoke up. "I suppose you're wondering what's going on between Pip and me."

"The thought crossed my mind."

"It's nothing, really. I was mad at him for a while but I'm over it now. I really was busy this morning when you called and couldn't make it."

"Is that so?"

"You don't sound convinced."

"So, convince me." Zeb sat back and stretched his considerable length out in front of him, crossing his arms over his chest and waiting.

Bo took a deep breath and then sat back as well, mirroring Zeb's posture. "I might as well start at the beginning. I have - *I had* - feelings for this girl that I had no right to feel. So, when Pip seemed interested in her I got jealous, which was stupid since she doesn't return my feelings anyway and probably never will. The part that I really don't like is that he and Reba were using her to get what they wanted."

"Using her how?" Zeb asked.

"Reba's crazy over Cory, the owner of the Urban Cowboy, but he seems interested in Viann as well."

"Viann. That's 'er name?" Zeb asked.

"Yes."

Zeb nodded. "Jacques's sister?"

Bo turned his head to look directly at Zeb. "I see you already know all the details. Jed, no doubt?"

"Go on. I wanna hear your side of things."

"And Angela, Jacques's girlfriend at the time, was jealous of Viann -"

Zeb interrupted. "Of his own sister? That's sick."

"They're step brother and sister," Bo explained. "So, Angela was jealous, and Reba wanted her out of the way, so Pip offered to use his charms on Viann and solve both their problems. According to Jed, Pip says he just wanted to make things right between him and Reba, since she was mad at him for a bunch of stuff from the past, including coming between her and her friend Pat Tibbett."

"Patsi Mae," Zeb said absently.

"Yes. You know this part, too?"

"Not really. What's she got to do with it?"

"Pat thought Reba was coming on to her ex-boyfriend - which she probably was - and was mad about it cause she still likes him, apparently. Not sure what that has to do with Pip except that he was also pretending to date Pat to make the other guy jealous."

Zeb furrowed his brows. "I'm getting confused. This is a sorry mess as far as I can see, and very high school."

"I agree, which is why I'm not mad at Pip anymore."

"So why wouldn't you come out for lunch today?"

"I'm getting to that," Bo answered. "So, Pip said he was trying to make it up with Reba by getting Viann out of the way. But then Jacques found out and banned them both from the Urban Cowboy."

"He what?" Zeb's voice rose a notch. "Now that doesn't seem fair."

"I know, and he hasn't really enforced it. Reba still comes once in a while, but she lays low. Pip on the other hand, hasn't shown his face since the night Jacques kicked him out. Jed says he's really depressed. Won't talk, won't go to the Urban Cowboy, goes off on his own who knows where."

"Have you talked to 'im?" Zeb asked. "Told 'im you're not mad at 'im anymore? He'd listen to you."

Bo sighed. "Not sure anyone will listen to me anymore. To be honest, I'm tired of trying to figure out everyone else's problems. I've got enough on my own plate without carrying theirs, too."

"Hm." Zeb rubbed his beard. "You still haven't told me what was so all-fire important that you couldn't come for lunch."

"Will had texted me that he needed to talk. His only time was right at lunch."

"And what's up with Will?"

"Not sure I should tell. You can ask him yourself when you see him tomorrow."

Zeb sat up straight and stretched. "All this drama. Seems to me there's a simple solution to all of your problems."

"And what would that be?"

"Youse all need to get laid."

Bo snorted. "Why am I not surprised? That's your solution to everything."

"I'm no psychiatrist, but all this lovesickness needs an outlet. Just sayin' is all. It's kept me free of it for - oh, for a long time, now."

Bo shook his head. "If it was that simple, why hasn't it been working for Jed?"

"That I haven't figured out yet." Zeb glanced at Bo. "You know anything about the one he's pinin' after?"

"Maybe. Her name's Andrea Carravagio, one of the hairdressers where Reba works."

"And?"

"I think she likes him, too, judging by the way she looks at him when she thinks no one else is looking. But she's religious and won't go out with him on account of it. Not to mention the fact that he drinks way too much these days. I'm worried. I think he needs help."

"And the sister - what's her name? She used to go with the French bartender but they broke it off, you say?"

"Angela, and yes. Did I say that?" Bo looked up quizzically.

"Somewhere back there."

"You're actually a better listener than I gave you credit for," Bo said with a laugh.

"Don't you worry. Long before you got labeled the family go-between, I was gettin' Jed outta scrapes you know nothing about."

"Are you sure you weren't the cause of them?"

Zeb grinned. "That's neither here nor there!"

A plan was beginning to form in Zeb's mind. He wasn't quite sure what it was or how he would carry it out. All he knew was that this time around, he was coming to the family's rescue. Lord knew he was the only sensible one left.

ZEB SAT on the couch in Jed's living room, drumming his fingers on the armrest. By his calculations, Jed and Pip should be walking through the door any minute.

As if on cue, he heard the lock rattling and then the door creaking on its hinges as it opened. "Anybody home?" Jed called.

"In here," Zeb responded.

"I'm off to take a shower," Jed announced and shuffled down the hallway toward the bathroom.

Pip appeared in the entrance that adjoined the hall and living room. He waved. "Hi, Zeb. Good to see you."

Their eyes held for only a second and then Pip's gaze focused downward.

"What kind a greeting is that?" Zeb hoisted himself from the depths of the couch and opened his arms wide.

He and Pip embraced, slapping one another on the back in typical Malloy fashion. Zeb gave Pip an extra big squeeze which brought an 'Oomph' of air from Pip's solar plexus, before releasing him.

"I saw you on the couch last night when I came in, but I didn't want to disturb you. You were sleeping like a baby."

"Always do," Zeb said. He cocked an eyebrow and sat down at the same time. "Sounds like I'm the only one in the family who does."

Pip rolled one shoulder in a half shrug and turned to go down the hallway.

"Where you think you're goin'?" Zeb called after him. "I wanna talk to you while Jed's in the shower."

Pip came back and stood in the entrance again. "What about?"

"Sit down," Zeb ordered.

Pip silently lowered himself into Jed's armchair, waiting like a teen about to be grilled by an angry father.

"First off, I'm not gonna lecture, so relax, for Ga's sake!"

Pip's shoulders sagged with the gust of breath he expelled.

"Second, I'm not one to give advice since I nary take to it. I just wants to know from your own mouth why you ain't gettin' on with the other members of this family."

"Everyone's mad at me. Even Jed."

"Not without reason, by the sounds of it." Zeb folded his arms across his chest.

"Sure, there's been some mix-ups, but none of it was intentional."

"So explain it. And hurry up about it before Jed gets outta that shower."

Pip sighed, then went on to explain the deal he'd made with Patsi, pretending to be her boyfriend to make her former boyfriend jealous. He talked about Reba, and Cory, and even Viann - pretty much the way that Bo had explained it earlier that day.

"Have you talked to Bo? Or Reba? Apologized?" Zeb asked.

"Why should I apologize? I didn't really do anything -"

Zeb raised a hand to cut him off. "That's your first mistake. Apologizing goes a long way - even if you don't mean it."

"Isn't that a tad hypocritical?" Pip asked.

"Not if it's for the right reasons, which in this case is mending fences with your siblings. Bo talked to me today and he don't harbor no ill feelings. Reba might be a little more tricky since she's stubborn, but she'll come around if I talk to 'er first. I'd even go so far as to try it with the rest of 'em, too. Patsi, Lester, Jacques, Viann…"

"I thought you said you weren't gonna give advice." Pip gave Zeb a sidelong glance and scowled.

"And I also said I rarely take it - even my own." Zeb grinned. "This whole mess is gonna blow over like a Nor'easter. A bit o' damage but in the end, everything is gonna be fine."

"You think?"

"I know it." Zeb rubbed his beard and surveyed his young brother for a moment. "But somethin' tells me this isn't the only thing eatin' at ya. You look as down in the mouth as a dead fisherman's cassock."

"That's one I haven't heard before." Pip smiled.

"Good, cause I just made it up. What's got you so low?"

Pip blinked, focusing on the interlaced fingers lying in his lap.

"G'wan! We don't got all day," Zeb urged.

Pip expelled a deep sigh, a sound much too melancholy for one so young. "I think I bit the big one for real this time."

"Meaning?"

"I'm in love, duffus! What'd ya think I meant?"

"Just checking." Zeb kept rubbing his beard. "And what brings you to that conclusion?"

"It's in here." Pip tapped his chest where his heart was. "And here." He patted his stomach. "I never felt this way before. Like I'm sick, or on pins and needles. And I can't concentrate. All I can think about is 'er."

"Never 'aving felt that way myself, I'm not sure I can relate," Zeb said. "But I hear them's the signs. So which one is she? Young Patsi or Frenchie's sister?"

"Neither."

Zeb furrowed his brows. "Oh right. There's another."

"Her name is Ophelia and she's way outta my league."

"Says who?"

"Says me. Left for California after we… well, we did have a bit of a fling one night, but then she left." He sighed again. "Every time I'm in my room I remember. I'm goin' outta my mind."

"You shouldn't put too much stock in sex," Zeb advised. "Get back on the horse, so to speak, and you'll probably be fine."

Pip scowled at Zeb. "You make it sound like it's the first time I ever done it. I'm no kid. But this time was different somehow. I don't know why, but it just was."

"Sorry. You know what they say. Wait a fair wind and you'll get one."

"Thanks, but it's not working."

"That's cause you haven't given yourself enough time."

"I'm outta time. I might just hop on the next flight to California and see what happens."

"That's a bad idea. Then you look desperate."

"Maybe I am desperate."

Zeb shook his head. "Well, I'm all outta suggestions. I'd say you and Jed make a good pair."

"What do you mean?" Pip asked.

"Two grown men pining for a woman he can't reach."

"Jed told you that?" Pip asked, his expression curious.

"In a manner. Does Jed know all the particulars about… what's 'er name? Ophelia?"

"Not all, I don't think. I certainly didn't tell 'im I brought 'er back here."

"Why not? Jed's a good listener - when you can get 'im to stop talking! He's worried sick about you. About all of you."

"Jed's too much like Pops. I'd be too embarrassed."

"Suit yourself. One thing's certain. You're coming with us to the Urban Cowboy tonight and that's final."

"I... I don't go there much anymore," Pip said.

"I heard. Cause Jacques says you can't." Zeb raised a brow and waited for Pip to deny it.

"Who told you?"

"Bo. And I say it's time we Malloys started stickin' together again, like in the old days. We'll show Frenchie who can and can't come into that bar." They heard Jed coming out of the bathroom. "Now, go shower so you don't scare the ladies away. The brothers are gonna be on the prowl tonight and no mistake."

"Eh, Spitfire! I knew you'd come!" Zeb lifted Reba off her feet and swung her around. Despite her stubborn streak, he had a soft spot for his youngest sister.

Reba gestured with her head to a scowling Jacques who was standing further down the line at the bar. "The place isn't as welcoming as it used to be."

"So I heard."

She sat down on the barstool to Zeb's right. She was the last of the clan to arrive at the Urban Cowboy. Zeb had managed to get her to agree to join them despite the fact that Pip was also coming. They were lined up in a row at the counter in front of Bo's station: Pip, Jed, Zeb and Reba. Zeb and Jed had agreed to purposely make it happen that way to keep some distance between the two youngest ones for the time being.

Bo thunked four steins of beer down in front of his siblings.

"I ordered vodka and water," Pip spoke up.

"Tonight you're drinkin' beer," Bo said. "Boss's orders."

"Who? Him?" Pip glared in Jacques's general direction.

"No, me," Zeb stated. "Hard liquor just makes people ornery and we're here to make up and get along, not start another round of fighting."

Pip sullenly took a sip of his beer but didn't say any more.

"Couldn't a said it better myself," Jed agreed. "It's about time youse made up. Stayin' mad isn't the Malloy way."

Reba rolled her eyes. "Can't we talk about something else?"

"I think Jed's right," Bo said. "I'm sick of the petty fighting. It's time we moved on."

"Petty is it?" Reba sat forward, ready for an argument. "I'd like to know who was being petty besides you."

"Whoa!" Zeb put an arm around Reba's shoulder and squeezed. "That's enough, Spitfire. Bo's trying to apologize for his part in the mess."

"Um… that's right," Bo agreed.

"And now Pip wants to do the same." Zeb flung Pip a meaningful stare. "Right Pip-squeak?"

Pip sighed but nodded. "Right. I'm sorry for all the things I did to make you mad. And all the things I did that I didn't even know I did to make you mad."

"There. See?" Jed's grin was triumphant.

"And…?" Zeb hadn't let go of his sister yet and gave her shoulder another squeeze before doing so.

Reba pursed her lips for a moment and then let out a gust of air. "Oh, alright. I'm sorry for being so crooked contrary. And I forgive Bo for moving into his own place without me." Bo raised his eyebrows. "And I forgive Pip for trying to help me out in his own weird way. I don't forgive 'im for Brianna, though. That I'll never forgive."

"Brianna?" Zeb scrunched his brows.

"After you moved away from home," Bo said.

"That's what he told me, too," Jed offered. He saluted Zeb with his beer stein and took a swig.

"So, what say we play a game of pool for old time's sake? Me and

Spitfire against Jed and Pip?" Zeb looked down the row at Jed and Pip and then back at Reba.

"I haven't had enough beer yet," Reba said.

"G'wan! No bein' contrary again, woman! Bo'll send another round to the tables right quick, eh Bo?" Zeb looked to Bo for affirmation.

"Sure. Whatever you say."

The foursome took their steins and headed to the pool tables. There was a table free, so they claimed it and Jed started racking the balls. They tossed a coin to see who would go first and Jed came up the winner.

"Good luck, b'y," Zeb teased. "Once it's my turn you won't get another."

He and Reba stood to the side as Jed broke the balls with a smash. One of each kind rolled in. "I'll take striped," Jed said and proceeded to make the next shot.

Zeb looked over at Reba, her countenance more quiet than usual. Not the fiery red-headed sister he knew and loved. "What's eatin' ya?"

She shrugged. "Nothing."

"I knows that's a lie, so you might as well tell me."

"It's hard being here with 'im around." She glanced toward the bar.

"You mean Frenchie? I'll tune 'im in if you want, sometime," Zeb offered. "Course, not here, but later on if you like."

"No, not 'im."

Zeb squinted over toward the bar. Cory Roberts was also there, talking animatedly to Jacques. "Oh, you mean that one. He's the one you're sweet on, I take it."

Reba frowned. "Shut yer trap! I don't want no one hearing you."

"Think it's a bit late for that, sis. Rumour has it you been throwing yourself in front of 'im at every turn."

"You're up!" Jed called to Zeb. He passed his cue to Pip and Zeb sauntered forward to take his turn, surveying his options before bending over to take his shot.

Zeb sliced the first ball into the side pocket, but then scratched on the next. He went back to Reba's side as Pip stepped up and handed her his cue. "You want I should tune that Cory fella in, too?" Zeb asked, trying to make a joke of it.

She shook her head. "Not funny. Besides, we all gotta play nice because Will is coming tomorrow for the bull riding tournament. We'd all be out on our ear if you did something like that."

"I wasn't serious," Zeb said. "Geez, Spitfire, you know better than that."

"Reba's turn," Jed called, like an announcer at a tennis match.

She took her turn, doing better than any of her brothers by downing three shots in a row. Finally, Jed was up again.

Reba sighed once back by Zeb's side. "What I really miss is Pat. I don't have any real friends in this city. Andrea's good to me, but Angela hates my guts."

"But she still lets you live with 'er."

"Only because of Andrea. She's real nice, but she doesn't get me."

"And Patsi does?" Zeb asked.

Reba nodded.

"Then why don't you make up with 'er? Seems simple to me."

"It's more complicated than that," Reba said.

"Only cause you're makin' it that way," Zeb replied. He held up a hand when she went to continue. "I heard all about it and it seems to me real friends don't let that kind of B.S. stand between them."

"I don't know…"

"Why not test it out?" Zeb gestured toward the entrance where Patsi was just arriving with her brother Lester and his girlfriend Sherri.

Zeb waved them over and after they got their drinks they headed their way.

"Good to see you again, Zeb," Lester said, shaking Zeb's outstretched hand. "How are you?"

"Best kind," Zeb replied.

Jed made the final shot, sinking the eight ball, and let out a whoop. "Now that's how she's done!"

"Shall we find a table big enough for all of us?" Sherri suggested.

"Sounds good. How about around the corner near that bull contraption?" Zeb asked. "I always wanted to see how it works."

They moved as a collective to the larger section which housed the mechanical bull. The bull was made of leather and metal, shaped like a large barrel with a saddle, stirrups, and a horn in front. It was roped off, with a layer of thick padding on the floor beneath it.

Zeb noticed that Reba and Patsi had not spoken to one another yet, but then it was hard to get a word in with a passle of Malloys around.

Good natured banter continued around the table, some of it to do with tomorrow evening's event.

"Trust Will to want to break 'is neck on that thing," Zeb said with a laugh.

Lester shrugged. "It just takes practice, like anything else."

"I've always wanted to try," Reba said.

"You?" Zeb's brows rose as he looked at his sister.

"Sure. Why not?"

"Come on. I'll teach you." It was Patsi who said it. She pushed her chair back and stood.

"Um…" Reba looked from Patsi to Lester to Zeb and back.

"Maybe you should let Lester," Sherri said.

Patsi dismissed the idea with a wave of her hand. "I've seen him do it a thousand times. I'm as good a teacher as he is. And, he probably never told you that I used to ride in the girls' events."

All eyes turned to Lester. "It's true," he said. "Patsi can probably teach her as good as anybody."

"It's settled then." Patsi reached out a hand to help Reba out of her chair.

Zeb smiled. The two were making up without him even having to interfere.

"First, someone has to go get Cory so he can man the controls," Patsi said.

"Oh, I don't -"

Lester was already up. "On it."

"Jump on," Patsi said.

Reba did and placed her feet in the stirrups. "Now what?"

"Hang onto the reins," Patsi directed. "No, with one hand only, and let the other hand go free for balance. Like this." Patsi demonstrated raising her hand above her head. "Then let your hips do all the work. You'll get the feel of it."

Lester arrived with Cory a moment later. Zeb watched the unspoken exchange of tension between him and Reba, but the other man put on a good facade as he stepped up to the console.

"Just start the darn thing!" Reba said impatiently.

Cory complied and the 'bull' jerked into a slow rock and roll. Reba screamed and clutched at the horn with both hands. In a few seconds she slid off, landing in a slow motion heap on the padded floor.

Zeb and the others let out a whoop.

"That was too fast!" Reba complained as she dusted herself off.

"It's as slow as it goes," Cory said with a laugh.

"You forgot to use your free hand for balance," Patsi said. "Remember?" She demonstrated again.

"Show me," Reba said.

Patsi vaulted onto the bull with ease and Cory started the machine again, still slow, but just slightly faster than he had with Reba.

"You've gotta let your body become one with it," Patsi said as she demonstrated how her body absorbed each rock. "And see how I use my free hand like this? It's to keep your balance."

"Let me try that again," Reba said.

Patsi jumped down as soon as the beast came to a stop and Reba got on again. This time she did better, but she still fell off, even though it wasn't going that fast.

"Good for you, Spitfire. They'll make a right cowgirl outta you yet," Zeb yelled his encouragement.

The evening wore on and Zeb's grasp of reality became a little unsteady. He was just glad that his siblings were together again, happy and smiling. And by the look of it, Reba had made amends with her friend, too. Life didn't get much better.

He told Bo so near closing time, his arm slung around his one sober brother's neck.

"You're drunk. I'm ordering you a cab," Bo said.

"Nah, I'll 'ave one more before I go, b'y!"

"Nope. You're cut off." Bo helped Zeb back around to the proper side of the counter and forced him onto a stool.

Zeb leaned heavily on the shiny surface of the counter with both elbows. "You know that girl of Lester's? What's 'er name?"

"Sherri Chan, " Bo supplied as he mopped around Zeb's elbows with a rag.

"Ya, that's it. Sherri Chan." Zeb's words came out slurred. "She's a pretty little thing, ain't she?"

Jed, who was sitting next to Zeb, frowned and then slung a half-hearted punch near Zeb's bicep, missing by an inch. "Watch it, b'y! Lester'd kill you if 'e thought you was lookin' at his woman!"

"Just statin' a fact." Zeb tried to focus on Jed's face, without much success.

"Maybe Zeb is just attracted to Asian women," Pip said reasonaly from his position further down the line.

Reba was nowhere to be seen, having left earlier with Patsi and crew.

"Maybe so. Maybe so." Zeb squinted and then burped loudly.

He didn't recall anything else after that.

A POUNDING noise woke Zeb with a start. He rubbed his eyes and swore, wondering where he was for a moment until Jed's living room came into focus. Why in blazes wasn't Jed answering the door?

Zeb sat up with a grunt and swung his feet to the floor, letting them rest there for a few minutes until he got his bearings. If Jed felt anything like he did, he had his answer. "Just a minute," he growled to no one in particular.

It took some fidgeting with the deadbolt but he finally managed to open the door to find Will standing on the other side, in his typical jeans and plaid shirt, grinning like a Cheshire cat. The hug was brief, with no slapping from Zeb's end.

"Bo told me you tied one on but good last night, so I thought I'd come over and torment you for a bit."

"Thanks. I love you, too, Bro." Zeb shuffled back to the living room and lowered himself into a sitting position on the couch that was also his bed. "I feel like 'ell."

"You look like it, too," Will teased. He sat down opposite in the armchair. "I wasn't expecting the whole cavalry to come and watch me kill myself tonight."

"Too bad. Cavalry's here in full force." Zeb rubbed his head, mussing his longish strawberry blonde hair into a nest that rivalled his thick beard.

"Doesn't start for a few hours yet, so I figured we could go out for a bite to eat or something."

"Not hungry yet." Zeb bent slowly to retrieve his phone from the floor beside the couch. "What time is it anyway?"

"Four o'clock. You b'ys slept the day away."

"Hmph." Zeb grunted. "So, your girlfriend coming to watch or what?"

"Girlfriend?" Will frowned. "Who told you that?"

"Jed said you've taken up with some artsy-fartsy type." Zeb watched his brother intently, gauging his reaction.

Will shrugged. "Not sure it's gonna work out."

"Why not?"

"What's it to you?" Will looked up defensively.

"It's nothing to me. Just makin' conversation. Geez."

Will sighed. "Sorry for snappin'. Her dad is my boss, and things could get complicated."

"Why? Don't you get on?"

"Yes, as a matter of fact we do." Will shifted in the chair.

"Hm." Zeb grunted again and stroked his beard. "So what's the problem?"

Will let out a small self-depreciating laugh. "Not sure. Marigold is beautiful, smart, cares about the environment... although, maybe a little too much." He stopped and smiled but then sobered again. "Not sure I'm ready for a serious relationship. Maybe jumped in a little too soon, you know?"

"I hear ya, b'y! Finally, someone talkin' sense!"

Jed emerged from the hallway, looking as haggard as Zeb felt. "Time for some orange juice and coffee," he said, rubbing his short bristled hair.

"On it." Will lurched from the chair and headed to the galley kitchen. "I'll rustle you up some grub while I'm at it. Can't have my cheering section down in the mouth."

"He gots too much energy, that one," Jed mumbled and sat in the vacated chair. "It's givin' me a headache."

"Beer and tomato juice. That's the best cure for a hangover. Any tomato juice in that fridge?" Zeb called to Will.

"I'll check," Will hollered back.

"Never fancied beer and tomato juice," Jed said, looking up at the ceiling.

"Whatever works. Gots to get some grub in our guts, too, so we can party hard again tonight."

Jed groaned. "I'm gettin' too old for this."

"Not that again." Zeb shook his head, wished he hadn't, and then got up slowly to use the washroom. A Malloy didn't give in, no matter how hung over.

By eight o'clock Zeb was feeling much better, thanks to his beer and tomato juice remedy, a couple of pain killers, some carbs, and a nice hot shower. He almost felt human again.

It was a packed house at the Urban Cowboy, the crowd of spectators who'd come to cheer on their favourite contestants outnumbering the usual clientele.

"Good luck."

Zeb turned to the newcomer, a middle aged First Nations man with slicked back hair.

"This is Buck Stone," Will introduced. "He works out at the camp."

"Pleased to meet you." Jed stuck out his hand and made the rest of the introductions.

"I'm surprised to see you here," Will said to Buck. "I thought you avoided bars."

"I do," Buck said. "But I'm making an exception this once. I wanted to see how much damage I'll have to put up with afterwards."

Will grinned. "Buck used to be a rodeo cowboy himself, once upon a time."

"Got injured and had to quit," Buck explained. "Well, I better go get a coffee and then find a good place to watch." He nodded before moving away.

"Coffee?" Zeb asked. "What's the point in that?"

"Buck's an alcoholic," Will said. "Goes to AA. I been catching a ride to town when he has meetings or when he comes to visit his daughter."

"How old's his daughter?" Pip asked.

Will gave Pip a withering look. "Don't know and don't care."

"You'll need to go over there and register," Jed said to Will, pointing to a table with two rows of people lined up in front.

Will nodded and with a salute to his brothers, sauntered to take his place at the end of one of the lines.

Zeb surveyed the other contestants, wondering how Will would fare in their midst. His brother was a natural born athlete, and Jed said he'd been practicing, so his chances were probably pretty good.

Reba sidled up to Zeb and gave him a squeeze around the middle.

"What's that for?" Zeb asked.

"Just cause I felt like it," she said.

Zeb smiled. She was obviously much happier now that she'd mended fences with her good friend Patsi.

"Here comes Lester," Jed said, elbowing Zeb in the ribs. "He's been coaching our Will." Jed waved Lester and his group over.

"Oh good!" Reba scurried to meet them halfway.

"Maybe I'll go sit somewhere's else," Pip said.

"G'wan!" Zeb said. "You met up with Patsi just fine last night."

"I don't want to jinx anything."

"Not gonna let you bail on us now. Scout for a table near the bull thingy."

Pip did as he was bid and headed in the direction of the mechanical bull.

Zeb watched as Lester and his entourage approached. There was Lester, Patsi and Reba, Sherri Chan and two other Asian women that Zeb didn't recognize.

Somewhere in the back of his mind he had a vague recollection about saying something awkward last night that involved Sherri Chan. He turned to Jed. "Did I say something weird last night when we were getting ready to leave?"

"You always say something weird," Jed responded.

Zeb shrugged. Probably nothing to worry about.

"Pip's gone to round us up a table," Jed said as soon as the party arrived.

"Good, good," Lester said with a nod. "I'm gonna go talk to Will. Make sure he remembers everything I told him. Sherri, can you make the introductions?"

Lester hustled toward the line up where Will was still waiting, just as Pip returned.

Sherri gestured to the tallest of the two other Asian women. "This is my cousin, Lily Chan." Lily nodded politely. Her hair was long and straight, framing her face and shoulders like a shining black waterfall. "And this is my friend, Tiffany Yuen." Tiffany also nodded. Sherri turned to the group of Malloys. "Lester's friend, Jed Malloy…" She let out a small, tinkling laugh. "And I'm afraid Jed should do the rest in case I get it wrong."

Jed went through the line-up, pointing as he went. "My brothers Zeb and Pip, and sister, Reba. Bo's behind the bar servin' up drinks, and Will is riding tonight, but you probably know that already." He turned his gaze toward Sherri, a look of mock offence in his expression. "And I hope I'm more than just 'Lester's friend'."

"Of course!" Sherri touched Jed's arm.

"I remember meeting all of you at the restaurant," Lily Chan said.

Zeb blinked, then nodded as a smile spread across his features. "I remember that! You was our waitress." He surveyed her more closely. "I'm surprised you remember us, seeing as you serve so many people."

Lily chuckled. "You made quite an impression. As I recall, you ordered way more food than expected, but then didn't even have to get to-go containers to take any home."

"We Malloys can pack it away." Jed patted his stomach.

"And you're just a friend?" Zeb turned his gaze to Tiffany.

"I don't know about *just*, but yes." Tiffany smiled at Zeb. She was shorter than Lily, but not as small as Sherri. She had a more exotic look about her than the others. They were all pretty, no doubt, but Tiffany had a worldliness, due perhaps to the dark eyeliner and makeup, which gave her an aura of mystique that the others didn't quite possess.

"Our mothers are best friends," Sherri supplied. "They immigrated at the same time when they both got married. Our families are very close."

"You found a table?" Jed asked Pip.

Pip nodded. "We better sit down before someone else grabs it."

They moved to the table that Pip had picked out and found enough seats by sliding in a few extra chairs from an adjacent table.

"Here comes Lester," Patsi said as her brother approached.

"They're about to get started," Lester said to the group. "We should go stand next to the perimeter so we can see." Without waiting for the rest, Lester strode toward the outer limits of the roped off area around the mechanical bull.

"Goodness!" Sherri said. "He seems more excited about this than when he was in it himself!"

The rest of the group followed and took their place among the gathering crowd around the bull. Zeb, aware of his height, made sure the ladies were in front of him so that they could see. He was having trouble keeping his eyes off the lovely Tiffany Yuen. He scooted a little to the left so that she was right in front of him, almost touching. Her swinging ponytail caught in his beard and she turned around and gave him a coy smile. He shrugged and smiled back. "Sorry."

"No problem."

A few minutes later, Cory Roberts jumped onto a small platform, microphone in hand. "Welcome to the Urban Cowboy's second mechanical bull riding competition! Hopefully one of many more to come!"

The crowd cheered. Cory held up his hand for quiet. "For those of you new to this gig, here are the rules. Stanley, here, our certified operator, gives everyone the same ride in round one. Stay on the bull for eight seconds, and you go on to round two. We'll go as many rounds as necessary to declare a winner." There was more clapping and a few whistles.

"And…" Cory held up his hand again. "We have in our midst tonight, Urban Cowboy royalty. He's not riding, cause he wants to give the rest of you a chance, but…" He pointed at Lester. "Winner of the first Urban Cowboy mechanical bull riding competition, Lester Tibbett!"

The crowd cheered even louder. Lester looked embarrassed, a slight pink glow forming around his ears, but he took off his cowboy hat and waved to the onlookers.

The contestants were gathered in an area off to the left of the bull. Each one wore a fabric tunic with a number on it, just like in a real rodeo.

The competition finally got under way and one by one the true amateurs lost their balance and tumbled to the mats. When it was Will's turn, only half of the contestants had remained on the bull for the full eight seconds.

"Give 'er heat, my son!" Zeb called across the cacophony.

Will grinned and tipped the borrowed cowboy hat that rested on his head - courtesy of Lester Tibbett, no doubt. He mounted the bull with one fluid jump and straightened himself in the saddle, just like a real cowboy. Zeb's chest swelled with pride.

Will lifted his free hand, gave a quick nod to Cory, and the ride began. Zeb held his breath for the full eight seconds, although by the look of it, Will was just enjoying the ride. The animal rocked back and forth with a few slow twists as Will's body swayed in rhythmic time. He jumped off at the end of it all, a wide grin never leaving his face.

Zeb expelled his pent up breath.

"You seem nervous," Tiffany noted, turning her head so that she could look up at him.

"Me? Nah!" He grinned.

"That's Weston Drake up next," Lester said, loud enough that everyone around him could hear. He pointed to the sinewy young cowboy that was just mounting the bull. "He was my only real competition last time."

Zeb took note of the confident aura that emanated from the young man. He finished the first round easily, jumped off the bull at the end, and swaggered back to the bull pen with the rest of the remaining contestants.

Round two saw many more contestants take a tumble as the bull's erratic movements increased. By round three, they were getting flicked off the bull's back like boogers. Round four would probably be the deciding one, since there were only three contestants left: Will, Weston Drake, and another lanky cowboy named Johnny.

Johnny went first. Stanley, the operator, started up the machine and almost immediately the bull started jerking Johnny around like a rag doll. After one too many jolts, he flew sideways and Stanley hit the stop button just as Johnny tumbled headfirst onto the mats. He got up slowly, retrieving his hat on the way, and then lifted it high for the onlookers. The crowd clapped and whistled their appreciation. The poor bugger had put on a show and now it was Will's turn.

Will, still grinning from ear to ear, vaulted onto the bull's back and raised his arm. The machine flew into motion, bucking and jerking beyond anything that Zeb had seen before. "You can do it, b'y! Hang on!" Zeb bellowed, his voice getting lost in the crowd. About six seconds in, Zeb saw it all in slow motion detail. Will jerked to the left, then to the right, one leg slipping from its grip until he flew head over arse and landed square on his backside. Will shook his head and stood slowly to his feet, orienting himself to the tilt of the room. Then the grin split his face again and he raised his hand as the crowd cheered.

Zeb let out his breath - again. As long as the competition didn't go longer than six seconds, Will would be the winner.

The tension was palpable and Zeb wished he had his beer handy to calm his nerves. His brain was buzzing, due perhaps to the lingering hangover, but also from the excitement. Weston Drake jumped on board the bull and began his ride with the practiced flourish of a seasoned cowboy. He was jerked and thrown about but managed to hang on, and eight seconds later, the machine shut down with a buzz. Weston had ridden the full eight count without getting bucked off.

Reba swore loudly in disappointment.

Zeb looked her way and let out a grunt. He noticed that Will was the first in line to congratulate the winner, and Lester Tibbett was making his way through the crowd to offer his congratulations as well.

"It was a good ride," Patsi Tibbett said. "He deserves to win."

"I suppose, but it doesn't mean I can't be disappointed," Reba said.

Zeb was just glad to get back to his beer. "I feel plumb worn out! You'd think I was the one ridin' that contraption and not Will!"

"I noticed you seemed a bit tense," Tiffany said, her eyes twinkling in amusement.

"I don't really get it," Lily Chan offered. "It doesn't look like fun at all. Don't they get whiplash?"

"It's about taming the beast," Tiffany said, and let her gaze swing back to Zeb.

"Couldn't a said it better myself." Zeb lofted his beer and took a swig, never taking his gaze from Tiffany's.

"Wonder if Bo got a chance to watch?" Jed wondered and looked around.

Zeb glanced over his shoulder and spotted Bo standing just around the corner, a white rag slung over one shoulder. "There he is." Zeb waved and Bo waved back.

"At least Jacques let 'im watch a bit," Pip said.

"Let's go congratulate the winner." Patsi elbowed Reba and the two girls took off in that direction. There was still a fairly large gathering around Weston Drake. Will was just heading their way.

"I think I'll go find Lester, " Sherri said. "Anyone coming?"

"Okay." Lily stood up. "Excuse me." She nodded at Pip and Zeb.

"Actually, I think I'll join you," Pip said, standing also. He flashed an almost imperceptible signal with his eyes at Zeb.

Zeb smiled and nodded. Good. His little brother was getting 'back in the saddle', as he'd advised. Zeb watched for a moment as Pip and company stopped to talk to Will and shake his hand.

"Looks like it's just you and me," Tiffany said.

"Not for long." Zeb gestured to Will's approaching figure.

Will pulled out a chair and sat down. "Phew! Did you see that? I almost made the full count!"

"But you didn't," Zeb teased. "How does it feel to be the first loser?"

Will just laughed and rewarded Zeb for his trouble with a punch in the arm. "He's just sore cause he didn't have the guts to try it."

"Probably never gonna, either. I'm not daft like you."

"Will Malloy, by the way." Will stretched his arm across the table to shake Tiffany's hand. "I don't think we met."

"No. You were signing up when we came in. I'm a friend of Sherri Chan's."

"Nice." Will nodded then looked around. "How does a guy get a drink around here? I'm thirsty as 'ell!"

Eventually the rest of their group gathered around the table once again and it was hard to keep track of all the conversations that were going on at once. Somehow Will had moved closer to Tiffany, effectively cutting Zeb off from pursuing any further conversation with her. That he had been making plans, of sorts, that involved the lovely Tiffany Yuen for later that evening, was something he wasn't ashamed to admit. She'd seemed interested enough, if his ability to read body language hadn't slipped any. But now, watching his brother Will talking animatedly with her, another plan was formulating. Will was leaving tomorrow and he wasn't sure his outdoorsy brother and Tiffany would make a good match, anyway, but Bo on the other hand... Plus, Pip and Lily were also deep in conversation. The cogs were definitely turning.

Maybe this confirmed bachelor was cut out for matchmaking.

~

ZEB LEANED back in the kitchen chair and patted his stomach. "Nothin' like Newfie breakfast on a Sunday mornin'. Good on ya, b'y. You cooks as good as Ma."

"Thanks." Jed nodded in response and then got up to clear the plates. All six of the 'Alberta Malloys' were crowded around Jed's tiny table. Will had opted for the folding lawn chair since there were only four regular ones, and Reba was sitting up high on a stool that normally served as Jed's bedside nightstand.

"I don't know why we all had to come over so early," Reba said. "Sundays are for sleeping in. Besides, I saw all of youse last night."

"I don't get to see my siblings that often, all together," Zeb said. "Can't you humour me just this once?"

"Seems like you're getting sentimental, now that you're over thirty," Will said and laughed.

"Him and Jed, both," Pip piped up.

"Watch your mouths. Zeb and I can still lick the lot of ya," Jed said from his position by the sink.

"I could lick the lot of ya by myself," Zeb said. "Jed included."

Jed made a scoffing noise. "What odds!"

"You wanna give it a go?" Zeb challenged.

"Not on the Lard's day, thank you very much," Jed said.

The rest of them burst out laughing.

"Jed only cares about religion when it suits," Bo said, smiling.

"You know nothin' about what I care about," Jed countered. "Least of all religion."

"Say, I know Will has to go back to work right off, but what say the rest of us do it again tonight?" Zeb suggested. "Down at that Chinese place we went to last time?"

"You mean I have to put up with you bozos for more than one meal in a day?" Reba asked.

Pip didn't look convinced and neither did Bo. "Come on. Bo gets the night off, and I'll be headin back to Fort Mac in a couple days. It could be our last chance cause I know you all get busy during the week." Zeb smiled encouragingly from one to the other.

"Why you so interested in family time all of a sudden?" Bo asked.

"It ain't all of a sudden. I've always been big on family."

"Well... " There were more sounds of dissension from the majority.

"My treat," Zeb offered.

"I'll have to check my schedule," Reba said.

They all laughed at that.

"What? Can't a girl have other interests besides hanging out with a bunch of lummox's like you?"

"If Bo's gonna make it back in time we better get going," Will said. "I wouldn't want to keep 'im from 'family time'." He grinned and gave Bo a shove.

Bo just rolled his eyes. "Be nice or I'll make you walk back to the camp."

"Can I come?" Pip asked. "I haven't seen the place yet."

"Sure," Bo said. "But we won't be stayin' long."

The rest of the siblings rose from the table. Jed was filling the sink with water and had dumped the plates into the suds.

"Why don't you go along, too, Jed?" Zeb suggested. "You don't get out much. It'll be a nice Sunday drive. Reba and I'll do up the dishes."

"What? What if I wanted to go?" Reba asked.

Zeb stared her down, trying to communicate with his eyes without saying anything. She seemed to get the message and immediately shut her mouth.

"You could go," Jed said to Zeb. "I can go out there anytime."

"No, you go ahead. I have a few other things I need to attend to this afternoon."

"Mysterious," Pip said as he walked out of the kitchen.

It didn't take long for the four brothers to exit the apartment, leaving Reba and Zeb behind to do the clean-up.

"So? What's up?" Reba asked as soon as the others had left. She already had a dishtowel in hand ready to dry, meaning she expected Zeb to wash.

He dipped his hands in the soapy water and then snatched them out again. "Lard of a duck but that's hot!"

"So? Talk to me while it cools. I haven't got all day." She waited expectantly.

Zeb turned his frame and leaned his backside against the counter, folding his arms across his massive chest. "I've got a little something planned for tonight and I might need your help."

"Figured as much."

"First off, do you think you could figure a way to get them twins you work for to meet us down at the Chinese restaurant?"

Reba furrowed her brow. "Andrea and Angela? Why?"

"Don't ask questions. Do you think you can do it?" He lifted a brow as he surveyed his sister.

"Maybe. Not sure that Angela will want to come. She pretty much still hates me. But Andrea I can probably swing. I can say it's to pay her back for being so nice to me or something."

Zeb nodded. "Good, good. What about getting the phone number for that Tiffany Yuen that we met last night?"

Reba scrunched up her forehead. "How am I supposed to do that? I only just met 'er, same as you."

"Can't you get it from Patsi Mae? She's Sherri Chan's friend and Sherri goes with Lester…"

"I don't see that that makes a difference."

"Can't you find 'er online or something?"

"Why can't you?" Reba asked.

"You know I don't go in for all that social media crap. I wouldn't know where to start!"

"What am I supposed to say if I do find 'er?"

"Girl stuff? I don't know! You could tell 'er your big brother wanted to know. That's honest enough."

"You like 'er, then?" Reba asked, raising a brow.

Zeb just shrugged. "Let's just say she may come in handy." He turned around and dipped his fingers again. "Much better."

As he washed the dishes he thought about the last errand he had to run before this evening's dinner. This one might be a bit more difficult, but he was willing to take a shot.

∼

ZEB HAD CALLED AHEAD to make sure Lily was working that evening and reserved the largest table available at the Fortune Cookie Restaurant. "What time you off?" he'd asked.

"Seven - unless there's still customers in the restaurant. We always have family dinner after hours on Sunday."

Zeb frowned. He'd forgotten about that detail, but it couldn't be helped. Hopefully, Pip would be able to figure it out on his own from there.

Zeb ushered his brothers into the restaurant and Lily met them just inside the door. "This way." She led them to a large, oval table and set the menus on top. "I'll be right back with water."

"She's a looker, eh, Pip?" Zeb elbowed his youngest brother in the ribs. "You should ask 'er out on a date sometime."

"Um… maybe?" Pip's confused expression did not bode well.

"Why such a big table?" Bo asked.

"I likes to spread out," Zeb said.

"Where's Reba?" Jed asked.

"She's coming later. Had a few other errands, I suspect."

Pip, Bo and Jed found seats and Zeb distributed the menus.

Lily came back with glasses of water.

"We'll be needin' some more of those in a minute. My sister and 'er friend are on their way."

"What friend?" Jed asked.

Zeb just shrugged. He looked over at Pip, who was perusing the menu. "Say, Pip? Why don't you see if Lily can help you out deciding what we should order?"

Pip furrowed his brow. "Why me?"

Zeb ignored him. "Lily? You got a minute to sit by Pip and explain the menu?" He looked around the room. "Doesn't seem too busy at the moment."

"Um… sure." Lily walked to Pip's side of the table and leaned over his shoulder. "If I recall, you ordered the dinner for eight last time…"

Zeb glanced at the entrance.

"Expectin' someone?" Jed asked.

Zeb swung his gaze back to Jed. "Hm?"

"You seem awfully antsy. Are you expectin' someone other than Reba?"

The bell over the outer door tinkled and Reba walked in, followed by Andrea Carravagio. Zeb smiled widely.

Jed's eyebrows rose and he blinked. "You invited 'er, didn't ya?"

"So?" Zeb said.

Jed went to stand up, but Zeb put his hand on Jed's arm and he settled back down. "I suppose Reba's in on it, too?"

Zeb just grinned. "What do you *think* I wanted to talk to 'er about?"

"Hi everyone." Reba waved. "Well, isn't this just a coincidence! You all remember my boss Andrea Carravagio?"

"Grab a seat," Zeb said. "There's plenty of room."

"You... you don't mind?" Andrea asked. "I'd hate to spoil a family get together."

"Don't be daft! There's a seat right next to Jed." Zeb pointed to the vacant seat.

"Oh... well, maybe I should sit over here..."

"No, no, I insist." Zeb was up and acting the gentleman by pulling out the chair next to Jed. She had no choice but to occupy it.

The door opened again and Tiffany Yuen walked in. Zeb waved as soon as he saw her and her eyes widened. She walked over to the table and stood by Zeb. "Oh... when you asked me out, I thought it was just the two of us. I didn't realize you meant the whole family."

"Have a seat," Zeb said, standing up. "I'll just move down one. This here is my brother Bo. Not sure if you met 'im last night since he was tendin' bar." Zeb indicated the now vacant chair beside Bo. As soon as Tiffany had been seated, he took the chair on her other side.

"Oh." Lily straightened her spine and surveyed the additional patrons. "Perhaps you *will* need the dinner for eight after all."

The bell over the door rang again and all eyes turned to see who had entered this time. It was Cory Roberts.

"Make that dinner for ten," Zeb said. "I'm starved." He waved Cory over to the table. "Come join us. The more the merrier."

Cory stopped at Bo's chair and slapped him on the back a few times. "Happy birthday, man. I'm honoured to be invited to the celebration."

Bo's gaze swung from Cory to Zeb. "What? It's -"

"There's a seat for you down by Reba," Zeb bellowed, effectively cutting Bo off. Reba's eyes were now as wide as everyone else's.

"But -" Bo sputtered.

"Play along!" Zeb whispered to Bo and then said loudly, "Well, I think we're all Here, so let's get that order in."

EVERYONE HAD enough to eat and there were even a few left overs which Zeb requested be packaged up for his lunch the next day. The bill, when it came, was hefty, but it was worth it in Zeb's eyes, if it meant he'd succeeded in setting up his siblings. Well, all except Will, but that one seemed to have a head on his shoulders.

Zeb glanced around the table and smiled. Reba and Cory were involved in an intense discussion, Cory's dreadlocks bobbing close to Reba's red mane as he explained something or other about the ins and outs of electronic music. Zeb couldn't make head nor tail of what the other man was saying, but Reba seemed riveted - if not by the conversation, then by Cory's attention.

Jed and Andrea seemed to be hitting it off as well. Jed was doing more listening than talking, which was a first, nodding at the correct moments as Andrea talked about an event coming up at her church.

Pip hadn't fared as well. He looked bored, spending more time checking his phone than conversing with anyone. Unfortunately, Lily was too busy to pay him much mind, but hopefully Pip would figure things out and call her some other time when she wasn't at work. At least he'd brought them together again.

Tiffany was the real enigma. She seemed to be flirting with both himself and Bo, going back and forth between them. Extended eye contact here; an exuberant laugh there. He'd caught himself a time or two responding to her wiles. It would be easy to get caught in the trap of her exotic eyes.

"I must say, I was a little overwhelmed when I first came in tonight." Tiffany batted her eyes at Zeb. "So many virile males all in one room." She laid her hand on Zeb's forearm.

Zeb tamped down his own growing interest. "You know, Bo is the nicest one of the bunch. He's a real gentleman." He removed his arm from under her grasp and put it safely in his lap. "And he's smart, too. Reads lots of books, don't you, Bo?"

Bo let out a small laugh. "That's the best recommendation you can come up with? He reads lots of books?"

"I like reading." Tiffany smiled at Bo.

"Oh? What do you like reading?" he asked.

"You first."

Bo shrugged a shoulder. "Westerns, mysteries. Sometimes I even like Science fiction. I don't have TV so it passes the time when I'm not at work."

"I like real life adventures," Tiffany said. "I'm not really into fiction. Although, I did read that erotica series that everyone was raving about." She smiled coyly and blinked a few times at Bo.

Lily Chan came and stood near Zeb. She cleared her throat quietly to get his attention. "Um… if you don't mind, you're the last customers here and I'd like to clear up now. If you don't mind," she repeated.

"Oh! Of course." Zeb gathered his napkin and threw it on the table. He should have realized. Several of Lily's family had arrived a few minutes earlier, including Sherri Chan with Lester in tow. They'd stopped to say hello, but then went through a set of double doors that Zeb presumed was a private dining room. "We'll clear on out and let you get to your family dinner."

Lily gave a slight bow and then scooped up a few glasses that still remained on the table. "Aunt Lani says you should stay for family dinner, also," Lily said to Tiffany.

"But I just ate," Tiffany said.

"I know, but it would mean a lot to her. She hasn't seen you since you got here and... well, you know how she can be."

"Yes, I know." Tiffany's lips formed a prim line. "Of course I'll stay for a bit. As long as she doesn't try to make me eat."

Lily shrugged her slender shoulders. "I can't promise anything." She hurried away with the glasses.

"Well, I guess that's my cue. Off to a second engagement!" Tiffany stood up. "We'll have to get together again soon." She was looking straight at Zeb with those darned exotic eyes.

"I don't live in Calgary, but Bo does." Zeb gestured to his brother.

Bo didn't make eye contact, choosing to focus his attention on a salt shaker instead.

"Oh, right. Well, see you around." She waved to the rest in general and then walked to the double doors, her hips swinging provocatively, and disappeared into the next room.

"Should we take this party elsewhere?" Cory asked. "I might be able to get us into this exclusive club I know downtown." He grinned. "And the birthday boy wouldn't have to lift a finger."

"Um..." Bo rubbed the back of his neck. "I don't know what line my brother told you, but it's not actually my birthday."

"Bo!" Zeb cuffed Bo's bicep.

"It's okay. Reba already told me," Cory said and raised a brow. "I just thought I'd see how long you'd keep the charade going."

Zeb blinked, his defence melting away. Cory didn't look upset and Reba was still smiling.

"So? Who's with me?" Cory asked.

"I'm in." Reba raised a hand to elbow height.

"Thanks, but I think I'll have to pass tonight," Andrea said. "I know we came together, Reba, but maybe you can catch a ride home with someone else."

"No problem," Cory said. "She'll ride with me." He glanced at Reba and smiled.

Jed cleared his throat. "I think I'll have to pass, too."

All eyes swung to Jed.

"What ya lookin' at?" Jed frowned. He reached for his ball cap and jammed it on his head.

"Nothing." Bo nodded in Jed's direction as if to say, 'Good job!'. Then he looked at Cory. "Thanks for the offer, but I spend enough time down at the Urban Cowboy, working or not."

"What's wrong with youse guys?" Pip piped up. "The night is young." It was the first time he seemed interested in anything since the dinner began.

"Actually, why don't Cory and Reba go on ahead, Jed can ride with Andrea, and the three of us will go in Bo's car." Zeb looked pointedly at Pip.

"But -"

"So it's settled," Zeb interrupted, still staring Pip down.

Pip nodded and they made their way to the door, Lily on their tails, ready to lock up behind them.

"Thanks again for everything," Zeb said to Lily on the way out.

"My pleasure," she said and smiled directly at him.

He blinked. It was the first he'd noticed that Lily Chan had exotic eyes, too.

THEY'D HARDLY STARTED DRIVING HOME when Bo spoke up. "So, you planning on hanging out a shingle next?"

"What's that?" Zeb let his gaze focus on the lights and signs that were passing by to his right.

"You. Starting a dating service."

Zeb chuckled and glanced at Bo's profile. "You noticed."

"Pretty hard not to."

"So that's what it was all about," Pip said from the back seat.

"Seriously? You just figured that out?" Bo glanced back at Pip and then turned his eyes forward to the street in front of him.

"How'd I do?" Zeb asked.

"Not so good." Pip leaned forward and put his hand on the head-rest. "Who was my date? Seems like you were one short."

"Make that two," Bo said. "He didn't have a date either, although Tiffany was trying hard enough."

"Lily Chan was supposed to be your date, dumb-nuts," Zeb said over his shoulder. "Shouldn't take rocket science to figure that one out."

"Thanks. My date had to work all night," Pip said.

"So? I done the hard part, now the rest is up to you."

"What hard part is that?" Pip asked.

"Set you up to see 'er again. I could tell you took a shine to 'er last night at the bull riding competition, so I thought I'd just give you a little boost. Back in the saddle and all that."

"Thanks, but I can find my own women," Pip said.

"Sorry for trying to be of service." Zeb scowled and looked out the window again.

"Besides, I'm not sure she's my type," Pip said.

Zeb scoffed. "Your type? And what would that be? She's got two legs. What else do you need?"

"Just cause you're into Asian women doesn't mean I am," Pip said.

"Hm. That almost sounded racist," Bo said.

"Sorry. Let me rephrase. I just don't see myself trying to date her. Not seriously."

"Who said anything about getting serious?" Zeb asked. "Getting back in the saddle is just that. Take a few for a test drive. Flush out the carburetor."

"Stick to one analogy at a time," Bo advised. "You're getting your metaphors mixed up."

"Whatever. The point is, the best way to get over a broken heart is to break a few yourself."

"That's the worst advice I've ever heard!" Bo glanced in the mirror at Pip. "Whatever you do, don't listen to him."

"And what about you? I hand you a hottie on a platter and what do you do? You talk about books," Zeb said.

"You're the one who brought it up," Bo countered.

Zeb grunted.

"Besides that, she seemed a lot more interested in you than she did in me." Bo looked his way.

"Ya think?" Zeb raised a brow.

"Yes, I think. You were so busy trying to push her at me, you missed the fact she was drooling over you."

"Drooling, you say? Now that's something I normally wouldn't go for, but in her case…"

Bo laughed. "You're your own worst enemy when it comes to women, although for some reason they fall all over you. I just can't figure it out."

"Well, at least I tried. My advice still stands, you know." Zeb looked over at Bo's profile. "The best way to get over a broken heart is -"

"I know," Bo interrupted. "Is to break a few yourself. I heard."

"I was gonna say, is to get laid, but you interrupted," Zeb said with a grin.

"Same thing. You're a piece, you know that?" Bo shook his head but smiled. "That might work for you, but it's not my style, so you can keep your advice to yourself from now on."

"Your loss."

"I'd say your days as a matchmaker are pretty numbered," Bo said.

"Oh, I don't know about that. Cory and Reba seemed to hit it off alright, and Jed and Andrea went home together. Two outta four ain't bad."

"Don't count your chickens…"

"You always this crooked contrary?" Zeb asked.

"Just being a realist. You can't fix everyone's love life in one evening," Bo said.

"Hmph." Zeb shut his mouth. Maybe he couldn't fix everyone's love life, but his own prospects just seemed a whole lot brighter.

ZEB LIFTED the coffee to his lips and took a tentative sip. His leftovers were still waiting back in Jed's fridge, but he just didn't feel like eating alone in the apartment. The Brew seemed like a nice alternative. He'd enjoyed the lunch he'd had with Jed the other day and thought he'd try it out again - without Jed's constant chatter.

From his table's vantage point, he had a view of the downtown traffic as it motored by - a steady but changing stream of cars, busses, delivery trucks and pedestrians. He also had a good view of that painting he'd seen earlier - the one with the mixture of mountains and skulls. It was quite cleverly rendered - not that he was an art critic by any means - but he could see that the woman who painted it had talent.

The attractive First Nations woman who had served his coffee came by with a pot. "Can I get you a refill?" she asked.

"Sure." He held his cup up while she poured the dark liquid. "You live in our - I mean, my brother Jed's building, right?"

She nodded. "That's right. I've seen you around a time or two."

He set his cup down and then stuck out his hand. "Zeb Malloy."

She took it, although barely touching his fingers with her own. "Tamara Spence."

"You know the gal that paints these pictures?" He chucked his head toward the mountain view.

"Of course."

He nodded absently. "Of course. You own the joint." He looked up at her again. "What's she like?"

Tamara's brows rose slightly. "Well… are you asking about her art or about her? I'm not sure I'm comfortable talking about her private life."

"One of my brothers, Will, is a… friend."

"Oh? Then why don't you ask him?"

"That's just it. I think he's sweet on her, so I can't really, without soundin' nosy."

"Ah." Tamara nodded. "You want to make sure she's good enough for your brother." Her tone was crisp - cryptic even, and she didn't look pleased.

"Not trying to offend you, Ma'am. And I'm sure she's a good gal. Just lookin' out for my brother's interests, like any brother would."

"I can't really tell you much," Tamara said and swept her considerable length of hair off her shoulder with a slight swing of her head. "I really don't know her other than to say she is a very talented artist with a social conscience. That's all I can say."

"That's a fact." Zeb squinted at the painting. "These for sale?"

"Yes. The prices are marked. Now if you'll excuse me?"

Zeb watched Tamara's graceful form glide through the French doors and back to the coffee station in the older section of the cafe. He rose and walked to the painting and stood looking at it for a while. His eyes widened when he saw the price and he blinked several times. He hadn't expected it to be that much! Then he stood back and rubbed his beard.

His cell phone bleeped on the table where he'd left it and he strode back to see who it was. It was an unrecognized number, but he opted to answer anyway. "Hello?"

"Hi. Is this Zeb?"

"You got it." He scrounged in the back of his mind to place the voice.

"This is Tiffany. Tiffany Yuen?"

His eyes widened and he sat down at his table. "Tiffany! What's up?"

"That was my question. What are you doing today? I thought maybe we could get together since we're both visiting from out of town."

"How'd you get my number?" he asked.

She laughed. "You called me yesterday, remember?"

"Oh, right." His mind was spinning. He'd pegged Tiffany for Bo, but Bo had made it clear in the car that he wasn't interested. "I'm just 'aving a coffee downtown. You wanna join? Or we could meet somewhere else if you'd like."

"That sounds fine. I was just visiting the tower since I hadn't been in years. What's the name of the place? I'll be there in a few minutes."

Zeb told her and then they said their good-byes and hung up.

"Well, I'll be jiggered," he said out loud to no one. "A fair wind is blowin' my way today and no mistake!"

~

"WELL, ISN'T THIS A NICE SURPRISE." Zeb lifted his mug and took a sip of his third refill. Pretty soon he was going to get a coffee hangover. The jitters were already starting from too much caffeine. The cause couldn't be the woman sitting across from him.

Tiffany smiled. "Yes, isn't it."

"So, you live in Toronto," Zeb stated and shook his head.

"By the sounds of it, you don't like Toronto. It's actually a very vibrant city."

"Wouldn't know. Never been."

"You'll have to visit sometime."

He considered that. "I do work shifts. Get a week off after every two."

"Excellent! Call me and we'll set it up." She smiled at him over the rim of her mug.

"And what do you do there?" He took another sip of his coffee.

"I'm a martial arts instructor," Tiffany said.

His eyebrows rose. "Is that so?"

"It is." She smiled coyly.

"So what you're sayin' is, I better watch my step."

"No. It just means I can take care of myself."

"Hm." He nodded. "That's good. I like a gal who's independent."

"You do, do you? The way you were trying to pass me off on your brother last night, I had my doubts."

Zeb laughed. "I was trying to do 'im a good turn. His hearts been broken by some French gal from Quebec, and I was trying to help 'im get over it."

"And you thought I was a good prospect?"

"Well…" He opted for another sip of coffee rather than reveal any more. To say that he thought she was 'easy' wasn't exactly the most flattering description.

"I liked him." Tiffany tucked a strand of her dark hair behind an ear. She was wearing it loose today and it suited her. Zeb was a sucker for long hair on any woman.

"Bo's a good, steady fella." Zeb folded his arms and leaned on the tabletop.

"I liked all of your brothers," Tiffany continued. "Will seemed especially nice, too."

Zeb grinned. "Will is easy to get along with. Most people like our Will."

"And then there's you." She captured his gaze with her exotic eyes and wouldn't let go. "What kind of man are you, Zeb Malloy?"

Zeb shrugged but couldn't look away. Perhaps she was a witch or into voodoo or something. Whatever it was she was doing to him was working. "I'm just a homeboy from the backwoods of Newfoundland. Nothing fancy."

Tiffany cocked her head to one side. "I don't know. To me you're the most interesting of the lot. You're certainly the strongest."

Zeb was finally able to break eye contact. "Now you're makin' me feel embarrassed."

"Why? Wasn't it obvious that I liked you best from the start?" she asked.

Zeb chuckled. "Ya, I'd say you were makin' it pretty obvious." He sat back and cleared his throat. The conversation was getting far too intimate for this early in the day. "Tell me again, what you're doing in Calgary?"

Tiffany sat back as well, relaxing her posture. "My mother wanted me to come. There's someone she wanted me to meet."

"Oh. For what?"

Tiffany shrugged. "Just personal reasons."

"None of my business, you mean." Zeb chuckled again.

"My mother and Sherri's mother are best friends. They came to Canada at the same time as brides - picked by their families to make sure they made a good match."

"Oh. Don't hear of that much anymore," Zeb said. He wasn't sure what that had to do with the earlier conversation, but he let it go.

"Maybe not in western culture," Tiffany continued, "but it's more common elsewhere than you'd think."

Zeb frowned. "Seems kind of backward to me. Lettin' someone else pick your spouse."

"Surprisingly, most arranged marriages work out rather well."

"You won't find me doin' narn a thing!" When she didn't say anything in response, he looked up at her. "You?"

She shrugged. "I'm undecided. It might just be the smart thing to do. It worked for my parents, after all."

"Ah…" The light bulb came on in Zeb's mind. "This person your ma wants you to meet is a prospective husband."

Tiffany nodded. "Yes."

"I'm surprised to hear you say that. You seem too… independent."

"You might think so, but I'm actually quite traditional when it comes down to it. I don't believe in romantic love. I think one can learn to respect and care for someone without it."

"Sounds kinda dry to me."

"Maybe, but once the commitment is made, there's no going back." She stopped and looked Zeb straight in the eye. "Which is why I need to make sure I've had enough other experiences to last a lifetime - just in case."

Zeb's eyebrows rose. "What kind of experiences?"

"I think you know."

"I see." He focused on the tabletop again.

She leaned forward and this time took one of Zeb's hands in between her own. She turned it over and looked at his rough palm, her two hands small compared to his one. "My favourite animal is a tiger. Do you like tigers?" She looked up at him.

"Sure. I guess. Not sure I have a favourite. Maybe a moose cause I like the meat."

She smiled. "You're so… honest and unaffected. It's one of the things I like about you. You just say what you think without trying to pretend to be someone you're not."

"Thanks, I guess."

She started tracing the lines in his palm with one of her fingers. "Do you know why I like tigers?"

"Why?" His own voice sounded breathless and he gulped, waiting for her answer.

"I like the untamed power. Kind of like you."

"I, uh… haven't tried in a while, but I think I can do a fair tiger impression." He grinned.

"Good. Is there anywhere we can go to test that out?"

"Jed won't be home from work for a few hours yet."

"Excellent. There's nothing better than a bit of afternoon delight." She dropped his hand and rose from the table.

Zeb blinked, his mind a muddled fog of desire mixed with apprehension. "But… what about that fella you're supposed to meet? The one you might marry?"

"What about him?"

"Have you met 'im yet?"

"Tomorrow." She flipped her hair out of her face. "He's not bad, really. I've seen a picture and I'll probably say yes."

"But… are you sure?"

She laughed and suddenly she didn't seem as attractive in his eyes. "Of course I'm sure. Come on. As a martial arts instructor I have some moves that I think you'll like."

"Hold on, now." Zeb stood up also. "I'm not sure I feel right about this. Not if you're about to pledge yourself to another man."

"Pledge myself? How quaint! And since when do you care about that?"

"I suspect you don't know me as well as you think."

She sighed. "Of all the brothers, I thought you'd be the one I could count on for one last fling."

A war was waging inside Zeb's chest. On the one hand he wanted to forget he'd ever heard that she was planning to get engaged to a stranger and just enjoy his time off, like he normally would. He'd slept with lots of women without any thought to ever seeing them again. Why was this any different?

He couldn't answer that question for certain except to say it was wrong, and somewhere in the core of his being he knew it.

"Sorry, but your gonna have to find some other gigolo. This one's takin' down his shingle."

"I never should have mentioned anything about why I was here," she said.

"Probably not," Zeb said. "But you did, and now that's the end of it."

She lofted her head, chin up, and marched through the French doors - and out of his life.

Zeb let out a deep exhale. He felt lighter, for some odd reason. He sauntered to the painting and perused it once again while rubbing his beard. Eight hundred dollars wasn't that much. Maybe instead of spending all his money on booze and women, he'd start buying art.

"Tamara?" he called. "Can I take this here painting now or should I come back for it later?"

EPISODE 7

NEIGHBOURHOOD RUCKUS

ED

JED SHIFTED his gaze away from the hockey playoffs on TV and looked down at the text message he'd just received on his phone. His stomach did a little jig when he saw the name: Andrea Carravagio. An expletive escaped his lips, more at his own silly reaction than at the woman. He opened up the message and read.

"Just wanted to remind you about the guest speaker at our church next week."

He grunted and closed the message without replying. She'd told him all about it the other night on their drive home together. Some former biker turned preacher was speaking at her church for several evenings in a row.

Not likely! The last thing he wanted was to listen to some holier than thou preacher trying to make him change his ways. He was happy just the way he was, thank you very much.

Or was he?

Jed refocused his attention on the game in progress but his mind began to wander once again. Less than a week ago he'd spent almost an entire evening in her company at the Fortune Cookie Family Restaurant. His brother Zeb had set things up, purposely inviting Andrea when he knew darned well Jed didn't have a hope in hell of making it with her.

He smiled at that. Hope in hell was right. Andrea was religious - the kind that went to church during the week and twice on Sundays. She was a good person, he had no doubt, but had made it clear a few months back that she would never consider dating a guy like him. She'd said it was because God didn't approve. 'Unequally yoked' she'd said. Hmph!

He'd gone to Catholic school for his entire education. Probably knew as much as most about the Bible when it came down to it. He'd just never subscribed to it, that's all. There were too many 'thou shalt nots' for his liking. No, he wasn't about to change for any woman, no matter how much he liked her.

They'd had a nice time the other night, though. She wasn't at all uppity - although she never had been - and she didn't even mention the fact that she and God had given him the thumbs down once already. She seemed genuinely pleased to see him and they'd gotten along like old friends, talking about his work, her salon, his sister Reba who worked for her, and various other topics. Then she'd gone and mentioned the biker dude preacher and things had gotten a little awkward.

He'd given her a ride home - thanks again to Zeb's orchestration. Not that he minded. He and Andrea lived in the same building and all, but it had been some time since he'd found himself alone in her company.

He'd forgotten how melodic her voice was… how her smile reached all the way up into her eyes, and how she seemed to have a positive energy that drew him in… made him want to accept her invitation - which was ridiculous, of course!

He downed the dregs of beer from the can he was holding and then set the empty on the floor beside his armchair. It was a silly fool notion to even be entertaining thoughts about Andrea Carravagio. He squinted at the TV and swore again. He'd missed a goal. With another huff he sat forward in the chair, determined not to miss another moment.

She was definitely a looker, that Andrea. He couldn't deny the attraction he felt every time he caught a glimpse of her, but that was only natural. He was a man and she was a well-endowed woman who was pretty in every way.

Jed shook his head. He'd dealt with these feelings, already! He was no schoolboy with his first crush. It would be downright foolhardy to accept her invitation, not only because he wasn't interested in religion, but he wasn't interested in Andrea, either. No, he was better off making an excuse and leaving it at that.

Zeb was no good at matchmaking and he was going to tell him so the next time he saw him, make no mistake.

THE HOCKEY GAME having failed to secure his attention, Jed did what he always did when he had nothing better to do. He headed for the Urban Cowboy. He sat up to his usual spot at the bar and ordered a beer from Bo, who was working behind the counter.

"Thought you were staying home tonight to watch the game," Bo said.

Jed shrugged. "It was a wash out."

"Too bad." Bo set the stein of draft in front of Jed and he took a long swig. "I thought the Canadiens had a real shot this year."

"They do. The series isn't over yet," Jed said.

"At least that is one thing we agree on," Jacques Marcett, the manager of the establishment, said from nearby.

"True enough," Jed said. "I know it's not popular to cheer for any team but the Calgary Flames in this town, but I've been a Montreal fan all my life and I'm not gonna change now."

"As I said, for once we agree," Jacques said.

Bo waved at an approaching figure. Jed looked over his shoulder and was surprised to see Buck Stone making his way toward them. Buck worked at the same campground as their brother Will.

"Fancy meeting you here," Jed said when Buck arrived by his side. "Can I buy ya a drink?"

Bo cleared his throat meaningfully. "Um, Buck doesn't drink, remember?"

"No, it's okay," Buck said. "I just came from visiting my daughter. Thought I'd stop in for one before I head back out to the camp."

Bo frowned. "Are you sure?"

Buck's face remained placid. "Of course. I'm not going to start drinking again. It's just one."

"I don't know…" Bo slung a towel over his shoulder.

"It is not your job to deny a customer," Jacques reminded, not far away.

Buck nodded his thanks at Jacques and sat up beside Jed. "I'll just have what he's having." He pointed at Jed's half empty mug.

Bo set his mouth into a line and silently filled the second stein with draft.

"Will didn't come with you tonight?" Jed asked, keeping the conversation going.

"No, not this time."

Jed shook his head. "I thought for sure now that things went south with that gal out there, he'd wanna come to town more often."

"Not everyone drowns their sorrows," Bo offered wryly as he set Buck's drink in front of him.

"That's for you to talk to him about," Buck said. "I try to stay out of people's personal lives."

"Good advice," Jed said with a nod of his head. "Makes for less ruckus later on."

Bo shook his head. "Says the one who loves to get his nose in other people's business."

"Do you like pool?" Jed asked Buck. "Looks like there's a table free."

Buck nodded. "Don't mind if I do."

"Good. That way we don't 'ave to listen to this mother hen."

~

JED HELD the cell phone to his ear and then glanced over at his living room couch where Buck Stone lay sleeping, one arm dangling on the floor, the other over his eyes.

"He's still sleepin' it off, b'y. I'll get 'im up and on 'is way shortly." Jed waited for his brother Will to respond and then winced when he did.

"I can't believe you went drinking with 'im last night!" Will chided into the phone.

"He was only gonna have one…" Jed looked over at his youngest brother Pip, who was leaning against a nearby door-jam with arms crossed, listening to the conversation.

"What's wrong with ya? Don't you remember he's an alcoholic?" Will continued on the other end of the line.

"It's not like I forced 'im," Jed defended.

"But you didn't stop 'im neither."

"How was I to know he's got no self-control?"

"That's the point. Alcoholic's don't have self-control. That's what makes 'em alcoholics."

"No need to yell at me. I'm not the one with the problem," Jed said. "Anyway, I didn't want to leave 'im on the couch and Pip and I are about to leave for work. Just be glad I phoned you this morning at all. Thought your boss might be wondering where he was."

"Oh he will," Will said. "I just hope it doesn't cost Buck 'is job."

"After one little slip?" Jed snorted. "Make some kind of excuse and I'll get 'im out the door right quick."

Will ended the call with a few choice words which Jed chose to ignore and he hung up.

"You could just let 'im sleep," Pip suggested.

"Better not. I told Will I'd get 'im up and goin', so I best do it." Jed walked closer to the couch and stood looking over Buck for a moment. He did feel bad, in a way, but how was he to know the other man couldn't stop at one?

Jed cleared his throat. ""Eh, b'y! Time to get a move on, as like."

Buck inhaled sharply and then stretched. He moved his arm from over his eyes and squinted at the offending morning light streaming through the patio doors. "What time is it?"

Jed checked his watch. "Seven fifteen. Pip and me are about to leave so we thought you'd best be up and at 'em, too."

Buck sat up and winced, swinging his legs onto the floor. "I never should have stayed. Now I'll be late for work."

"You were in no shape for driving last night. Your boss'll cut you some slack, I reckon."

Buck turned bleary eyes to Jed. "Not if he finds out why."

Jed just shrugged. "Will's gonna cover for you till you get there."

"Where's my truck?" Buck asked.

"Still parked outside the Urban Cowboy," Jed said.

"By the time I get back to my truck and then out of the city it'll be two hours before I make it back." Buck ran a hand through his hair and stood up. He seemed momentarily disoriented. "Where's your washroom again?"

"Down the hall." Jed pointed and then watched Buck shuffle in that direction.

"Hope he doesn't take too long." Pip looked at the time on his cell phone. "I don't wanna be late."

"Never you mind," Jed said. "I'll cover for ya if I have to."

When Buck reappeared a few minutes later he looked somewhat more presentable, although still red rimmed around the eyes. "Thanks," he mumbled.

"No trouble. Any time."

"I hope not."

Jed blinked. "What's that now?"

"I hope it doesn't happen again." Buck shook his head. "Not that I'm not grateful for keeping me off the roads, but now I've got some explaining to do and I'm not looking forward to it. Especially not my daughter."

"Why even tell 'er?" Jed asked. "What she doesn't know won't hurt her."

Buck shook his head. "No. Secrets lead to more secrets. It's best to just get it out in the open and let the chips fall."

"Suit yourself." Jed shrugged.

"Thanks again." Buck hesitated once more, the door to the apartment half open. "I'll be back next week. For my AA meeting. Now that I know where you live, maybe I'll pick you up."

Before Jed could formulate an answer, Buck was gone.

Pip smiled on his way past Jed. "That'll be the day, eh, b'y? You goin' to an AA meeting?"

"Shut yer trap and get a move on." Jed locked the door behind them.

EPISODE 8

NEIGHBOURHOOD HEARTACHE

o

"That scowl will be permanent if you don't watch it."

Jacques's French accent cut into Bo's consciousness and he glanced up from the case of bottles he was sorting to see his boss standing next to him with arms crossed, an easy grin on the other man's face. Bo purposely smoothed his brow as he straightened. "Not sure what you're talking about. I was just concentrating."

"Sure you were." Jacques didn't sound convinced.

Bo rolled one shoulder. "Okay, so I'm still miffed about last night. But I'll get over it."

"Last night?"

"Serving Buck Stone when he's a known alcoholic."

"A lot of people are alcoholics, but it's a free country. We can cut people off once they've had too many, but we can't legally refuse to sell to someone without cause. It's just part of the job."

"A part I don't like."

271

Jacques shrugged. "You should have thought of that when you decided to become a bartender."

Bo didn't say anything else. Jacques was right. He'd never really considered the moral dilemmas he might have to face when he'd taken the course back in Newfoundland. He just thought it would be fun. A way to be part of the action without actually having to participate.

Jacques turned his back on the crowd and leaned against the counter. "Did I tell you that Viann is finally leaving? I told her she didn't have to, but she's made up her mind."

Bo blinked. All concern over Buck Stone vanished. "She's leaving? When?"

"Next week. She's got her flight booked." Jacques smiled and stroked his goatee. "It's about time."

"Where will she go?"

"Back to Montreal." Jacques narrowed his eyes at Bo. "You seem surprised. I don't know why. She stayed longer than I expected."

"She has a habit of coming and going?" Bo asked, slipping back into his Newfoundland accent.

"You can say that again! Every time she has men troubles she comes running for help. This time she ran from one right into the arms of another. I could have warned her, but she doesn't listen."

Bo took that bit of information in. Viann was apparently as unstable as she appeared. It was probably for the best that she was going back to Montreal.

Bo heard a familiar holler coming from the direction of the entrance and watched as Jed and Pip made their way toward him. He definitely wasn't in the mood to see Jed. Or any of them for that matter.

"Just like old times, eh b'y?" Jed said loudly as he swung his body onto a stool. "I finally convinced this lubber it was time to get outta the 'house. You'd think 'e'd gone religious or something the way 'e avoids the place."

"Not everyone wants to drink their life away," Bo clipped.

"You tricked me," Pip said to Jed. "Said it had something to do with work."

"No, I said Lester Tibbett wanted to have a word with you. Which 'e probably does if 'e shows up."

Pip shook his head but smiled good-naturedly anyway. The youngest of the clan had been in a bit of a funk lately, so Bo was glad to at least see he was coming around and could smile again. That didn't mean he was in the mood for Jed's banter.

"Beer I take it?" Bo asked.

"Vodka water for me," Pip replied.

"Right."

"Good to see you're gettin' back to yourself." Jed slapped Pip on the back.

Bo made a snorting noise as he set their drinks in front of them.

Jed took a slurp of his beer and then pointed at Bo. "You seem a bit outta sorts. What gives?"

"Nothing. I just find it ironic that 'normal' to you means everyone gets drunk."

Jed raised his brows. "I'm not drunk yet. Lard tunderin'! Give me a minute or two!"

"He is upset about last night," Jacques informed from nearby.

"Last night?" Jed asked.

"Buck Stone." Bo crossed his arms.

"Don't blame that arn me! I never forced 'im."

"Still, you didn't discourage him," Bo said. "You know he's an alcoholic."

"He stayed over, if that means anything," Pip offered. "At least Jed didn't let 'im drive home."

"Thank the Lard for small mercies," Bo said under his breath.

"Sides, you're the one who served 'im. Seems to me you're more to blame than me."

"We cannot refuse a customer without cause," Jacques said, his tone slightly defensive.

"Anyhoo, 'e'll get over it, I reckon. Looked like death warmed over this mornin' and said 'e was comin' back next week for 'is AA meetin'. No harm done, I'd say." Jed took another swallow of beer.

Pip grinned. "Said 'e was gonna pick Jed up and take 'im along to the meeting."

"Now there's a good idea," Bo said.

Jed scowled. "Not likely."

"Really? When are you gonna admit that you have a problem?" Bo asked. "Or maybe it's easier to keep everyone around you drunk as well so you don't have to feel too bad about yourself." He looked meaningfully at Pip.

"I take exception to that," Jed said, his voice rising.

"Hold on a minute," Jacques cut in. "No sibling squabbles or I'll toss the lot of you." He looked squarely at Bo. "Including you. No intimidating the customers."

Bo threw his towel down on the counter. "In that case, they're all yours. I'm going to the back to count stock. You can serve."

Bo turned on his heel and stalked away. The job, his siblings, his own loneliness… it was getting to be too much for him. Something had to change - soon - before he tipped over the edge.

Bo LIFTED his hand to knock and then let it fall to his side again. What in the world was he doing standing outside Jacques's apartment? Hoping to see Viann one last time, that's what, but it was a stupid fool thing to do. First of all, Jacques might be home. Second of all, he had no claim to Viann. She had made that abundantly clear. So why was he torturing himself?

He strode down the hall and decided to take the emergency stairs instead of the elevators. His footfalls echoed in the tunnel like space and he emerged in the lobby just in time to see Jacques exiting the building through the front doors. Bo stopped in his tracks, thinking for a few minutes. With resolve, he went back through the stairwell door and took the steps two at a time back up to Jacques's floor.

This time he knocked before he could change his mind. There was a shuffling noise on the other side of the door followed by the rattle of the emergency chain. Then the door swung wide. Viann was on the other side.

Bo blinked when he saw her. Her face was splotchy and her eyes puffy and red. In fact, he hardly recognized her. Her face was devoid of all makeup - the first time he'd seen her like that. She looked ordinary and vulnerable, but even without makeup she was beautiful. And for some reason his heart started to pound.

"Jacques just left," she said and was about to close the door again.

Bo put out a hand to stop her from closing the door. "It's okay. I came to see you."

"Me?" She stared up at him.

He nodded. "Jacques told me you were planning to move back to Montreal and I... well, I just wanted to say good-bye."

She seemed at a loss for words.

"Can I come in for a few minutes?" Bo asked. "I won't stay long."

She sighed but opened the door wider for him to pass through. "I am a mess. But what does it matter? You will never see me again."

"You don't know that for sure," Bo said.

"True. Do you want coffee? I can make some."

"Sure. I'd like that."

She gestured for him to sit down at the kitchen table and he watched her mundane movements as she put the kettle on to boil and then readied the French press.

"I'm not sure anyone but Jacques has seen me without my makeup on." She ran a hand through her hair, which was unusually limp.

"I like you without makeup," Bo said. "It's like I can see the real you. No mask."

"I am good at wearing a mask, that is certain," Viann said with a shrug.

"Oh?"

"I learned from the best."

"Who would that be?"

Viann poured the boiling water into the press and positioned the plunger on top. "My mother. She was never happy, but she always pretended. I suppose I am just like her."

"How do you mean?"

Viann kept her gaze on the coffee pot, not making eye contact. "Moving from man to man. Never satisfied."

"And that's why you're leaving?"

"Men just seem to use me and I fall for it every time." She stole a glance his way and then pressed the plunger on the French press.

"Not all men are the same," Bo said.

"Aren't they?" She poured the coffee into two mugs and brought them to the table. "Perhaps you are different. Besides Jacques, you are the only man I feel safe with. See? I don't even mind that you see me like this." She gestured at her face.

"I don't care about makeup and fancy clothes. It's what's on the inside that counts."

"On the inside I feel ugly." She said it matter-of-factly and took a sip of her coffee. "Oh. I forgot to ask you if you needed cream and sugar."

"This is fine." Bo took a sip of his coffee as well. It was strong. Just what he needed this morning. "I think you're beautiful on the inside and out."

"You're sweet." She allowed a small self-depreciating laugh to escape. "You obviously do not know me very well."

"I think you're being too hard on yourself."

She shook her head. "No. I am a coward and a fool."

"Then don't run away. Stay here and face whatever it is. I'll help you."

"I have taken advantage of Jacques for too long already. It is time to move on. And the last thing you need is to get involved in my troubles."

"I don't mind."

She smiled a watery smile and Bo's heart leapt again. "I almost wish I could, but it would be no use. Maybe I feel safe with you because you have no other motives. Not like other men. You just want to be my friend."

Bo blinked, trying hard to maintain the same nonchalant smile he had been wearing thus far. "I'm glad you feel that way."

"With you I do not feel threatened. You aren't interested in me as a trophy and for that I am grateful. You are such a good friend. I wish more men were like you. I don't have to worry about falling in love with you."

Bo took a large gulp of the scalding coffee and swallowed. How could he tell her that his interest went way beyond friendship? That he *was* just like the others?

BO MOVED LIKE AN AUTOMATON, polishing, stacking, filling… it didn't really matter. He could serve drinks in his sleep. What did matter was that Viann was gone. For good.

She'd boarded her plane earlier that day. He wished he could have been the one to take her to the airport. To see her one last time. But of course, that was Jacques's job, not his. So he'd had to make due with a final, awkward hug in the lobby of their apartment building. She had been perfectly made up and wore her usual air of aloof confidence, something he was beginning to see was a defence mechanism.

Now here he was, back at work, going through the motions, even though his insides felt like they had been ripped to shreds.

Female laughter reached his ears and he glanced toward the three-some entering the establishment. Andrea and Angela Carravagio and his sister Reba. It had been awhile since any of the women had been at the Urban Cowboy. Angela and Jacques had been an item for several months but when Jacques broke it off, Angela had quit coming to the bar. Andrea didn't drink and had only come infrequently for moral support, and Reba had had some embarrassing moments with owner Cory Roberts, although that might be changing.

The three women sat up to the bar. Bo noted that Jacques, who was further down the line, purposely turned the other way.

"It seems like ages since I've been here," Angela breathed, looking around. "I hate to admit it, but I think I've missed the place."

"That's not all she's missed." The corners of Andrea's mouth turned up as she nodded in Jacques's direction.

Angela tossed her mane from her shoulders. "Whatever. A modern, independent woman doesn't need a man to make her complete."

"Agreed," Reba said, then added with a grin, "But it helps."

The three placed their order, Andrea opting for a fancy non-alcoholic drink while Reba had beer and Angela had the same as her sister, only with the alcohol added. Bo mixed the drinks and set them in front of the women.

"Is Cory working tonight?" Reba asked.

"He's not here if that's what you're asking," Bo replied. "He may show up later, though."

Reba nodded, a satisfied smile playing at her lips.

The three continued with their easy banter, talking shop since they all worked at Gemini's hair salon owned by the twin sisters. Bo tuned out most of the conversation, feigning busyness and serving other customers. He noticed Jacques was listening, even though the other man was trying to look nonchalant. It seemed as if everything was getting back to normal at the Urban Cowboy.

Except for Bo, nothing would ever be normal again.

EPISODE 9

NEIGHBOURHOOD GAMES

EBA

REBA HUMMED to herself as she restocked some beauty products on the display shelf. Last night had been a good evening. Cory Roberts had showed up at the Urban Cowboy after all.

"Guess who called me this morning before work?" Angela said over her client's head, deftly combing and trimming as she spoke.

Reba looked over at her boss.

"I know," Andrea said from her position behind the reception desk.

"No telling," Angela said. "So? Any guesses?" she directed at Reba.

Reba set a shampoo bottle beside its fellow and then screwed up her face in thought. "Someone famous?"

"No. Guess again."

"Someone with a French accent," Andrea supplied.

"No fair!" blurted Angela.

"Jacques?" Reba guessed. "I'm surprised. He wouldn't even look at you last night."

"I know, right?" Angela said.

"So what did 'e want?"

"It was the strangest thing. Just small talk, really."

"He obviously wants you back," Reba said.

"Maybe. I'm not going to make it too easy for him, though. At least now that Viann is gone we won't have that between us."

"Viann is gone?" Reba looked up from the shelf.

"So he says. I told him to take a hike."

Andrea frowned. "I thought you wanted to get back with him."

"Of course, but I can't come off as too anxious, now can I?"

"I don't know. It might be better to just be honest," Andrea said.

Angela made a scoffing sound. "You're a fine one to talk!"

"Angela…" Andrea pleaded with both her eyes and her tone. "Not here, okay?"

"Oh right. Wouldn't want to be too honest, now would we sister?" Angela kept on snipping. "So how was your weekend?" she asked the woman in the chair.

Reba felt sorry for Andrea. Angela was hard on her sister at times. Not that Reba agreed with Andrea's choices, especially when it came to religion, but she didn't see why Angela had to rub it in her face.

Reba finished up the shampoo and conditioner and took the now empty cardboard containers to the recycling in the backroom. On her way back with a carton of hair dyes she stopped at the reception desk. "Don't mind 'er," she said softly to Andrea so that Angela wouldn't hear. "She's still hurting."

"I know." Andrea smiled up at Reba. "I just wish she wouldn't judge me. I am trying to be honest with myself - and her - but sometimes she just throws it back at me. It's what I get for confiding in her, I guess."

"Oh?" Reba's brows rose. "Are we talking about a budding relationship, perhaps?"

Andrea just shrugged. "It's complicated."

"I see. Now I'm intrigued."

"That's all I'm going to say - for both our sakes. If it's meant to be you'll find out soon enough." Andrea pursed her lips and went back to checking through the day's list of clients.

"Well, I don't mind telling you that things are looking up for me in that department."

Andrea glanced up. "Oh? I noticed you and Cory seemed quite friendly last night. Maybe Viann's leaving is good for more than just Angela."

Reba nodded. "I'm hoping. He asked me out just before we left."

"Congratulations!" Andrea said enthusiastically.

"What's this?" Angela asked from across the room.

"I'm going out on a date with Cory later tonight," Reba said. She knew she was grinning but she couldn't help it.

"Nice work!" Angela said.

Reba tore open the container of hair dye and started arranging the products on the shelves.

A few moments later, Andrea was by her side. She picked up a jar of dye. "This looks interesting. If I wanted to change my colour I might try it myself."

Reba just shrugged. She wasn't interested in changing her own hair colour ever since the last time. It hadn't turned out that well.

Andrea put the jar back on the shelf and hesitated for a moment before speaking again. "Um, do you happen to talk to your brother Jed much?"

Reba snuck a glance at Andrea. "I haven't seen much of 'im since we all went out to the Chinese food place. Why?"

"No reason. I was just hoping he would come to the event at my church I was telling him about. I thought maybe you'd have some influence, that's all."

"Is that who you don't want to tell me about?"

"Don't be silly!" Andrea waved a hand dismissively. "Jed and I are just friends."

Reba smiled. "Jed's as stubborn as they come, but I'll see what I can do."

She turned away, still grinning from ear to ear. So… Zeb's match-making skills were having more effect than he realized.

∼

REBA ROCKED FORWARD on her ridiculously high heels and peered out the smudged glass doors of her apartment building. The late rays of sunlight streaming through the glass were warm and golden, highlighting every dust particle that danced in the foyer. Reba's insides were also doing a little jig. She was just so nervous! Cory Roberts was picking her up and they were going out on a real date. Just the two of them. It was about time!

Cory drove up in his sleek red sports car and idled it just outside the doors. As soon as she saw the car her heart did a little flip and she pushed through the glass doors. He got out and rounded the front end of his car but she had already clicked her way to the passenger side of the vehicle before he managed to get there himself. When she went to reach for the handle he called out, "Hold on, lady!" He opened the passenger door and bowed with a flourish. "Your carriage."

Reba giggled and slid into the low leather seat. She could get used to this kind of treatment.

"I hope I'm not over dressed," she said once they were both settled. "You didn't tell me where we were going." She smoothed the skirt on her dress, a more feminine affair than was her usual style, and examined the strappy heels that clung to her feet. Andrea had helped her dress for the evening. Her usual dress up style was a bit more edgy and probably more in line with Angela's taste.

"You look lovely." Cory gave her a winning smile, his teeth flashing whitely against his dark skin. "And I didn't want to spoil the surprise." He pulled out of the parking lot and onto the street. "You must think I'm a bit slow."

"No, I get it. Sometimes the traffic is bad this time of day."

He laughed. "Not what I meant. I meant slow as in making a move."

"Oh." For once Reba felt shy; at a loss for words. She looked down at her coral coloured toenails.

"Don't think I didn't notice your attempts at trying to make me take notice. I just had some other things on my mind. The timing wasn't right."

Things like Viann, she wanted to say, but didn't. Instead she said, "Oh dear. I guess I should feel embarrassed."

"It shows that you're a woman who knows what she wants. And a woman of good taste." He smiled over at her again and her insides did another flip.

"Some might call it bull headed. That's what my brothers say." She pasted on what she hoped was a worldly smile. She'd tried for so long to get Cory's attention and now that she had it she was acting like a teenager.

Cory shook his head and his dreadlocks bobbed. "I was actually a bit intimidated by all those brothers of yours! Another reason it took me so long."

"They're all bluster. I can handle them."

"I'll just bet you can." Cory veered onto Deerfoot Trail and merged into the rush of bumper to bumper traffic. "I guess there's no point in keeping it a secret any longer. I thought we'd go out for dinner first and then try this new club. Maybe get our freak on."

"The competition?" Reba asked.

"Not really," Cory said. "This is more of a techno-club. 'Biome' it's called. Ever heard of it?"

Reba shook her head. "No." She wouldn't let him know that she wasn't exactly a fan of his style of electronic music. "Are you playing there?"

"I wish! It's a pretty intimate space, but all the hot DJs want to get their turn. Something about the atmosphere, I guess. It's old school. You'll see once we get there."

"I can hardly wait." She hoped she sounded more enthusiastic than she felt.

"Of course nobody shows up until at least 10 or 11, so we'll have plenty of time to eat first. I hope you like Indian?"

"Sure. I pretty much just like food, so whatever you've got planned is fine by me."

"Good. Cause I'm taking you to my favourite Indian restaurant. Best butter chicken this side of India - not that I've been." He grinned over at her again.

They arrived at their destination - an out of the way restaurant in the middle of the industrial area. It seemed like an unlikely location, but the parking lot was full - a good sign. It was finally starting to get dusky, now that the days were lengthening for the summer, and Reba was starving. It had been a long time since lunch.

The interior was dim and smelled of curry and other spices. High backed booths upholstered in purple damask made it difficult to see just how many patrons were dining, but from the murmur of voices over the twang of sitar music, the place was full.

"Reservation for two," Cory said quietly to the hostess, a young woman sporting dramatically penciled in eyebrows. She scanned her list, nodded, and led them through the labyrinth to their own secluded booth.

Reba opened her menu and blinked. Everything sounded unfamiliar. She gave a little laugh. "I must admit the only thing I recognize is butter chicken."

"Like I said, it's the best. Would you like me to order for you?" Cory asked. "We could get a variety of dishes to try."

Reba nodded and closed the padded menu. "That sounds like a plan."

"I'll order some wine, too. Would that be alright?"

"Sure." What she really felt like was a beer, but she wasn't going to say so. Cory had gone to a lot of trouble to make this date special and she wasn't going to spoil it by coming across as a hick.

Cory placed their order and soon the waiter came with their wine and poured them each a generous glassful. Reba took a tentative sip and tried to smile. She really wasn't a wine person - beer was much more to her liking, but maybe this was for the best. At least this way she wouldn't get tipsy too early in the evening and make a spectacle.

Cory lofted his glass and took a sip. "Mm. That's good. So what really brought you all the way across the country, if I may ask?"

"What do you mean 'really'?"

He shrugged and swirled the liquid around in his glass. "I kind of know the basics, but I thought there might be more to it than that."

"Trying to find out my secrets?" Reba batted her lashes at him over the rim of her own wineglass and took another tentative sip.

"Sure. Why not? Everyone has them." Cory smiled mischievously. "What makes the lovely Reba Malloy tick?"

Reba felt herself warming under his gaze. Or maybe it was the wine. She shrugged, trying for nonchalance. "Adventure, I guess. I want to see the world and was tired of the same old same old. Jed and Zeb moved west years ago and it always sounded so… exotic."

"Calgary? Exotic? Hardly. This is red-neck central."

"Have you been to Newfoundland?" she asked. When he shook his head in the negative she smirked. "Then you don't even know the meaning of red-neck. Then again, maybe you do. You've met my brothers."

"True enough!" He laughed. "I hear it's very scenic."

"Oh, that it is. I miss the ocean most, I think." She inhaled deeply, her eyes far away. "And the smell of the salt sea air."

"Homesick?"

She shook her head to clear it. The wine was really taking her places she didn't want to go. "No way! Not by a long shot. I got things to see yet before I run home to Ma."

"So that's it? Just needed a change of scenery?" Cory asked.

Reba nodded. "My ma can be a bit… overbearing is one way to put it. When Bo decided 'e was coming for Christmas, I saw my chance and tagged along. The rest is history, I guess."

"So, not running away from a romance gone wrong? Nothing like that?"

Reba shook her head. "Nope. That's Viann's style, not mine." As soon as she said it, she bit her lip and blinked. "Oops. Sorry. I was just repeating what I've heard. I shouldn't a said it."

Cory rolled one shoulder nonchalantly. "No harm done."

"But you and her…" Reba trailed off.

"We what? Viann is simply the sister of my friend and manager. I was trying to help her through a rough patch. Nothing more."

Reba took this in. "Me and my big mouth. Zeb always says it'll get me in trouble." When she glanced at Cory she could see he was smiling and she felt even more foolish for what she'd said. If this was her way of making a good impression it was backfiring miserably.

"It's okay. It means you were jealous, which is a compliment."

"There's no hiding my shame around you, it seems."

"There's no need to. You're a woman who speaks her mind. I like that. I don't have to work to read between the lines."

"Oh gawd!" Reba rolled her eyes heavenward. "I feel like the hick you think I am."

"Hey. Relax." Cory took her hands in his own and held them on top of the table. "I like you. I find your 'hick' ways, as you put it, rather charming. I'm not in the habit of asking women out on a date if I don't find them attractive, so go ahead and be who you really are and quit worrying about the proper way to behave around me. I can smell a phoney a mile away."

"So things are stinkin' pretty bad then, eh?" Reba asked.

"I was wondering the moment you walked out the door. You looked different - not bad different - but just not like the Reba I've come to know this past little while."

"Cause I listened to Andrea about what to wear instead of going with my gut." She gestured down at her frilly skirt. "Who actually wears this stuff?"

"You look fabulous. But frankly, you could have come out wearing a paper bag and I wouldn't have batted an eye. You're a very sexy woman, Reba Malloy." His eyes twinkled and he lifted one of her hands up to kiss it.

Their food came and broke the spell. Reba felt like she was on cloud nine. Cory was attracted to her and she didn't have to pretend to be someone she wasn't. Her lucky stars had finally come into alignment.

They chatted some more about their families. Cory confided that his father, Tad, was getting married soon to a woman named Goldie Harper who had a young son.

"He's quite a bit older than she is, but they seem to be happy together, so who am I to judge?"

"I like your dad. He used to work at the Urban Cowboy a lot before you came back from Vancouver."

"Surprising, since he has a religious streak a mile wide," Cory said. "I think he's relieved he doesn't have to do it anymore and can go back to being the silent partner. He did me a good turn when he hired your brother Bo. He's a good bartender and a good employee."

"Yeah, he's always been a bit different, our Bo. Except for the look of 'im you'd almost think 'e was adopted. Instead of being the black sheep of the family, he's the only white one." She stopped and blinked at what she'd just said. "I mean… holy jumpin' that sounded racist and I didn't mean for it to. Sorry."

Cory just laughed. "I understood exactly what you meant and didn't take it as racist at all."

"Good thing. I really put my foot in my mouth, as like."

Cory frowned slightly at what she'd said and then his forehead cleared again. "Speaking of your lovely feet, how about if we head over to 'Biome' now and try out the dance floor. 'Bust a move', as they say."

"Is that the same as getting your freak on?" Reba asked with a grin.

"You're catching on. I'm a student of classic 90s lingo and can't help myself. Comes with the territory. I'm still a DJ Jazzy Jeff junkie. Him and the Fresh Prince. Those dudes had style!"

Reba didn't have a clue what Cory just said but nodded her head in agreement anyway. She wasn't sure how much dancing she'd be doing in the heels she was wearing, but determined she'd give it a shot.

Cory paid the bill and ushered her out of the restaurant, his hand at the small of her back. She leaned closer to him on the way to his parked car and allowed his gentlemanly side to open the door for her without protest.

Biome was small by club standards. 'Intimate' Cory had said, but the flashing neon and strobe effects made the size irrelevant. Who could actually see in a place like this? There were two bars along opposite walls and a raised stage where the DJ performed his beats. The rest was dance floor with only a few glass tables and plexiglass chairs around the outer edges. For the most part, if you weren't dancing you weren't sitting either, so it kind of made dancing the more attractive alternative.

"Come on." Cory grabbed her hand and pulled her out on the floor. Immediately he was moving with the beat. Reba put a hand over her mouth. If she didn't find Cory Roberts attractive she would almost find his movements comical.

She swayed, mostly in one spot, occasionally trying to emulate the moves of others on the floor who seemed more adept.

"You're too tense," Cory shouted. He grabbed her hand and still holding onto it, swung himself behind her so that his body was plastered up against hers. With his arms effectively pinning her to him, he started to grind and gyrate to the music, forcing her to move along with him.

Reba laughed and tried to follow his movements, but very quickly her eyes widened when she felt the unmistakable evidence of his desire pressing up against the small of her back. As brash as she might seem to most people, she wasn't used to this kind of intimate display on an open and public dance floor. She tried to pull away to make more space but Cory seemed oblivious to her distress. When she glanced around she saw that there were several other couples engaged in a similar 'style' of dancing.

She had tried to attract Cory's attention for quite some time now, hadn't she? Well, now she was getting her wish.

The song finished and Cory stepped back, still holding onto one of her hands. The DJ announced he was taking a break and was replaced by canned music. "Phew. That was fun." He didn't appear to be at all embarrassed. "I'm ready for a drink. How about you?"

She nodded her agreement, hoping that they served beer, and followed him to one of the bars. Before she could voice her choice, Cory had already ordered for them both. When the bartender produced a frothy stein of draft beer, Reba's face split into a grin. "Thank you. A thousand times thank you!"

Beer in her right hand, her left firmly enclosed by Cory's, they strolled down the line looking for a seat. There wasn't one to be had.

"Hey!" Cory released her hand for a moment and waved.

Reba focused on the object of his greeting and then her own face lit up. "Patsi!"

With renewed purpose, Cory led her to one of the highly sought after tables near the back where Patsi Tibbett and Brett McMillan sat. There were two empty plexiglass seats at their table.

Patsi jumped up and hugged Reba. Reba hung on for a few seconds longer than necessary. It was so good to be back in her friend's good books.

"I can't believe you're here," Reba said as she pulled away. Patsi was wearing leggings and a long T-shirt and suddenly Reba wished for her own more comfortable clothes, not the fancy-shmancy ones Andrea had insisted she wear for her date. She glanced over at Brett McMillan and nodded, then flicked Patsi a question with her eyes. Patsi's reply was just as subtle, as if to say, "I'll tell you about it later."

"These taken?" Cory asked.

"Saved them for you," Brett said. "Pat spotted you on the floor as soon as we got here and said we should grab the table before someone else did."

"Smart girl." Cory held out Reba's chair until she was seated and then sat down himself in the only vacant one left.

"So what did you think of that set?" Brett asked Cory.

"Old school new school. Loved it. And did you catch that extended mash-up?"

"I did so."

Cory leaned forward. "Since the DJs on his break, we should see if we can talk to him. Maybe we could even talk to the manager about bookings."

The men took their drinks and vacated with hardly a glance.

"They do love their music," Patsi said with a shrug.

Reba watched until they had disappeared into the crowd. Then she turned to Patsi. "So. You're here with Brett." There was no point in beating around the bush.

Patsi nodded. "I... he wore me down." She smiled sheepishly.

"So I see. Is that a good thing?"

Patsi just shrugged again.

"What does Lester think?" Reba asked.

"I didn't ask. Part of the deal when I moved back here was that he let me have some space. So far, he hasn't said much. How can he when he and Sherri are - you know."

Reba blinked. "Having sex? Isn't that what most couples do?"

"Not if you're supposed to be a Christian and saving yourself for marriage. Oh, I know Lester would never admit to it, but I mean, seriously? I've caught them on the couch a couple of times and it was hot and heavy. If they aren't, then they're close."

"You sound bitter."

"Do I? Sorry. I didn't mean to. I guess I've finally just grown up." Patsi sighed. "Anyway, to get back to Brett and me, yeah, we're back together again. I'm tired of being lonely and feeling like a naive little country bumpkin. Brett's into me and… and I like him, too, so why shouldn't I?"

"As long as you know what you're doing…"

Patsi leaned forward in her chair. "And I see you finally got Cory to sit up and take notice. Talk about hot on the dance floor. I thought you were gonna start making out!"

Reba waved a dismissive hand. "We were just dancing. And yes, I finally got him to take notice." She grinned widely.

"Is this your first date?" Patsi asked.

Reba nodded.

"So? Are you gonna sleep with him later? You know what they say. Once you've had black you'll never go back."

Reba frowned at her friend's crass remark. Who was this bold young woman and where had her clean cut country friend gone? "Oh, I doubt it. Not yet."

"Don't wait too long. He might lose interest."

The men were making their way back to the table. Reba was glad. Something was off with Patsi and she wasn't quite sure how to handle it.

"Do we dare risk leaving the table and dancing some more?" Cory asked.

"Go ahead," Patsi said. "I'm more into the two step."

Reba was about to heartily agree but Cory was already pulling her forward.

"Wait," she protested. When Cory stopped she proceeded to unlatch the straps from her heels and slipped them off her feet. Then she tossed them to Patsi who caught them both with the ease of an outfielder. "There. If you're gonna force me to dance, at least want to be able to walk in the morning."

Cory laughed.

She danced freely once they got started, deciding that she couldn't possibly look any more foolish than half the people out there, including Cory. A couple of beer helped, too. She was a Malloy and she was determined to have fun.

LATER THAT NIGHT - technically early morning - as Reba lay on her mattress on the floor in Andrea's room, she thought about the evening and all that had transpired.

She had finally scored a date with the delectable Cory Roberts. It had been fun, but it wasn't quite the dream she had imagined it to be. It was a lot like Christmas. The anticipation was better than the actual presents.

When Cory had dropped her off at her apartment building, he was the perfect gentleman. Despite the sexual innuendo on the dance floor, a chaste kiss outside the glass doors was all she got for her troubles. "Sure you can make it up to your own apartment all right?" he'd asked.

As if they'd have been free to do anything anyway, with Andrea and Angela under foot. Maybe that was the problem. She hadn't quite scored the big prize yet. Once she and Cory made out she would be satisfied.

A grin spread across her face at what Patsi had said. Almost immediately, Reba sobered. What was with her friend? Patsi's attitude had been so out of character. Something was up and Reba intended to find out.

EPISODE 10

NEIGHBOURHOOD QUEST

IP

PIP STEADIED the sheet of glass while Lester Tibbett set the screws in place. Floor to ceiling glass doors and walls were being installed on the eleventh and twelfth floors - a custom order from the new occupants that would be moving in once the entire building was complete. Jed and another member of the crew were working on the same floor but not near enough to carry on a conversation without yelling.

"That should about do it." Lester stood up with a grunt.

"One down, twenty-nine to go," Pip said with a grin. He'd been trying hard to get on the other man's good side after the misunderstanding that stood between them regarding Lester's sister Patsi.

"Is that all?" Lester asked, returning Pip's grin.

They worked for a while in silence until Lester spoke up. "You know, Patsi has started seeing Brett McMillan again."

"I heard," Pip said.

"I feel as if I need to apologize to you for the way I acted awhile back. She was going to do what she was going to do, and I shouldn't have blamed you."

"I coulda warned you, I suppose," Pip said.

Lester shook his head. "I've just got to let her be. She's old enough to live her own life and I've got to learn to let go."

"It's hard. Or so I'm told."

"I just hope it doesn't jeopardize her faith. She's really come around in the last few months."

"That's something I know nothing about," Pip said.

Lester surveyed Pip for a moment before focusing back on the work at hand. "You could change that. If you wanted to, that is."

Pip blinked, not sure how to respond. He glanced sideways to see Jed sauntering over, creating a small cloud of dust as he beat his work gloves against his thigh.

"What's up little brother? Ya looks worried."

"I was just telling Pip he could learn more about God if he wanted to," Lester said. "All he needs to do is ask."

"Not you, too." Jed rolled his eyes skyward.

"What do you mean?" Lester asked.

"Andrea's been trying to get me to come to something at 'er church."

"Why don't you go?"

"The place would cave in around us if I set foot in the door," Jed said with a laugh.

"Not true."

"Not gonna test the theory."

"Your loss," Lester replied.

Jed made a harrumphing sound. "Anyway, I better get back. Gary'll wonder where I got to."

Pip watched Jed stroll away, not in any hurry to get back to assisting Gary, and then turned back to Lester. "So… what if I was to ask?"

"Ask what?"

"About how to learn about God."

"Oh! I didn't mean ask me," Lester said. "I meant ask Him." He pointed toward the ceiling and grinned.

"Does he give directions on how to mend a broken heart?"

"His specialty," Lester said. Then he frowned. "Not Patsi, I hope."

Pip shook his head. "No. Someone else."

"Can't hurt."

Pip took that into consideration. He had to figure out a way to either get Ophelia to love him back or get her out of his mind for good.

PIP KNOCKED on the door to Lester's apartment and waited, hands in pockets. He hadn't bothered changing from his work clothes yet and noted the dirt clinging to the toes of his boots.

Lester opened the door and his brows rose in surprise. "I wasn't expecting to see you twice in one day," he said. "Come in." He gestured for Pip to enter.

Pip slid through the opening and hovered near the entrance after Lester closed the door.

"Can I get you something?"

"Actually, I wondered if I could talk to Pat."

Lester's brows rose again. "I'll get her. She just got home from work as well."

Lester left Pip by the door and disappeared down the narrow hallway that led to the bedrooms. Patsi emerged a moment later.

"Hi, Pip. What's up?"

Pip glanced toward the living room where Lester had just turned on the TV. "Wanna go for a little walk?"

Patsi followed his gaze to where Lester resided, understanding dawning in her eyes. "Sure. Hey, Lester," she called. "Be right back."

They stepped outside the apartment into the hall and Patsi swung the door partially closed without actually letting the knob click into place. "What's up?" she repeated.

Pip shifted his weight from one foot to the other. "I, um… I was wondering if you could do me a favour?"

Patsi crossed her arms. "I guess that depends. What is it?"

"I need… I mean, I was wondering if you could get me Ophelia Stanfield's number." Pip surveyed Patsi closely for her reaction.

At first her eyebrows shot up in surprise. Just as quickly they descended into a frown. "I don't know her, really. And we… didn't exactly get along when I did meet her. You know that."

"I know. But she's cousins with your friend Megan and now that you're with Brett again…"

"You heard about that."

Pip just nodded.

"And you thought one of them would have it?"

"That's right. They are cousins."

Patsi tucked a strand of hair behind her ear and let out a gust of breath. "I don't think Brett would be too happy if he knew who wanted it."

"So Megan, then?" Pip asked hopefully.

"I suppose I could ask…"

"Thank you. I mean it." Pip looked down at his toes sheepishly and then back up at Patsi. "It means a lot, especially since you and me didn't exactly part on the best footing."

"Water under the bridge." Patsi waved her hand dismissively. "Real friends don't hold grudges. Besides, without you around, Brett and I might never have gotten back together."

"Kind of chased you right back into 'is arms," Pip said.

"Something like that." She looked at him pointedly, her hand on the knob. "Anything else?"

"Actually, yes." Pip rubbed the back of his neck. "I wanted to ask you a question."

"Oh?"

"You might laugh. It's kind of personal…"

Alarm flitted across her face but she recovered quickly. "O-kay…"

"Do you pray?"

Pip studied the emotions that seemed to march across her features at his point blank question. Surprise. Relief. Confusion. And finally annoyance. "Do I pray?" she repeated, as if to give herself more time to formulate an answer.

"Yeah. I was talking to Lester about it earlier and I know that you go to church, so I thought maybe you could give me some pointers. I've never really tried it before but I thought it couldn't hurt."

"I um… yes, I pray. Maybe more sometimes than others, but the answer is yes."

"And has it worked for you?" He could see her agitation growing and almost wished he hadn't brought it up, but he needed some answers and now seemed as good a time as any.

"I used to think so. Right now I'm not that sure." Her frown deepened. "May I ask what this sudden interest is all about?"

"I'm just about out of ideas when it comes to Ophelia, but prayer is one thing I haven't tried yet. I figured if I prayed and asked the big guy if 'e could help me convince 'er to give me a chance, things might work out."

"Prayer isn't some kind of wish list, you know." Patsi's tone was crisp and reprimanding.

"Sorry I brought it up."

Patsi let out a frustrated breath. "I'm not the best person to be giving spiritual advice right now, okay? I've got enough stuff of my own going on at the moment. If you really want to talk about it, talk to Lester some more. Or Tad and Goldie. They know a lot more than I do and are much more reliable."

"Thanks. I might do that." He smiled in an attempt to soften the stricken look on Patsi's face. "And thanks again for agreeing to get Ophelia's phone number. I'll owe you big time."

"You have no idea," Patsi said under her breath. She gave him a half-hearted wave and let herself back into the apartment.

She was definitely stressed about something, Pip decided. He, on the other hand, felt lighter. He was one - make that two - steps closer to seeing Ophelia again. In his books that was a good day.

～

"PATSI WAS RIGHT when she said praying isn't just presenting a wish list." Tad Roberts leaned forward from his position on the couch in Goldie Harper's living room. Goldie's son Jason played 'Lego' nearby while Goldie was busy preparing supper in the galley kitchen. Tad's sincere brown gaze reached across the distance to where Pip sat in a matching chair.

Pip rubbed a hand over his hair, making it stand on end in spots. "Then what's the point?" He really felt confused about the whole thing. People kept telling him to pray about stuff but then in the same breath not to pray about stuff. Just what was fair game?

Tad stroked his smooth face - almost as smooth as his shaved head, and tried again. "Prayer is like a conversation between friends. There is nothing wrong with asking, but that's not all it's about. It's about the relationship. You wouldn't just go to one of your friends and start demanding things without talking about it first. Without knowing the context and the circumstances and such. Maybe your friend knows something that you don't. Knows that what you're asking for really isn't what's best for you. Does that make sense?"

"I suppose..."

"Supper is ready," Goldie called from the kitchen. She stuck her head around the corner. "You're more than welcome to stay if you like, Pip," she offered.

"Thanks, but Jed's probably waiting on me as it is," Pip answered. "I just thought I'd come ask since it was fresh in my mind."

"Tell you what," Tad said. "There's a speaker at our church all next week. Why don't you come to one of the meetings and we can talk more afterwards. It might help."

Pip furrowed his brow. "That the same speaker Andrea has been trying to get Jed to come and hear?"

"Probably." Tad smiled. "We go to the same church."

Pip nodded as he stood up. "I'll think about it. I know if I could get Jed to come with me I'd score big points with Andrea. Maybe even a free haircut."

Tad laughed. "Well, there you go! Wouldn't want to pass up an opportunity like that!"

"Thanks again. We'll be in touch." Pip waved and let himself out of the apartment. He had lots to think about. His conversation with Tad had been interesting if not totally enlightening.

His phone vibrated in his jean's pocket and he reached in to pull it out. A text from Patsi. *Good news. Ophelia is coming for a visit.*

Pip stopped in his tracks, his heart hammering in his chest. Then he dialled Patsi's number and waited for her to pick up. "When is she coming?" he asked without preamble.

"I'm not sure. Megan just said she talked to her recently and Ophelia said she was coming up for moral support."

"But did you get her number?" Pip asked.

"Well... Megan was kind of preoccupied and I forgot to ask."

"What?" Pip frowned and then kept walking.

Patsi hesitated. "You know that Brett's parents' trial is coming up soon? It's a very stressful time for them. For everyone. And with Megan pregnant..."

Pip pushed his way into the stairwell and then made for the stairs, descending at a brisk trot down to his own floor. "Right, right. What was that about again?" He reached into the back of his brain, trying to remember the details. Something about Brett's lawyer parents involved with fraud or embezzling money or something. He hadn't really paid that much attention.

"They were representing Nudara Oil, the company under investigation. I don't understand everything myself, but it's been kind of stressful," she repeated. "For Brett and Megan. And with Megan pregnant..."

"Of course." He emerged in his own hallway and strode toward the apartment he shared with Jed. "Thanks anyway."

He hung up and pocketed the phone. It wasn't ideal, but at least there was some good news. Ophelia would be back in Calgary sometime in the near future. Now if he could just figure out a way to connect with her again, everything would be golden. It was the closest he'd been to a plan in weeks.

EPISODE 11

NEIGHBOURHOOD NOR'WESTER

*W*ILL

WILL BUMPED past the little shed-cum-art-studio on the company ATV and sped up just a bit, making sure to look the other way should *she* suddenly emerge from the tiny door.

He wasn't quite sure where things had gone south between him and Marigold. Once he'd seen the portrait she had painted of him it had changed things. They'd made out that one time on the dusty floor of the shed but then everything came crashing down soon after. She'd wanted to 'tell' her parents about their relationship. And he... well, he just wasn't ready. It was too much too soon. At least that's what he told himself.

He did a little spinout with the back wheels when he came to a stop in front of the repair shop, gravel spurting out in an arc behind the machine. Then he swung off the ATV and crunched through the gravel into the dim interior of the shop.

"Done your rounds already?" Buck Stone glanced up from the work bench along the back wall. He had a piece of one of the water pumps locked in a vice and was trying to loosen a bolt with a socket. A lock of slick black hair fell across his forehead as he strained to budge the corroded bolt.

"Want a hand with that?" Will stepped up to where Buck was working and surveyed the pump.

Buck ignored the offer and continued what he was doing. "You must be flying over some of them ravines to be done this quick."

Will grinned. "Something like that." He loved the thrill of speed. Maybe he'd missed his calling as a motocross racer or stuntman.

"Besides the fact that you could smash up your sorry hide, the boss wouldn't take it lightly if you wrecked his machine just by being reckless."

Will frowned. Buck wasn't usually this snarky. "No worries. I'm a better driver than you."

Buck snorted. Suddenly the bolt gave way and the momentum brought Buck's knuckles into contact with the edge of the vice. He swore softly, shook the wounded hand a few times, and then proceeded to undo the bolt all the way.

Things had been a bit strained with Buck ever since Will had covered for him that one time. Buck had fallen off the wagon, thanks in part to Will's brother Jed, and Buck had been late for work. Other than a terse, "Thanks," Buck hadn't wanted to talk about it. Will couldn't blame him.

"How's that pump coming?"

Both Will and Buck turned to look at Jeremiah Reynolds, their boss - and Marigold's father. He was still sporting the same ball cap with the campground logo on it, his longish hair pulled into a ponytail down his back. A regular hippy, just like his daughter.

"I'm just about to see what the problem is," Buck said. "With any luck we'll have it back in operation tonight and ready to be put back first thing tomorrow."

Jeremiah nodded. "Good, good." He squinted at Will. "You done your rounds already?"

Will nodded. "All's quiet on the western front."

"Good. I have a little job for you before you call it a night. Follow me."

Will got into step behind Jeremiah's bow-legged and somewhat jerky gait. They stepped into the waning light of the evening, the sun about to wink out behind one of the mountain peaks. "What's up?"

"The top hinge is off Marigold's studio door and I figure it needs fixing before the whole darn thing falls off. Then how would she keep the varmints out of her paints and things?"

Will hesitated a step and then had to take a double skip to get back in line. "Oh. Okay."

Jeremiah looked over his shoulder at Will. "Should only take a couple of minutes. I'd do it myself but Maizy is already chomping at the bit. We have to get to town for some charity thing she booked months ago."

"No problem."

"I keep telling her not to slam the darn thing, but…"

"I'll have no trouble fixing it, for sure."

"I knew you would. You're handy as all get out. Well, I better get a move on. See you in the morning."

Maybe too handy, Will mused as he watched Jeremiah jerk his way to the main house. He took a deep breath and strode the rest of the way to the little shed. He might as well survey the damage before he went to get some tools.

The screws holding the hinge in place had popped out, leaving worn holes that might not hold the next set. He could move the hinge down a bit, but that would entail some chiseling on both the jam and the door. Looks like the fix wasn't as straight forward as it seemed.

"What are you doing?" Marigold's tone, from somewhere behind him in the waning light, was clipped. Accusing.

"Jeremiah - I mean your dad - asked me to fix your door. The hinges have popped loose. Too much bangin', he says." He smiled at her in a way that he hoped was friendly - that said, "No hard feelings." She wasn't buying it.

"I'd prefer Buck fix it." She crossed her arms.

Will took in her stance - feet apart, ready for an attack. The long peasant skirt she wore whipped across her legs as a sudden breeze stirred. It reminded him of how shapely her legs were. He shook his head, clearing the memory. "Buck's got other things to do. Your dad asked me to do it."

"Fine. But there's no point starting now. It's almost dark. Wait until tomorrow."

Wait until I'm not here, she might have said.

Will sighed and rubbed the back of his neck. "It is a bigger job than it looks. And I'll have to take the door right off so I can do a bit of work on it."

"It's settled then. I'm going to do some painting, now, so if you'll excuse me." Marigold strode past him, her head held high, about to go into the small building.

Will reached out and grabbed her arm. "Wait." The moment he touched her he knew it was a mistake. He dropped his hand and shuffled his feet. "Can we talk?"

She turned blazing eyes to him, boring a hole right through his soul. "About what? You made it perfectly clear you were only interested in one thing and now that you've got that out of the way, you're on to the next adventure."

"It's not like that!" Will shoved his hands in his pockets. Of course she'd think that. Hadn't he acted in exactly that way, practically scrambling to get out of there once the deed had been done?

She crossed her arms again. "No? Then tell me how it is. From where I stand, you saw an opportunity, took it, and now you regret it ever happened."

"That's not true. I... I don't regret it." He searched her face for any sign of softening and saw none. He thought back to that fateful night. The storm had been crashing around them, confined as they were in the small studio with no power, shrouded in darkness. It was intimate. Her personal space and she'd let him in. Then he'd seen the portrait she had painted of him, flashing to life with a crack of lightning. It hit him in the gut with more force than the storm outside. Next thing he knew they were locked in an embrace, sliding to the floor, all hands and mouths and desperately flailing body parts.

When it was over and they were spent, they sat together on the floor, him leaning against the wall with Marigold tucked under his arm, purring like a cat. His plaid work shirt lay open, not quite discarded in their hurry to come together, and she'd traced his pecks with her finger where his chest was exposed.

"I was wondering when we'd get around to this," she'd said, her lips curving up in a satisfied smile.

"Oh really, now?" he'd teased. "A wanton woman on my hands."

She'd sat up to look at him, her face shrouded in the darkness. "I think I might be in love with you, Will Malloy."

The instant tightness in his chest had absolutely nothing to do with desire and everything to do with fear. At that very moment the lights had come back on and he'd scrambled to his feet, careful not to look at Marigold's half naked body as he donned the remnants of his own clothes.

"I suppose we'll have to tell my folks about us," she'd said on a sigh. "Not that they'll mind, I don't think."

"Um, listen. Can we hold off on that?" He tucked his shirt into his jeans. "We shouldn't move too fast."

The hurt look in her eyes told him he'd needed more tact. Instantly her gaze shuttered. "Of course you're right."

With awkwardness they'd parted, without so much as a final kiss. They'd been avoiding each other ever since.

Marigold's voice brought Will back to the present. "Then why have you been avoiding me? I've hardly seen you since..."

"I know. I'm sorry." He rubbed the back of his neck. "I just... I don't know how to explain it, really. I got spooked."

"Because I said I love you," she stated, her tone flat.

"Maybe." He peeked at her through hooded lids.

"Stupid. Stupid!" She turned away, locking her arms around her body as if to keep herself from falling apart.

Will stepped up behind her and put his hands on her forearms, rubbing up and down. She didn't jerk away - a good sign. "You're not stupid. I'm the stupid one for putting you in that position. I never should've -"

She spun around to face him. "So, you do regret it."

"No!"

"But you just said -"

"What I meant was, I'm sorry for not being a gentleman, like my ma taught me." He searched her angry face. "I like you, Marigold. A lot. But I liked what we had before, too, before it got... complicated. Can't we just go back to being friends?"

She inhaled sharply then straightened her spine, increasing her height. "I don't think so. In fact, I think it's best if we keep on avoiding one another. I'd be too embarrassed to do it any other way."

"There's nothing to be embarrassed about..."

She was already striding away, her arms embracing her body once again.

"I thought you were gonna paint tonight," he called after her. "Marigold?"

She ignored him, making her way to the main house with determined steps.

He'd gone and really put his foot in it, now. With a deep sigh, he took off in the opposite direction toward his own bunkhouse. The hinges would have to wait.

WILL SWUNG the door back and forth on its new hinges a few times and then gently pulled it forward, noting the smooth click as it shut without a hitch. The door was better than it had ever been, he'd wager. With a satisfied grin he stood back and surveyed his handiwork. He'd gotten up extra early in order to fix it before he had to start on his regular chores. He hoped Marigold would be pleased.

She was nowhere in sight, but then it was early. If she wasn't still in the house she was probably off painting somewhere else already. He still worried about her traipsing in the mountains alone when there was so much wildlife nearby, but as she said, she'd been doing it for years, and he couldn't take the time to be her personal bodyguard.

After what had transpired between them, he doubted she would let him anyway.

He heard the crunch of gravel underfoot and waited for Jeremiah as he strode toward the shed. The older man examined the door up and down, opened it and tried the hinges, and then shut it again. "Nice job."

"Thanks. It needed a bit more TLC than expected so I waited until daylight to do it."

"I see that. You're up early. I'm sure Marigold will appreciate it."

"Um, yeah." Will kept his eyes focused away from Jeremiah's probing gaze.

"Say. Is there something I'm missing?" Jeremiah asked, frowning. "Between you two?"

Will straightened his spine. "Not sure what you mean."

"Don't you, now?" Jeremiah let out a short bark of a laugh. "I might be getting on, but I'm not stupid. Maybe it's just the overprotective father coming out in me, but I coulda swore you two were taking a shine to one another."

Will's stomach dropped to the soles of his shoes. "I, uh... we're just friends." He hesitated. "What did she tell you?" He snuck a glance Jeremiah's way and wished he hadn't. The other man was scrutinizing him like a hawk about to swoop in on its prey.

"Not much, really. Marigold is closed mouthed when it comes to her private life. An introvert. Guess it's the artist in her. And I've quit trying to pry. Once in a while she tells her mother things, but I figure if she wanted me to know, she'd tell me herself."

Will felt the air whoosh out of his lungs on a wave of relief.

"She didn't have to tell me, though," Jeremiah continued. "I saw something for myself yesterday when I noticed the door needed fixing. I don't normally go into her studio without being invited - another one of those artist things - but I thought the screws might have fallen onto the inside." He looked square at Will, forcing him to meet his eyes. "Maybe you should see for yourself."

Will knew what was coming next and waited, his insides a mass of pins and needles again as Jeremiah opened the door with a fluid swing. Of their own accord, his feet stepped into the interior after his boss.

"What the?" Jeremiah stopped abruptly and Will almost ran into him.

He looked over the other man's shoulder at the easel in the far corner. His portrait stared back at them - make that one eye of the portrait. The other drooped forward, a huge slash slicing through the centre of the canvas.

Jeremiah jerked forward to inspect the damage. "It wasn't like this yesterday." He turned to look accusingly at Will. "I'd say you better tell me what's going on before I toss your sorry hide off the property."

Will rubbed the back of his neck and let out a gust of wind. "I'm really sorry, Sir. We, um… I suppose we were becoming more than just friends. But things didn't work out. We, uh… had a fight. I promise you, it won't affect my work."

Jeremiah turned back to the painting. "I'm more concerned about my daughter and by the look of this, I'd say she's upset."

Will nodded. "I'd say so."

"Are you going to elaborate?" Jeremiah asked.

Will stood for a minute, not meeting the other man's gaze. Then he shook his head. "No, I don't think so, Sir. Respectfully."

Jeremiah sighed. "Well, I guess I can't expect much more. It's your business - and hers. Not mine." He swung his gaze to Will. "And since when did you start calling me 'Sir'?"

"Sorry, Sir. I mean… just sorry."

"Well, better come get your breakfast before Maizy has a fit. And don't worry. Your job's safe for now and I won't say a word to her - or Marigold."

Will followed the older man out of the studio and shut the door, all pleasure in the smooth sound of the door latching in place now gone. Summer had just begun, and it looked like it was going to be a long one.

WILL KNOCKED on the outer door of Buck's bunkhouse and waited for the older man to answer. The crickets were chirping, and an owl hooted. The warm glow of lights from the main house reached out deceivingly with a calm that he did not feel, casting shadows along the edges of the trees.

Buck swung the wooden door open, flooding the small step with golden light from within.

"What's up?" Buck asked.

"I was wondering if we could talk for a minute or two," Will said.

"Sure. Step in before the place fills up with mosquitoes."

Will entered the bunkhouse, similar in design to his own with its log A frame interior and two sets of bunkbeds. Buck apparently slept on one of the bottom bunks, his pillow showing an indent where his head must have been moments ago. Buck's personal belongings were lined up neatly on the two top bunks. There were other markers of his presence like a photograph tacked to one log. A youngish woman and a little girl smiled back from the portrait, both holding fish. "Nice catch," Will said.

"My daughter and granddaughter," Buck said. "Taken last father's day. One of the first I spent with them since I been sober."

"Nice." Will nodded his approval.

"But you didn't come here to talk about that." Buck gestured at the empty bunk across from the one he slept in. "Have a seat."

Will lowered himself onto the bunk, ducking his head on the way down until he was settled. Once seated there was only about an inch of head clearance. He took a deep breath and then started right in. "I'm not sure what to do about Marigold."

"Marigold..." Buck's eyes narrowed. "O-kay... Is there more information that would help me out with my answer?"

Will sat forward, his hands clasped between his knees. "We, uh... we kind of made it with each other one time, if you know what I mean."

Buck's eyebrows rose. He clearly hadn't known. "I see. And...?"

"I really like her, you know? But then when she started talking about 'love' and telling her parents, well, it kind of spooked me."

"I wondered if you two liked each other, but I had no idea you moved so quickly."

"That's just it. It's too soon," Will said.

"So you rejected her and now she's mad at you," Buck filled in the blanks.

Will nodded. "Something like that. But what was I supposed to do? Go along with it when I'm not sure - about anything. I didn't mean to hurt 'er, and I still like 'er and all. I'm just not ready for a 'relationship', as she calls it. And now she's so mad she won't even be friends with me."

"Can you blame her?" Buck asked.

"I guess not."

"You've wounded her pride. That takes a lot to get over."

"I never thought of it that way. So what should I do?"

"What do you want to do?"

"I don't know. That's why I'm asking."

"You still care about her?" Buck asked.

"I… guess so," Will said.

"I guess so isn't strong enough. I'd say you were best to stop it before it got out of hand. If it's meant to be then things will work themselves out."

Will nodded his head in agreement, but on the inside, he was frowning. Exactly what were his feelings for Marigold Reynolds? Right up until the moment when he had actually taken her in his arms and kissed her, she was the only thing he could think about. After that, the worry of getting tied down superseded his desire to be with her. Maybe he was incapable of love.

"I think you should know that I've got things back under control," Buck said.

Will looked up in surprise. "What's that?" He'd been a million miles away.

Buck was standing up beside his bunk. "My little slip the other night. I won't be doing that again, I guarantee." He looked at the picture of his daughter. "I've got too much going for me now to make that mistake again."

310

"I'm sorry. Jed didn't know any better," Will defended his brother.

Buck shook his head. "Don't blame your brother. When you're an alcoholic like I am, every day is a challenge not to drink."

"I'm glad to hear it," Will said. "Not sure I'm up for covering your behind again."

"You know, I've got plans for your brother," Buck said with a grin.

Will's eyebrows rose. "Oh?" Buck didn't seem like the kind to want revenge.

"Yup. Next time I'm in town I'm taking him to an AA meeting."

Will smiled. He wasn't sure how successful Buck would be, especially if Jed knew beforehand what was coming. But he liked the idea. Maybe the whole family needed to go.

EPISODE 12

NEIGHBOURHOOD SURPRISE

 EB

ZEB RAPPED his knuckles soundly on the apartment door and then waited, a broad grin splitting his shaggy red beard. He loved surprises - especially if he wasn't on the receiving end. He'd managed to slip into Bo's apartment building on the tails of a large party that were exiting. No need to ring for Bo to open the security lock on the front doors. Perfect.

After a few seconds, the door swung wide. The look of surprise on Bo's face was exactly what Zeb had hoped. "What the? How'd you get in? What are you doing here?"

"What kind of greeting is that?" Zeb slapped Bo on the back as he pushed past him. "Aren't ya happy to see me?"

"Course I am. I just wasn't expecting you. Not on a weeknight."

"They had to shut our crew down for a few days for repairs. Costing 'em big time, but..." Zeb shrugged. "I don't mind a few extra days off. Thought I'd see how the family was gettin' on."

"Come in, come in. I was just, uh… on a video call with someone. Let me go say good-bye."

"No rush." Zeb watched as Bo scurried to the open laptop on the kitchen table. He heard the distinct melodic sound of a woman's voice. Before he could get a look at the screen they had said their good-byes and signed off.

"Looks like you landed yourself a girlfriend," Zeb observed. "Nice. You've been holding out on me. Anyone I know?"

"Just a friend." Bo snapped the laptop shut and pushed it aside to make room on the tabletop for his elbows.

Zeb sat down opposite Bo. "You sure?"

"Absolutely. You can get rid of that matchmaking shingle anytime now. I'm not interested."

"Hmph. Just trying to do a good service. So? How's about the others?"

"What do you mean?"

"Since last time I was here. It was a lot of work settin' everyone up. Hope it wasn't for nothing."

"You'll have to ask them. I'm not keeping tabs."

"You're not much help."

"I think Reba and Cory might be dating, if that helps," Bo said. "And what about you? Here to visit anyone in particular?"

"Besides you, you mean?" Zeb shook his head. "Nah. Just had a few days off, like I said. Say, that painting looks right nice on the wall. I'll have to remember to take it home sometime." He pointed to the large painting he had purchased at the Brew the last time he had visited.

"Anytime. It's yours, after all. I just thought I might as well hang it on the wall as have it leaning against it."

Zeb nodded. "Next time I drive down, I guess. It's too big to take on a plane."

"I'll be heading to work in a couple of hours. What do you want to do until then?" Bo asked.

"I've got a couple of errands to run. I'll head down to the Urban Cowboy later on. Surprise Jed and the rest."

"Errands? What kind of errands?"

Zeb shrugged. "Just stuff."

He wasn't about to admit to any of them that his next stop was the Fortune Cookie Restaurant.

THE FORTUNE COOKIE Family Restaurant hadn't changed one bit. Same red and gold decor. Same vinyl booths. Same smells - which were delicious. Zeb inhaled deeply as he found a seat in one of the corner booths. He hadn't eaten since leaving Fort Mac so he might as well make it seem like that's why he was here. To be honest, he wasn't quite sure *why* he was here. All he knew is, he had an urge to visit the place and so he'd followed his gut.

An unfamiliar waitress came to him with a menu, a glass of ice water, and cutlery wrapped in a paper napkin. She was short and blonde and a bit thick around the middle. Everything that Lily Chan was not.

"I'll just give you a few minutes and I'll be back to take your order," she said.

"Just a minute. Is Lily Chan working tonight by any chance?"

The girl's eyebrows rose slightly. "You a friend of Lily's?"

Zeb nodded. "Yes. A... family friend. Is she here?"

"She's not working today," she informed.

Zeb scowled. He hadn't considered that possibility.

"But she just happens to be here at the moment."

Zeb's countenance shifted just as quickly to a smile.

"Stopped in to talk to her folks. I'll go tell her someone is here to see her."

Zeb watched the waitress retreat to the swinging kitchen doors and disappear into the back. He waited, drumming his fingers on the tabletop without bothering to look at the menu. He didn't take his eyes off the doors until he saw Lily's tall, lithe form swing through the opposite side from whence the waitress had entered.

She scanned the room until her gaze landed on him sitting in the far booth. He thought he saw mild surprise register across her features but then her face became an unreadable mask of calm that seemed to be her signature. He raised a hand in greeting and smiled. She acknowledged him with a slight nod but her facial expression did not change as she approached.

"Hello, Zeb. Chandra said there was someone here who wanted to speak to me." Her voice was just as he remembered. Melodic and sweet like a cool brook on a hot day.

"Yup. In town for a quick visit. Thought I'd stop in for a bite. Love the food here."

She nodded. "Thank you. I'll tell my parents. They'll be pleased."

"Your parents? Oh right. They run the place."

"Yes. The family business."

He suddenly felt awkward. Just what had he wanted to say to her? "Uh… I thought you'd be workin' but I guess you get time off like anybody. Just wanted to say hello."

"Yes. I'm taking summer classes, so my schedule has been changed. Another advantage of working for family."

He surveyed her standing there, ram rod straight, her hands clasped in front of her, that pleasantly detached look on her face.

"You wanna sit for a minute?" he asked.

Her eyebrows rose ever so slightly.

"You know, so we can talk. Catch up."

"Um… alright." She slid gracefully onto the vinyl bench seat across from him. "Is there something you want to talk to me about?"

"Not particularly. Just thought it might be nice to have some company."

"Oh. I see."

They sat for a moment, an awkward silence stretching between them. Lily reached out and straightened the salt and pepper shakers.

"So? How've you been?" Zeb asked.

"Fine. Busy with classes."

"Summer school you said?"

She nodded. "Yes. Trying to get through my degree a year early."

"And what degree would that be?"

"Business. Not sure what I'll do with it afterwards. Maybe help

316

the folks. Get a job. Start my own business…" She shrugged, keeping her gaze fixed on the napkin holder beside the salt and pepper.

Zeb tried to guess her age based on what she'd just said. It was hard to tell with some people. "So… when will that be? When will you finish, that is?"

"I just finished my first year, so two more for sure. Maybe two and a half depending on how many summer courses I can take."

Zeb blinked. "Wow." He wasn't good at hiding his feelings. Not like Lily.

"Wow what?" she asked.

He smiled sheepishly. "Nothin'. I was just thinkin' that you're probably younger than I thought."

"I'm nineteen, since you're asking." She finally looked at him for the first time since sitting down.

Zeb's eyebrows shot up at the revelation. Nineteen! He shook his head and laughed. "Mary, Martha, and Lazarus! I'll be jiggered as not! I wasn't expecting that one."

"Really? And you?" she asked.

"I'm ancient. Thirty. Well… coming thirty-one later this year, but let's just keep it an even thirty for now. I hope that's not a problem."

"Why would it be a problem?" She maintained her calm demeanour but had added a subtle air of confidence. "We're just acquaintances. 'Family friends' as you told Chandra."

"Right…" He stroked his beard, then risked looking her in the eye. He grinned. "I must be losing it."

"Losing what?"

"My touch. If you haven't already guessed, I was hoping we could go out sometime."

"I see." Lily's gaze flitted downward.

"Then again, what would a young thing like you want with an old fart like me?" He laughed.

"I'm flattered, but…"

"You don't need to say it. I've got too much pride for that. You've been a good sport, though. Sorry if I embarrassed you."

She shook her head. "I'm not embarrassed. I'm just…" She furrowed her brow. "Surprised."

"Why's that? You're a good lookin' gal. You're friendly, nice to talk to… any man would be interested."

"That's very kind, but I can't help wondering about your motives."

"What do you mean?"

"I hate to think the worst, but some men like to prey on 'inexperienced' girls. Add them to their list of conquests. Show them the ropes, so to speak." She ducked her head slightly - a sign of subservience or maybe just embarrassment.

Zeb's eyebrows shot up. "That's what you think this is about?"

"Isn't it?" She dared a glance. "Why even bother with someone like me? I'm plain and shy. Not like Tiffany."

Zeb frowned. "Tiffany's got nothing to do with this."

"Or is it that things didn't work out between you so you're settling for second best?"

"Let's get one thing straight. I'm not remotely interested in Tiffany."

"Now that you've slept with her, I suppose."

"Is that what she told you?" Zeb asked.

"She didn't have to. I know Tiffany. And, well… I think I know you, too. At least your kind."

"You know nothing, if that's what you think. I never slept with her, for the record. Oh, she offered, but I refused. I'm not into a woman who would cheat on her intended just for a few laughs." Zeb took a deep breath, trying to control the anger he felt rising - anger at her assumptions or anger at his own stupidity, he wasn't sure.

"She didn't end up getting engaged, by the way. Just in case you're still interested."

"I already said I wasn't."

Lily shrugged one delicate shoulder. "Anyway, I think our conversation is over." She went to get up.

Zeb stopped her with a hand on her arm. "Wait. Also for the record, you are not plain."

"Oh. Thanks for saying so." She dipped her head in a bow, as if to thank him.

"No, I mean it." He let out a gusty sigh. "Listen. I, uh… well, I know there's a bit of an age difference, but would you consider it? Going out for coffee or dinner or something before I go back to Fort Mac? Maybe we can start off on a better foot."

"I doubt it. I'm very busy with classes and work."

"Right, right. The age thing. I get it." He drew back his hand and let it rest on the tabletop.

"For the record, as you say, it's not the age thing. It's just…" She lifted one delicate shoulder. "I've never even dated before. My parents brought me up to be cautious and this," she gestured between herself and Zeb, "is totally out of my comfort zone."

"Sometimes steppin' outside your comfort zone can be liberating. You'll never know until you try." He smiled hopefully.

Lily shook her head. "I'm flattered, as I said. But now, if you'll excuse me?" She stood up with one fluid motion and gave another slight bow before turning and walking calmly back to the kitchen.

How could she maintain such a serene demeanour, Zeb wondered as he watched her go? His own insides were rumbling like a volcano about to erupt.

Chandra was approaching, likely ready to take his order. He stood up before she'd made it all the way. "I've changed my mind," he said. "Sorry about that."

The Urban Cowboy was probably a better place to go tonight. He needed to kill the embarrassment - not to mention douse whatever flame had ignited - with a few cold ones.

EPISODE 13

NEIGHBOURHOOD WISHES

"Did I tell you I applied for a job today?"

The excitement in Viann's voice made Bo smile. He was happy to hear her sounding so upbeat. He folded his arms on the tabletop and leaned closer to the computer screen. "No you didn't. I guess we got interrupted earlier. That sounds exciting. What kind of job?"

"As a personal stylist for a well-known woman. A... how do you say... 'socialist'?"

Bo frowned. "A socialist? That sounds strange. A socialist needing a stylist."

"She is very wealthy. From old money. One of the elite."

"Do you mean a socialite?" Bo asked.

"*Oui*! This is what I meant to say." Viann smiled and nodded, clearly happy with herself.

"Is that something you've done before?" Bo asked.

"Been a stylist or had a job?"

"Either, I guess," Bo said with a laugh.

"It will be my first paying job. Of course, I know a few things about style."

"Of course you do."

Viann giggled and flipped her hair off her shapely shoulders. "You haven't forgotten? Perhaps you are judging me because of the way I look right now?"

"Never." Bo smiled. To him, she was the most beautiful creature on God's green earth. Even devoid of makeup - a state he had been privileged to see more than once, now - he thought she was the most gorgeous woman he'd ever met.

Viann sighed dramatically. "But what if I don't get the job?"

"Well, first off, do you need the money?" Bo asked.

"Of course not. I am looking for something - what did you say? Meaningful to do with my life."

"So if you don't get it, then it probably wasn't right for you in the first place. The right thing will come along at the right time."

"I don't know what I would do without you, Bo Malloy. You are so sensible! You are the best friend I have ever had."

Bo swallowed and forced a bright smile. "Thank you." He wished for so much more with Viann, but if all she wanted was to be his friend, he was willing to be there for her.

A knock sounded at the door. Bo frowned. Zeb had gone out on his 'errands' and he wasn't expecting him back. "Can you hold on a sec? There's someone at the door."

"You have a lot of visitors tonight," Viann said.

"Not normally. I'll be right back."

Bo scurried to the apartment door and peeked through the security peep hole. His eyebrows rose in surprise. Will.

He unlocked the deadbolt and swung the door wide. "Hi there! I wasn't expecting you. Come on in." After a few brief slaps on the back, he went back to the computer. "Listen, it's my brother Will this time, so I guess I'll have to sign off for good. You take care and I'll call you again tomorrow, okay? Same time?"

"I'll be waiting." Viann blew him a kiss and his heart jumped - again. It wasn't the first time she'd done it and he knew it was a show of sisterly affection, like she probably did with Jacques. But he couldn't help it that every time she did, his heart did a little happy dance.

"You got a girlfriend I don't know about?" Will stood over his shoulder as Bo clicked the laptop shut.

"What? No! Just a friend."

"'I'll be waiting,'" Will mimicked and then blew Bo a kiss. "Sounds like more than just friends to me."

"That's just her way. The French thing, you know?"

"If you say so." Will turned around and surveyed the kitchen. "Not much else has changed."

"Nope. So what brings you to town?" Bo asked.

"Buck was going to his AA meeting and I thought I'd tag along. Not to the meeting - to town. It's been awhile since I been out."

"Things still going okay at the camp?" Bo asked.

Will shrugged. "Good as they can be, I guess." He changed the subject. "Buck says he's gonna take Jed to the meeting with 'im. Kind of as payback for what happened last week. I told 'im good luck with that. If 'e can drag Jed to an AA meeting then more power to 'im."

"Amen to that. Jed needs it."

"You off to work soon?" Will asked.

"Pretty soon. Zeb's in town, if you didn't know. Said he'd be coming to the Urban Cowboy later. You wanna tag along?"

"Why not? Got nothing else to do." Will sauntered into the living room and stopped short as soon as he rounded the corner. "What the? How did this get here?" He marched up to the large painting and stared at it.

"Oh, I guess I didn't tell you. Zeb bought it last time he was out. He didn't want to have to transport it all the way to Fort Mac by air, so he left it here until the next time he drives down. Looks good, doesn't it?"

Will flopped down onto the sofa, staring at the painting.

"What's wrong? Don't you like it?" Bo asked.

Will shook his head. "You don't know, do you?"

"Know what?"

"Who painted this."

"Sure I do." Bo walked to the painting and squinted down at the signature on the right hand corner. "M. Reynolds." Realization dawned on his face. "The same M. Reynolds that caught your eye and then broke your heart, as I recall."

"That's not quite the way it happened, but, yeah. That's 'er."

"You never did tell me the finer details. I take it there's more to the story than just, 'It didn't work out'?" Bo asked.

Will sighed. "You could say that." He looked at Bo. "I'm not much for spilling my guts, if you know what I mean, but I think I'm gonna puke if I don't."

"About time." Bo sat down next to Will. "I'm good at listening. Fire away."

"Well, we - me and Marigold - were getting to be good friends. Then I found out by accident that she was painting my portrait. It kind of freaked me out, but then… well, we ended up making out. Well, you know, more than just making out. After she said she loved me and wanted to tell her parents about us. I freaked. Got cold feet or something and that's pretty much it. She left the camp without even saying good-bye and hasn't been back. Her parents won't tell me where she is, so…" Will shrugged. "There you have it in a nutshell." He turned his gaze to Bo. "Was I wrong to panic? It just seemed like too much too soon, you know?"

Bo shook his head. "I'm not the best one to be giving advice. I spend every evening talking to a woman who thinks of me as her best friend - nothing more." He looked up at the ceiling and laughed. "The last thing in the world I want is to be her friend, but I can't tell her that."

"That the same one you were sweet on before? What's his name…" Will snapped his fingers. "Jacques's sister?"

Bo nodded. "Yup. She's moved back to Montreal so all I have left is our nightly talks."

"Seems kind of sadistic to me," Will said.

Bo shrugged. "Maybe you're right, but I'm not sure what else to do. It would be worse to not ever see her again."

"You're right about one thing," Will said.

"What's that?"

"You're definitely the wrong person to ask advice from!"

They both laughed.

"I CAN'T BELIEVE Jed went to an AA meeting," Zeb said for the third time. He shook his head and took a swig of his beer. He was sitting side by side with Will, across from Bo's station on the other side of the Urban Cowboy's long, shiny bar.

"It's a good thing, believe me," Bo said as he polished a glass and set it with its fellows. "It's one thing to have a few drinks, but with Jed it's getting out of control. Even Will agrees."

Will just shrugged. "All I know is, Buck said it was payback for the time 'e came to town and had to stay over after 'e got partying with Jed."

"Don't expect me to be next," Zeb said.

"Nobody said that and you know it. Every time you're around, of course the two of you party hard, just like old times. But with Jed it's every night of the week. Going to one AA meeting can't hurt." Bo looked first at Zeb and then Will. "That's all I'm saying," he added.

"No argument here," Will said.

"I'm thinkin' about slowin' down, myself," Zeb offered.

"Now that would be a miracle," Will said with a laugh.

"I'm serious. When a person gets to a certain age, they have to start thinkin' about the future. I don't want to end up in a spot where I have to start goin' to no AA meetings."

"Cause you're practically over the 'ill," Will teased.

"Feelin' my age at times, b'y, and no mistake," Zeb countered.

"Good for you," Bo said. "Any particular reason?"

"Nope."

"How did your errands go?" Bo asked.

Zeb just shrugged. He glanced to the side and called over to where Reba was sitting several seats down, engaged in a conversation with Cory Roberts, their heads close together over the counter. Cory was leaning forward from his side and she was perched on the edge of her stool. "Eh, Spitfire! You gonna come visit with your brothers or are you gonna be gaga all night with your new boyfriend."

Reba looked over, annoyance mixed with embarrassment on her face. Cory just laughed. He planted a quick kiss on her lips and stood up straight. "Better go. I don't want to mess with them."

"The only one to work out," Zeb said, shaking his head. "And I tried so hard, too."

"Like I said, matchmaking is not your forte," Bo said with a laugh.

"You're not out of the woods, yet. Remember I saw you on the computer with your new girlfriend," Zeb said. He leaned conspiratorially toward Will. "And 'e says they're just friends.".

"What's this?" Reba asked as she sat down next to Will.

"Bo's got an online girlfriend," Zeb said. "She's French."

"What will Viann say?" Reba teased.

"Sh!" Bo frowned. "For your information it is Viann, and it's not like that. We're just friends. She needs someone to talk to and I'm… well, I have nothing better to do…"

"Nothing better to do?" Zeb whooped.

"Sh!" Bo scolded again. "Jacques might hear."

"Oh." Reba nodded knowingly. "So this is all behind Jacques's back, is it? Don't worry. I won't say a word, although I must say, why you're interested in such a snob, I'll never know."

"Maybe you should let 'im alone," Will defended quietly.

"I shoulda known you two would stick together," Zeb said.

"Viann's not a snob," Bo said between tight lips. "You don't know her the way I do."

"Somebody is awfully defensive," Reba said.

Bo clamped his mouth shut and kept on polishing glasses. He wished he'd never told any of them about his nightly ritual with Viann. None of them - not even Will - could possibly understand.

EPISODE 14

NEIGHBOURHOOD CONSCIENCE

ED

JED SLOUCHED FORWARD, fidgeting with his hands which were draped between his knees. The stiff wooden chair, arranged with about twenty others in a circle in the basement of the downtown Anglican church, was becoming more and more uncomfortable. Some woman was droning on about her drinking problem. That was fine for her, but he didn't have a problem.

Did he?

The person leading the small group, a dark haired man named Benny with a full beard and John Lennon glasses, thanked her for her story and then turned his attention to Buck. "Buck? Why don't you introduce your friend?"

Jed blinked and sat up straight, realizing Benny meant him.

"This is Jed Malloy." Buck stuck a thumb in his direction.

"Hello Jed," came the chorus of voices.

"I'm embarrassed to admit he and I tied one on last week after the meeting, but he was gracious enough to come with me tonight as a way of apology."

Jed almost snorted, but managed to check himself in time. Gracious? Apology? Buck hadn't been honest about where they were going when he made a surprise visit to Jed's apartment. He thought they were headed to the Urban Cowboy. Boy, was he wrong.

"Why don't you tell us about last week?" Benny invited.

Buck went into his story, mentioning how the news affected his daughter when she found out. He'd assured her it was a one-time deal - not like last time he'd fallen off the wagon.

Jed felt a twinge of guilt for his part in the affair, but squared his shoulders against it. He wasn't responsible for Buck's choices.

"Thanks for sharing," Benny said when Buck had finished. He turned to Jed. "Is there anything you'd like to share tonight, Jed? You're safe here. Among friends."

Jed thought for a minute and then shook his head. "No thanks. I'm good."

"That's perfectly fine, Jed. No one is judging you here. We've all been there. When you are ready to share, we'll be happy to hear you out."

There were murmurs of ascent from the rest and Jed hunkered down in his seat once again. The sooner he could get out of there the better.

"In the meantime, I hope everyone is looking to their higher power for help. Here's a copy of the twelve steps for you to take home, Jed, in case you want to read it." Benny handed Jed a small, bound book.

Jed turned it over in his hands, ready to discard it once the meeting was over. He didn't want to do it in front of these people, though. They all seemed genuinely friendly and obviously needed the crutch of a 'higher power' - whatever that meant - as well as the twelve steps. He, on the other hand, could regulate his alcohol intake just fine without any of it. He simply didn't have a problem.

After the meeting, when he and Buck were safely on the road away from the church, Buck spoke up. "So? What did you think?"

Jed shrugged. "Not as scary as I imagined. It's good, I guess, if it's what you need."

Buck nodded. "And everybody there does. It works, you know, hokey as you may think it sounds."

Jed didn't have a response. He looked out the window instead. "Say, can you drop me off at the Urban Cowboy?"

"Exactly where I was headed. Will texted me and said that's where he'd be when I was ready to head back to the camp."

"Good, good." Jed looked sideways at Buck. "You're not afraid to go there? After what happened last time?"

Buck shook his head. "No. I've learned my lesson for a while. Besides, I plan to stay in the truck and wait for Will, just in case." He glanced at Jed and smiled. "I'll always be a recovering alcoholic, no matter how much time I put between myself and a bottle. I learned that the hard way last week. Thanks for helping me with the lesson."

Jed grunted. "Not sure thanks are in order, but okay."

"I mean it. Some lessons are harder than others. I'm just grateful this one was short lived."

"Whatever you say, b'y. Whatever you say."

The sooner he got safely back on his own turf the better.

JED STRETCHED out in his armchair and switched on the TV. First game of the season for the Calgary Stampeders. He wasn't a huge football fan. He preferred hockey but there would be no more games for a few months. Maybe there'd be a Blue Jays baseball game on instead.

"Is that what you're wearing?" Pip appeared in the hallway, fresh from the shower.

Jed looked down at the sweats and T-shirt he'd donned after his own shower. "What do you mean? I'm not going anywhere tonight. Gonna watch a bit of ball instead."

"Really? The one time I want to go out with you and you're bailing?"

Jed frowned. Pip hadn't been that sociable lately. As often as not he was the one to stay home when Jed went to the Urban Cowboy - or went somewhere else on his own after Jed was gone. Jed grunted. He wasn't his little brother's keeper. "You go on. I need a breather."

Pip smiled, crossing his arms as he leaned against the wall. "Tied one on after that AA meeting last night?"

"None of your business."

"I seen the pain you were in all day at work, don't you worry. You can't keep secrets from me."

"So? You my mother now?" It was true. He had had a few too many last night after the AA meeting, but that was just anxiety after the stress of it all. Plus, it was Zeb's last night in town. That counted for something. Tonight he'd show them all. He had as much self-control as the next guy.

"Come on. Rocky Carravagio is picking us up, so we don't even have to worry about getting a cab later."

"Rocky? What in blazes are ya doin' hangin' out with the likes of 'im?" Jed asked.

"Don't let the tatts scare you. He's actually a really nice person. Plus, since he doesn't drink, he's the perfect DD."

"Hm. Let me think about it."

It didn't take much thought, really. Pip was finally coming out of his funk and Jed didn't want to be the one to set him back again.

Jed quickly changed into jeans and a button up plaid shirt and the two Malloys headed down to the foyer. Rocky Carravagio was waiting for them, dressed in his standard black leather jacket and jeans. Same bald head, pointy goatee and inked up skin that Jed remembered.

"Thanks for waiting," Pip said to Rocky.

"No trouble. Andrea went on ahead in her own car."

Jed furrowed his brow. Andrea was going to the Urban Cowboy, too? He shrugged. It wouldn't be the first time. Maybe this was Pip's way of trying to set them up. As if that stood any chance.

They piled into Rocky's beat up SUV - a shortened version of a GMC Suburban with a hole in the muffler and rust around the wheel wells. Pip sat in front with Rocky and Jed got into the back with the litter - paper coffee cups, chip bags, and general debris.

"Sorry about the mess," Rocky said as he pulled out onto the street. "I've been meaning to clean it, but… Maybe I'll wait for one of those fundraisers. Let the kids make a little money for a trip or whatever it is they do."

It took a few turns for Jed to realize they weren't headed to the Urban Cowboy as he'd been led to believe. "'Eh, b'y. You're goin' the wrong way."

"I don't think so," was all Rocky said. Pip was curiously close lipped.

"What's goin' on?" Jed asked. "Where we goin'?"

"You'll see." Pip grinned like a Cheshire cat.

Jed furrowed his brow and sat back against the ripped upholstery. Realization hit like a lightning bolt. He sat forward again. "Are we goin' to that church thing? Are we?" he demanded.

"Relax. I'm going too, so it can't be so bad," Pip said.

Rocky glanced in the rearview mirror at Jed's unhappy face. "You didn't know? Man! We're almost there. I could turn around if you want."

Jed's 'Yes' was drowned out by Pip's resounding 'No!' Pip turned around to look Jed full in the face. "I told Andrea and the others you were coming. She's expectin' you. You wouldn't want to disappoint 'er now, would you?"

"What others?" Jed growled.

"Tad, Goldie…"

"The whole world plans my life without even consulting me," Jed huffed.

"It's just once," Pip said. "You know how much this'll mean to 'er."

Rocky glanced in the mirror again. "It's true."

Jed sat back in his seat for the duration, decidedly grumpy and nervous as all get out at the prospects of seeing Andrea in her element. What if he did or said something stupid?

They arrived at the church - a sprawling complex with a huge parking lot - and Rocky pulled up beside Andrea's little car. Jed mumbled some choice expletives as he got out of the back seat.

"What's that?" Pip asked with a grin. "I didn't hear you."

"You darn well did, you little weasel."

They walked to the large glass doors and Rocky opened one, standing aside like a gentleman as Pip and Jed passed through. The hum of people milling around hit Jed's ears, along with some instrumental music coming from the main auditorium.

"You came!" Andrea Carravagio rushed to his side and grabbed his hand. "Pip said he was bringing you but I wasn't sure if he meant it." Her eyes were wide.

Jed nodded and rubbed his short hair with his free hand. "Seemed like an interestin' night out," he lied.

Pip just kept on grinning.

"They're about to start. I saved us some seats," Andrea said. "Come on."

She led the way into the main room. It was a hexagonal shape with rows and rows of seating that sloped downward toward the main stage. It was unlike any church Jed had ever been in before. Back home he was used to stained glass, unforgiving wooden benches, and a crucifix at the front depicting Jesus in perpetual agony as he hung on the cross.

A man of about Jed's age took the stage and the murmur of the crowd quieted. He thanked everyone for coming and welcomed any folks that were there for the first time. After a short prayer, a group of musicians took their places and started into the first song. Jed kept glancing at Andrea to make sure he didn't do anything out of order. He wasn't much for singing - at least not until he'd had a few beer, but he mouthed the words the best he could as he followed along.

Andrea seemed to be enjoying herself, that's for sure. At one point she even raised her hands. Jed quickly looked away. It seemed like a private moment. Something he didn't want to interrupt.

Finally they sat down and the guest speaker - the one Andrea had been raving about for so long - took the stage. The man looked like an older version of Rocky. Shaved head, tattoos, and a leather jacket. Jed prepared himself for an onslaught of religious jargon, but after about five minutes he found himself actually listening to the man.

Could it be true? Could God actually love him enough to die just for him? Could Jesus wipe away every bad thing he'd ever done? Could he start over with a clean slate, like the biker turned preacher said?

Jed stole a glance at Andrea. She was jotting notes in a little note-book, flipping to the passages the preacher referred to with ease of practice. No. He would never be on the same level as Andrea Carravagio. She was too pure. Too fine. Too good for the likes of one Jed Malloy.

Jed slouched in his seat and endured the rest of the message, tuning most of it out. If God really was a God of mercy, this whole evening would come to an end - and soon.

The guest speaker asked everyone to bow their heads and pray. He said that if anyone wanted to say the 'sinners' prayer' and ask Jesus into their heart, to just silently repeat after him. Then he asked for a show of hands with strict instructions for everyone to remain with their head down. The temptation to take a peek was strong, but Jed purposely kept his eyes squeezed shut. There was no use tempting fate, real or not.

Finally, the prayer ended. Merciful heavens, it was finally over! With a sigh of relief Jed opened his eyes.

With a grin he cast a sidelong glance at Pip, about to elbow him in the ribs for enduring such agony along with him. To his surprise, Pip's eyes were still shut. Jed blinked.

Next thing he knew, Pip was going forward for prayer along with a slough of others. Andrea clutched Jed's forearm and leaned into him. When he looked down at her rapt face he could see tears of joy glis-tening in her eyes as she focused on the throng making their way slowly to the front.

She looked up at him and smiled. "Sorry. I just get so emotional when someone comes to the Lord." She let go of Jed's arm and smoothed her skirt over her lap. "So? What did you think?"

Jed opened his mouth and then shut it again. For once in his life he had absolutely no words.

"His last night is tomorrow," Andrea went on. "It's been such a wonderful series! Are you coming again tomorrow?" She looked up at him hopefully.

Jed blinked. Not likely.

"I think Jed's had enough for one night," Rocky said gently. "He can decide later." He turned to Jed. "I can take you home now, if you like." He put a hand on Jed's shoulder. "I'm sure Andrea can give your brother a lift when he's ready."

"Absolutely," Andrea said, her voice sounding overly bright.

Jed nodded his head and let Rocky lead him from the auditorium.

This was definitely a night he would remember. And not for the reasons Andrea hoped. The truth had been solidified in his mind. There was no way he and Andrea Carravagio could ever be together. He just wasn't good enough.

EPISODE 15

NEIGHBOURHOOD CHANGES

IP

PIP OPENED his eyes and a rush of peace enveloped him. It was like nothing he'd ever experienced before. He wasn't sure exactly what had happened, but last night's decision changed everything.

After a few more minutes just lying in bed, he rolled to the side and sat up. He could hear Jed rustling about in the kitchen. Pip wondered what, if anything, Jed would say to him this morning. When Andrea had dropped him off last night, Jed was already in bed.

He showered, got dressed, and sauntered out into the kitchen. "Mornin'. You went to bed early last night. What gives?"

Jed shrugged, avoiding Pip's gaze. "Tired is all. You better get a move on. I'm leaving in ten minutes."

Pip downed a glass of milk, threw a sandwich together for his lunch, and grabbed a banana on the way out the door. Jed was uncharacteristically quiet on the drive to work. Obviously, he wasn't in any mood to talk and Pip wasn't exactly sure how to broach the subject even if he had been.

It wasn't until he was working side by side with Lester later that morning that Pip was able to share what was on his mind. "So, uh, I did what you told me to do," Pip said, holding two sheets of drywall board steady while Lester used a carpet knife to cut the paper holding them together.

"What's that?" Lester said, not looking up.

"Prayed." Pip waited for the word to sink in. It only took about one second.

Lester blinked and focused on Pip's face. "Come again?"

"I prayed. Went to that meeting at Andrea's church." Pip smiled and shook his head. "I kind of tricked Jed into going with me. Figured it would score me some points with Andrea. As it turns out, I went up for prayer after."

"I see. And?"

"I said the sinners' prayer, I think they called it." Pip grinned. "I never felt so good in all my life."

Lester let his own smile split his face. He slapped Pip on the back. "That's awesome news. I'm happy for you. And Jed?"

"Took outta there like a bat outta 'ell." Pip stopped and surveyed Lester sheepishly. "I mean, 'e left before I could talk to 'im. Was already in bed when I got home and 'e hasn't said a word to me since."

"Getting saved is a wonderful experience for those who take the leap, but it can be awkward for those who don't understand. Jed probably doesn't know how to bring it up or even what to say. He might even feel betrayed - like you think you're better than he is, now."

Pip frowned. "I never thought of it that way. The guy I prayed with gave me a Bible and told me to start reading."

"The book of John?" Lester asked.

"No, Mark, he said. Is that a bad thing?"

Lester shook his head. "Not at all. Mark's as good a place as any, I suppose. Different people suggest different places. In the end it's all God's word, so…"

"He showed me where, since I had no clue. Andrea and I talked for a long time in the parking lot, too, so I guess it was late when I got home. Still, Jed's not one to go to bed too early. I think I scared 'im."

"Probably."

"I read lots, too, once I got home. I think I pretty near read through the entire book of Mark, so maybe I'll start on John next."

"Good idea. Would you like me to talk to Jed for you?" Lester asked.

"Would you?" Pip looked at Lester hopefully. "I just don't know what to say. It's all new to me and I don't want to give 'im the wrong idea. Like I think I'm better than 'im, like you said."

"I'd be happy to do it," Lester said.

"I'm going again tonight," Pip said. "It's the preacher's last night and I don't want to miss it. I just wish I woulda gone sooner."

"God's timing is always perfect."

Pip nodded. He wanted to say a hearty 'Amen' to that.

THE PREACHER WAS WELL into his sermon when Pip got the text from Patsi.

"Ophelia arrived today. Cory and Brett are playing tonight and she'll probably come. Here's the address if you're interested."

If he was interested? What an understatement! He'd been saved for twenty-four hours and already God was answering his prayers! Sweet!

He leaned over to whisper in Andrea's ear. "I just got a text and I gotta go. Don't worry, though. I'll take a cab."

Andrea turned anxious eyes toward him. "Is everything alright?"

"Couldn't be better." He grinned. "Let's just say it's an answer to prayer."

"Okay. As long as you're sure. I could drive you," she offered.

Pip shook his head. "No need. I'll check your notes later."

He slipped out of the cushioned bench and headed for the exit. He knew he was grinning like a fool, but he just couldn't help it. Jed didn't know what he was missing.

Pip put on his best swagger as he walked up the steps to where a rented security guard stood with arms crossed. "I'm with the DJ." The not-so-private private house party was in a mansion, as far as Pip could tell. The double doors were wide open, music and the hum of partiers within spilling out into the darkened street. So this is how the other half lived.

The guard, a burly man with a shaved head and a full beard didn't seem impressed. "ID?" He held up a tablet, ready to scan Pip's ID.

Pip's brows rose ever so slightly. He'd never been to a party where you had to have your ID scanned before. He was just about to claim he'd lost his wallet when Patsi came to the rescue.

"There you are." She looked at the guard. "He's with me."

The guard gave a curt nod and let him pass. Apparently she had some pull.

"Impressive," Pip said as he followed her into the house.

"Not really. I told him in advance you were coming but might not have your ID. Since I'm with the DJs, he seemed to be okay with it."

"Thanks."

"I'm not sure why I'm bothering," Patsi said. "I don't like telling lies."

"The guy upstairs don't mind a little white lie now and again, if it's for a good cause." At least Pip hoped that was the case. He'd have to ask Lester about it.

"Not sure if that's how it works," Patsi said. "Anyway, Ophelia's not here yet, but Brett said she was coming."

Pip glanced around the room - a large open concept that flowed onto a back deck through wide open French doors. A magnificent double staircase flanked one wall with a balcony above. Several people had already gathered there to look over into the main room. It reminded him of something out of a movie.

Brett and Cory had set up in the space between the staircases. The sound would travel well to both floors. Right now, canned music was playing over the speakers and neither man was to be seen.

"This is some set-up," Pip said.

Patsi shrugged. "Cory and Brett do a lot of private parties. Brett and I had our first date at one."

Pip nodded, still taking it all in. It was probably still early by party standards, but more people were coming through the front doors.

"If you want a drink, the bar's in the kitchen through there." Patsi pointed to her right.

"A hired bartender, too, I suppose?" Pip asked.

"Of course. Here comes Brett now." Patsi's voice became a staged whisper. "He doesn't know I told you about Ophelia. Pretend that you were invited."

Brett sauntered to where Patsi and Pip stood and surveyed Pip up and down for several seconds. "Hm. I wouldn't have expected to see you here."

"No? Surprising the connections one makes," Pip said with a shrug.

"How do you know the Stanislovskys?" Brett asked.

"You know me. The friendly sort. I forget where it was exactly, but here I am."

"So I see. Why don't you go say hello to the host?" Brett's scowl matched his skeptical tone but he didn't question Pip further. He took Patsi's arm possessively. "The pool and deck are very romantic. We'll be seeing you around." He led Patsi away toward the French doors.

Pip looked around, trying to decide which socialite was the owner of the mansion. His attention was short lived when someone tapped him on the shoulder.

"What in blazes are you doin' here?" It was Reba, decked out in a skimpy purple dress and high heels.

"I could ask you the same thing," he countered.

"I came with Cory, of course." She gestured to the turntables and other equipment. Cory had donned what looked to Pip like huge earmuffs. "He's about to start 'is first set."

"Nice. I always wanted to hear 'im."

Reba rolled her eyes but didn't say anything.

Pip surveyed her grim expression and smiled. "What? You don't care for your boyfriend's brand of music?"

"Not really, but I gotta be supportive," she said.

Cory made some intros and then started into his first set. As far as Pip could tell it sounded like a lot of scratching and repeating, like the needle got stuck in one spot. The bass was catchy, though. He tapped his foot in time and watched as several people got up to dance. He glanced at Reba. "You wanna?"

"What? Dance? With you?"

"Yeah, dance with me! I gots the moves, or at least I'm told." He grinned.

Reba shook her head, but smiled. "Still got a swelled head, too, I see."

Pip spun his sister onto the area that had been cleared for dancing. It didn't take long for her mood to change from somewhat sour to bubbling with laughter. They'd been fighting far too long and over things that didn't matter in the long run. Maybe now that he was a new person inside, his relationship with his family - especially Reba - would improve as well.

"I need a drink," Reba said when the song ended and Cory launched into the next one. She put her hand on Pip's forearm and leaned forward, puffing. "You gonna be a gentleman and get me one?"

"Why not?" Pip said.

"Good. I'm going to find Pat. Don't be long."

"Okay, boss. I think she's outside."

Reba headed for the French doors as Pip made his way in the opposite direction to the kitchen. It was huge - a chef's kitchen with the biggest island Pip had ever seen. The hired bartender was using it as a counter to mix drinks.

"One beer on tap and one vodka with a little water. Make it a -" Pip cut himself off. He'd usually go for a double but now that he was a new creation he thought better of it. "Just a single, thanks."

Pip tapped in time with the music as he waited. He tossed the bartender a ten dollar bill as a tip and headed back to the main room. He almost bumped into someone on his way through the wide doors. "Ophelia!" His heart skipped a beat. Good thing his hands were full or he might have grabbed her right there and then and kissed her on the spot.

"Pip?" Ophelia's eyes were wide. "Wow! I wasn't expecting to see you here. What a surprise."

"A good one, I hope."

"Of course. I just got here. I was going to get myself a drink before I tried to find my cousin."

"Brett and Pat are out on the deck, as far as I know. I was goin' that way myself." Pip lofted the drinks. "I'll wait for you."

"I heard that Brett got back together with that little country bumpkin." Ophelia laughed. "She must be good in bed to keep Brett's interest." She turned to the bartender and ordered her fancy drink.

Shock at Ophelia's insensitive words washed over Pip but he tamped it down and tried for a smile. "Pat's a nice person."

Ophelia turned a suitably contrite gaze toward Pip and blinked, her false lashes sweeping her cheeks. "Oh right. I forgot that you and she were an item at one time, too. Well, sort of."

"We've only ever just been friends. But… well, she's a good person, like I said." This wasn't the way he had pictured their meeting, that was for sure.

Ophelia took a sip from her frothy pink drink. "Mm. Just what I needed. Now which way were you going?"

Pip led the way to the main room and then out through the French doors. The night was calm and mini-lights twinkled over the deck and throughout the trees, glistening off the water of the luxurious pool. It would have been serene had there not been so many other people gathered around. Pip spied Brett and Pat standing under some trees talking to Reba.

"Cousin!" Ophelia gave Brett a pseudo-side hug, careful not to spill her drink.

"It's about time," Reba said, taking the beer from Pip. "I see now why it took you so long." She offered Ophelia a none-to-friendly nod.

"You've met my cousin Ophelia?" Brett asked.

"Briefly," Ophelia supplied. She turned to Patsi. "So? Still horseback riding or whatever it is you do?"

"I'm back in the city working at a coffee shop downtown," Patsi said.

"Wonderful. You're moving up in the world."

"I like my job," Patsi said.

"And what do you think of that, Brett? Now that you've got your life straightened around and are heading for the hallowed halls of the court house, how do you feel about your girlfriend's job as a waitress?"

"We'll see," Brett said with a shrug. "Maybe she'll go back to school next year."

"I'm not much for college," Patsi said.

"And there's nothing wrong with *honest* work," Pip put in.

"Of course not. You're an unskilled labourer," Ophelia said pointedly. "I just meant that Brett might want someone a little more… shall we say, upwardly mobile once he passes the bar."

Brett rubbed the back of his neck, looking decidedly uncomfortable, but he didn't defend Patsi further. "Listen, I've got to go catch up with Cory. It'll be my turn to take over soon. Good to see you, Ophelia." He gave her a quick peck on the cheek, turned to Patsi and did the same as if on an afterthought, and strode into the house.

"Well, there's one thing about us unskilled labourers, as you put it," Reba said once Brett was gone.

"What's that?" Ophelia blinked dramatically as she took another sip from her straw.

"We sure as 'ell aren't as affected as some people," Reba said.

"Meaning?"

"You're nothin' but a snob."

Ophelia smiled coyly. "I don't deny it. At least I know who I am. I'm not pretending to be someone I'm not."

"Why you…"

Pip cut Reba off by quickly stepping between the two women. "That's enough. Why don't you two go in and see your men? Cory'll be done soon and Brett'll be starting up. You're supposed to be having a good time."

Reba didn't look convinced.

"Good idea," Patsi said. She took Reba's arm. "Let's go."

Pip watched them maneuver safely to the house. Once they disappeared inside he turned to Ophelia. "My sister is right. You seemed a bit harsh. What's gotten into you? Certainly not the person I remember."

Ophelia laughed, the sound a humourless tinkle. "And what person would that be? I hardly know you."

"I wouldn't say that. Not after the way we…"

"Had sex?" she finished for him. "It was fun, by the way. Just what I needed at the time. But that's all it was. Sex."

Pip felt like he'd been punched in the gut. All his pining after her; all his dreams. Vanished. Poof into thin air. Maybe that's all Ophelia Stanfield ever was. A figment of his imagination.

Ophelia reached into her purse and drew out a cigarette. After taking the time to light it, she surveyed Pip under hooded lids. "Don't tell me you thought there was something to that?"

"Well, I…"

She blew out a puff of smoke and cut him off. "That is rich." She shrugged. "Oh well. Sorry to disappoint you."

Ophelia's lashes looked garish now in the shadows, making her eyes into nightmarish hollows. Her white blonde hair was brittle and stiff, and her nails were like talons. Pip took a step back. How had he ever been taken in by her brazen wiles? Everything about her was fake, right down to her personality.

"I'm tough," he said, putting on his best brave face and straightening. "I won't be cryin' over you anymore, if that's what you think."

Ophelia shrugged. "Too bad. I said it was just sex, but it was good sex. If I get bored this trip I might want to look you up."

"Not likely." He looked over the top of her head at the French doors. "I think I'm going to go in now, too." Without a backward glance, he walked away.

Before he got to the entrance he looked down at his half-filled glass and then tossed the contents into the grass. His emotions were reeling but he didn't want to numb the pain with alcohol.

Here he thought God had answered his prayers by bringing

Ophelia back to Calgary. Maybe He had. He no longer felt anything for her except pity.

He spotted Patsi and Reba standing together. Brett was just starting his set. Cory joined them and gave Reba a kiss before leaving them and heading for what Pip assumed was the washroom.

Pip stopped in his tracks and gazed at Patsi. She was watching Brett, swaying to the music, but if he read it correctly, she wasn't a fan either. Patsi was a down to earth girl who liked country music. She was fresh and wholesome and naive despite her experiences - polar opposite to Ophelia. Her hair, although tamed tonight by a straightener, was still soft and a few curling wisps had already found their way free with the humidity. Patsi's complexion was clean, enhanced by a light application of makeup that still allowed her true colours to shine through. She was everything Ophelia was not - and she was beautiful, inside and out.

Yet, when she had hinted at wanting more than friendship from him, he had rejected her in favour of a plastic version of perfection. His loss. And now she was back with Brett McMillan. How long would it be before he got tired of her again and traded her in for someone higher on the social scale? Ophelia thought Brett deserved someone better, but the truth was, Pat deserved better than Brett McMillan.

With a sigh, Pip turned around again. He needed some air. The deck was large and surely he could find a spot somewhere out of the way of Ophelia, if she was still out there.

He circled around the pool and headed for a clump of trees in the shadows. Once he got closer he heard the unmistakable sounds of a couple in heat. He smiled. He'd have to scram and give them some privacy.

Then he heard the voice. Ophelia. It was unmistakably her. He'd heard those sounds from her before. He shook his head. She worked fast. It hadn't taken her much time at all to find a replacement.

The man spoke and Pip froze. He recognized that voice, too. At least he thought he did. He stepped closer, feeling like a peeping Tom, but needing to know if what he suspected was indeed true.

One more step around the tree and Pip stopped and cleared his throat. A head full of dreadlocks bobbed up from the shadows.

"I can't say as I enjoyed your set, Cory," Pip said. "I don't think my sister liked it either. Probably less once I tell 'er I caught you in the bush with yer pants down."

EPISODE 16

NEIGHBOURHOOD WHIRLPOOL

J ED

JED DRUMMED his fingers on the arm of his easy chair. He just wasn't sure what to make of it all.

Pip's conversion had taken him by surprise. He hadn't had the guts to talk to the youngster about it. He didn't know what to say. The preacher's words had gotten to him, too, if the truth be told, right on the heels of the AA meeting he'd been coerced into by Buck. He supposed he deserved that one, but Pip's tricksy ways had him flummoxed. He certainly hadn't seen that one coming. Unless Lester had put him up to it. He had overheard them talking about Pip's new faith yesterday when they thought he wasn't listening.

What was all that about, anyway? He'd heard of people going religious before, but he'd never thought it to be more than a bid for attention. A person either believed or they didn't and that was the end of it. All this talk of a 'new creation' and 'born again' gave him an unsettled feeling in the pit of his stomach. It wasn't something he'd been taught, that's for sure, yet his own mother believed in God and she was a good person as far as he could tell. Heck, he believed in God when it came down to it. He just didn't go flashing it about, that's all.

Pip entered the living room. "I'll see you in a bit."

"Where you goin' this time on a Saturday morning?" Jed asked.

"I just have a couple of things to do. I probably won't be long." Pip surveyed Jed closely. "Why? You got something for me to do?"

Jed shook his head. "Nope. Get along, then."

"Oh. I thought maybe you wanted to talk. You know, about what happened the other night."

Jed waved a dismissive hand. "Later."

"Okay." Pip headed for the door and was out without another word. He didn't seem anxious to approach the topic either.

With an 'oomph' Jed reached for his cell phone which had fallen to the floor beside his chair. Without analyzing his motivation too much, he dialled Lester's number and waited. As embarrassing as it might be, he just had to know what was going on.

REBA

"Oh, you poor dear!" Patsi put her arms around Reba and squeezed.

Reba leaned into her friend's embrace for a moment, but then gently extracted herself when her limbs started to protest. They were sitting cross-legged on Patsi's bed. "I shoulda known. I just don't seem to have good luck when it comes to relationships."

"Did you ever…? You know?"

"Sleep with 'im?" Reba asked. "One time too many, apparently. Live and learn, I guess."

"Oh, you poor dear!" Patsi repeated.

"I'll get over it."

"Men!" Patsi bounced off the bed and extended a hand to help Reba up. "Come on. There's some ice cream in the fridge that'll cheer you up. Now that Lester finally took off we can take over the living room."

Reba followed Patsi down the narrow corridor but waited in the living room until her friend appeared with a small bucket of ice cream and two spoons. Patsi handed her one of the spoons and they flopped almost in unison onto the couch.

"I've seen them do this in movies," Reba said as she took a scoop. "Does it really help?"

Patsi shrugged and dug in with her spoon. "I don't remember. I tried it when I broke up with Brett the first time, but..."

Reba sighed. "You're so lucky to have found Brett."

Patsi didn't answer right away, possibly because her mouth was full of ice cream.

Someone knocked on the door and both girls looked at each other before Patsi got up to answer it. Reba took another bite of ice cream, savouring the delectable smoothness in her mouth as she closed her eyes and relaxed against the cushions. As soon as she heard who it was she sat up again, frowning. What was he doing here?

"Come on in, Pip," Patsi said from the entrance. "Reba and I were just indulging in some ice cream therapy. Care to join us?"

"Ice cream therapy? Now that sounds like something I could use," Pip said. "As long as I'm not interrupting anything."

"I'd say you deserve it as much as anybody," Patsi said.

Pip waved at his sister as he entered the living room and sat down in Lester's easy chair. "Eh, Sis. I didn't expect to find you here. You doin' okay?"

"As well as can be expected." Reba shoved another spoonful of ice cream into her mouth to avoid having to explain further and instantly scrunched her face as searing cold pain shot into her forehead. "Oh! Ice cream headache!"

"I'll get bowls," Patsi said and disappeared into the galley kitchen. She came back a minute later with three small bowls and a spoon for Pip. "Take as much as you want."

Pip scooped a mound into his bowl and passed the carton back to Patsi who filled her own bowl before handing it over to Reba.

"I'm really sorry about what happened last night," Pip offered. "I coulda just let it go until another time, but you don't deserve that. I was real proud of you for not makin' a scene, too."

"I wanted to, believe me," Reba said with a sigh. "But then I decided 'e wasn't worth it." She surveyed Pip over the spoonful of ice cream waiting to disappear into her mouth. "I know it wasn't easy for you either, seeing as you liked Ophelia and all."

"If you'd a told me a few days ago, I might a done something stupid - like kill 'em both." Pip let out a small laugh and shrugged. "But it didn't take me long to see Ophelia for who she really is. I guess I was blind before."

"You and me both," Reba said. "I guess you were finally the hero for once."

"I've always looked out for you! You just didn't know it."

"Hm. Thanks, I guess."

"Does this mean I'm forgiven?" Pip asked.

Reba frowned. "Forgiven for what?"

"Brianna. I figure we should be about even by now."

Reba grinned. "Forgiven."

"Who's Brianna?" Patsi asked.

Reba shook her head. "Old news."

"Oh." Patsi let it go. "Well, I knew Ophelia was a snob the first time I met her, but nobody listens to me." She turned a sympathetic gaze toward Pip. "I hope you'll be okay."

"Me?" Pip waved a dismissive hand. "I'm already over it. Like, gonzo."

"Well, I'm not," Reba said. "I'm just so humiliated! To think I fell for 'is…'is… 'is charms!" She shook her head in disgust and took another bite of ice cream.

"It is going to be awkward since he and Brett are friends, not to mention all the other connections," Patsi said.

"Maybe I'll just hightail it back to Newfoundland," Reba said. Both Pip's and Patsi's eyes widened. "What?" Reba looked from one to the other. "There's nothing to keep me here but bad memories."

"There's family. And friends." Pip glanced at Patsi.

Reba set her empty bowl on the coffee table. "I know. I guess I'm getting tired of my living arrangements, too. Not that Andrea hasn't been nice, but it feels like I'm still visiting, not like I really live there."

"Well…" Patsi sat forward. "I might be in the market for a room-mate soon." She looked around the room as if to make sure no one else was listening. "Please don't say anything because it isn't official yet, but I think Lester and Sherri are getting married - soon."

Reba's brows rose, her interest piqued. "How soon?"

"Like this summer," Patsi said. "They haven't announced anything yet - not even to me, but I overheard something Lester said the other night when he didn't know I was listening."

"Will they move into Sherri's place? Maybe we can just take over this lease," Reba said.

"Maybe. Please don't say anything, though," Patsi repeated.

"My lips are sealed." Reba ran her index finger over her mouth. Then she turned to Pip, pinning him with her gaze. "So what brings you over?"

"I just wanted to make sure you're okay."

"I thought you said you didn't know I was here," Reba said.

"Oh. Right. Well, I thought Pat might know how you were doin'."

"Now you're lying through your teeth," Reba said. "You never could pull one over on me."

Pip squirmed in the easy chair.

"Come on, b'y! Spill yer guts!" Reba ordered.

Pip frowned, obviously trying to formulate an answer before opening his mouth. Finally he sighed heavily. "I came to talk to Pat about something, that's all. Something private."

Patsi blinked, the look on her face suddenly shuttered.

"I could leave if you want. Since you're my new hero and all." Reba made a motion to stand but Pip waved her back down onto the couch.

"It's private but not *that* private," Pip said. "Besides, Andrea said it would be hard the first time. To tell people, I mean."

"Andrea? What's she got to do with this?" Reba asked.

"Well, see it's like this. You know there was this preacher doing special meetings at Andrea's church?" He paused, probably to gauge their reactions.

Patsi nodded. "I've been to that church. Used to go there before I moved. Lester thought it would be better for me than the one we went to because there was more stuff for the youth." She gave a slight laugh. "I guess it didn't do much good. I still got into trouble."

"Everybody makes mistakes," Pip said. "But we all deserve a second chance."

It seemed like a strange thing to say, coming from Pip, but Reba kept her mouth shut, unsure of what was coming next.

He continued. "I kind of tricked Jed into going, sort of as a favour to Andrea. I thought it would be good for 'im and maybe be a good way to get back at 'im, too, although now I don't know why." He paused again and grinned. "Except lo and behold if *I* didn't give my life to Jesus."

Reba exhaled sharply, not realizing until that moment that she had been holding her breath. "What... what do you mean by that?"

"I went forward for prayer after the meeting. Gave my life to Jesus. It's called being 'born again.'"

"Is this some kind of joke? Cause if it is, it ain't funny!" Reba looked to Patsi, whose expression was still unreadable. "Well? You go to church. Is 'e gonna get struck with lighting for blaspheming?"

"I'm not blaspheming!" Pip cut in. "I'm telling the truth. I went forward and said the sinners' prayer. I got saved. I'm a new creation."

Patsi smiled and shook her head. "I doubt he'll get struck with lightning, although I'm surprised you know a word like 'blaspheming.'"

"We both attended Catholic school," Reba said. "Were forced to learn a few things." She shook her head. "But I can't believe you've gone and got religious on me. Not you of all people." She turned pleading eyes toward Pip but he was still sitting calmly in the easy chair.

"It's not a bad thing," Pip said. "I've never felt better in my life. And to be *h*onest, I think it's what helped me get over Ophelia so fast." He turned to Patsi. "It helped me see that things - people - aren't always what they seem. Everybody makes mistakes, but now that I'm saved, I'm hoping others will give me a second chance, too, just like Jesus did."

Patsi was silent and Reba looked from her friend to her brother without knowing what to think. Suddenly Patsi stood up.

"I'm happy for you, Pip," she said. "But I forgot I have somewhere to be this afternoon and I'm going to have to run." She turned to Reba. "Like I said, once Lester and Sherri announce their engagement we can start thinking about moving in together if you still want to."

"Course I do," Reba responded. She stood also.

Her own heart was still aching but she would mend, she knew. Of more importance at the moment was what was going on between her brother and her best friend.

WILL

Will took his time whipper-snipping around the little studio. Even if Marigold wasn't around to see it, he wanted it to be perfect.

His scouting trip around the perimeter had been torture the last few evenings. Previously, knowing Marigold would be out there painting, it had been the highlight of his day - something to look forward to. Now? Nothing but the same scenery… which was a strange thought since he loved the outdoors. Somehow it just wasn't as pretty.

He cut the small motor and let the whir of the machine die with a final buzz. He frowned when the sound seemed to still be echoing behind him and he turned around to see Buck Stone nearby, cutting down some errant shrubs with a chainsaw.

Buck finished one final branch and then let the chainsaw sputter into silence. "You're spending an awful long time on that little shack," he called, leaning on the chainsaw like a cane.

Will hoisted the weed-whacker and walked toward Buck. "You got something better for me to do?"

"There's always something to do," Buck said. "We've got firewood coming out the yin-yang that needs stacking."

Will nodded. "I'll just clear up the debris and get right on it."

When Will went to move away toward the workshop, Buck stopped him. "You never asked me how things went with your brother. I thought you'd be curious."

"Oh, right." Will blinked and focused his full attention on Buck's chiseled features. "How'd that go? I know it surprised the heck outta the rest of the family, but I never got a chance to talk to Jed about it."

"It made him think. That's about all I can say. I guess you've been kinda preoccupied with your own issues, am I right?"

"You could say that."

Buck motioned to the machine shop with his head. "Come on. We'll clean this up together and then do the wood together, too." Buck hoisted the chainsaw and started walking, Will close behind with the whipper-snipper. "I'm not the best one to give advice when it comes to relationships, but I'd say if you can't stop thinking about her, you should go after her."

"But she's moved back to the city. How am I supposed to do that?"

They entered the relative coolness of the building and Buck set the chainsaw down on a low workbench. "It's not rocket science. Go into town sometime and talk to her."

"I don't know where she lives. And I'm not about to ask the boss for 'er address."

"Scared?" Buck teased.

"Does a dog have fleas?"

Buck smiled. "I don't blame you. The good news is, I happen to know exactly where she lives. Dropped her off there a few times. And I know the address of her studio, too."

Will turned incredulous eyes to Buck. "You do? And you didn't tell me?"

Buck shrugged. "You didn't ask."

Will let out a gust of wind. A sense of excitement like the anticipation of Christmas had started jumping in his gut. But if he did go to

Calgary to see her, what was he going to say? He still wasn't sure where he stood when it came to making a commitment.

"Don't look so anxious," Buck said.

"I don't know what I'm gonna say," Will admitted.

"You want to see her? Then go see her. Let the rest work itself out."

"But how am I gonna get there? I don't have a vehicle and I'm sure as heck not gonna ask her father to lend me his."

"You can borrow my truck. Take off a little early. I'll cover for you."

"You'd do that?"

"You covered for me. It's the least I can do."

"Thanks. I appreciate that."

Buck handed Will a rake and then grabbed the wheelbarrow. He looked over his shoulder as he pushed it out the shop doors. "My advice would also be to say a little prayer about the whole situation. It never hurts to have the big guy on your side."

JED

"Thanks for comin' over." Jed waved Lester to the couch. "Can I get you anything? A coffee?"

"No thanks, and no problem. You sounded... anxious. What's up?" Lester asked.

Jed lowered himself into his chair and rubbed the bristly hair on his head. "I might as well get right to it, although I don't quite know where to start."

"You want to talk about what's happened to Pip." Lester's gaze was steady.

Jed blinked. "Well... yes. How did you know?"

Lester smiled. "I just had a feeling."

"So? What does it all mean? I heard of such things on TV - being 'born again' and such - but I thought it was all for show. And to get money."

"Unfortunately, there have been some bad examples on TV, although not all. Some are genuine. Where should I begin?"

"Well, for starters, should I be worried? Is 'e gonna change?"

"You heard when the preacher said the other night that we all need to be born again?"

"Yeah, I heard it."

"So the answer is 'yes', Pip is going to change. He's a new creature in Christ, now. His past, with all its sins and other baggage, are forgiven and it's like he's got a brand new start. A clean slate with Christ as his helper. Of course, that doesn't mean he's going to be perfect, but with God by his side he's probably going to make different choices - live different. Have a different focus."

Jed stroked the stubble on his chin. "I still don't know what all the fuss is about. Either you believe in God or you don't."

"Even the demons believe and tremble," Lester said.

Jed looked up sharply. "So I'm a demon, now?"

Lester put up his hands and laughed. "I never said that! You just took it that way. I was just quoting scripture."

"A regular walking Bible."

"You seem awfully defensive," Lester noted. "You're the one who wanted to talk about it. And as for quoting scripture - I don't know it as good as I should, but I know a few key verses."

"Like what?"

"'For all have sinned and fall short of the glory of God'. That's Romans 3:23. Then Romans 6:23. 'For the wages of sin is death but the gift of God is eternal life through Jesus Christ our Lord'."

"I'm impressed."

"Don't be." Lester gave a slight laugh. "I know there's another one I'm supposed to say to lead someone to Christ, but I can't think of it right now. The point is, trying to be good isn't enough. We can never be good enough for God and because He is holy, He can't let sin go unpunished. But that's where Jesus comes in. He paid the price for us on the cross, so that we can have a relationship with God. 'For God so loved the world that He gave His only begotten son, that whosoever believes in Him should not perish but have eternal life'. John 3:16."

"That one I do know," Jed said. "The nuns beat it into us in elementary school."

"I'm not sure what else I can tell you, then," Lester said. "You already know the basics. You just have to believe it for yourself, like Pip did."

Jed let out a disgusted puff of air. "I doubt the big guy would want the likes of me. Pip? Sure. He's still young, but me? I've crossed too many lines."

Lester shook his head. "You're missing the point entirely. It's not about being good, or being bad. It's about accepting the free gift. Surrendering your life to Christ. 'I am the way the truth and the life,' Jesus said. 'No one comes to the Father except through me.'" Lester smiled. "Maybe that was the one I was thinking of before."

Jed squinted, rasping the stubble on his chin. "So I don't need to be worried, then? About Pip?"

Lester shook his head. "If anything, you should be glad for him. The Bible says that the angels are rejoicing in heaven when someone gets saved."

"Stop with the verses already!" Jed said in exasperation.

"Sorry." Lester smiled sheepishly.

"Next thing you'll be convincing me to say that sinners' prayer or whatever it is the preacher called it."

"Not such a bad idea if you want to."

"Watch it before I throw you out on your ear."

Lester just smiled.

Jed took a deep breath and let it out very slowly. "I appreciate you talking to me. I just wasn't sure how to bring it up with Pip, or even if I should. I didn't want to make 'im embarrassed, especially if it's just a passing fancy."

"I hope it isn't," Lester said. "I suppose your best bet is to let him decide if and when he's ready to talk about it."

Jed nodded. "Good idea."

Lester hoisted himself to a standing position. "Well, if that's it, I suppose I should get going. Got a pretty full list of things to do today now that..." He hesitated. "Well, anyway. If you ever want to talk about it again, you know where I live. Or if you ever want to say the sinners' prayer and don't know how to start..." He grinned.

Jed grunted. Then he surveyed Lester under hooded lids. "Now that what?"

Lester furrowed his brow. "Now that what...?"

"You said you had lots to do now that... what? What's happening that you're keeping a secret all of a sudden."

Lester looked down at the floor and then up again and smiled. "I'd make you promise to keep a secret but it's going to get out in the open soon enough anyway."

"Well?" Jed prompted.

"I asked Sherri to marry me." Lester beamed.

"Ya didn't, b'y!" Jed vaulted from his chair and thumped Lester's back in a bear hug. "Way to go!" He stood back, holding Lester at arm's length. "It's about time, although as you said, it's not even a year. When's the big day?"

"Um... pretty soon, actually. As soon as we can arrange it."

"Can't wait any longer?" Jed surveyed Lester with a twinkle in his eye. "I forgot you religious types aren't supposed to do what comes natural till you tie the knot, although I'd wager most don't follow that rule anymore."

Lester rubbed the back of his neck. "Well, actually..."

Jed's eyebrows shot up. "Ya done gone and got 'er knocked up, I suppose?"

Lester frowned. "Not exactly the way I'd put it, but yes. She's pregnant. And for the record, we wanted to wait, but..."

"Things got outta hand a time or two," Jed finished for him. "I gets it."

"I am only human," Lester offered with a wry grin.

"Which I'm glad to hear ya admit after all that Bible quotin' earlier."

"Which just goes to prove that every one of us is in need of a Saviour," Lester said. "I never said I was perfect or that I haven't made mistakes. But with Jesus, every day is a fresh start."

"Hmph." Jed furrowed his brow, the thunder taken out of his next response.

"Please don't tell anyone. We're going to tell Sherri's parents' tomorrow night at family dinner and then we still have to pick the date and send out the invitations."

"But it'll be soon, you say?" Jed asked.

Lester nodded. "Yes. Sherri wants it that way. Before the end of summer, for sure."

"Good luck findin' a place in that short a time."

"Her family have some connections, apparently. It shouldn't be a problem."

"Good, good."

"Well, I guess now that you know why, I better get going," Lester said.

Jed walked Lester to the door but before he opened it, he looked down at his feet, shifting his weight back and forth for a few seconds. "Say. About that sinners' prayer…"

Lester's eyebrows shot up. "Yes?"

"Before you leave, do you think you could say it for me - in case I decide to pray it myself later on?"

"Why sure."

Jed nodded and waited.

Lester closed his eyes. "Lord Jesus, I admit that I'm a sinner and in need of a Saviour. I come to you now believing that You died for my sins and took my penalty on that cross. I surrender my life to you now and commit to live for you from here on in. In Jesus name. Amen." Lester opened his eyes.

"That's it?" Jed asked.

Lester nodded. "It doesn't have to be fancy. Just from the heart." He looked squarely at Jed. "So?"

"I'm still mulling it over."

Lester smiled and shrugged. "At least that's something. Can I ask what made you change your mind? To at least consider it?"

Jed grinned. "When I found out my saintly neighbour ain't no saint after all, I figured maybe there's hope for a rascal like me."

EPISODE 17

NEIGHBOURHOOD TURN AROUND

IP

Pɪᴘ ᴘᴜᴛ on the only button up cotton shirt he owned and then tucked it into his jeans. On second thought, he untucked it. He wasn't sure what people wore to church on a regular basis, but it would have to do. They were clean jeans, anyway.

It had been liberating yesterday telling Reba and Patsi about his new life in Christ. It was awkward in some ways, yes, but at least now he didn't have to skirt the subject if it came up. He'd been surprised by Patsi's lack of reaction, though. He'd thought someone had said she was religious, but her non-reaction made him wonder if she really was saved after all.

Talking to Jed was going to be the next big item on the list. He needed to fortify himself with going to church first, though, before he tackled that one.

He'd texted Andrea the night before to see if he could catch a ride. He was just about to text her to say he was ready when he reached the kitchen and stopped in his tracks.

Jed was pouring himself a cup of coffee, which wasn't unusual in itself. What was different was that Jed was wearing a plain white shirt and a pair of dark dress pants. He'd never seen Jed in dress pants before. Jed lofted his mug in a salute. "Almost ready?"

"Um… for what?"

"To go to church! Are ya stun?"

"You're going to church with me?" Pip asked.

Jed nodded. "I thought I'd drive ya since you don't have a car of yer own. Unless you wanna take transit, but that's a nightmare on a Sunday, or so I'm told." He took a sip of his coffee.

"Sure. That'd be great." Pip looked down at his phone. "I'll just text Andrea and say I don't need a ride."

"Don't tell 'er why, though," Jed said. "I want it to be a surprise."

Pip blinked. "Okay."

What was going on? Unless aliens had invaded the planet and taken over the bodies of his loved ones…

JED

Jed smiled to himself as the closing song swelled around him. In fact, he couldn't stop smiling. This was the best surprise he'd ever planned. He glanced over at Andrea Carravagio, seated three down from him with her brother Rocky and Pip in between. That was the only unfortunate thing about the whole morning. It was an issue that would soon be remedied if he had anything to say about it.

He and Pip had arrived just in time to find a seat. Much to their good fortune, there were two seats in the same row as Rocky and Andrea.

The pastor said a closing prayer and Jed had trouble keeping his excitement at bay. As soon as the man said 'Amen' his eyes popped open and he sought Andrea's gaze with his own. She smiled tentatively and then looked shyly down at her hands resting on the seat in front.

He moved out into the aisle and shook several people's hands as they moved past before Rocky and Andrea finally emerged from the row.

"Good to see you this morning," Rocky said, pumping first Pip's hand and then Jed's. "Both of you."

"Pip needed a ride." Jed gestured with his thumb at Pip.

"I told you -"

Jed cut him off. "Actually, I was wondering if I could talk to you for a minute." He looked directly at Andrea. "In private?"

Andrea nodded to Rocky that it was alright and stepped further into the aisle. "Perhaps over there by the side would be quieter. We won't be long. Rocky, why don't you introduce Pip to some people?"

Rocky nodded and led Pip away to the large foyer where many of the congregation had gathered to chat.

"Shall we?" Andrea gestured to a row of seats along the right wall. Jed followed, suddenly tongue tied and feeling shy. When they both sat down, he wasn't sure exactly how he was going to begin. He was glad when Andrea started the conversation.

"I was so happy to see you here, today. I was a little surprised, but in a good way. I thought for sure you got scared away the other night."

"I was." Jed smiled.

"But you came back. A good sign." She waited.

He rubbed his bristly hair and then sat up straighter. "So... you're wondering what it is I wanted to say."

"Take your time."

"It's like this, see." He stopped and swallowed, then took a deep breath, determined to just get it out there. "I, uh... I said that sinners' prayer like the preacher said." He looked at her hopefully. "This Newfie's born again."

He waited a beat as a myriad of emotions played across Andrea's face. Then she did the most unexpected thing. She burst into tears and covered her face with her hands as her shoulders shook.

It wasn't the reaction he was expecting. "There, there. I wasn't expecting water works. I thought you'd be happy is all." He patted her back awkwardly.

It was several seconds before she was able to pull herself together.

She dug for a tissue from her purse, blew her nose and then sniffed as she straightened her posture. "I am happy, silly. I'm ecstatic."

"Ex… you are?" Jed surveyed her reddened eyes and nose.

"Of course I am." She took one of his big hands in her own and he thought his heart would melt. "When? When did it happen? After the meeting?"

He shook his head. "Yesterday. Last night, actually. I called Lester and he explained a few things to me. I didn't want to at first, and put it off until I went to bed. I started thinking about what you said that one time, a long time ago, and couldn't get it outta my head. About us not ever being more than friends, and I thought what a stubborn fool I've been. So I just did it. I prayed and… God did the rest, I guess you could say."

"I hope that's not the only reason you prayed." She dropped his hand and clasped hers in her lap. "It has to be from here." She pointed to her heart. "It's a big commitment - with or without me."

Jed felt his elation deflating but he nodded. "I know. I'm not holding you to anything you said back then. I wouldn't expect it of you. I just wanted you to know, even if we are only ever friends."

She nodded primly. "Good. Friends is a good place to start."

"Friends." Jed extended his hand and after a second's hesitation, they shook. He smiled his most convincing smile and stood up. "Suppose we find Pip and Rocky now?"

"Good idea."

Yes, he had committed his life to Christ and he didn't regret it. The peace that had flooded him after saying the prayer had taken him by surprise. But he had expected a bit more reward for his efforts. Maybe this is what it meant to suffer for Jesus.

∼

WILL

It was a tight squeeze, but Will managed to parallel park Buck's truck in the available space right in front of The Brew. Some amateur had parked a delivery style van at a weird angle, taking up more than one spot and making it difficult for the next person to fit. Oh well. Parking was usually at a premium downtown, but considering it was a Sunday afternoon, he was lucky to get a spot at all.

Buck had given him directions to both Marigold's studio and her apartment, but for some reason he wanted to look at her paintings again before he took the plunge. Seeing her work might help to ground him.

He headed to the glass entrance, but when he went to pull it open, it was stuck fast. With a frown he read the posted hours on the door. Closed Sundays and holidays. Of course! He hadn't thought of that.

He turned to leave but before he made it back to the truck, he heard the deadbolt click and the door opening. "Hey! Will, right?"

He swung around and recognized Patsi Tibbett poking her head out the door.

"Hi. I never thought about the fact that you might be closed on Sundays."

"Not as much foot traffic. But you can come in if you want. I had to meet one of the artists so she could collect the pieces that didn't sell."

Will's stomach jumped into his throat. "One of the artists, you say?"

Patsi nodded.

"Okay. Just for a minute."

Patsi propped the heavy door wider with her foot and Will stepped over the threshold.

"She's almost finished, I think. I told Tamara I didn't mind. It saves her having to come down when she has her son to look after and all. So? You in town for the weekend or just the day?"

"Just the day. Say, would you mind if I took one last look at the paintings that are left? I... might want to buy one myself. Take it off her hands before she has to pack it up."

Patsi shrugged. "Suit yourself. I'll just re-secure the door."

Will took a deep breath and then strode through the French doors into the new part of the establishment. He heard a rustling sound behind one of the dividers that had been put up so that more art could be displayed. His breath hitched when he saw Marigold's familiar figure, her hair falling straight down her back. The muscles of her bare arms and shoulders flexed as she lifted a large canvas from its hanger.

"That's a heavy one. Let me help you." Will stepped forward and grasped the painting from Marigold before she could gather her thoughts.

Her eyes were wide. "What? What are you doing here?"

He gently set the painting against the wall with the others and straightened, a sheepish grin playing at his lips. "Tryin' to get you outta my system, I suspect."

Her eyebrows rose. "Is that so?"

He nodded. "Or maybe get you back into it." He took a step toward her and stopped a mere hand's breadth away. "I came looking for you but thought I'd stop by here first to have one last look at your paintings. I wasn't expecting to find the real thing."

She searched his face with her eyes and it was all he could do not to cover her mouth with his own. "You came looking for me. Why?"

"'Cause I want a second chance? Cause I'm a dumb lummox and spoiled everything cause I have commitment issues?"

"Do you? Have commitment issues?" she asked.

He nodded. "I think so. I never really tested the theory before, but I think so."

"And?"

"I'm willing to try to get over them if someone will help me."

"Someone?" She smiled.

"A certain someone," he clarified.

"I see." Her lashes fluttered downward. "Will, I…"

He placed a finger on her lips. "Sh. Don't say anything more. I just want to kiss you. Can I kiss you?" He tilted her chin up and looked hopefully into her eyes.

He could see the struggle to resist, but she finally gave an almost imperceptible nod. He didn't wait for further encouragement.

It felt like heaven having Marigold back in his arms, their lips touching. He didn't want this moment to end and he encouraged her by increasing the pressure on her mouth.

After a few seconds, Marigold stepped back, breaking the sweet contact and pulling out of his embrace. She folded her arms across her chest. "This doesn't really change things. I'm still mad at you."

"Course you are. I deserve it."

"And just because I let you kiss me does not mean I want to take up where we left off."

"Hm. You're one tough cookie." Will scratched his head. "Okay. So what will it take to convince you?"

"You hurt me, Will. I'm not sure I'm up for that again."

He took her face in his hands. "I know. I'm sorry." He kissed her again, gently. She didn't resist.

"I'm just not sure," she said. "How can I know you won't hurt me again? I told you straight up how I feel about you and that hasn't changed, but it doesn't mean I want to make myself vulnerable."

He rubbed his hands up and down her arms, willing her to meet his gaze and see the sincerity there. "Listen, I won't tell you I'm not afraid, cause I am. But I think I'd rather try this… this relationship thing afraid than not try it at all."

"And that's it?"

"Commitment issues, remember?" He grinned and then sobered almost instantly. "I'm being straight up with you, too. It's about all I've got to offer at the moment, although I have a feeling I could be convinced."

"You could, could you?"

He nodded. "If someone is willing to convince me…"

"I'm not sure," she said again.

Will captured her mouth with his again and kissed her until she was breathless.

"You make it awfully hard to resist," she said, disentangling herself from his grasp.

"Good. That's my plan."

She smiled. "I'll think about it. In the meantime, since you're here, you might as well help me lug these to the van." She gestured to the stack of paintings leaning against the wall.

"Since when do you drive a van?"

"It belongs to a friend," she said.

"Should I be jealous?"

"Only if you think I prefer senior citizens."

Will frowned. "Come again?"

She laughed. "Vance is part of our artists' co-op and shares the studio space. He lets the rest of us use his van whenever we need it."

"Nice of him."

"Very. So? Time to start using those muscles you're so famous for," she teased.

Will picked up the first painting and held it back as far as he was able. "I like this one. Almost as much as that other one you did overlooking the mountains." He glanced at her and smiled. "You were doing sketches for it the first time I saw you."

"You remembered."

"How could I forget?" Their eyes held for a moment.

Marigold picked up the next painting in the stack. "I liked that one, too. I almost put 'not for sale' on it, but it sold."

"I know. My brother bought it."

Her gaze swung sharply to his. "What? Really?"

He nodded. "I saw it last week at Bo's place."

"Bo bought it?" She nodded, a slight smile on her face. "I remember him. He seemed to know something about art."

"Actually, he's not the one who bought it. Just storing it for now. My brother Zeb bought it. I don't think you've met 'im."

"How about that?" She shook her head. "I'd like to see that painting again, sometime."

"That can be arranged."

~

BO

A knock sounded on the apartment door, jolting Bo out of the gunfight that was absorbing his attention. He set his book down open faced on the crate-cum-end-table, hoisted himself from the couch, and ambled barefoot to the door. He wasn't expecting anyone and had decided to spend his Sunday off in the company of a good book.

A slightly distorted version of Will appeared through the peep hole. So much for avoiding family, although Will brought less drama than the rest.

Bo unlatched the deadbolt and swung the door wide. His brows rose slightly when he saw that Will wasn't alone. "Come in, come in." He stepped aside so the pair could enter. "It's Marigold, right?"

She nodded. "You remembered."

"Of course. I don't know if Will told you, but I have the pleasure of looking at one of your paintings every day."

"I told 'er about it," Will said. "That's why we're here."

"Oh. Great. This way." Bo gestured to the living room, still sparse by most standards, but gaining in a few pieces since he'd moved in. The addition of the painting made it seem less spartan. "Will probably also told you that I didn't actually buy it. Our brother Zeb did, but he asked if I'd store it till he figures out how to get it to Fort Mac."

"Yes, he told me that." Marigold stood back and viewed the painting, cocking her head to one side. "It's one of my favourites. I almost didn't want to sell it but thought I'd put an outrageous price on it, just in case."

"Zeb's got money to burn, so I guess he didn't mind," Bo said with a laugh. "I'll be sorry to see it go if he ever decides to take it."

"You can always replace it," Marigold said.

"I'm afraid my budget doesn't have room for art at the moment," Bo said.

"There are lots of art sales throughout the summer where you can buy something original and unique for a really good price." She smiled. "Who knows? I might even have some work for sale that would be in your price range."

"I'll keep that in mind. So? You guys want a drink or something? Iced tea, coffee?"

"We're probably keeping you from something," Marigold said.

Bo pointed to the book sitting face down on the crate. "Nope. I was just reading."

"You and your books." Will shook his head.

"If you'd ever invite me to go fishing sometime, maybe I'd do something else for entertainment. In fact, I was reading a book the other day about all the different birds in the area. I was thinking about buying a set of binoculars."

Will smiled. "See? Read it in a book!"

"There are some really good spots for birding near the camp-ground," Marigold said. "People come there all the time for that exact reason."

"Really?" Will's eyebrows shot up. "You never told me that."

"That's because you're always ripping around on one of your loud machines. I didn't want you to scare them away." Despite the scolding tone of her voice, Marigold's mouth was turned up in a coy smile.

"Women," Will said. He had his hands jammed in his jean's pockets, but he gave Marigold a playful bump with his hip.

Bo smiled. If he wasn't mistaken, the flirtatious banter was a sign that the two had made up, or if not, at least were headed in that direc-tion. He wished he could say his own progress with a certain someone fared as well. He straightened. "Who's for iced tea, then?"

As he was pouring three glasses of iced tea, the security buzzer sounded. "Can you get it?" he called to Will.

"You don't give everyone a key to the front door?" Will asked with a grin.

"Don't make me regret I gave you one."

It was Jed and a few minutes later, he ushered himself into the room. "I wasn't expectin' to see you here, Will." He stopped abruptly when he saw Marigold. "Well, I'll be jiggered! If it isn't the artist. Nice to see you again." He pumped Marigold's hand.

"My brother Jed," Will said under his breath.

"I remember."

"Pip's on his way up, too. I let 'im drive for a change."

"The whole family is congregating, I see," Marigold said.

"Oh no," Jed replied. "There's nine of us in all."

"She knows," Will interrupted.

By the time Bo had poured two more glasses of iced tea, Pip had arrived, and Bo distributed the refreshments. "And before you ask, no I don't have anything stronger. Not today, anyway."

"I'm good with this," Pip said.

Bo raised a skeptical brow but didn't argue. He pulled two kitchen chairs into the living room to make enough seating. "I don't know if I've ever had this much company at one time. What brings you two over - together, no less."

"Can't a man want to spend time with his siblings?" Jed asked.

"Sure. It just doesn't usually happen without some ulterior motive."

"Like Zeb's dinner," Pip said with a grin.

Bo nodded. "My point exactly."

"Well, there was something we wanted to discuss with you," Jed said. "But there's no hurry seeing as Will's here with 'is friend."

"Oh. I can go if it would be better," Marigold said.

Bo frowned. Trust Jed to say something to make her feel awkward. "I'm sure whatever it is can wait."

"It's not like it's a big secret anyway," Pip said.

Bo looked first at Jed and then Pip. "Okay then. Shoot."

"It's like this, see," Jed began. He stopped and rubbed the afternoon bristle on his chin. "We got invited to this here meeting. At Andrea's church?"

Bo's eyebrows rose slightly but he kept his mouth shut.

"Pip actually tricked me into going, but that's another story. Anyway, I probably had it coming since I've been a stubborn mule for such a long time when it comes to that kind of thing. If I'd a known what I know now, I wouldn't have taken so all fired long to make up my mind. As it is, Lester Tibbett's been trying to convert me for some time, now, and I guess you could say I seen the writing on the wall a few times. That AA meeting..." He stopped and levelled a gaze at Will.

"Which I know you knew about - but I'm not holdin' it against you - although I might have a few days ago -"

Pip cleared his throat. "What Jed's trying to say is, we both got born again. Gave our lives to Christ and that's about it. We're not the same. At least, I'm not." He grinned over at Jed. "This lubber, I'm not certain about yet, but we had a good long talk this afternoon and I think it's genuine."

Whatever Bo had been expecting it wasn't this. He glanced over at Will, whose expression mirrored the shock that he was feeling at the moment.

"I can see by the look on your faces that we've caught you off guard," Jed said. "I know the feeling, believe me!" He gestured at Pip. "When this youngun went for prayer the other night I pretty much hightailed it outta there! But then I got to thinking. And after talking to Lester some about it, it just seemed to make sense, somehow. And I asked myself, what was I afraid of? It couldn't hurt to say the prayer, like they said. If there was something to it, why take the chance on missing out? And if not, well, no harm done. But when I did, it was like the shutters were suddenly open and I could see clear." He shook his head. "I don't quite understand it myself, yet, but I know there's been a change somewhere deep in here." He patted his chest.

Bo shifted in his chair. "I... I don't know what to say. Congratulations, I suppose? I mean, it sounds like a good thing..."

"My grandmother is very religious," Marigold said. "I've heard her talk that way."

"And Buck," Will put in.

"See?" Jed beamed. "Speaking of Buck, can you tell 'im I want to go to the next AA meeting with 'im when 'e goes? Now that I know Jesus, all that higher power business doesn't seem like such hocus-pocus."

Will nodded. "I'll tell 'im."

"I wonder what Zeb's gonna say?" Bo asked. He blinked and looked to Jed, realizing he'd inadvertently said it out loud.

"I'm gonna call 'im later. That lummox needs Jesus as much as anybody!" Jed grinned.

Will stood up abruptly. Judging from his body language, he was decidedly uncomfortable with the revelation. "Listen. We should get going. We still got to unload all Marigold's paintings back at 'er studio and I should try to get back before dark."

"Why?" Jed asked. "You gonna turn into a pumpkin?"

"No. I..." Will trailed off, looking to Marigold for support.

"Thanks for letting me come by and see the painting," Marigold said, taking Will's hand as she stood. "Let me know when Zeb takes it and I'll see what I can do."

"Oh, before you go, did you hear that Lester and Sherri Chan are gettin' married?" Jed asked.

"How'd you know that?" Pip sat up in his chair. "Pat said it was a secret."

"Then why'd she tell you?" Jed countered.

"When's the wedding?" Bo cut in.

"Not sure yet," Jed said. "I guess I wasn't supposed to tell yet, but they're lettin' 'er folks know tonight. " He turned to Will and Marigold, who were now standing by the door. "That'll be a good excuse to come to town, eh b'y?"

"What if I'm not invited?" Will asked.

"His favourite rodeo student?" Jed shook his head. "You'll be invited."

After a few more good-byes, Bo saw Will and Marigold out.

"So what do you make of that?" Jed asked once they were gone. "Think our Will is serious?"

Bo shrugged and sat down on the couch in the spot vacated by Will. "I don't know. She seems nice enough."

"Looks like he's the only one to get 'is girl after all." Jed shook his head once again.

"I'm surprised to hear you say that," Bo said. "I thought maybe that was your motivation for... for your conversion. So that you could date Andrea."

"The thought crossed my mind, I won't lie, but if the good Lord sees fit to put us together then He's gonna have to do some work, and that's a fact."

"What do you mean?" Bo asked.

"Seems she's only interested in bein' friends."

"Oh." Bo blinked. The similarity to his own situation was obvious. He looked down at his hands.

"Sometimes we think we want something and then God shows us it was the wrong plan after all," Pip said.

"Aren't you the giver of sage advice, now!" Jed said with a snort.

"I'm the first one to give my life to Jesus, so I guess I must be the smartest one, anyway."

"Hmph." Jed had no other come back.

"I think that's part of the point," Pip continued. "God wants you to surrender everything to Him - including people. Least that's what Andrea said. If you're hangin' on to something then you haven't really surrendered."

"She said that, did she?" Jed asked, surveying Pip out of the corner of his eye.

Pip nodded.

"Maybe we should have a talk about that sometime. The three of us."

Pip grinned. "Sure. But don't think I don't know what you're actually hoping for."

"A man can surrender but still have hope, can't 'e?" Jed asked.

Bo leaned against the door for a moment once Jed and Pip finally took their leave. He'd been hoping for a stress free afternoon; getting lost in a book so he wouldn't have to think about his own state of emotional turmoil. Instead, he felt even more wound up, and he wasn't exactly sure why.

He flopped back onto the couch and took up his book. One paragraph in he closed it all together and tossed it on the floor. There was no point.

Pip and Jed had become born again Christians! Pip and Jed - of all people! He'd had conversations about faith with Tad, Andrea, and even Lester. He'd felt the void inside his own soul for some time and had been curious enough to do some research online. Heck, he'd even watched an evangelist on the internet a couple of times.

He'd stopped short of praying the sinners' prayer when he thought about what his family might say. And now Jed and Pip had beat him to it!

He shook his head and smiled at the silliness of that thought. Of course that didn't matter and he really didn't mind. It wasn't a competition and he was too cautious a person to make such a decision lightly. One day, maybe very soon, he would try it for himself. As Jed said, he had nothing to lose. He just wasn't ready yet.

He checked the time on his phone and then closed his eyes, relaxing back against the cushions with a sigh. Viann would be calling soon. But rather than feel excited about the prospect of talking with her, he felt tired. Worn out.

He'd thought he could be satisfied with friendship alone, but he'd been fooling himself all along. It might be better to cut ties, even if his heart did bleed out.

If he fell asleep, though, he'd miss her call…

The last thing he remembered as he drifted off were Pip's words. "God wants you to surrender everything to him - including people." Including Viann.

EPISODE 18

NEIGHBOURHOOD TIGHTROPE

EB

"I GOT an invitation to Lester Tibbett's wedding," Zeb said into his phone. "It surprised me, too, seeing as I don't know 'im that well."

"There's actually a funny story behind that," Bo said.

"Oh? What's that?"

"Sherri Chan's mother felt the guest list was too lop-sided. She insisted Lester find more people to invite to balance things out."

"So I'm an afterthought, is what you're sayin'," Zeb said. "Thanks."

Bo laughed. "I guess we both are, but think of it this way. You're helping Lester out with his new mother-in-law and getting a free meal at the same time. Win-win."

"Sounds like a way to get more presents."

"Spoil sport. Jed thought it was a hoot."

"Speaking of Jed… what you make of 'im gettin' religion? He phoned me last week and nearly blew my socks off with it."

"It's a good thing, I think," Bo responded. "He's made some changes for the better, like going to AA."

"Hm. I guess, although that's going to change things between us, I expect. Now who's gonna be my drinkin' buddy?"

Bo laughed. "Count me out."

"Looks like I'll have to rely on Spitfire, and that's a sorry situation when the only drinkin' buddy left in the family is your sister."

"Maybe you need to slow down, too."

"Don't start," Zeb warned. "And what's this about Pip, too? I never spoke to 'im directly, but Jed says he's the one who started it all."

"True enough. They both went to an evangelistic meeting at Andrea Carravagio's church. You remember Andrea?"

"Course. Well, they better not expect me to follow suit. Next thing you know, you'll be telling me you got religion, too."

"Well, now that you mention it…" Bo trailed off.

Zeb blinked and physically took a moment to stare at his cell phone before putting it back to his ear. "You don't mean…?"

"It's not as bad as you make it sound. And it's not 'getting religion' either. It's having a relationship with God."

"Now I've heard everything. Who's next? Will?"

Bo laughed on the other end. "That'll be up to him. I haven't heard anything, if that's what you're wondering, although he and Marigold - the artist - seem to have made up."

"You don't say. If it makes 'im happy…" Zeb frowned. "Wait a minute. You're trying to distract me. Get me off topic."

"No I'm not."

"I can't believe you fell for all that religion stuff, too. You're supposed to be the sensible one. The one with the level head. Now you're telling me you went and turned on me, too?"

"You're being melodramatic," Bo said with a laugh. "Nobody's turned on anyone. We've just turned to God. But what you decide to do is totally up to you. No pressure."

"Hm. That's not what Jed said." Zeb rubbed his beard.

"Jed's pretty excited, I will admit. You should see him, actually. He's not shy, that's for sure. And he's definitely taking everything he's learning to heart. I guess he just cares enough about you to want the best for you."

"You sound as cracked as Jed."

"You're the one who brought it up. We can talk about something else if you want."

Zeb exhaled sharply. "I don't want a sermon, I just wanna know why in blazes my whole family seems to be going off the rails. Must be something in the water down there."

"It's really not that much of a stretch when you think about it," Bo said. "We went to church as kids. Went to catechism. Learned about the Bible at school."

"Don't I know it. It's taken an awful lot of beer to help me forget." Zeb laughed, but the sound was hollow, even to his own ears. "What made you do it?"

"Actually, it was something Pip said."

"If that don't beat all! Now I heard everything!"

"I'll tell you about it sometime, but you said you didn't want a sermon. So are you going to the wedding, then?" Bo asked.

"I'll check my schedule and see if I have that week off. I don't see why not if I can make it. I've got nothing better to do." Zeb laughed. "Although I'm afraid of what might happen if I come to Calgary. The three of you might gang up on me."

"Don't worry. We won't. Well, I won't at least. I can't speak for Jed and Pip."

It was exactly what had Zeb worried.

BO

"How are you this evening?" Viann smiled at Bo over the computer screen.

"Good, good," Bo responded. "Getting ready to go to work later. You know - the usual."

"Of course. It isn't evening in Calgary yet," Viann said. "I'm still running on Montreal time." Her smile hadn't faded.

"You're looking particularly happy. What's up?"

She shrugged. "Can't a girl be happy without a reason?"

"I suppose so. How's the job? Tired of shopping with other people's money yet?"

"Well... It didn't work out."

Bo's eyebrows rose. "You quit?"

"More like I got... what is the term? Laying off?"

"Laid off."

"*Oui*, laid off."

"You seem awfully happy about it."

Viann shrugged. "My employer and I did not see eye with eye about certain things. It is for the best.

"Eye to eye."

"Pardon?"

"You meant 'eye to eye'. You and your employer didn't see things 'eye to eye.'"

Viann shook her head and smiled again. "That's what I love about you, Bo Malloy. You don't try to protect me when I make a mistake. I like that. It helps me not to look like the idiot."

Bo immediately picked up on the word 'love' but then tamped his breathing into regularity. It was just a phrase. "No problem. It's what friends do."

"So, I am unemployed once again." She sighed but the smile remained. "And what is new with you?"

"Well, let's see." Bo hesitated, unsure how much he should share about his conversion. "There've been a few changes in my life, too, but I don't want to scare you."

She blinked, her smile fading. "Oh. You have found someone nice to date?"

He frowned. Where had that come from? "No, that's not it."

She looked relieved. "Oh good. Not that I would stop you, but a girlfriend might complicate our friendship."

He couldn't agree more. He barrelled forward. "What's your take on God? Religion? Stuff like that?"

She cocked her head to one side. "We went to mass at Christmas and Easter, but our parents were not the most devout."

"Catholic I presume?" Bo asked.

"Of course."

"Same," Bo said. "I went to Catholic school as a kid."

"So did I," Viann answered. "I'm not sure how much effect it had on what I believe, though."

"Same." Bo laughed. "See? More things we have in common." He sobered. "So, what do you believe, exactly?"

She furrowed her brow in thought. "I'm actually not sure. After I left school I just ignored it. Thought of it as a pretty myth not worth my time. But when I got back to Montreal this time, I..." She shrugged and smiled wryly as if embarrassed. "You will think it silly, but I went to confession. I've even gone to mass a few times."

"I don't think that's silly. I think that's good," Bo said.

"It is strange, but I felt this emptiness inside and I just felt the urge to go to mass. To see if that is what is missing."

"And?"

She shrugged. "So far I am not sure. I am still... what is the word? Exploring?"

"Fair enough."

"What does this have to do with the changes you mentioned?" Viann asked.

Bo took a deep breath. "Well, I was feeling exactly the same way you just described. Empty inside and unsettled. Like I was missing something important but I didn't know what." He paused and looked her straight in the eye. "I think I've figured it out."

She raised her elegant brows. "Oh?"

"Yes. I accepted Jesus as my personal Saviour. You know, like you may have heard about? It's called being born again." He tapped his chest. "And guess what? That empty feeling is gone."

She still seemed lost in thought.

"So if anyone is going to laugh, now, I suppose it's you," Bo said. "You probably think it sounds kind of looney-tune."

"Looney-tune?" Her brows furrowed more deeply.

"Crazy in the head." He tapped his.

"No. I trust you and if you say it is real and a good thing then I believe you."

"That's a relief. I thought you might not ever want to talk to me again."

"Of course not. I would never want to stop talking to you, Bo Malloy. You are my best friend."

There it was again. The friend reference. Bo rubbed his head. "Thanks."

"This change must have really affected you. You usually aren't this slow."

"It has." He stopped and frowned. "What do you mean 'slow'?"

"It usually doesn't take this long to notice things." She smiled.

"Notice things?"

She nodded. "Look around." She gestured to the room behind her.

He squinted, not sure what she meant, trying to take in the background on the screen. Suddenly his eyes opened wide. "You're not in your apartment."

"*Oui!*" She giggled.

Her surroundings were vaguely familiar but he couldn't put his finger on why. He squinted some more, trying to find something that would trigger his memory.

"Look." She turned her tablet so it faced the room, slowly sweeping it from one side to the other so he could get a full view.

"Is that...?" Sudden realization almost choked him. "That looks like Jacques's apartment!"

Viann clapped her hands. "Surprise! I am not in Montreal, but right here in Calgary."

"But..." His face split open in a wide grin. "You're pretty sneaky, you know that?"

She giggled again. "I know. It was difficult not to just tell you. I wanted to see how long it would take."

"Too long, apparently."

"But now you know!"

"But why? When?"

"When I got laying off -"

"Laid off," he interrupted.

"Yes. When I got laid off, I decided there was no reason to stay away any longer. I wanted to visit and - *voila*! Here I am!"

"But the other reason you left… to get some space because of your last relationship. What about that?"

She waved dismissively. "I didn't need to move to get over that. You helped me, Bo. I could have stayed right here."

Maybe she did need to move, Bo thought. Having her near again would be torture. Instead he said, "That's super. I bet Jacques will be happy."

"I hope you are happy, too."

"Of course."

"You are quiet," she observed.

He forced a smile. "Just in shock. I'm thrilled."

She nodded her approval. "Jacques doesn't know I'm here yet."

"He doesn't?" Bo asked.

Viann sat up straighter. "I am becoming much more independent. I took a cab to his apartment and I have my own key."

"Wow. That is something."

She wore a happy smile, like that of a child who had just accomplished something for the first time. "*Oui*."

"So what's the plan now? Are you going to stay? Are you just visiting?" Bo felt his insides knotting up at either prospect.

"I am not sure yet. We will let the time tell, hm?"

"Right. So… are you coming to the Urban Cowboy tonight? When will I get to see you in person?"

"Are you that anxious?" she asked.

"Of course." Bo smiled in what he hoped was a brotherly way. "We're friends."

"I will come tonight, then. Do you think Cory will be there?"

Bo's excitement hit the floor like a lead balloon. "Um, probably."

Viann nodded. "I will see all of you then. Cory, my brother, and you - my best friend."

Bo nodded, a lump forming in his throat. If he could call in sick without having to lie, he would. Maybe he would have to be the one to leave Calgary next.

∼

WILL

Will stood on the sidewalk outside Marigold's Calgary studio, looking at the nondescript grey siding and bank of windows along the top one quarter of the rectangular building. The bland exterior of the former warehouse did not even hint at the vibrancy within. The artists' co-op had multiple studio spaces, all suitably cluttered by an explosion of creativity.

He'd helped Marigold unload her paintings that one time, and although he'd been to town since, she always seemed to be otherwise occupied. Maybe she was just avoiding him.

He tried the outer door and when it opened, he took the stairs two at a time to her studio space on the second floor. He could hear the melodic sound of her humming even before he reached the entrance to her studio.

He rapped softly on the open door jamb with his knuckles and then stepped across the threshold.

"Ah!" Marigold jumped.

Will lifted his hands. "Sorry. I didn't mean to scare you."

"How did you get in?" Marigold asked, still breathless.

"The front door was open."

"Really?" Marigold frowned. "I told Savard to make sure he locked up when he left since I'm the last one here. I guess he forgot."

"You're alone?" Will asked. "That seems dangerous."

"Don't start. He must have just forgot." She smiled mischievously. "Although, I wouldn't want just anyone coming in off the street."

Will smiled. "I'll go lock it for you."

"Would you?" She glanced at her painting, which was facing away from Will. "You made me make a big streak right across this piece and I should try to fix it before it dries."

Will headed back down the stairs, clicked the deadbolt into place, and then went back the way he'd come.

"So what are you working on?" he asked, coming around behind

384

her so he could see the painting. He frowned. He could have sworn the canvas was larger.

"Just a landscape." She dabbed at some bushes in the foreground.

Will squinted at the painting. "You fixed it up pretty fast. I don't even see a streak."

Marigold kept dabbing, her head to one side. "I'm just that good, I guess."

Will rubbed his chin and stood back. "Are you hiding something?"

"Don't be silly!" She dabbed some more, avoiding his gaze. "Now, what brings you here?"

Hardly the welcome he'd been hoping for. He cleared his throat. "I just happened to be in the city. Thought I'd stop by, that's all."

"Oh. That's nice."

Will waited a beat and then crossed his arms over his chest. "I get the definite feeling you've been avoidin' me. I thought last time I was here that we'd worked things out between us. That we had an... understanding."

"Oh you did, did you?" Marigold said. Dab, dab, dab.

"Yes, I did. You even kissed me."

"Let's get one thing straight. You kissed me." Dab, dab, dab.

"You didn't stop me."

"True, but..." Dab, dab, dab.

"Damn it, woman!" He threw his hands up in the air before jamming them in his jean's pockets. "Can ya stop paintin' for one second and look at me?"

Marigold carefully placed the paint brush in a jar of liquid and turned slowly around on her stool. With deliberateness she met his gaze. "Alright. Is that better?"

"Yes." Will let out a heavy sigh. "No. I mean, what happened? I thought I made it clear last time that I was still... you know. Interested."

"In what? Taking up where we left off?"

"Yes." Now he wished she wouldn't keep staring at him so intently. He looked away.

"If it's sex you want, may I suggest a prostitute?"

"That's not all I'm interested in!"

"Isn't it?" She turned back to her canvas and started applying paint, more forcefully this time in thick, ragged strokes.

"You're ruining all the nice work you done."

"Now you're an art critic, too?" she bit out.

Will sighed. He put his hand gently on hers, noting the way hers was shaking, removed the paint brush, and put it back in its bath. "I don't know what's made you so all fire mad, but whatever it is, I'm sorry." He drew her up to stand in front of him. "I said I wanted a second chance and I meant it."

Marigold glanced down at her feet. When she looked up again there were tears glistening in her eyes. "You also said you had commitment issues. I've had time to think about it and I'm not sure I'm ready to set myself up to be hurt."

Will expelled a long breath through his teeth. "I knew that was a stupid thing to say."

"It's how you feel," she stated.

Will took both her hands in his. "Look. I think I'm ready for a little bit of commitment. I mean, I'm not proposing or anything, but how about 'I'd like to date you,' kind of commitment?"

She hesitated, blinking away from his gaze.

"Please?"

She let out a small laugh, her shoulders visibly relaxing. "I suppose that's a good place to start. And I wasn't asking for a proposal, by the way!" Her tone was a bit miffed, but she was trying not to smile, so Will took it as a good sign.

"Good. So how about right now? We could go get something to eat. You could give me your number so I don't have to keep driving into the city every time I want to talk to you..."

"You don't have my number?"

He shook his head.

"No wonder you never called me," she said. "Why didn't you ask my parents?"

"You kidding? Your dad already lectured me about breaking your heart. I wasn't gonna go through that again."

"That explains a few things."

"Like what?"

"Why you never called."

"I know I been a stun-lubber about the whole thing," Will said, "but if you'll just give me second chance…?"

"I don't even know what a stun-lubber is, but I'll take your word for it." She smiled up at him.

"Good. Cause this one is about to kiss you again before you change your mind."

BO

Bo wasn't sure how he was going to work. His hands were shaking, his stomach churning, and his mind was everywhere but on serving customers.

Jacques glanced his way a time or two, but Bo kept his mouth shut. He wasn't sure how much the other man knew about his secret online rendezvous with Viann, and tonight Jacques was in for one big surprise.

Cory sauntered behind the counter and Bo purposely kept his back turned, busy with some pop canisters underneath the counter.

"Your father back from his honeymoon soon?" Jacques asked Cory.

"This weekend. Took me by surprise when he and Goldie just up and eloped at the courthouse. I thought they'd want the whole church thing seeing as they're both so religious."

Bo let out an inadvertent snort.

Cory turned to him, his eyes narrowed. "You have something to say about it?"

Bo shook his head. "No. I just think you've got a wrong view of what it means to be religious, that's all. But it's none of my business, so…"

"Exactly. It's none of your business, so next time keep your opinions to yourself." Cory stomped down the aisle, his dreadlocks bobbing.

Ever since Pip had caught Cory with Ophelia Stanfield, things had been tense at the bar. He obviously assumed that the whole Malloy clan was now out to get him, reinforced by the fact that Jed and Pip no longer frequented the place. The fact that they no longer drank weighed into it, but Malloy loyalty had something to do with it, too. It was a strong force to be reckoned with.

Bo sensed Viann's presence before he actually saw her. When he glanced at the door she was sashaying ever so elegantly toward the bar. She was heading straight for Jacques, whose back was turned, and winked at Bo on the way past.

She said something in French and Jacques whipped around. He rushed around the counter and enveloped her in an embrace worthy of a Malloy.

"When did you arrive? How did you get here?" he asked.

"Earlier today. I came to your apartment but you were already gone, so I decided to surprise you." She was beaming. She glanced over at Bo and smiled.

Jacques noted the small exchange and looked square at Bo. "Did you pick her up from the airport?"

"She did it all herself," Bo said, not able to disguise the pride in his voice. "Booked her own flight, took a cab. Everything."

Jacques turned back to Viann. "Becoming very independent, *non?*"

"*Oui*. Well, I have had encouragement." She looked at Bo again and smiled.

Cory Roberts came around the counter and enveloped her in his own hug. "So good to see you." He rubbed her back up and down.

Bo scowled when the hug went on a bit too long. Finally Viann stepped free. She took a deep breath and stood straighter. "It is good to be back. I am surprised to say it, but I missed you. All of you."

"That's so sweet of you." Cory put his arm around her and led her to a stool. He sat down on the one next to her and took one of her hands. "Now, what can I get you to drink after your long trip? Anything you want. It's on the house."

Viann removed her hand from his and placed them together on the counter top. "What is that one I like, again?" She looked to Jacques.

"Cosmo," Bo and Jacques said simultaneously.

"*Oui*. I had it the first time I was here." She looked at Bo and smiled. "You made it, if I remember."

"I certainly did. One Cosmo comin' up." Bo went to work on the drink, all the while keeping an eye on Cory.

"Excuse me for a moment," Jacques said. "I have a call I must take. But I will be right back and we will catch up, *non?*"

Viann nodded.

Cory put his arm around Viann as she waited. When Bo set the drink in front of her, he was certain she tried to shrug the other man's arm off, but Cory wasn't getting the hint.

Maybe she liked it, he mused. She had seemed to be interested in Cory the last time they were together. But she didn't know what kind of man he really was.

"Can I talk to you for a second?" Bo said, trying to keep his tone light. He smiled at Viann, purposely keeping his eyes on her and away from Cory.

"It'll have to wait. You're working," Cory said, his friendly tone iced with underlying malice. He removed his arm from around Viann but took up her free hand instead, on top of the counter.

Bo couldn't keep it in any longer. "Maybe she doesn't want to hold hands with you." He pointed at their hands. "Especially if she knew what kind of man you really are."

Cory's hand slackened and Viann slid hers safely into her lap. She looked from Cory to Bo, her eyes wide. "I do not want to cause trouble. Not on my first night back."

"You're not causing trouble." Cory stood up lazily and straightened to his full height. "In fact this is a perfect opportunity to do what I should have done the minute I got back from Vancouver." He paused for effect. "Fire your sorry ass."

Viann's eyes widened even more. "You can't do that."

"I own the place."

"Tad won't be 'appy when 'e gets back," Bo said evenly. He was determined not to take Cory's bait and lose control, although he had slipped back into his Newfoundland brogue. "'E's the one who 'ired me."

"He's so glad to be rid of the responsibilities he won't even blink. Besides, he's got that hot young wife to keep satisfied. He won't care."

"Now that's disrespectful," Bo said.

"Face it. You're redundant. I don't need you anymore."

Viann was standing up now, clasping one of Bo's hands on top of the counter. "I am so sorry," she whispered.

Bo hardly heard her. He slung the towel from his shoulder. "No trouble. I was thinkin' of findin' other employment anyway. I quit."

It was true. Serving drinks at the Urban Cowboy hadn't been sitting well for some time now. But getting sacked in front of the woman he loved was not the way he had imagined a career change.

"Good. Saves me the hassle of writing you up." Cory stopped, a smile playing at his lips. "Oh. And tell your sister it took one roll to make me want to drop her like a hot potato."

Crack! Bo's fist connected with Cory's face. Viann started to cry but there was no going back now.

Without a backward glance, Bo strode from the establishment, his ears burning with what might have been. For he had no chance with Viann now. Not after tonight.

EPISODE 19

NEIGHBOURHOOD FIREWORKS

J ED

JED LADLED some of the sweet, non-alcoholic punch into the ridiculously small glass he'd been given and took a sip. Glass in hand, he strolled away from the refreshment tables, surveying the crowd of people milling about on the green lawns. He recognized several people from work, the Urban Cowboy crowd including his own relatives, and a few others like the owners of The Brew. Other than that, he assumed the majority were Sherri's relatives. Large canvas gazebos provided relief from the summer sunshine for those who needed it, although the sun was beginning to set. Sherri's parents knew how to put on a shin-dig, that was for sure.

He spotted the happy couple shaking hands with some older Chinese folks and he headed their way. "Are ya over the jitters yet?" He thumped Lester Tibbett's back with his broad hand.

"I think so," Lester said. "Thanks again for standing up with us."

"Yes. Thank you," Sherri echoed. She slipped her hand through the crook of Lester's arm.

"No, thank *you*," Jed countered. "To be your best man - well, I can't think of a bigger *honour* than that."

Lester smiled and bent to give his bride a quick kiss.

Jed smiled, too. They were obviously very happy and he couldn't blame them. "I have to say I nearly didn't recognize you at the church without your cowboy hat, but you clean up okay."

Lester laughed.

"And you are the picture of the perfect bride, Mrs. Tibbett." Jed winked at Sherri. She had changed into a short, lacy dress for the evening.

She beamed. "Thank you."

"Everything went off without a hitch, I take it?" Jed asked.

"I think so," Lester replied. "From where I'm standing, anyway. I got the girl, so what else matters?"

"There's still the whole evening ahead," Sherri said. "Sherman said mother has a surprise planned, which has me worried."

"I'm sure it'll be fine," Lester said. "You worry too much."

"Looks like a success, anyway, as far as I can tell. There were flowers, a priest, and the prettiest bride I ever seen."

"Such flattery, Jed!" Sherri teased. "Now we just have to get you married off."

"Oh, I don't know about that…" Jed cleared his throat and changed the subject. "I never been to one of those Chinese tea ceremonies before. Real elegant."

"My mother insisted," Sherri said. "It was hard enough on her that we weren't doing everything the old fashioned way, so I conceded and let her plan the tea ceremony."

"It was nice." Jed glanced at Lester and smirked. "And you looked real smart in that fancy Chinese jacket."

"Don't remind me," Lester said.

Sherri laughed. "I had a time keeping it down to three outfits, believe me. My mother wanted a different dress for the church, the tea ceremony, the reception, the dance, and for going away."

"You are her only daughter," Lester said.

"You're actually taking my mother's side of things?" Sherri asked. "I can't believe my ears."

Lester bent down for another kiss. Jed looked away.

"And now, speaking of mother, I have to go talk to Sherman for just a minute. Make sure he's keeping her in line. Do you mind?" She looked up at Lester.

"Go ahead. But don't be long." He held her for another kiss before he let her go.

Jed shook his head. "You're one lucky son-of-a-gun."

"I think so." Lester looked at Jed through narrowed lids. "Seems to me you could have the same luck with a certain someone, if I'm not mistaken. You and Andrea seem to be hitting it off pretty well these days. You took her to the Stampede when it was in town, didn't you?"

Jed shrugged. "Just once. To the chuck wagon races. She's not interested in bein' more than just friends."

"Give her time."

Jed laughed. "Seems like all I've been giving 'er is time."

"It hasn't been that long!" Lester laughed. "Besides, it wasn't that long ago that you said you'd never let a woman tie you down."

"A man can change 'is mind, I guess," Jed said. He looked around at the guests, not seeing the woman in question.

"Listen, I better do a little more mingling. Don't forget you need to dance with Lily once the band starts - which should be soon. The whole bridal party thing."

"I know my best man duties, alright," Jed said.

"Good. Talk to you later."

Jed watched Lester stride toward his new bride, now in deep conversation with her twin brother Sherman and his girlfriend Carmen Lamont. They'd be next, if he wasn't mistaken.

Someone tapped him on the shoulder and he turned. It was Pip. "Well? Never thought I'd be this far into a wedding and be completely sober."

"I hear ya, b'y! Who'd a thought, eh?" Jed shook his head.

"You should come sit with the rest of the family now that your duties are over," Pip said.

Jed glanced at one of the covered tables where Bo, Zeb, Will and Marigold were sitting together. Tamara Spence, part owner of The Brew, was standing nearby talking to Marigold. He didn't see Reba, but she was probably with Patsi. He turned his attention back to Pip. "I've got orders to be ready to dance with the maid of *honour* when the time comes. I think I'll go find 'er instead. I'll see youse later."

"Suit yourself."

Jed watched Pip walk away then headed toward a cluster of Asian guests, Lily Chan among them. On his way he spotted Andrea, Angela, and Rocky Carravagio. Jacques was sitting next to Angela, his arm slung along the back of her chair. And if he wasn't mistaken, his sister, Viann, was also there. Funny. Last he'd heard she'd moved back to Montreal. Oh well. Maybe she was better friends with Lester and Sherri than he knew.

He reached Lily's group and waved when a few people turned his way. Sherri's mother rushed forward and bowed several times. "Thank you for being the best man. We are honoured."

"No trouble," Jed said. He'd actually said it already - more than once. It seemed every time Mrs. Chan saw him she wanted to thank him.

"You come with me." The tiny older woman grabbed his arm and started steering him away from the group. He looked over his shoulder, but the rest had gone back to polite chatter in Chinese and didn't seem to notice he was being manhandled by a very pushy midget.

"Um... what can I do you for, Missus?" he asked.

"I need your help with the surprise."

"What surprise?"

"If I tell you it won't be a surprise," she stated matter-of-factly.

He nodded. "Gotcha." He could see why Sherri was worried. Lani Chan might be small in stature but she wielded a lot of influence in this family. He leaned in. "Can I at least get a hint? So's I know what I'm in for?"

She slapped his arm playfully. "You so silly! Now I know why Sherri says you a funny man."

"She thinks I'm a funny man, eh? Well, I guess that's better than an arse. But seriously, if I'm gonna be in on your secret, you have to give me a little somethin'."

She swatted his arm again, but her grin was a mile wide. "Okay, but you no tell!"

Jed leaned his ear downward so that she could whisper more comfortably. His eyebrows shot up when he heard what the surprise was. "Wow. That's right generous."

Lani nodded happily. "Nothing too much for my only daughter. The cowboy is okay, too. He will make good grandchildren."

Jed laughed outright. "Your secret is safe with me, don't worry. Why not tell your son Sherman?"

Lani waved a dismissive hand. "He would have tried to interfere. My children. They don't trust me to make good choice."

"Well, I need to talk to Lily, now, if you don't mind. Apparently we need to dance together soon."

Lani clapped her hands. "Ah yes! The wedding party must dance. Then the surprise!"

Jed smiled as he sauntered back to the circle of relatives. He recognized Sherri's father from the ceremony, but other than Tiffany Yuen, whom he'd met awhile back, he didn't remember anyone's name or how they fit into the family dynamic. Oh, he'd been introduced already, but it had gone in one ear and out the other.

"Thought I better not shirk my duties since Lester warned me we'd have to do that dance soon," he said to Lily. Hope I don't step on yer feet. I'm not much of a dancer."

"Me neither, so we should be fine," Lily said.

$\sim$

ZEB

Zeb swirled the inch of wine around in his glass. The Chans had spared no expense at renting the park, that was for sure. Jed had told him it was going to be a small affair, but it was hardly simple from his standpoint. Who ever heard of two ceremonies?

He took a sip of the wine he'd poured himself from the bottle on the table, and then grimaced. He never did care much for wine, but besides what was left over from the toasts, there was no alcohol to be found. Who ever heard of a wedding without alcohol?

"You better stop frownin' or people will think the Malloys are unsociable," Will teased.

Zeb just made a grunting noise. He'd enjoyed meeting Will's artist girlfriend. They'd had a good chat about the painting. He liked her. Will had done alright for himself. The rest of the family hadn't fared as well.

A live band was set up on the park's permanent bandstand and had just finished tuning up. The leader announced that the bride and groom would have the first dance, followed by the wedding party.

Zeb watched as Lester Tibbett led his bride onto the dance floor - a wooden rectangle in front of the stage with strings of mini-lights criss-crossing overhead. They looked as a bride and groom should - totally in love and oblivious to the onlookers around them.

Zeb grunted again. He'd never wished for that kind of ball and chain. At least not before. Now, he almost felt envious. Almost.

"This should be good," Pip said to the rest. "The rest of the bridal party are joinin' them. Let's see if Jed can keep from steppin' on Lily's toes."

Sherman Chan, Sherri's brother, and Patsi Tibbett rounded out the bridal party. Zeb watched as the three couples swayed and pivoted. Jed was holding his own. Zeb wished he was the one holding Lily Chan so close, though.

Zeb stood abruptly. "Gonna stretch my legs a bit." He turned his back on the dance floor and strode to the refreshment table.

Reba was there filling a glass with punch.

""Eh, Spitfire. I haven't seen much of you since the reception. Where ya been?"

"Hanging out with Pat. She needs the moral support."

"Any particular reason?"

"Just girl stuff. She had to go do the dance thing, though."

"Yes, I know. You holdin' out okay?" Zeb asked. "I know it must be awkward with Cory here, but…"

"I'm okay. You know me. Tough as nails." Her eyes found their way to where Cory Roberts was laughing and talking with another group.

"You're too good for the likes of 'im, anyway," Zeb said.

"Thanks, I guess. Sometimes I think I might end up all alone, though. I know the old saying is there's plenty of fish in the sea, but I think my line might be broke."

"The right one will come along. You just need to be patient."

"Seems a bit ironic coming from you," Reba said.

Zeb shrugged. "Whatever."

"I'm just glad that nasty Ophelia went home - for both my sake and Pip's. I might have lost it if she showed 'er face."

"Never mind 'er and forget Cory Roberts, too. He's a player if there ever was one."

"Takes one to know one?" Reba teased.

Zeb just laughed. "*Touche*. I might be growing out of that phase, though."

"Wonders never cease."

"I mean it. I'm getting tired of playin' the field. It might be nice to find a good woman and settle down, like Lester."

"I'm going to drop from shock pretty soon if you don't stop."

"I mean it," he repeated.

Reba set her now empty glass on the refreshment table. Next she surprised Zeb by flinging her arms around his neck and squeezing. "I love you, you know?"

"I know." He patted her back.

"I mean, I really love you. All of you." She stepped back. "Did I ever tell you that?"

"I think so." Zeb rubbed his beard. "But even if you didn't, I knows it. And I love you, too, Spitfire. You'll always be my baby sister. You know that?"

Reba nodded. "I'm beginning to see why family is so important.

I've been some crooked contrary at times, but I don't know what I would do without you guys. Even Pip."

"He might like to hear you say it."

"Let's not get carried away," Reba said with a laugh. She pointed. "The dance is over. I'm going to go find Pat."

He allowed an indulgent smile as he watched Reba's retreating figure. Then he took a sip of punch and grimaced. Too sweet.

"You don't care for the punch, Mr. Malloy?"

Zeb looked over the rim of his tiny glass in surprise. It was Lily Chan and he suddenly felt tongue tied. "Just too sweet is all. I'm not used to sweet drinks. And it's just Zeb. Mr. Malloy is my pop's name."

"Of course. Enjoying the rest of the wedding, though, I hope?" she asked pleasantly.

He nodded. "Real nice. Not that I've been to a lot of 'em. They look real happy. The bride and groom, I mean."

"Yes. My aunt wasn't too happy with Sherri's choice at first, but I think she's come around."

"Good, good. You and Jed looked nice dancin', too."

"Thanks." Lily allowed a tiny smile to creep over her small, bow shaped mouth. "I was so nervous. I don't actually know how to dance, but your brother seemed to know what he was doing."

A quick stab of jealousy flitted through Zeb's gut. "I'm not much of a dancer, either, but maybe we could give it a whirl. What'd ya say?"

"Um… why not?" Lily smiled shyly.

Zeb was about to lead Lily away when a voice stopped them from behind.

"Well, hello Zeb. I wasn't expecting to see you here, although I must say I'm pleased."

Zeb turned around and frowned. "Hello Tiffany. Me and Lily were just about to dance."

"Wonderful. Save one for me, later," Tiffany said.

"Actually, I should get back to see if Sherri needs anything." Lily gave a slight bow and quickly walked away.

Zeb watched her retreating figure, a deep scowl marring his face.

"Don't be too glum. I'll dance with you," Tiffany said.

"I, uh… I don't think so. See you around."

"Wait." Tiffany put a hand on Zeb's forearm. The sleeves of his dress shirt were rolled up to the elbow and the warmth of her hand branded his skin like fire.

He shook off her hand but waited to hear what she had to say.

"For the record, I didn't accept that other offer. So you don't have to keep up your chivalrous indignation."

"I know. I heard," Zeb said.

"Good. I was thinking… no, hoping, that we could start off on a better foot. Maybe take up where we left off before that unfortunate revelation spoiled things. What do you think?" She batted her eyelashes.

Zeb stared at her exotic features for a moment, perfectly made up with everything in place. The dress she wore hugged her curves and the V-neckline dipped to reveal just enough cleavage to make most men want more. He let his gaze travel slowly up to her face again and shook his head. "Thanks, but no thanks."

Her eyes widened momentarily. Then she smiled. "Don't tell me you have eyes for little Lily Chan? Why, she's just a baby, not at all experienced, if you know what I mean. You'd be bored to death after the excitement of the initial conquest. Besides, her parents have a very short leash and she's too… what's the word? Sensible. I can't imagine a goody-two-shoes like her even giving you a second look."

"Is that so?" Zeb asked.

"It is." She folded her arms, pushing her breasts further up for his viewing.

He shook his head and looked away. "Why don't we test that theory?" Without a further glance, Zeb strode away.

BO

"You doing okay?" Bo placed a hand on Reba's back. She was sitting with her friend Patsi Tibbett.

"Sure. Why wouldn't I be?" she asked.

"No reason. I just never got to talk to you after the… Cory debacle."

"Forget him!" Reba waved a hand. "I'm over it. Although I pity you, having to work with 'im every night."

"For your information, that's changed," Bo said.

Reba frowned. "What do you mean?"

"I quit." Bo's mouth turned up at the corners.

"You what?"

"You heard me. Not before I punched him in the face, though."

Reba sat up. "You what, now?"

"Clocked 'im one good."

"Holy… I can't believe it. Our quiet Bo gettin' into a bar room fight?"

Bo laughed. "It was hardly a bar room fight. He just said some things I took exception to, and I gave 'im what for."

"What did he say?" Patsi asked. "It must have been bad for you to punch him."

"Not worth repeatin'. Anyway, I just wanted to check on you before I go back to my table."

"You can stay here," Reba said. "It's just me and Pat."

"I told Marigold I'd watch 'er purse and what not so she and Will could dance. I better go keep my promise."

"She seems nice," Reba said.

"Will's a lucky b'y."

With a final nod, Bo walked back to his own table. Zeb was still nowhere to be found, but Pip, Will and Marigold were still seated. He plopped down in his own chair.

"May I join you?"

Bo looked up to see Viann standing over him, a glass of punch in her hand.

Bo quickly stood again and pulled out a spare chair. "Please sit down. May I introduce my brother Will and his girlfriend Marigold? And of course, you know Pip…"

Viann nodded to Will and Marigold as Bo pushed in her chair.

"You have been avoiding me all day," Viann said. "I finally must take matters into my own hands."

"No I haven't," Bo said. "I've just been hangin' out with the family."

"Actually, Marigold and I were just about to go for a dance," Will said. He stood and helped Marigold up as well. "Nice meeting you."

"And I'm going to talk to Pat and Reba," Pip said, also making his exit.

Bo waited until they'd all vacated. His siblings had perfect timing, he'd give them that. "I'm surprised to see you here." He looked sheepishly down at his water glass. "After the other night, I didn't think you'd want to talk to me again."

"You thought wrong. What kind of person abandons her best friend in his time of need?"

There it was again. The friend reference. He smoothed the scowl off his face. "I didn't know you knew Lester or Sherri that well."

"I don't. I convinced Jacques to let me come as his date since Andrea and Angela received their own invitations anyway."

Bo furrowed his brow. "Why would you do that?"

Viann said something under her breath in French. "Men! You are so... what is the word? Thick in the head."

Bo blinked. "Pardon me?"

Viann reached forward and took Bo's hands in her own. "Why did I come to the wedding of people I do not even know? To see you, of course."

"Oh."

"Why did I quit my job back in Montreal and fly all the way back to a cowboy city where I have no friends? To see you, of course."

"You quit? I thought you said you got laid off?"

She waved a hand. "No matter. I am here. And you still must ask why?"

Warmth started to flow through his body. "I... I think I'm beginning to see. I hope I'm beginning to see. But, I don't want to jinx anything."

"I love you, you silly lummox!" She leaned forward and kissed him on the lips. A light, feathery, angel touch that was far too fleeting. She sat back and grinned. "Lummox? Is this not a word you English use?"

Bo laughed. "Well, maybe not every English speaker, but we Malloys like it." He sobered. "Can you repeat that, please."

"The kiss, 'I love you', or the part about you being a lummox?"

Bo smiled. "Actually, it doesn't matter. It was all good to me."

Viann sobered and blinked, never taking her gaze off Bo. "I love you, Bo Malloy."

"That's what I thought you said." He leaned forward to receive her kiss, not caring who saw them. Her lips were soft, as he knew they would be, and he let out a sigh of contentment before pulling away. He smiled. "I guess it's pretty obvious that I feel the same way."

Viann sat up primly. "Let me hear you say it."

"Okay. I love you Viann-Patrice Marcett." He sighed. "There. You don't know how long I've wanted to say those words. I just never thought it was possible for you to return the sentiment."

She laughed. "Silly man. And why not?"

Bo shrugged. "I don't know. I'm not very interesting. Not for a woman like you."

"You are not my usual type, it is true, which is probably what attracted me at first. But then I saw your true self. How caring you are and how honourable. I think I started loving you right after the accident, but then I let my old habits - my insecurities - take over."

"Just what is going on here?" Jacques Marcett looked down his nose at first Viann and then Bo. Angela Carravagio was close behind, holding his hand.

Bo took Viann's hand, cradling it between his. "I love your sister. That's what."

"Hooray!" Angela clapped. "You make such a cute couple!"

Jacques frowned his disapproval but didn't say anything about her outburst. "What do you have to say, Viann?"

"It's true. Bo and I are in love and there's nothing you can do to stop it!" Traces of her old defiance bubbled to the surface as she stuck out her chin.

Jacques's stern countenance suddenly melted and he slapped Bo on the back, laughing as he bent over double. "Just teasing. Of course I know all about it. I couldn't be happier for Viann. You are the first decent man she's dated."

Bo let his own smile creep back into place. "So you're not mad?"

"Of course not. Viann told me why she came back to Calgary when I grilled her about it. I told her she had my blessing. It's why she came along today to the wedding."

Bo looked to Viann. "And you played along just now?"

Viann nodded. "You should have seen your face, my love. You were white as the spirit."

"White as a ghost," he corrected.

"*Oui*. What you said."

They all laughed. Jacques and Angela sat down at the table.

"And what about what happened with Cory?" Bo asked. "I never meant to just quit on you. Feels like I'm lettin' you down. He just got my goat and -"

Jacques held up a hand. "That is between you and him. I will not get involved. Tonight it is all about love, *non*? *L'amore*."

"I love it when you talk French," Angela said.

"That was Italian, my love." Jacques gave Angela a lingering kiss.

Bo couldn't resist and did the same with Viann.

Jacques interrupted by tapping Bo on the shoulder. "Mind you take good care of her, *mon ami*. I will be watching."

"Don't worry. I will." He had finally found his home.

PIP

Pip wandered toward Patsi and Reba and sat down in a vacant chair. "Mind if I join?"

"Why ask when you've already plunked your arse on the chair?" Reba asked.

Patsi giggled.

Pip ignored the jibe and turned to Patsi. "So? You wore out yet?"

"Almost." Patsi took off one of her heels and rubbed her arch.

"High heels are so - ridiculous! I'm sure they're a trap to keep women in bondage or something."

Pip laughed. "You've had a busy day. But now you can relax. Put your feet up."

"Not likely."

"Why's that?"

"It's not every day my big brother gets married." She put her shoe back on. "I'm gonna tough it out for his sake."

"Why I wore flip-flops." Reba pointed to her own feet.

"You're so smart. I wish I would have thought of that for later," Patsi said.

"You're part of the bridal party. I, on the other hand, have nobody to impress," Reba said.

Patsi snorted. "As if I have anyone to impress either."

"There's me," Pip said with a smile.

"You don't count."

"Fine. Then come dance with me," Pip said.

"My feet are killing me."

"Go barefoot."

"I might get a sliver," Patsi said.

Reba tossed her flip-flops in Patsi's direction. "Borrow these."

"No excuses now," Pip said with a grin.

He took Patsi's hand and led her to the dance floor. Will and Marigold were already dancing together and Pip gave them the thumbs up.

It was a lively beat and by the time is was over Pip and Patsi were smiling and panting for breath.

The next song was slow and Pip held out his arms - a silent invitation to dance again. With a nod, Patsi moved into his embrace and they began to sway together to the music.

"You know," Patsi began. "Brett and I broke up again."

"Reba mentioned it," Pip replied. "I thought when you wanted me to know, you'd tell me."

"I actually need to thank you," she said.

He drew back enough to look at her face. "Why's that?"

"It happened right after you told me that you had accepted Jesus."

"Oh. I wondered. And?"

"It made me think about all the things I was doing that weren't pleasing to God, dating Brett being one of them. He wasn't right for me before and he's not right for me now. I thought that things might be different this time, but they weren't. Not really."

"But if you love him…?"

Patsi shook her head. "I don't think I ever loved him. Not really. I just got caught up in the excitement. In thinking someone so… so worldly could ever be interested in little old me."

"I'm interested," Pip said.

Patsi laughed. "But you're not worldly."

"Eh! I resent that! I can be as worldly as the next guy." He grinned.

"I don't think so. You don't have a snobbish bone in your body."

"If that's your definition of worldly, then okay. I concede."

"I don't think I ever really loved him. I loved the idea of him. But after you told me about your conversion, well… it made me think about my own priorities. I want to get married someday. To a guy who believes the same way I do. Who has the same values." She looked up at him. "Despite what you may think, I do love Jesus, you know. I just keep backsliding a lot."

Pip laughed. "Good to know."

The song ended and they stood there on the dance floor for a few seconds until they simultaneously jumped away from each other. Pip rubbed his neck. "Well, thanks for the dance. And for telling me. About Brett, I mean."

"Okay." Patsi looked down at her feet. "I should get Reba's flip-flops back to her."

The next song started to play.

"You wanna dance one more time?" Pip asked. "Might as well get some use outta them sandals."

The song was livelier but they chose to hold onto one another instead.

Pip tightened his arms around her trim form. "I'm glad to know you still love Jesus."

"You weren't sure?"

"I'm still a baby, so I don't know much of anything," he hedged.

"But you wondered?"

He shrugged. "Maybe a bit."

She was silent for a moment before she spoke again. "Thanks again."

"For what?"

"For making me see what's important. Like my faith. Your honesty brought that back into focus for me."

"Honesty is the best policy, my ma always says."

Patsi smiled. "Since we're being honest, I really liked you at one time. I'm sure it was just a silly infatuation, but I would have been glad to date you for real, not just pretend to date you."

"But there were things in the way," Pip said. "Reba's silly notions, Lester, my own bad rep..."

"It worked out for the best. I'm glad you're just my friend."

Pip pulled away to look at her better. "You know, I realized something that night I caught Ophelia and Cory together. I was so focused on what I *thought* I wanted that I didn't see what I *actually* wanted. What was right there in front of me all the time."

Her breath hitched. "Meaning?"

"I'm glad we're friends, too, Pat, I really am. But I think I might want to be more than just friends. I think I have feelings for you that go beyond friendship. But if that's not possible, then I'm okay with staying friends, too."

Patsi let out a gust of breath and then giggled. "I lied. I still like you - in that way. I always have. I just didn't want to embarrass myself again if you didn't feel the same way."

Pip laughed and tightened his hold, drawing her body firmly against his own. He stopped suddenly and took her hand, hurrying them off the dance floor.

"Where are we going?" Patsi asked, scurrying behind him.

Without answering, he pulled her into the shadow of some trees. Then he bent to kiss her full on the lips. After a few breathless seconds he pulled away, although his hands still cupped her face.

"There. Now it's sealed. I wanted to kiss you on the dance floor, but I didn't want to start another ruckus. Not today."

"You're right. We'll act like nothing's happened and wait to tell the others after the wedding."

"Good idea."

"You do know that as a Christian, there are certain rules about what one can and can't do while dating."

Pip frowned. "You mean the 'no sex', rule, don't you?"

Patsi giggled and nodded.

Pip sighed. "More suffering for Jesus. Oh well. It'll be worth the wait if we decide to get hitched."

"I'm too young to get married," Patsi said.

"Says who? Ma and Pops were married right after her eighteenth birthday."

"We're not in Newfoundland."

"Just one more kiss?" Pip asked.

"Oh, all right."

Pip didn't hesitate. This was what he had been wanting all the time.

WILL

"Let's go find a quiet place away from everyone else for a few minutes," Will said, leading Marigold from the dance floor. "I think Bo needs more time."

"Is she his girlfriend?" Marigold asked.

"He wants her to be his girlfriend," Will said. "I just hope he's as lucky as me when it comes to getting the girl."

He leaned in for a quick kiss.

Marigold swatted him away. "Behave. We're in a public place."

"So?" Will grinned.

They found a park bench on the outskirts of the perimeter and sat down.

Will slipped his arm around Marigold's shoulders and she leaned against him. "This was very lovely. Just the way a wedding should be." Marigold sighed.

"It was pretty good - as weddings go," Will agreed.

"Oh right," Marigold said with a laugh. "People with commitment issues don't enjoy weddings, as a rule."

Will laughed, too. "I admit it. I thought it was going to make me uncomfortable. But, actually, it didn't."

"No? Well, that's good news, I suppose."

Will straightened and turned to look at Marigold. He took both of her hands in his. "Actually, what it did do is make me see how foolish I been over the whole thing."

Marigold blinked and waited. "Oh?"

Will nodded. "See, I was thinking… what better time than right now, under the stars, to tell the woman I love that I, well, that I love 'er?" He waited, a silly grin on his face.

Marigold's hand went to her mouth, a small cry on her lips. Before she could say or do more, Will covered her mouth with his and kissed her long and hard. When he pulled back he smiled again. "Yep. I finally got the courage to say it. I love you. There." He cleared his throat and said it again. "I love you. Now, how hard was that?""

"As long as you mean it," she said.

He nodded. "I mean it with every breath. I love you, Marigold Reynolds, and I'm not afraid to say it." Will took her hand in his and stroked it between his roughened thumb and forefinger, content to just be with the woman he loved.

She sat up. "I have a confession to make."

"O-kay…" Feelings of uncertainty began to resurface.

"You know that time you came looking for me at my studio?"

He nodded.

"I was hiding something from you that day."

He let out a deep breath. "Phew! I knew it!"

She laughed. "What did you think I was going to say?"

"I didn't know, but it scared the be-jiggers outta me."

"You're so eloquent!"

"I try," he said wryly.

"It's another painting. Of you."

"What?"

"I couldn't help myself!" She turned soulful eyes toward him. "I love you, Will Malloy. My feelings haven't changed. You're on my mind all the time. But I didn't want you to see it in case it ended up the same way it did the other time."

"We made love that time. That wasn't so bad," he said.

"No! I mean after that. You know, in disaster."

"That was my dumb fault, not yours."

"Anyway, I regretted ruining the other painting. So I wanted to do another, but I didn't want you to know."

"Can we go and see it when we leave here?" Will asked.

"I suppose."

"Good. Maybe I'll get lucky."

She swatted him across the arm.

"Ow! Just teasing. I don't want you to ever feel like I'm in it just for that," he said.

"Promise?"

"I love you, Marigold. Did I say that already?"

"You did, but you can go on saying it for eternity if you want to."

EPISODE 20

NEIGHBOURHOOD WRAP

EBA

REBA YAWNED and checked her phone. What was taking Pip and Pat so long? She didn't see them dancing anymore. She smiled. She could almost bet they liked each other. This time she wouldn't discourage it. She owed Pip that much, at least.

"Excuse me?"

Reba looked up. A lanky cowboy was standing at her table. Dark jeans, huge belt buckle, plackets on his western shirt, and a cowboy hat. The only one in sight, if she wasn't mistaken.

"Looking for someone?" she asked.

"You're Patsi Tibbett's friend, right?"

Reba nodded. He looked familiar, but she couldn't quite place him. "She's off dancing, or something. I can tell 'er you're looking for 'er."

"That's okay. It was you I wanted to talk to." He took off his hat and fingered the rim. "The name's Weston Drake. I saw you sittin' all alone and thought you might like some company."

Reba blinked. Where had she heard that name? "Um... sure. Sit down." She gestured to the vacant seats. "Take your pick."

Weston sat down opposite, and put his hat on top of the table.

Reba leaned forward. "You look awful familiar. Do I know you from somewhere?"

"The Urban Cowboy," he replied. "I've seen you there with Patsi and Lester."

Reba surveyed him a moment longer and then snapped her fingers. "You're the buddy who won the bull riding competition."

He beamed. "That's right. Well, I lost the first one to Lester, but I managed to pull out a win the second time."

"Against my brother, Will," Reba said.

"Will Malloy is your brother?" Weston asked. "He did very well, considering he has no real rodeo experience."

"That's our Will. A natural born athlete."

"Say. Since everyone else is up dancing, I don't suppose you'd like to go for a whirl?"

Reba took stock of the newcomer. He wasn't half bad, really. She pointed to her feet. "Got no shoes. Lent 'em to Pat."

"Oh. That's too bad. Maybe next time." He smiled shyly and looked down at his rough and weather worn hands. "I'm more into the two step, myself, anyway. I'm a country music fan through and through."

Reba took that information in and a smile spread across her features. "What the heck." She stood up. "I'm not afraid of a few slivers." She held out her hand and let Weston Drake lead her to the dance floor.

ZEB

For all his bluster, Zeb wasn't feeling as confident as he'd let on to Tiffany Yuen. Lily Chan had flat out rejected him - twice. The difference in their ages seemed to be the likely culprit, although Tiffany had given him a few more reasons for Lily's lack of interest.

The funny thing was, now that he had his sights set on her, he was determined to win. He wasn't used to taking no for an answer when it came to women, but the lovely Lily had turned him out on his ear.

He spotted her sitting at a table with several of her relatives, including the bride and groom. Zeb hesitated in mid-stride. It was a fool's errand and he'd be better off high-tailing it back to his own table.

Too late. Lester had spotted him. "Hi Zeb! Thanks for coming all this way for the wedding."

Zeb walked more slowly toward the group and nodded. "I was right *honoured* to be invited. I appreciate the gesture."

"You did me a favour by accepting, believe me." Lester laughed.

"So I heard," Zeb said.

"Gotta love Aunt Lani," a young man said. "She's got her own way of keeping the world in alignment."

"Would you like to join us?" Lester asked. "We could squeeze in another chair somewhere."

Zeb shook his head. "I, uh, I actually came to collect that dance Lily promised me." He smiled when he saw her start. A break from her cool demeanour meant he was finally getting through.

Lily glanced around at the curious faces. "I, um, well…"

Zeb held out his hand. "You can't reject a man in front of all these witnesses, now can ya?"

Lily put her slim hand in his large one and stood up. Zeb nodded to the group and then led her to the dance floor.

"I'm not much of a dancer," she said.

"So you said already. I think you're just makin' excuses cause you're scared."

She blinked mutely and he took her left hand in his right and rested the other on the small of her back, then proceeded to move effortlessly to the music.

"I thought you said you weren't much of a dancer," Lily said after a few seconds. "You're even better than your brother."

"I lied," Zeb said. "It's actually in the genes. We Newfies got the rhythm." He twirled her around once and she giggled nervously.

"Oh my! I might trip on my own feet."

"Just relax and let me lead," Zeb said.

She nodded.

Zeb laughed. "And don't concentrate so hard. Relax and enjoy it."

She smiled tentatively. "Okay."

They danced until the song ended and Zeb released her body but not her hand. "See? That wasn't so bad."

"No, you're right. It was fun."

"Good. We'll give it another go, then."

Before she could protest, Zeb had reclaimed his position and was twirling her against him again.

"For the record, Tiffany propositioned me again," Zeb said. He felt Lily stiffen in his arms. "I told 'er to take a hike. I'm not interested in 'er kind, no matter what you might think."

"Oh. Well, it's really none of my business anyway," Lily said.

"I thought I made that clear the last time I came to your restaurant. I want to make it your business."

Lily blinked. "Oh."

"Tell me straight. Is it the age thing?" Zeb asked.

"No. I don't care about that."

"Okay. You just don't fancy me then."

"No... I wouldn't say that either."

Zeb couldn't help the smile that threatened to split his beard in two. "Good. I thought I was losin' my touch."

"I think it's more that aspect that bothers me," Lily said. "The fact that you're so sure of yourself while I'm so... unsure."

"You unsure?" Zeb's eyebrows rose. "You seem as cool as a cucumber most of the time."

"My defence mechanism," Lily admitted, the corners of her mouth turning up. "I've been perfecting it for years."

"I'm not asking for your hand in marriage," Zeb said. "I just wants to get to know you. Go for coffee a few times. Maybe to dinner. No pressure at all for anything else. My word."

Lily pulled back a bit to look at him. She had to gaze upward since he towered over her. "But why? Why me?"

Zeb shrugged. "That's the age old question, isn't it? What attracts a certain man to a certain woman? What chemistry makes one couple fall in love and not another?" He chuckled. "I'm no matchmaker, as my siblings will attest to, but I know a good thing when I see it. A good feeling when I get it." He looked down into her darkly exotic eyes. "There's just something about you that I find unexplainably attracted to, Lily Chan, and I can't quite put my finger on it."

She blinked. "Oh." She smiled suddenly and looked up at him again. "It's kind of hard to argue with that."

He laughed and whirled her away on the dance floor.

JED

Jed slumped into a chair and loosened his tie, exhaustion about to overtake his weary bones. He'd been dancing most of the night. Seems all of Sherri's female relatives had to take a turn dancing with the best man. In the commotion he'd hardly said two words to Andrea. He'd been hoping to get her up on the floor to dance at least once, but so far it hadn't come to pass.

"You look about ready to pass out."

Speak of the she-devil. Andrea had just joined him. "I'm right tuckered," he responded. "Who knew bein' best man was such a workout?"

Andrea laughed. "I know. I've been watching you all evening. I think some of those younger girls have a crush on you."

"Nah!" He waved a hand. "Now you're seein' things. Nobody'd be interested in a old beggar like me."

"Oh, I wouldn't say that."

Jed glanced at Andrea's face; at the way she couldn't look him in the eye and the way her cheeks were flushed.

Jed undid his tie altogether and whipped it free, taking the time to fold it before stuffing it into his suit pocket. "A comment like that could get a man to hoping. But I don't want to jump the gun, so I'll just content myself with askin' what you meant by it."

She blinked rapidly, her eyes making contact with his. "You read me so well. I can't hide anything from you, can I?"

"Well, I wouldn't say that exactly." Jed rubbed his hand over his hair. He'd let it grow some for the wedding and the motion made a few course strands stand on end. "I've been gettin' a lot of mixed messages from you lately, so if you'd give it to me straight, I'd be much obliged."

"Total honesty?" Andrea asked.

"Yes please. The old me would want to fortify myself with a drink first, but since there's nary a drop to be found around this shin-dig, just give it to me straight."

"Well… I've been thinking a lot about what you said that time at church when you first got saved. That you knew we could never be together if you didn't…"

Jed nodded. "It's true. I haven't changed my mind, but I'm tryin' to be respectful of your wishes. I've had eyes for you right from the start and it's been killin' me inside. But the last thing I want to do is chase you away. Your friendship means more to me than anything. If that's all you want, then that's all it'll be." He snorted derisively. "What would such a perfect woman want with a lummox like me?"

"Well, I have news for you, you big lummox." Her tinkle of laughter was like a balm to Jed's heart. "Yes, I want to be your friend, but I also think I've had eyes for you since the day we first met, too."

"You have?" His eyes widened. He felt like his chest was going to burst.

She nodded and a stray tear slipped down her cheek. She dug in her purse and then dabbed at her eyes with a tissue. "And not only that. I… I felt as if the Lord told me one time that you were the one, but that I had to be patient. I felt so confused. You weren't a believer and I knew He wouldn't want that for me. I just had to trust Him to do what He thought best."

"He does that?" Jed's eyes widened even further. "Talks to you?"

"Not in an audible voice," Andrea clarified, "but sometimes, yes. It's just a feeling. A still small voice on the inside. I just couldn't figure out how it could ever be. Then when you got saved I needed to be sure it was for real, not just wishful thinking."

"And? Did I pass the test?" Jed asked.

She nodded. "With flying colours!"

Jed squinted, his eyes straying to her mouth. "Can I kiss you? Or is that not allowed yet?"

"I think we've waited long enough."

Jed didn't need to be told twice.

A tap on the shoulder interrupted his sweet bliss. "Not now! Can't you see I'm kissin' my woman?"

"Young people! You said you would help me with the surprise."

Jed jerked away from Andrea to stare at Lani Chan's miniature form, standing next to him with arms crossed.

"Oh right! Sorry about that. I'll get right on it."

JED LUGGED the awkward burden all the way from Lani's parked van to the head table. It was carefully concealed under a wool blanket.

Lester and Sherri were seated with Sherman, Carmen and several others nearby.

"Now!" Lani said and pointed at Jed. He flung the blanket off, matador style, to reveal a perfect model of a bungalow. "Surprise!" Lani called, clapping her hands.

"Oh." Sherri smiled. "It's lovely. What is it? A doll house for the baby?"

"Baby? What baby?" Lani demanded. When nobody dared answer she waved a frustrated hand at the model. "It a house, silly. A house for you and your new husband."

"It's a model," Jed clarified. "Of the one your parents bought for you."

Sherri's eyes widened. "What? You bought us a house?"

Lani nodded vigorously and rushed to squeeze her daughter tight. Lani's husband Joseph wasn't far behind.

"It's ... it's too much." Lester said. "I couldn't expect you to buy us a house."

"She my only daughter. What else I have to spend my money on?" Lani said.

"Why didn't you let me help you choose?" Sherman asked his mother.

"Poo! What you know about houses? You just an architect."

Everyone laughed.

"Now we sing 'For they a jolly good fellow' and then go! We all tired and still need to clean up." Lani started the song off key but it swelled to cover any discord by the time it was through.

After they all waved good-bye to the newly married couple, a few volunteers stayed behind to start taking down the decorations. The park needed to be left as it was found before the last person left.

"This was the best wedding I've ever been to," Jed said to Andrea as he wound some mini-lights into a bundle.

"I couldn't agree more. And by the look of it, your family feels the same way."

Jed glanced to where his siblings worked, all seemingly paired off. Will and Marigold, Bo and Viann, Reba and some cowboy who looked somewhat familiar, Pip and Patsi Tibbett, and even Zeb with Lily Chan.

"We should treat them to another one real soon," Jed said.

"What do you mean?"

"I mean, I'm not gettin' any younger. Since the Lord told you I was the one anyway, why not just agree to marry me right now, as soon as possible?"

Andrea's eyes were wide.

"So? What's your answer?" Jed asked.

"Yes?"

"That's my girl." He spun her around and then kissed her soundly, not caring who saw it.

∼

NEIGHBOURHOOD CAST

The Malloys:

Jed Malloy: 32 – back woods boy from Newfoundland is the head of the 'clan'.

Zeb Malloy: 30 – rough around the edges; likes to party, and likes his 'freedom'.

Bo Malloy: 27 – quiet and more sensible than the rest. Works at the Urban Cowboy.

Will Malloy: 26 – into sports, the outdoors, and anything fun!

Reba Malloy: 24 – fiery redhead with a stubborn streak.

Pip (Steve) Malloy: 22 – the 'baby' of the family and a bit of a 'ladies' man'.

The Rest:

Andrea Carravagio: identical twin to Angela. Owns Gemini's Beauty Salon.

Angela Carravagio: identical twin to Andrea. The 'wild one' of the two.

Jacques Marcett: manager of the Urban Cowboy, originally from Quebec.

Lester Tibbett: former cowboy and Jed's friend.

Patsi Tibbett: Lester's younger sister back from the country.

Brett McMillan: Patsi's former boyfriend and one of the 'elite'.

Marigold Reynolds: artist and environmentalist. Her parents own a campground.

Ophelia Stanfield: rich California girl visiting her relatives, the McMillans.

Cory Roberts: owns the Urban Cowboy and a DJ. A bit of a player.

Viann-Patrice Marcett: Jacques's step-sister from Montreal.

Sherri Chan: college professor engaged to Lester Tibbett.

Tiffany Yuen: Martial arts instructor visiting from Toronto.

Lily Chan: Sherri Chan's cousin who also works at the family restaurant.

Some Minor Players:

Tamara Spence: co-owner of the Brew café where Patsi works.

Carmen Lamont: co-owner of the Brew café where Patsi works.

Sherman Chan: Architect. Sherri's brother. Dating Carmen Lamont.

Rocky Carravagio: Scary looking brother of Andrea and Angela.

Jeremiah Reynolds: Will's boss who owns a campground. Marigold's dad.

Maizy Reynolds: Jeremiah's wife and Marigold's mother.

Buck Stone: First Nations' man who works at Jeremiah's camp with Will.

Tad Roberts: Cory's father and financier of the Urban Cowboy.

Dr. Lawler: has a brief relationship with Viann.

Crystal: waitress at the Urban Cowboy.

Millicent Peacock: nosy neighbour who lives in the apartment building.

Weston Drake: a cowboy

Ma and Pops Malloy: The parents who started it all.

Fanny: 33 - Malloy sister still in Newfoundland, married to Joe with 3 kids

Mary: 29 - Malloy sister still in Newfoundland, married to 'Dr.' Trent with two kids

Sissy: 28 - Malloy sister still in Newfoundland, married to Hank with four kids

Characters from *Neighbours Series I* referenced in *Series II*:

Megan McMillan: Patsi's friend and sister to Brett.

Emmanuel Fernandez: Megan's boyfriend whom she eventually marries.

Elaine and Bruce McMillan: Brett's lawyer parents involved in a scandal.

Steve Russell: Newspaper columnist who dates Tamara Spence.

Matonabee Spence: Tamara's young son.

Goldie Harper: Lives in the apartment and goes with Tad Roberts.

Jason Harper: Goldie's son.

Vinny Kirkpatrick: retired newspaper reporter.

Renee Tucker: Carmen Lamont's niece, who used to date Cory Roberts.

MORE IN THE SERIES

Did you enjoy reading *KEEPING UP WITH THE NEIGHBOURS SERIES 2*? An honest review would be most appreciated and are a tremendous boost in today's marketplace.

In case you missed where it all began, check out the first book in the series: *Neighbours Series I*, starring handsome cowboy Lester Tibbett and an entire cast of other characters.

https://www.tracykrauss.com/books/neighbours-a-contemporary-christian-romance-series-1/

OFFER

Join Tracy's mailing list and get up to date info on all new releases, promos and giveaways when they happen. You'll also get a free book!

https://tracykrauss.com
- fiction on the edge without crossing the line -

If you enjoyed this novel, or any of Tracy's books, please consider writing a review online. Reviews help readers find books they'll love and are tremendously helpful for today's authors. Thank you in advance!

ABOUT THE AUTHOR

Tracy Krauss writes contemporary Christian romance with a twist of suspense and a touch of humour. Her books strike a chord with those looking for a hard hitting yet thought provoking read. She also writes stage plays tailored to a high school audience, and has contributed to several anthologies, devotional books, and one illustrated children's book. Tracy has a Bachelor's degree from the University of Saskatchewan and taught secondary school Art, Drama and English – all things she is passionate about. She is a member of ACFW, The Word Guild, and is on the executive of Inscribe Christian Writers' Fellowship, a Canada wide organization for writers of Christian faith. She and her husband have lived in five provinces and territories including many remote and unique places in Canada's far north. They have four grown children and now reside in beautiful Tumbler Ridge, BC where she continues to pursue all of her creative interests.

Visit her website for more:
https://tracykrauss.com

ALSO BY TRACY KRAUSS

<u>Novels</u>

Wind Over Marshdale

Lone Wolf

Play It Again

Conspiracy of Bones (And the Beat Goes On)

My Mother the Man-Eater

Neighbours Series I

Keeping Up with the Neighbours Series II

Three Strand Cord

Blood Ties

Tempest Tossed

Aliens Among Us

Out of This World

Whispering Winds

<u>Stage Plays</u>

Dorothy's Road Trip

Ebenezer's Christmas Carol

Hook's Nemesis

Ali and the Magic Lamp

Mutiny On Mount Olympus

A Midterm Eve's Phantasm

The Western Tale

Little Red In the Hood

King William Travels The World